and perhaps wrongly sought to shield you from has
returned. And now you, like your parents before you,
are in grave danger.

In the year 1888, when your father and I were still
young, we learned that evil lurks in the shadows of our
world, waiting to prey upon the unbelieving and the
unprepared.

As a young solicitor, your father was sent into the wilds
of Transylvania. His task was to help Prince Dracula
conclude the purchase of a property in Whitby, an
ancient monastery known as Carfax Abbey.

During his stay in Transylvania, your father
discovered that his host and client, Prince Dracula,
was in truth a creature thought to exist only in folktale
and legend, one of those which feed upon the blood of the
living in order to attain immortal life. Dracula was
what the locals called Nosferatu, the Un-Dead. You may
more readily recognize the creature by its more common
name: **vampire.**

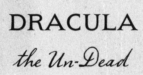

DRACULA

the Un-Dead

DRACULA
the Un-Dead

DACRE STOKER

AND

IAN HOLT

VIKING
CANADA

VIKING CANADA

Published by the Penguin Group
Penguin Group (Canada), 90 Eglinton Avenue East, Suite 700, Toronto, Ontario, Canada M4P
2Y3 (a division of Pearson Canada Inc.); Penguin Group (USA) Inc., 375 Hudson Street, New York,
New York 10014; U.S.A.; Penguin Books Ltd, 80 Strand, London WC2R 0RL, England; Penguin
Ireland, 25 St Stephen's Green, Dublin 2, Ireland (a division of Penguin Books Ltd); Penguin Group
(Australia), 250 Camberwell Road, Camberwell, Victoria 3124, Australia (a division of Pearson
Australia Group Pty Ltd); Penguin Books India Pvt Ltd, 11 Community Centre, Panchsheel Park,
New Delhi – 110 017, India; Penguin Group (NZ), 67 Apollo Drive, Rosedale, North Shore 0632,
Auckland, New Zealand (a division of Pearson New Zealand Ltd); Penguin Books (South Africa)
(Pty) Ltd, 24 Sturdee Avenue, Rosebank, Johannesburg 2196, South Africa

Penguin Books Ltd, Registered Offices: 80 Strand, London WC2R 0RL, England

First published in Viking Canada hardcover by Penguin Group (Canada), a division of Pearson
Canada Inc., 2009. Simultaneously published in the United States by Dutton, a member of Penguin
Group (USA) Inc.

1 3 5 7 9 10 8 6 4 2

Copyright © Dacre Stoker and Ian Zisholtz, 2009

Grateful acknowledgment is made to the following for permission to reprint:
Pages 415–417. Bram Stoker, notes for *Dracula* EL3f. S874d MS pp. 1, 31b verso,
and 38a. Courtesy Rosenbach Museum & Library, Philadelphia.

Set in Adobe Caslon Pro
Designed by Amy Hill

Manufactured in the U.S.A.

ISBN: 978-0-670-06986-6

Library and Archives Canada Cataloguing in Publication data
available upon request to the publisher.
American Library of Congress Cataloging in Publication data available.

Visit the Penguin Group (Canada) website at **www.penguin.ca**

Special and corporate bulk purchase rates available; please see **www.penguin.ca/corporatesales**
or call 1-800-810-3104, ext. 477 or 474

For Bram,
thank you for your inspiration,
and your guidance

DRACULA

the Un-Dead

PROLOGUE

LETTER FROM MINA HARKER TO HER SON, QUINCEY HARKER, ESQ.
(To be opened upon the sudden or unnatural death of Wilhelmina Harker)

9th March 1912

Dear Quincey,

My dear son, all your life you have suspected that there have been secrets between us. I fear that the time has come to reveal the truth to you. To deny it any longer would put both your life and your immortal soul in jeopardy.

Your dear father and I chose to keep the secrets of our past from you in order to shield you from the darkness that shrouds this world. We had hoped to allow you a childhood free from the fears that have haunted us all our adult lives. As you grew into the promising young man you are today, we chose not to tell you what we knew lest you think us mad. Forgive us. If you are reading this letter now, then the evil we so desperately and perhaps wrongly sought to shield you from has returned. And now you, like your parents before you, are in grave danger.

In the year 1888, when your father and I were still young, we learned that evil lurks in the shadows of our world, waiting to prey upon the unbelieving and the unprepared.

{ 1 }

As a young solicitor, your father was sent into the wilds of Transylvania. His task was to help Prince Dracula conclude the purchase of a property in Whitby, an ancient monastery known as Carfax Abbey.

During his stay in Transylvania, your father discovered that his host and client, Prince Dracula, was in truth a creature thought to exist only in folktale and legend, one of those which feed upon the blood of the living in order to attain immortal life. Dracula was what the locals called Nosferatu, the Un-Dead. You may more readily recognize the creature by its more common name: vampire.

Prince Dracula, fearing that your father would expose the truth of what he was, imprisoned him in his castle. Dracula himself then booked passage to England on the sailing vessel the *Demeter*, spending the many days of his voyage hidden in one of dozens of crates in the hull. He concealed himself in this strange fashion because although a vampire may have the strength of ten men and the ability to take many forms, he will burn to ash if struck by the light of the sun.

At this time, I was staying in Whitby at the home of my closest and dearest friend, Lucy Westenra. A storm had blown in off the sea, and the treacherous Whitby cliffs were shrouded in a dense mist. Lucy, unable to sleep, saw from her window the storm-driven ship heading for the rocks. Lucy raced into the night in an attempt to raise the alarm before the ship was wrecked, but she was too late. I awoke in a panic, saw that Lucy was not beside me in bed, and raced out into the storm to search for her. I found her at the cliff's edge, unconscious and with two small holes in her neck.

Lucy became deathly ill. Her fiancé, Arthur Holmwood, the son of Lord Godalming, and his dear friend, a visiting Texan whom you know as your namesake, Quincey P. Morris, raced to her side. Arthur called every doctor in Whitby and beyond, but none could explain Lucy's illness. It was our friend who owned the Whitby Asylum, Dr. Jack Seward, who called in his mentor from Holland, Dr. Abraham Van Helsing.

Dr. Van Helsing, a learned man of medicine, was also acquainted with the occult. He recognized that Lucy was suffering from the bite of a vampire.

It was then that I finally received word from your father. He had escaped from Dracula's castle and taken refuge in a monastery where he, too, was deathly ill. I was forced to leave Lucy's bedside and travel to meet him. It was there in Buda-Pesth that we were married.

Your father told me of the horrors he had seen, and it was from this that we learned the identity of the vampire that had attacked Lucy and now threatened all our lives: Prince Dracula.

Upon returning from Buda-Pesth, we were told that Lucy had died. But worse was to follow. Days after her death, she had risen from her grave. She was now a vampire and was feeding on the blood of small children. Dr. Van Helsing, Quincey Morris, Dr. Seward, and Arthur Holmwood were faced with a terrible decision. They had no choice but drive a wooden stake through Lucy's heart in order to free her poor soul.

Shortly thereafter, Prince Dracula returned in the night to attack me. After this attack, we all swore an oath to hunt down and destroy the vampire, and rid the world of his evil. And so it was that we became the band of heroes and chased Dracula back to his castle in Transylvania. There, Quincey Morris died in battle although, like the hero he was, he managed to plunge a knife into Dracula's heart. We watched as Prince Dracula burst into flames, crumbling into dust in the light of the setting sun.

Then, we were free, or so I thought. But about a year after you were born, I began to suffer horrible nightmares. Dracula was haunting me in my dreams. It was then that your father reminded me of the dark prince's warning and how he had claimed, "I shall have my revenge. I shall spread it over centuries. Time is on my side."

From that day onward, your father and I have had no peace. We have spent our years looking over our shoulders. And now I fear we are no longer strong enough to protect you from his evil and I have made a terrible misjudgment in character.

Know this, my son, if you are to survive the evil that is now hunting you; embrace the truth I speak in these pages. Look deep within your young self and, as your father and I were once forced to do, find the brave hero within. Dracula is a wise and cunning foe. You cannot run, and there is nowhere to hide. You must stand and fight.

Good luck, my dear son, and do not be afraid. If Van Helsing is correct, then vampires are truly demons, and God will be at your side as you do battle.

With all my undying love,
Your mother, Mina

CHAPTER I.

---◆---

OCEANS OF LOVE, LUCY.

The inscription was the only thing Dr. Jack Seward could focus on as he felt the darkness overtake him. In the darkness was peace, with no harsh light to illuminate the tattered remains of his life. For years, he had devoted himself to fighting back the darkness. Now he simply embraced it.

Only at night could Seward find peace with the memory of Lucy. In his dreams, he still felt her warm embrace. For a fleeting moment, he could go back to London, to a happier era, when he found meaning through his place in the world and his research. This was the life he had wished to share with Lucy.

The early morning din of milk wagons, fishmongers' carts, and other merchant vehicles rattling hurriedly across the cobblestone streets of Paris intruded on Seward's dream and thrust him back into the harsh present. Seward forced his eyes open. They stung worse than fresh iodine on an open wound. As the cracked ceiling of the stale Parisian flophouse room he had been renting came into focus, he reflected on how much his life had changed. It saddened him to see all the muscle tone he had lost. His bicep sagged, resembling one of those hand-sewn muslin tea bags after it had just been removed from a teapot. The veins on his arm were like rivers on a tattered map. He was a shadow of his former self.

Seward prayed that death would come quickly. He had willed his body to science, to be used in a classroom at his alma mater. He took comfort from the fact that in death he would help to inspire future doctors and scientists.

After a time, he remembered the watch, still nestled in his left hand. He turned it over. Half past six! For an instant, panic overtook him. *Damn it to hell.* He had overslept. Seward staggered to his feet. An empty glass syringe rolled off the table and shattered on the grimy wooden floor. A small, smoked brown bottle of morphine was about to follow the fate of the syringe, but he quickly caught the precious liquid, untying the leather belt from his left bicep with a practiced movement. Normal circulation returned as he rolled down his sleeve and returned the silver monogrammed cuff link to his frayed dress shirt. He buttoned up his vest and slipped on his jacket. Wallingham & Sons were the finest tailors in London. If his suit had been made by anyone else, it would have disintegrated ten years ago. *Vanity dies hard,* Seward thought to himself with a humorless chuckle.

He had to hurry if he still wanted to make the train. Where was that address? He had put it in a safe place. Now, when he needed it, he could not recall where exactly that was. He overturned the straw-filled mattress, inspected the underside of the wobbly table, and peered under the vegetable crates that served as dining chairs. He sifted through piles of aged newspaper clippings. Their headlines spoke of Seward's current preoccupation: gruesome stories of Jack the Ripper. Autopsy photos of the five known victims. Mutilated women posed, legs open, as if waiting to accept their deranged killer. The Ripper was deemed a butcher of women—but a butcher is more merciful to the animals he slaughters. Seward had reread the autopsy notes countless times. Loose pages of his theories and ideas written on scrap paper, torn cardboard, and unfolded matchboxes fluttered around him like windblown leaves.

The sweat flowing from Seward's brow began to sting his bloodshot eyes. *Damn, where had he put it?* The Benefactor had taken enormous risks to get him this information. Seward could not bear the thought of disappointing the only person who still believed in him. Everyone else—the Harkers, the Holmwoods—all thought he had taken leave of his senses. If they could see this room, Seward knew, they would feel justified in that belief. He scanned the crumbling plaster walls, which bore the evidence of his morphine-induced rants, his wild insights handwritten in ink, coal, wine, even his own blood. No madman would be so obvious. He was certain that these writings would one day prove his sanity.

Amidst it all, there was a page torn from a book, stabbed into the wall with a bone-handled bowie knife whose blade was stained with old blood. The page featured a portrait of an elegant, raven-haired beauty. Beneath the picture, an inscription: *Countess Elizabeth Bathory circa 1582.*

Of course, that's where I hid it. He laughed at himself as he pulled the knife out of the wall, seizing the page and turning it over. In his own barely legible handwriting, he found the address of a villa in Marseilles. Seward removed the cross, wooden stake, and garlic wreaths that hung next to Bathory's picture and scooped up a silver knife from the floor. He placed everything into a false bottom in his medical bag and covered it all with standard medical supplies.

The train left the Gare de Lyon exactly on time. Seeing it pull away just as he was paying for his ticket, Seward sprinted across the flood-stained building to reach the chugging behemoth as it left the seventh bay door. He managed to catch the last Pullman car and hoist himself on before it had a chance to pick up speed. His heart surged with pride as he made the daring leap. He had done this sort of thing in his youth with the Texan Quincey P. Morris and his old friend Arthur Holmwood. *Youth was wasted on the young.* Seward smiled to himself as he recalled the reckless days of his innocence . . . and ignorance.

The doctor took a seat in the elaborate dining car as the train lumbered southward. It wasn't moving quickly enough. He glanced down at his pocket watch; only five minutes had passed. Seward lamented that he could no longer pass the time by writing in his journal, as he was unable to afford the luxury of such a thing. They were not scheduled to reach Marseilles for ten more hours. There, he would finally have the evidence to prove his theories and show those who had shunned him that he was not mad, that he had been right all along.

These were going to be the longest ten hours of Seward's life.

"Billets, s'il vous plaît!"

Seward stared wide-eyed at the conductor standing over him with a stern look of impatience.

"Forgive me," Seward said. He handed the conductor his ticket, adjusting his scarf to cover the torn breast pocket.

"You are British?" the conductor asked with a heavy French accent.

"Why, yes."

"A doctor?" The conductor nodded toward the medical bag between Seward's feet.

"Yes."

Seward watched the conductor's gray eyes catalogue the threadbare person in front of him, the ill-fitting suit and well-worn shoes. He was hardly the image of a respectable doctor. "I will see your bag, please."

He handed over the bag, for it was not as if he had much choice in the matter. The conductor methodically pulled out medical bottles, read the labels, and dropped them back in with a clink. Seward knew what the conductor was looking for and hoped he wouldn't dig too deeply.

"Morphine," announced the conductor in a voice so loud that other passengers glanced over. He held up the brown bottle.

"I sometimes have to prescribe it as a sedative."

"I will see your license, please."

Seward searched his pockets. Over a month ago, the International Opium Convention had been signed, prohibiting persons from importing, selling, distributing, and exporting morphine without a medical license. It took him so long to find it that by the time Seward finally produced the license, the conductor was about to pull the cord to stop the train. The conductor examined the paper, frowning, then turned his steely eyes to the travel document. The United Kingdom was the first to use photo identification on their passports. Since that picture had been taken, Seward had lost a tremendous amount of weight. His hair was now much grayer, his beard wild and untrimmed. The man in the train bore little resemblance to the man in the photo.

"Why are you going to Marseilles, doctor?"

"I am treating a patient there."

"What ails this patient?"

"He's suffering from a Narcissistic Personality Disorder."

"*Qu'est-ce que c'est?*"

"It is a psychological instability causing the patient to inflict preda-tory, autoerotic, antisocial, and parasitic control on those around them. As well as—"

"*Merci.*" The conductor cut Seward off by handing him back his papers and ticket with a deft flick. He turned and addressed only the men at the next table. "*Billets, s'il vous plaît.*"

Jack Seward sighed. Replacing his papers in his jacket, he checked the pocket watch again, a nervous habit. It seemed as if the interroga-tion had lasted hours, but only another five minutes had passed. He rolled down the fringed window shade to shield his eyes from the day-light and reclined into the plush, burgundy upholstered seat.

Oceans of Love, Lucy.

He held the beloved watch close to his heart and closed his eyes to dream.

It was a quarter century ago. Seward held the same watch up to the light the better to read the inscription: "Oceans of love, Lucy."

She was there. Alive. "You don't like it," she said, and pouted.

He couldn't break his stare away from her green eyes, soft as a sum-mer meadow. Lucy had an odd idiosyncrasy of watching a speaker's mouth as if trying to taste the next word before it passed by his lips. She had such a lust for life. Her smile could bring warmth to the cold-est heart. As she sat on the bench in the garden that spring day, Seward marveled at how the sunlight illuminated the loose strands of red hair that danced in the breeze, haloing her face. The scent of fresh lilacs mixed with the salty sea air of Whitby Harbor. In the years since, whenever he smelled lilacs, he would remember this beautiful, bitter day.

"I can only conclude," Seward said, clearing his throat before his voice had a chance to break, "since you wrote on the gift card 'Dearest

Friend' rather than 'Fiancé,' that you have chosen not to accept my proposal of marriage."

Lucy looked away, her eyes moistening. The silence spoke volumes.

"I thought it best that you hear it from me," Lucy finally sighed. "I
have consented to wed Arthur."

Arthur had been Jack Seward's friend since they were lads. Seward
loved him like a brother, yet always envied how easily everything came
to Arthur. He was handsome and rich, and had never in his life known
worry or struggle. Or heartbreak.

"I see." Seward's voice sounded like a squeak in his ears.

"I do love you," Lucy whispered. "But . . ."

"But not as much as much as you love Arthur." Of course he could
not compete with the wealthy Arthur Holmwood, nor was he as dashing as Lucy's other suitor, the Texan Quincey P. Morris.

"Forgive me," he went on in a softer tone, suddenly afraid he'd hurt
her. "I forgot my place."

Lucy reached out and patted his hand, as one would a beloved pet. "I
will always be here."

Back in the present, he stirred in his sleep. If he could just see the
beauty in Lucy's eyes . . . The last time he had gazed into them, that
terrible night in the mausoleum, he had seen nothing but pain and torment. The memory of Lucy's dying screams still seared Seward's brain.

After leaving the train, Seward walked in a torrential downpour through
Marseilles's labyrinth of white buildings and cursed his timing. Of
course, his quest brought him to the French Riviera in March, the only
rainy month.

He slogged farther inland, glancing back to see Fort Saint-Jean
standing like a stone sentinel in the indigo harbor. Then he turned about
to study the Provençal city, which had been built around a 2,600-year-old
village. Artifacts of the city's Greek and Roman founders were found
throughout the streets. Seward lamented that he was in this picturesque
haven for such a sinister purpose. Though it would not be the first time
malevolence had made its presence felt here: Over the last century, this
seaside town had been marred by plague and pirates.

Seward stopped. Looming in front of him was a typical two-story Mediterranean villa with large wooden shutters and wrought-iron bars on the windows. The winter moon peering through the rain clouds cast a spectral glow on the traditional white walls. The roof was covered in red terra-cotta tiles that reminded him of some of the old Spanish houses he had seen when he visited Quincey P. Morris in Texas so many years ago. It created a decidedly foreboding ambience, even unwelcoming, for an ornate villa on the French Riviera. It appeared entirely devoid of life. His heart sank at the thought that he might be too late. Seward looked again at the address.

This was it.

Suddenly, he heard the thunderous approach of a horse-drawn carriage splashing along the cobblestones. He ducked into a vineyard across from the building. There were no grapes on the dripping, weblike branches. A black carriage with ornate gold trim sailed up the hill, pulled by two glistening black mares. The animals drew to a stop without a command. Seward looked up and, to his surprise, saw there was no driver. *How was that possible?*

A strapping figure emerged from the carriage. The mares nipped at each other and squealed, necks arched. Then, again to Seward's amazement, they moved off, in perfect step, with no coachman to direct them. The figure held a walking stick aloft with one black-gloved hand, and dipped into a pocket with the other for a key, then stopped suddenly as if becoming aware of something.

"Damn," Seward muttered to himself.

The person at the door cocked his head, almost as if he heard Seward's voice through the rain, and turned slowly toward the vineyard. Seward felt waves of panic and adrenaline wash over him but managed to hold his breath. The gloved hand reached up to the brim of the velvet top hat and Seward choked back a gasp as he saw the top hat removed to reveal sensuous locks of black hair cascading onto the figure's shoulders.

His mind reeled. *It is she!* The Benefactor had been right.

Countess Elizabeth Bathory stood at the doorway of the villa, looking exactly as she had in the portrait painted over three hundred years ago.

CHAPTER II.

———◇———

Lightning danced across the sky, illuminating the raindrops like gems on black velvet cloth. Seward knew he should move for cover, but he could do nothing except stare, entranced, at the exotic—and dangerous—beauty before him. Bathory's fair skin contrasted sharply with her midnight hair, and she moved with the silent grace of a predator. Her icy blue eyes searched for any movement in the street as another flash of lightning brightened the grounds before her. When she turned toward the vineyard, he quickly threw himself into the mud to avoid detection.

There, he held his breath, trying not to move and ignoring the cramp in his legs. He desperately longed to glance up, but the lightning flashing on his pale face would reveal him immediately, and so he remained pressed to the ground, his nose a mere inch from the mud. After what seemed like an eternity, he finally allowed himself to look up, half expecting Bathory to be waiting next to him like a cobra ready to strike. But she was nowhere to be seen.

Fighting his rising fear, Seward freed himself from the mud's grasp with a revolting slurp. Too loud. His eyes darted. He needed to move, but he had to wait for the blood to flow back into his legs. He felt like wet burlap, with his oversized clothes weighing heavily on him.

The wind whistled, and he turned with a start. Still no one in sight. Setting his resolve, he took a determined step toward the stone building—and felt wet mud soaking his bare foot. Seward looked back to see one of his shoes stuck in the mud. He cursed under his breath and nearly toppled over while balancing to replace it. He continued, stumbling, across the marshy laneway and tripped into a palm tree. Seward was certain he was making a terrible amount of noise but hoped the rain would drown it out. At last he reached the tree adjacent to the villa. He had been good at climbing trees when he was a schoolboy, but five decades later, that was hardly likely to be the case. But there was nothing for it. He took a deep breath and hauled himself up onto the lowest branch.

From the tree, he was able to hoist himself to the roof of the front walkway. The clay shingles were slick with rain. Seward steadied himself by gripping the decorative wrought-iron railing for support and glanced about, terrified that Countess Bathory was laughing in the shadows as he made a fool of himself. He spotted an awning over one of the second-story windows and scurried to its shadow for protection, taking a moment to catch his breath. He listened, and heard nothing except the pounding of rain beating in time with his heart.

He peered into the window and found that it overlooked what must have once been a grand ballroom. Now, devoid of life and full of shadows, it unnerved him. It was like looking into a museum at night. Or worse . . . a tomb.

His thoughts were interrupted by two glowing white figures moving across the ballroom floor. They glided effortlessly and seemed to be carrying something that resembled a crate or chest. Wary of staying in one place too long for fear of being spotted, he gripped the rails, hoisted himself from one balcony to the next, and edged his way to another window.

On this level, the only light came from a few scattered candles and the embers in the fireplace. It was enough for Seward to see that what had seemed like two spirits were in fact beautiful young women dressed in flowing, sheer white gowns. Where was Bathory? Seward still couldn't get over the creeping dread that she was standing behind him.

His heart threatened to burst from his chest at the sound of the

French doors flying open. Countess Bathory swept into the ballroom. Seward, relieved, shrank back into the shadows.

Bathory untied her cloak from around her neck and tossed it carelessly over her shoulder, revealing her full statuesque form. She was dressed in an evening jacket, complete with fitted, starched white, wing-collared shirt and black tie. In its severe lines, her tailor had found a way to accentuate her voluptuous feminine figure while projecting a masculine strength.

She strode toward the other two women. "My sweets," she greeted them; and beneath the languorous tone of her voice, Seward detected something infinitely more sinister. He shivered as Bathory kissed each of these "Women in White" on the lips passionately.

"What toy have you brought me?"

The blond woman broke the heavy padlock on the captain's chest with her bare hands, a shockingly casual gesture for one so delicate in appearance. She opened the lid with a flourish, like a waiter proudly presenting the main course. Inside the trunk was a young woman, bound, gagged, and clearly terrified.

Bathory reached into her boot and unsheathed a curved metal blade. Seward immediately recognized the knife: It was a medical amputation lancet.

The young woman's eyes widened at the sight of the blade. In a movement too fast for Seward to see, Bathory sliced the lancet toward the young woman. The gag and the ropes binding her hands fell to the bottom of the chest. Bathory placed the blade's tip under the girl's chin. Seward gripped the handle of his silver throwing knife.

Instead of inflicting a bloody wound, Bathory used the blade to gently guide the girl out of the box. Seward relaxed his grip. The girl touched her face and wrists to feel whether the blade had cut her. There did not appear to be even the slightest scratch.

Seward watched the countess walk around the young woman, appraising her attire. She was dressed in a French teal wool dress, chastely covering her from her neck to her ankles. He felt enraged at the thought of what Bathory's eyes must be seeing—a beautiful package just waiting to be unwrapped.

The girl kept perfectly still. The lancet sliced. Her dress and under-garments fell away like puzzle pieces, leaving her delicate skin unscathed. Despite the young woman's frantic efforts to recover the fabric, more fell away until she was completely revealed.

Bathory's eyes did not blink once as she drank in the sight. Shivering with fear, the girl pulled herself back into the shadows, covering her body. The Women in White laughed.

Seward moved to the next window to get a better view. Once there, he noticed Bathory's eyes narrow. Flickering candlelight reflected from the small gold crucifix around the young woman's neck. Bathory's lancet flashed forward and back so quickly that Seward almost doubted it had moved at all. But there was no mistaking the *ting* of the cross hitting the marble floor, the broken chain gathering around it in a smooth pile. The young woman gasped in surprise—a small drop of blood glittered like a gem at the base of her throat. The Women in White leapt upon her like wild dogs.

"Mary, Mother of God, protect her," Seward prayed, the words coming out as a plaintive whine under his breath. He watched in horror as the Women in White hoisted the naked young woman and hung her upside down by her ankles on a pulley system, suspending her from the ceiling. The dark-haired demon handed Bathory a black leather cat-o'-nine-tails, with curved metal hooks tipping each lash. The countess's red lips curved into a humorless smile, her otherworldly eyes remaining focused on the single drop of blood now sliding down her victim's chest. With a quick flick of her wrist, Bathory stung the flesh with the whip, watching eagerly as the blood began to flow more freely.

Seward turned away from the sight, but he could not shut out the screams. He clutched the cross around his neck, but it gave him no comfort. His instinct was to rush in to save this poor girl—but that would surely be a foolhardy decision. One old man was no match against these three. They would tear him apart.

No matter what you see or feel, nothing must distract you from your duty. That had been the last message from the Benefactor. Seward finally gathered the nerve to look again though the windowpane into the depraved insanity of the villa.

Bathory was maintaining a steady momentum now as the metal lashes whined through the air. The force of each blow caused her young victim to sway like a pendulum. The blood dripping from the young woman had turned into streams. The Women in White, meanwhile, lay upon the floor beneath her, their mouths open to catch the precious crimson drops that fell like some hellish form of rain.

Seward knew that he was witnessing true madness. When the sun rose, these three creatures would be lying in their coffins, asleep and vulnerable, and it would be his only opportunity to rid the world of their evil. He would drive the silver-plated blade into their hearts, sever their heads, stuff their mouths with garlic, and burn the remains.

Yet he felt tormented by the guilt of standing idle while this innocent girl was tortured. He curled a hand around his blade, squeezing until drops of blood seeped from between his own fingers. If he could not spare this young woman her pain, the least he could do was share it. The girl's screams had finally quieted—but they continued to echo eerily in his head, evoking painful memories of Lucy's second death. A death that Seward himself had helped bring about. Again, the memories came rushing back to him: the anger he had felt at the desecration of his beloved's tomb; the shock of discovering her body still warm and rosy, apparently full of life; the sight of Arthur driving the stake into her heart, as the creature that looked like Lucy cried out in bloodcurdling screams; and the tears he had quietly shed as he stuffed the monster's mouth with garlic and soldered her tomb closed for good. Yet none of these emotions were as shameful as the one he had hidden all these years, even from himself—the secret satisfaction of watching Arthur lose Lucy. If Seward could not have her, at least no one else would. It was a horrible emotion, and every bit of the darkness that had fallen upon his life after this was well deserved. Accepting this final mission was his act of contrition.

He was drawn swiftly back into the present by the sudden silence. In the ballroom below, the young woman had passed out from the pain. He could see her chest still heaving, so she was not yet dead. Bathory threw down her whip, as irritated as a cat when the mouse will not play after its neck is broken. Seward felt hot wetness on his face, and touched his cheek only to realize that he was crying.

"Prepare my bath!" Bathory ordered.

The Women in White propelled the young woman across the pulley system's metal track and thus transported her into another room. Bathory turned to follow, purposefully stepping on the gold cross as she did so, twisting her foot and crushing it beneath her heel. Satisfied, she continued into the adjacent room, stripping off her clothes one by one as she went.

Seward leaned out over the balcony to see if there was another window looking into the adjacent room. The rain pattered to a stop. Its din would no longer hide his footfalls on the clay shingles. Slowly and cautiously, he made his way over to the next window and peered through. The pulley system ended directly above a Roman-style bath. Dozens of candles now illuminated the sight of Bathory slipping delicately out of her trousers. For the first time, Seward had a clear view of her—without a stitch of clothing. She looked nothing like the prostitutes he had encountered in the back rooms of Camden district brothels. The wanton curves of her body, white and smooth as porcelain, would have distracted most observers from ever noticing the calculating cruelty of her eyes—but not Seward. He had seen a gaze like that before.

Yet nothing in the doctor's bleak past could have prepared him for the macabre scene he witnessed next. The young woman, pathetic gurgles issuing from her throat, was suspended above the edge of the empty mosaic bath. Bathory stood at the bottom; arms outstretched, neck arched back, magnificently naked. She turned her palms upward. It was a signal. In that instant, the dark-haired Woman in White used her fingernail to slit the young lady's throat and pushed her to the end of the track just above where Bathory waited. Seward saw Bathory's fanged mouth open wide as she orgasmically bathed in a shower of blood.

Damn them all to hell! His thoughts were inflamed as he reached into the false bottom of his medical bag for a small crossbow, loading it with a silver-tipped arrow. If this rash decision should be his death, so be it. Better to be dead than to allow this perverse evil to continue a second longer.

Seward aimed the crossbow between the wrought-iron bars and prepared to fire on Bathory. That was when he spotted something. His eyes widened in shock. There was a large advertisement poster lying on the desk by the window. The poster seemed to glow eerily as if it were painted by moonlight. The oversized embossed letters stood out:

William Shakespeare's
"The Life and Death of King Richard III"

7 mars, 1912
Théâtre de l'Odéon
rue de Vaugirard 18
Téléf. 811.42
8 heures
Paris, France

Avec l'acteur roumain
BASARAB
dans le premier rôle

He took an involuntary step back, forgetting the incline of the roof. The tile under his foot cracked and slid down to shatter on the cobble-stoned walkway below. He froze.

In the grand ballroom, the blond Woman in White spun at the sound outside. She flew to the door, her soulless eyes scanning the horizon for any sign of life. She saw no one. Remaining in the shadows, she moved around to the side of the house from where she had heard the noise. Again, she saw nothing and was about to return inside the villa when she spotted a broken clay tile on the ground—stained with a drop of fresh blood. Human blood. Its pungent aroma was unmistakable. She tasted it eagerly and immediately spat it out. The blood was polluted with chemicals.

With reptilian agility, she scaled the wall to inspect the villa further. On the rooftop, she spotted a bloodstained silver knife beneath one of the windows. Only an inexperienced vampire hunter would be naïve enough to carry a silver blade.

But the Woman in White knew that her mistress was no longer safe.

They had to flee Marseilles tonight. She quickly scurried back into the house.

Seward knew that Bathory and her banshees would not stay in Marseilles this evening. They would assuredly flee to Paris and, once airborne, the dead travel fast. But thanks to the advertisement he had seen, Seward realized he once again had the advantage. He knew their plans. Countess Bathory and her companions would be at the theatre tomorrow night.

He allowed himself a grim smile. *That is where the battle will take place.*

CHAPTER III.

———◇———

"**I** charge thee to return and change thy shape," cried out a young man in a bowler hat, arms stretched out imploringly, speaking in a determined yet trembling voice. "Such is the force of magic and my spells: No, Faustus, thou art conjuror laureat, That canst command great Mephistopheles: *Quin regis Mephistopheles fratris imagine.*"

A hiss. A wall of smoke. Then flames erupted out of thin air. From the surrounding gas lamps sparked an extra roar. The small crowd that gathered in the Luxembourg Gardens gasped in unison.

Quincey Harker, his back turned to his audience, felt a surge of pride at his ingenuity. With a whiplash smile as he threw off his bowler hat, stuck on a false goatee, placed a pointed hat upon his brow, threw a cape over his shoulders, and, in what seemed a well-practiced continuous motion, leapt up and spun around onto the edge of La Fontaine Medici. The perfect setting for a one-man pantomime of *Faust,* for the Medici family had been a prominent Florentine family, patron saints of avant-garde artists and long rumored to be in league with the Devil. Quincey, completely at ease on his makeshift stage, reveled not only in his performance but also in his cleverness.

He did what was known as chapeaugraphy—changing hats to change characters. It was a well-known but seldom-used performance technique due to the high level of skill required and was thus attempted only by the most talented actors . . . or the most arrogant.

Quincey used the shadow cast by the figures on the fountain to ominous effect as he spread his cape and held himself with poised menace and growled in a deep, devilish voice, "Now, Faustus, what wouldst thou have me do?"

Quincey paused, expecting applause from his audience. There was none. This was odd. Quincey glanced up and was surprised to find the audience distracted. Something was drawing their attention to the north end of the park. Quincey tried not to let this momentary diversion throw off his concentration. He knew his talent was up to the challenge. He had performed this part at the London Hippodrome, and was so good that he'd even managed to secure the "deuce spot" just before the main attraction, Charles Chaplin, a master of physical comedy. Rumor had it that Chaplin was going to leave London to find his fortune in America. Quincey had hoped to win Chaplin's spot. But Quincey's overbearing father, Jonathan Harker, had smashed that dream by paying off the theatre manager and shipping Quincey off to a Paris prison with no bars—to study law at the Sorbonne.

Panic set in for Quincey as his meager audience began to disperse, heading off to investigate the commotion at the park's north end. Checking his false beard to see if it was crooked, Quincey hurriedly bellowed one of Mephistopheles' soliloquies as he ran down the fountain steps, in a desperate attempt to regain his audience's attention. "I am a servant to great Lucifer, and may not follow thee without his leave: No more than he commands must we perform!"

For a moment, it appeared as if the power of his performance would recapture his audience, but all hope was lost when Mephistopheles slipped on the fountain's wet stone, crashing onto his arse. Laughter erupted as the last of the crowd walked away.

Quincey pounded his fist on the ground and ripped off his beard, thankful for once that at the manly age of twenty-five, there were no whiskers beneath. That was when he saw him, laughing with that familiar sneer. That most loathsome waste of flesh, Braithwaite Lowery, Quincey's fellow lodger at his digs at the Sorbonne. *What was he doing here? The clod had no appreciation for anything artistic.*

Braithwaite peered over his spectacles at the few scanty coins the audience had carelessly tossed about the cobblestones. "Daft as a brush. Are you aware of how much a real barrister earns in a day, Harker?"

"I don't give a fig for money."

"That's because you were born under the comfort and protection of an inheritance. I am the descendant of Yorkshire fishermen. I will have to *earn* my fortune."

If only Braithwaite knew what Quincey had had to give up to secure his family's financial support.

"What do you want?" said Quincey as he scooped up his earnings.

"This post arrived for you. Another letter from your father," Braithwaite replied with venomous glee. The sod enjoyed watching Quincey squirm as he received the scolding letters from his father. "Do you know what I like about you, Braithwaite?"

"I can't imagine."

"Neither can I," Quincey said as he snatched the envelope from Braithwaite's grasp with a flourish, and waved him away with the other hand.

LETTER, JONATHAN HARKER, EXETER, TO MASTER QUINCEY HARKER, THE SORBONNE UNIVERSITY, PARIS

29 February 1912

Dear Son,

I have received a most disturbing letter detailing your progress, or lack thereof, in your studies and have been advised that you are once again devoting far too much time to your extracurricular activities off campus. This is unacceptable. Though you have not been home these past three years, a fact that has injured your dear mother deeply, I should remind you that it is my money that is paying for your studies and lodgings. Should you fail this term, even my connections will be unable to prevent your expulsion. Of course this would mean the immediate termination of your per diem and

Quincey stopped reading. More and more people continued to hurry past him going northward, and he was only too glad for the distraction from hearing his father's condescending voice in each typed word. His fingers rifled through the rest of the letter. *Blast! Thirteen pages!* The Harker family was famous for their voluminous letters, yet their dinner table was void of any conversation. Another gaggle of people hurried past. "Whatever is going on?"

Without breaking stride, a man called over his shoulder, "Basarab! He's arriving. Here! Now!"

Basarab? Quincey recalled reading some weeks ago in *Le Temps* that Basarab, the great Shakespearean actor who billed himself under a single name, was due to perform in Paris. And although he longed to see the world-renowned actor on the stage, he had put it out of his mind, knowing he could never justify the cost of a ticket on the expenditure report he filed monthly for his father to audit. He had lied so many times before that his father knew all of his tricks.

What good fortune! Or was it fate that Quincey should be here at the moment of Basarab's arrival in Paris? Suddenly, he felt at ease, realizing that it was not his performance that chased away his audience. He had simply been upstaged by a true star. Forgetting his props and costumes upon the fountain, he found himself running along with the crowd, hoping to glimpse the magnificence of the great Basarab with his own eyes.

Quincey emerged from the park onto the rue de Vaugirard and found a throng of people crowding the street. They were turned toward the Théâtre de l'Odéon, a white building with Roman-style columns adorning the front steps. The moonlight made the brass-lettered name of the theatre glow as if illuminated from within.

Quincey tried to move closer and found himself trapped in the roundabout, pressed against the monument to French playwright Émile Augier. Undeterred, he scaled its pedestal to get a better look.

A Benz Tourer motorcar circled the roundabout toward the theatre's front steps. It honked, clearing a way through the crowd. Quincey climbed higher. The car stopped short of the front steps, and the driver walked around to the other side of the vehicle to open the door for his passenger. During the two years Quincey had struggled as an actor, he had come to the realization that since Shakespeare's days, the profession was considered the vocation of sinners, drunks, prostitutes, and vaga-bonds. Yet here before him was an actor who was regarded like royalty, and all of France seemed to have turned out for his arrival.

The dashing young Romanian stepped out of the car and stood on the ride rail. Quincey recognized the dark hair and chiseled features of Basarab from the picture in *Le Temps*. The actor was wearing a cloak similar to one worn by Prince Edward, yet his was cut from crimson-dyed leather, very decadent for a mere actor. Reporters with cameras mounted on wooden legs waited on the steps to capture the first images of his arrival. When he turned to them and smiled, the flash powders ignited like lightning. After a few moments, Basarab stepped down from the motorcar and moved through the crowd with arms out-stretched, palms up, allowing the adoring public to touch him. Quincey laughed when a woman touched Basarab's elbow and fainted. If only he could evoke this sort of reaction from a crowd.

The portly figure of André Antoine, the theatre manager of l'Odéon, waited on the top step to greet his star. A man with a wooden film cam-era stood close by and wound the handle like an organ grinder as Basarab mounted the steps to shake the manager's hand. Next to the handsome form of Basarab, Antoine's pleasant face seemed like a dot in the center of his large round head. The crowd cheered Basarab's name. Caught up in the frenzied energy, Quincey found himself chanting along: "Basarab! Basarab! Basarab!"

No wonder people adore him, Quincey thought. Even he was in awe. Basarab had not uttered a single word, yet he controlled everyone before him. How magnificent he must be to watch onstage. He would bring such life to Shakespeare's words.

Basarab motioned to Antoine, and the two men disappeared into the theatre. The crowd lingered for a moment as if waiting for an encore. A small man emerged from within to announce that the box office would be extended for the night, selling tickets to the performances of *Richard III*.

The crowd turned into a mob as people pushed their way toward the door. Quincey's spirits sank. Now he would never be able to put it out of his mind again. He desperately wanted to see Basarab perform, but he had not a franc to spare. The per diem his father gave him was measured out barely to cover the essentials—in order to prevent Quincey from wasting money on what Jonathan Harker would see as frivolities. *Bloody hell. What is life without the theatre?*

Quincey counted the coins he had made from the earlier performance. He was young enough to take risks, even if it meant dipping into his per diem and spending the last franc he had, even if it meant enduring his father's wrath. He would attend Basarab's opening performance at the Théâtre de l'Odéon tomorrow night.

CHAPTER IV.

———◇———

It had been thirty years since Seward last traversed these waters, and it had been daylight at the time. He rowed the boat he had "acquired" into the port of Villefranche-sur-Mer, after traveling by cart to Antibes from Marseilles. It would count as stealing only if he were caught.

He had to get to Paris. Even if he had enough money for the fare, the train would not depart Marseilles until ten o'clock in the morning, arriving in Paris at eleven o'clock at night. It was imperative that he reach the Théâtre de l'Odéon by eight the next evening.

Using a slipknot to secure the boat, he stumbled along the wooden dock until his land legs came back. The sight of the old Lazaret made Seward brighten. As an idealistic young physician, he had become involved with research funded by the French government, working with brilliant scientists like Charles Darwin. The study attempted to correlate the behavior of animals such as chimpanzees, rats, and mice to that of humans, hoping further to validate Darwin's theory of evolution. During his time there, Seward had become fascinated with the one or two percent of the test subjects whose actions could be considered anomalous. Why did these anomalies exist? Could the anomalous behavior be corrected? Seward smiled, recalling walks along the sea with other scientists from the Lazaret during which they had debated and challenged the archaic views of the Church about creationism. Their studies were so controversial that the government had decided to put an end to the work, and converted the building to an oceanographic laboratory. To keep them quiet, the scientists received financial compensation. This was the money Seward used to purchase his asylum in Whitby.

Seward continued up the hill overlooking the port. As he surveyed the familiar seaside town that had hardly changed since he left, he recalled the groundbreaking work he had done on the R. N. Renfield case. Seward had diagnosed Renfield with the rare mental condition of zoophagy, or "life-eating." The fact that Mr. Renfield had spent his entire young adult life as "normal" before showing signs of mental illness made him the perfect test case.

"Renfield," Seward muttered aloud. He had been so hopeful when Renfield came to the Whitby Asylum. Once a promising barrister, Renfield had suddenly de-evolved into a raving, insect-devouring lunatic. If Seward could have cured Renfield, he would have proven that mental illness was a disease and was not inherited, which would have proven his theories from his days at the Lazaret and helped to strengthen Darwin's arguments that all mammals evolved from a common ancestor. Poor Renfield, a hapless pawn taken too early in the game, had sadly become yet another addition to a long line of Seward's failures.

Within a short distance from the port, Seward would find his old friend Henri Salmet, whom he had first met at the turn of the century when he had just lost everything: his asylum, his practice, and his family. They had most recently crossed paths four summers ago, outside Le Mans at an incredible historic event: the Wright brothers' demonstration of their successful flying machine. The series of flights lasted only two minutes, but a new era had been born in Europe. Seward shook his head in bewilderment at the rapidly changing world around him. The French might have an antiquated railway system, but they were investing heavily in the race for the sky.

Withdrawal fatigue began to overtake his system. He could feel every bruise and cut from his tumble off the villa rooftop. He was getting old. Valiantly, he fought the urge for a fix, certain he would need his wits about him for the battle to come.

From the top of the incline, he beheld the familiar sight of Henri's farmhouse nestled in foothills of the Alps. The once-prosperous vineyard had been plowed to create a runway. The barn now housed planes and a workshop rather than livestock. Mounted on the roof of the barn, the weather vane had been replaced by a radiotelegraphy tower.

A light flickered in Henri's kitchen window.

"Thank God, my friend is home."

"Jack Seward!" Henri Salmet opened the door of his modest farmhouse. "Where is the rest of you? *Mon dieu*, what happened to your hand?"

"*Bonsoir*, Henri," Seward said. He looked down and saw that the blood had soaked through the handkerchief. "I know the hour is late, but . . ."

He couldn't help but notice that Henri had hardly changed. *His handlebar moustache is a little longer.* This was the last thought to cross the doctor's mind before he succumbed to his fatigue and passed out.

Daylight forced Seward's eyes open. He was drenched in sweat. He focused on the fresh bandage wrapped around his hand. *He had to get to the theatre.* Seward jerked himself out of bed and stumbled out of the room.

"Henri?" he called out. "How long have . . . ?"

Upon entering the kitchen, he found himself in the company of Henri, his wife, Adeline, and three children who had grown much since he had last been there. The children sniggered at the sight of him; Seward was not quite presentable. He could feel the blood rushing to his face.

"*Regardez*, Adeline," Henri chuckled. "From death he has finally risen."

"I need to get to Paris," Seward stammered through the withdrawal symptoms that were causing his entire body to shake. He prayed Henri would think he was merely tired.

"You wish to fly to Paris?"

"I know that reaching Paris is impossible, but as close to it as your aeroplane can reach . . . perhaps Lyon . . ."

"I think you do not know what you ask. But I have always said I would do anything for a friend in need. First, you stay and rest for a few days. You frightened us last night."

"I appreciate your hospitality, but I need to get to Paris by tonight."

"Tonight!" cried Henri, trading an incredulous look with Adeline. "You are so worn out, you can barely stand. What could possibly be this important?"

"It's a matter of life and death, a patient." The lie sprang all too easily to Seward's lips. "If she doesn't receive a special elixir from my medical bag by . . . seven o'clock tonight . . . I fear the worst."

Henri looked at his wife again. She nodded. "Very well," said Henri. "A life is at stake and it's our Christian duty to act. Sit and eat, regain your strength. We leave in an hour."

Seward sat in relief at the table, quickly relenting to Henri's wisdom. "I cannot thank you enough, my friend." Adeline shushed him by placing a heaped plate of food before him.

Henri turned to his children. "Come help your papa prepare for his flight."

One hour later, Seward carried his medical bag into the barn. He had not eaten so much in years. He hoped the food would give him the strength he needed to hold off his intensifying morphine withdrawals.

A mechanic carried metal canisters of petrol out to the field. Henri, bent over his wireless telegraph, glanced up when Seward appeared beside him. "I am wiring a friend to expect us at his field in Vichy," he explained. "It is the halfway point, and we'll need to refuel there."

"May I send a message as well?" asked Seward.

"Of course."

Seward retrieved a small card from his pocket book. "It needs to reach a person at this private wireless station at the Théâtre de l'Odéon. The post code is on the card."

Henri tapped the wireless key. "And the message?"

TELEGRAM—Dr. Jack Seward to Basarab,
Théâtre de l'Odéon—Paris
COUNTESS BATHORY IS IN PARIS. BEWARE.

Moments later, they were walking toward Henri's Bleriot monoplane. From a distance, Seward thought it looked like one of Da Vinci's designs, pieced together from papier-mâché and string. He could see that the "skin" was fitted plywood. Two bicycle wheels supported the cockpit, and the propeller had only two blades. "There she is," Henri said, beaming. "Fifty horsepower, and capable of a height of two thousand feet."

Seward choked on his response as Henri's son took his medical bag and strapped it into a storage compartment at the back of the cockpit, then helped him into the rear passenger seat. Seward was giddy with delight as he watched Henri kiss his wife and two young daughters and march boldly toward the plane. He could hardly believe that he would be in the air in only a few moments.

"Put on the goggles!" Henri called out, placing his own large goggles over his eyes. Seward copied him. "And keep your mouth closed as we take off. Unless you enjoy eating flies."

Henri's son spun the propeller, and the engine grumbled slowly to life. The mechanic held up the tail section as Henri lurched the craft forward. *This might have been a very bad idea*, Seward thought, watching the machine move ever closer to a dangerous precipice. His jaw clenched in terror. But mere seconds before reaching the edge, the aircraft jolted unceremoniously upward, causing Seward to feel as though all of his internal organs had dropped into his legs. Scanning the coastline, he recognized the familiar shape of the Chateau d'If, the famous prison off the shore of Marseilles. It had taken him several hours to row from Marseilles to Villefranche-sur-Mer. And now, in a matter of minutes, they were soaring above it. He knew that Bathory, like all the un-dead, enjoyed the power of flight. Now he did, too.

Four hours later, they were in a farmer's field in Vichy, refueling the monoplane. It took all three men to roll the barrel of petrol on its side from the barn out to the field where Henri's aircraft had landed. After the exertions of standing the barrel up on end, it was Seward's task to use the hand-pump mechanism to siphon the petrol from the barrel. The farmer held the hand pump's hose firmly in the aircraft's tank, monitoring its fuel level carefully. The fumes of petrol mixed with paraffin stung Seward's eyes. Turning his head away, he caught sight of Henri walking around his aircraft, checking every bolt and the delicate plywood skin for any damage. Seward's mind wandered, his attention drawn to the creeping shadow cast by the monoplane as the sun moved across the midday sky. The shadow of the aircraft's wings resembled a large bat gliding low across the ground. It was then that the darkness overtook him again.

"Don't stop pumping!" Henri called out to Seward. "We need to be airborne before the wind changes direction. We won't have enough fuel to reach Paris if we're fighting a headwind. I don't know about you, *mon frère*. But I don't want my destiny to be dying by crashing into some stranger's barn."

The petrol overflowed the aircraft's tank. Henri motioned for Seward to stop pumping and cried out, *"C'est tout!"*

Seward snapped back from his dark thoughts.

CHAPTER V.

— ◇ —

After the plane came to a rolling stop in a horse farm's grazing pasture, Seward untied himself, tumbled onto the ground, and kissed it.

"I am never going to fly again as long as I live," he said shakily as the engine cut silent. He glanced up to see Henri Salmet dancing on the fuselage like a child on Christmas morn.

"From our last fuel stop, I have estimated we have flown two hundred and fifty miles," he cried. "We did it!" Henri began to calculate aloud. "Now, how far would two hundred and fifty miles be from Paris?"

"I believe London," Seward said somberly, thinking of his home as he retrieved his medical bag.

"Now that I know for certain she can reach the distance, I will fly to London and have the press meet me there to document that I will be the first man to cross the English Channel and fly from London to Paris. It will make me *très fameux*! I must hurry into the city and purchase much petrol. How the devil am I going to get it out here?"

"Thank you for everything, Henri," Seward said, forcing a smile. *"Bon chance, mon ami."*

Henri kissed Seward on both cheeks and pumped his hand.

Seward watched as Henri ran off toward the road. He knew this could well be the last time he'd set eyes upon his friend's cheery face. He could think of no words more meaningful, so he kept his farewell simple and called out as he waved, "Good-bye, old friend!"

Seward turned in the opposite direction and checked his pocket watch. There was barely enough time to return to his room, gather his arsenal, and double back southward to the theatre. He would meet Bathory and her harpies fully armed. As the sun continued to set, he stopped to stare at the magnificent color in the heavenly sky. For too long, he had taken such grandeur in the natural world for granted, living alone in darkness. Tonight, he was glad, one way or the other, that he would at last bask beside God in His light.

Quincey arrived early at l'Odéon to purchase his ticket and took his time walking through the foyer of the old theatre. Each wall was adorned with busts, medallions, and portraits of actors. He drank them all in, recognizing a large portrait of Sarah Bernhardt mounted in a gold-leafed frame. Beneath the photo were her name and the title: *La reine de l'Odéon*. Quincey stopped at the photograph of Sir Henry Irving from his touring production of *Hamlet*. Irving was considered by most to be the greatest actor ever to voice Shakespeare's prose. Most actors used their talent to affect the emotions of their audience through the strength of their own emotions. They watched for opportunities to tear the heartstrings of their listeners. In contrast, Irving approached a character from an intellectual perspective, taking into account the author's intention and the character's personal history. Though greatly ridiculed by other actors, Irving's new approach captivated audiences. Much of the press said the same of Basarab; one reviewer had even raved that Basarab had inherited the mantle of "World's Greatest Actor" from Sir Henry Irving.

Quincey became aware that he was still holding the envelope that he had carefully put together. He had purchased fine writing paper and paid a few francs for a local street artist to decorate the envelope with theatre masks in blood red. With fine calligraphy, an art he'd learned from his mother, Quincey addressed the envelope: *To Basarab—*

from Quincey Harker, Esq. After seeing the pandemonium of adoring fans the night before, Quincey needed to make his envelope stand out from the countless other letters of admiration Basarab was sure to receive. He hoped that it would look important, and prayed it was not too much.

Quincey saw a short, elderly, uniformed man with a large set of keys in one hand and an electric torchlight in the other. Quincey knew this must be the head usher.

"Excuse me," he said, extending the envelope toward him. "Could I ask you to deliver this backstage for me?"

The head usher read the name on the envelope, shook his head, and answered simply, *"Non."*

Quincey's mind raced. "Very well, I must speak to Monsieur Antoine at once."

"André Antoine? He cannot be disturbed."

"I think the theatre manager would like to know why Basarab won't be performing tonight."

The head usher studied Quincey. "What are you talking about?"

"Monsieur Basarab is expecting this letter. He is so anxious, I fear that he may be too distraught to perform if he doesn't receive . . ."

"Very well," the head usher interrupted, stretching out his hand. "I will take it to him."

"Merci." As Quincey gave him the envelope, the head usher's hand remained outstretched until Quincey gave him some money. Then the man retreated. The lie had come so easily to Quincey.

Quincey turned to see that the wealthy and cultured, dressed in their best evening attire, had begun to pour into the opulent theatre. He knew that most of them were here to be seen rather than to see the play. Many of them shared his father's view that actors were vagabonds and heathens. *Hypocrites.* His father was the worst of them; he seemed to have forgotten he was the son of a cobbler, a mere clerk at law fortunate enough to inherit the firm upon the death of its owner, Mr. Hawkins. The senior partner, Mr. Renfield, who had been destined to inherit the firm, had committed suicide in an insane asylum. Quincey suddenly felt a cold sensation as if the temperature in the room had dropped significantly. He glanced about, wondering where such a blast of cold could have come from, when a striking vision caught his eye. A woman had entered the foyer, towering over all others. The nearby crowd hurled disapproving glares. She was dressed like a man, in an extremely well-fitted dinner jacket.

Elizabeth Bathory could hardly believe this was le Théâtre de l'Odéon. She rested her hand on the gilded column as she looked about the theatre. The last time she had been here was March 18, 1799. The night of the great fire. The theatre rebuilt seemed smaller now. She glanced upward at the glass painting on the ceiling, which was illuminated by new electrical lights. In Michelangelo-style artistry, the painting depicted dancing women who seemed to be floating in the air. Some of the women were cloaked in virginal white flowing robes, chaste and angelic, but most were in various forms of undress, and yet appeared more like little girls than women capable of desire. Of course, the artist did not understand that women were sexual beings, with needs like men. Only a God-fearing man would depict a woman with such contempt.

Bathory's eyes were fixed on the image of a raven-haired young maiden running with her white robe carelessly trailing behind her as if she had not a worry in the world. Bathory knew well enough from her own dark past that such a creature did not exist.

A fifteen-year-old Elizabeth Bathory had gasped in horror as her bejeweled wedding gown had been ripped violently from her body. Her terrified eyes had looked up at her assailant as he groped her breasts—her new husband, Count Ferenc Nádasdy, a fat, drunken slob of a man more than twenty years her senior.

"You are my wife. . . . As such you have an obligation to God to consummate this marriage . . . *Bathory!*" slurred Nádasdy, and his wine-drenched breath was rancid. The way he emphasized her surname confirmed he was still outraged that she was allowed to retain her maiden name since her family was more powerful than his. When she didn't move quickly enough, he struck her backhanded across her face, the full weight of his girth behind the blow. The signet ring on his hand had cut her lip. She tried to scream, but the bastard covered her mouth. She could still smell the manure since he had not cared to wash his hands after coming in from the fields. That had been the very first time she tasted blood and it had been her own.

In her youth, she had read countless books and poems written in Hungarian, Latin, and German. The stories always portrayed "romance" as a magical fairy tale sealed with a kiss. At fifteen she knew nothing of sexual intercourse or the pain of losing one's virginity. Such things were meant to be handled gently and with care. Every young girl dreamed of their wedding day. But for Bathory the dream had become a living nightmare from which she could not wake up.

Hers was an arranged marriage, to secure military alliances and lands; romance had no part in it. For Count Nádasdy, she was nothing more than a bucking mare to be broken. Every orifice in her body became his plaything. Her flesh meant no more to him than paper to rend and tear.

After the fat oaf had fallen at last into intoxicated slumber, Bathory had stolen away from her wedding chambers and tried to flee into the night. The Castle Csejthe, which was his wedding gift to her, was situated deep in the Carpathian Mountains. Unlike the lively, edifying estate where she had grown up in Nyírbátor, Hungary, this picturesque setting offered a bucolic tapestry of small fields and meandering stone walls. The castle itself was set high among the jagged outcrops of the frozen mountains. It was May, but at this altitude, it was as cold as winter. Bathory had stood naked, exposed, the freezing air soothing her wounds, her blood frosting on her skin. To freeze to death would surely be better than life with the grotesque monster to whom she had been given. But even in this, God had shown her no mercy. The servants ran from the castle and covered her with blankets. When she fought them, they subdued her and forced her back to her master. There was no escape. Bathory was a prisoner in her own life.

"What is it, mistress?" the pale-haired Woman in White asked, concerned. Her touch startled Bathory back to the present.

She said nothing, but as her rage boiled, she was haunted by the lie of the blissfully ignorant, raven-haired girl running in the painting above. *They say blood will have blood, but everything in its time. My ven-geance has just begun.*

Could it really have been nearly two days since Seward had last taken his "medicine"? His hands shook violently. Time was running out. He needed his fix soon, or he would be too ill and weak to mount an effec-tive assault on Bathory.

He was grateful to find that the Benefactor had left a complimentary ticket for him—a seat in the orchestra section, under his name at the box office. The Benefactor must have received the telegram and antici-pated his needs. In his deteriorating condition, sneaking into the theatre would have been impossible. Alas, in spite of the excellent seat, he would not have the luxury of enjoying the play as a spectator. He was sweating profusely and felt nauseated as he stumbled up to the door beneath a sign: *"Personelles du Théâtre seulement."* It was locked. He was about to search for another door leading backstage when he spotted Bathory and the two Women in White at the back of the theatre.

He was not ready! He peered from behind a Romanesque column, his clammy hands clutching it for support. He saw Bathory staring at the ceiling and he followed her gaze to a magnificent Renaissance-style painting. One pale, painted figure caught his attention. She was taller than the other women in the scene, with piercing blue eyes contrasting with her flowing black mane. A dark-haired Aphrodite, the perfect stand-in for Bathory. It seemed that Fate had decreed this theatre to be the ideal setting for the immortal to meet her end.

The sound of rattling keys startled him. He turned to see a short man approaching, carrying an envelope adorned with red illustrations. The man looked nervous as he unlocked the door and went inside. Seward slipped his toe in the door before it closed again. Making sure no one was watching, he strolled through as casually as if he belonged there.

Half-dressed performers dashed about. Men carried papier-mâché boulders to the stage. A seamstress sewed a costume onto an actor as he did vocal exercises. Seward had to find a safe place before he was discov-ered and thrown out.

"What are you doing back here?" a Russian-accented voice called.

Seward spun so quickly that his eyesight momentarily blurred. Had he been caught?

His teary, bloodshot eyes focused on the Russian, who stared down at the small man with the keys—obviously the head usher. Seward was safe . . . for now. Not wanting to press his luck, he ducked into the shadows behind a high-backed prop throne.

The head usher looked up at the large Russian and said, "I have a delivery for Monsieur Basarab. He is supposedly expecting it."

"I will take it to him." The Russian snatched the decorated envelope. He stalked toward a door marked with a star and the name *Basarab* carved in it as the head usher scurried back the way he had come. The Russian knocked and slid the envelope under the door. Seward, near the point of passing out from the need for drugs, remained hidden by the throne. His strength quickly ebbing, he looked up into the rafters, which were filled with ropes, pulleys, and sandbags. He would await Fate's fortune above, but first he needed a fix.

He thought of a fitting quotation from the play that was about to begin as he quietly drew his medical bag from under his overcoat. "Let not our babbling dreams affright our souls; Conscience is but a word that cowards use." Safely obscured on the floor behind the throne, he withdrew a leather belt and tightly cinched it around his sagging bicep. He filled a glass syringe with morphine. *Only half a dose this time. Merely enough to quell the nausea.* Seward knew that doping up was a gamble, but he could no longer function without the morphine. He felt the drug surge through his veins. It took only a few minutes for him to regain control of his body, and once he felt his legs were steady enough, he began his climb into the rafters.

While the War of the Roses played itself out on the stage below with wooden swords and fake sugared blood, Seward would set the stage for the truly bloody battle. He drew his weapons from a hidden compartment in his coat. The pieces were set, and now the game was in motion.

CHAPTER VI.

⊶——◇——⊷

It was now twenty minutes to nine. Only two minutes had passed since Quincey last pulled on his watch fob and checked the time. Curtain was supposed to be at eight o'clock sharp, and the audience was growing restless. Having spent time working in a theatre, Quincey was well aware of all the possible complications that could delay curtain time. Terrifying thoughts crept into his mind. What if Basarab couldn't perform? They could be refitting Basarab's costumes onto some poor understudy. Under usual circumstances, it was a stroke of luck for the understudy, but tonight the audience had paid to see Basarab. Quincey had paid dearly to see Basarab. A substitute would be most unwelcome. If the actor were unable to perform, it would all be for naught.

A gentleman complained to his wife in French, a language Quincey knew well: "This Basarab is as bad as that Englishwoman Sarah Bernhardt. I saw a performance of hers when she began almost an hour late. A Frenchman would never . . ."

Quincey was about to say something in defense of British performers when the houselights flickered off, section by section, and the theatre was plunged into blackness. Quincey expected a spotlight to appear, but nothing happened. The audience fidgeted in their seats. Still nothing happened, and Quincey strained his eyes in the hope of seeing into the darkness.

Without any warning, a soft baritone voice reverberated throughout the Coliseum-like theatre: "Now is the winter of our discontent made glorious summer by this son of York."

A single footlight sparked to life, illuminating the pale face of Basarab with an eerie glow from below. His piercing black eyes fixed on the audience from under his dark brows. Quincey was in awe of the impressive transformation of the handsome actor into the hideous Richard III. He was, of course, dressed all in black, his left arm withered, sporting a hump on his back. Despite the heavy costuming, his mannerism and tone left no doubt that the figure on the stage was an aristocrat.

"But I, that am not shaped for sportive tricks, nor made to court an amorous looking glass . . ."

The stage light slowly grew brighter. Quincey could see the pain in Basarab's eyes. He was not merely reciting Shakespeare's words, but rather drawing forth the thought and meaning behind them.

"I, have no delight to pass away the time unless to spy my shadow in the sun and descant my own deformity."

Basarab stopped, focusing his attention on one of the box seats. Quincey glanced over, immediately recognizing the dinner-jacketed woman from the lobby. "And therefore—since I cannot prove a lover—I am determined to prove a villain. . . ."

Bathory was surprised to see Basarab looking so intently in her direction. With the luminous stage lights blinding him, could he actually see her, or was it pure chance? She stared coldly back at the actor. The dark-haired Woman in White whispered, "Is it he, mistress?"

"It is he," an unblinking Bathory replied. She ran her fingernails across the arm of the seat, causing tiny wood shavings to fall to the floor, as she realized that the arrogant bastard was doing the unabridged version of this horrid play. Having to sit through four hours of this tripe was going to be far more torturous than any device she had acquired from the Spanish Inquisition. The actions of the actors on the stage hit far too close to home.

. . .

Ferenc Nádasdy was not an intelligent man. Elizabeth soon learned that he had no thought that originated from above his waist. It was this flaw in his character that ultimately enabled her to outwit him. She lulled him into a false sense of security by pretending to enjoy his sexual sadism and violent debauchery. Three years after they were married, in the hope of ridding herself of him forever, she had used his vanity against him and manipulated the count into taking command personally of the Hungarian troops in a war against the Ottomans. Through victory in war, he would enhance the Nádasdy family name, she had told him, assuring him that upon his victory parade, she would change her name to Countess Nádasdy in front of her entire family.

During the count's absence, his guards had initially kept a close watch on her, but she had tricked them as well, leading them to believe she was less interested in escaping than in running the affairs of the estate. She provided assistance for the Hungarian and Slovak peasants, even medical care. There were several instances in which she interceded on behalf of destitute women, including a woman whose husband was captured by the Ottomans and a woman whose daughter was raped and impregnated. Each night, alone in her bedchamber, she secretly prayed to God for her husband's death on the battlefield.

As a student of science and astronomy, Bathory had waited for the right moment. On the night of a lunar eclipse with total darkness as her ally, she had dressed in a black hooded cloak and vanished from the castle. With the assistance of the peasants whose loyalty she had bought and paid for with her husband's wealth and her own calculated generosity, Bathory escaped to find refuge with her aunt Karla.

Karla was said to be a pious woman. In the safety of her aunt's home, Elizabeth had hoped at last to find the soothing love and protection of God's embrace.

Aunt Karla wore her dark matronly look with pride. Her clothes were crisp, black from head to toe, except for the large gold cross around her neck. Young Bathory assumed that she was merely in mourning for one of her husbands. Aunt Karla had been married four times, each husband having met some horrible inexplicable death. When Bathory arrived wearing a crimson velvet gown, instead of giving her niece a warm greeting, Aunt Karla had sneered, "Wearing bright colors is for the vain. Vanity is one of the seven deadly sins. God would not approve."

Although Aunt Karla seemed to be cold and strict in public, in private she was far kinder and gentler. She listened attentively to her niece's tale and comforted Bathory. They grew close, close enough for Aunt Karla to confess during a night of drinking what seemed to be gallons of wine that she had murdered her husbands because they had discovered the true reason why she refused their bed. It was not because Aunt Karla was so in love with God that she took the Bible literally and believed lovemaking to be for the sole purpose of childbearing. The truth was that she gained no arousal from the male form. Aunt Karla could find satisfaction only with other women.

Bathory stared at the cross around Karla's neck, shocked by this murderous hypocrisy. Yet as a result of Karla's revelation, so much of her own self that she did not understand at last became clear to her. Bathory, as a budding young lady, had "played" with several servant girls until discovered by her mother and scolded severely. Her parents had called in a priest to pray with their sinful daughter. Her marriage to Nádasdy came shortly thereafter.

Seeing the confusion on young Bathory's beautiful face, Aunt Karla had comfortingly stroked her hair, all the while staring longingly into her ocean-blue eyes. Before Bathory had known what was happening, Karla's lips were upon hers.

Bathory had pushed Karla away. The idea of touching her elderly aunt in such a way seemed repulsive. "Does the Bible not say that murder and those desires are sinful? Are you not sinning before God?"

Karla stood up, self-righteously enraged. "You foolish, naïve child. I could not risk any of my husbands exposing me! At best, I would have lost my wealth and been forced penniless into the wilds, my flesh branded by a hot poker with the sign of the heretic. At worst, I would have been burned alive at the stake. It was not murder, but self-preservation! You would do well to not judge me so harshly. The way I see it, you have three choices. Stay with me, love me, and I will protect you from your husband. Go to a convent and let your unparalleled beauty waste away until you become as fat, old, and wrinkled as I. Or you can go back to the brutality of Nádasdy. The choice is yours."

Bathory needed time to sort out her thoughts, but Aunt Karla was not a patient woman. She had no choice but to give in to all of her aunt's desires.

Bathory had never experienced lovemaking like this. Why couldn't her husband learn to touch her this way? As she climaxed for the first time in her life, she no longer gave any thought to what she was doing, and with whom she was doing it. At last Bathory had found her true self. How could something so enjoyable be called a sin against God? Was not love God's way? It was in that moment when Bathory's rebellion against God began.

Bathory jolted suddenly in her seat as an actor screamed onstage. She couldn't sit through another moment of this performance. She rose.

"Mistress, what is it?" the blond Woman in White asked.

Bathory's eyes were firmly focused upon the stage character of Christopher Urswick, the priest. "I need to leave this place."

"What of Basarab?"

"You know what must be done. Do not fail me."

Quincey had no idea what fortuitous extravagance this evening would bring. He had never seen a production of *The Tragedy of Richard III* performed in its entirety, nor could he have ever imagined it being so spectacular. The costumes looked authentic, the scenery detailed and grandiose. The performers were magnificent. Most wonderful of all was Basarab, who played the Machiavellian king with such conviction that, for a short time, Quincey forgot he was watching a performer. Basarab made the lines sound as if they were the first words that came to his mind. Quincey had memorized the entire play years ago, but then it had only been words on a page. Now those words lived and breathed.

The play soared to its climax. Basarab's entire presence seemed so filled with remorse that Quincey truly believed he repented his evil deeds. He could feel the tragedy of the character who realized it was too late. As King Richard, Basarab thundered onto the stage, waving his sword. "A horse! A horse! My kingdom for a horse!" Quincey's heart pounded like a war drum. He was completely unaware that he was gripping the seat in front of him so tightly that he was almost pulling the unfortunate patron who occupied it backward. A battle cry rang out. Several actors playing soldiers sprang onto the stage to attack Basarab, who swung his mighty sword with the deft skill and agility of a true warrior knight. Lost in the moment, Quincey was about to stand up and cheer when more soldiers appeared. It seemed that an army of a hundred men was attacking King Richard. Quincey was in awe at the most stunning display of sword choreography he had ever seen. There were no words to describe the vicious reenactment of the battle that ended the Plantagenet dynasty.

He gasped when Richmond plunged the sword into the king's chest. All characters on stage froze in tableau as the stage lights, with the exception of the solitary footlight, went out. Quincey knew that the death of King Richard ended the play, but he found himself frozen along with the rest of the audience. No one breathed. Basarab stumbled and, in a splendid fashion, died.

The audience applauded madly, so much so that Richmond's final soliloquy could not be heard. No one cheered louder than Quincey.

Basarab returned to the stage, gave his final bow, and then made eye contact with the wildly applauding Quincey. The young man's heart soared. Basarab's attention drifted over to the dinner-jacketed woman's box seat. It was empty. Who were those women? Did Basarab know them? When he looked back to the stage, the curtain had already descended, separating Basarab from the adoring audience. He could not wait to meet this magnificent man face-to-face.

There was no longer any doubt in Quincey's mind. The theatre was where he belonged, not in some oppressive law firm. He needed to find the quickest way backstage to see if Basarab had received his letter. He waited for the crowd to begin to disperse before attempting to exit to the aisle. As he started to make his way out of the row, he noticed the head usher pointing him out to Antoine, the theatre manager. Antoine approached the end of the aisle, intercepting Quincey.

"Allons," Antoine whispered. "Monsieur Basarab will see you now."

CHAPTER VII.

———◇———

Quincey felt like a present-day Theseus as he followed the manager through the backstage labyrinth of the opulent Théâtre de l'Odéon. He noticed the "horses," men who now resembled centaurs as they struggled to free themselves from their elaborate costumes. Half-dressed female performers with nymphlike bodies scurried by. Antoine stopped in front of a door bearing Basarab's name.

He knocked. "*Excusez-moi*, Monsieur Basarab? The young gentleman is here."

There was a long moment of silence. As Quincey began to think that he would not meet Basarab after all, the baritone voice resonated from behind the door, "Send him in."

Quincey took a deep breath, swallowed his nerves, and stepped through the door. Basarab sat in front of his makeup mirror, reading Quincey's letter. The actor did not look up, but, as he continued to read, he gestured gracefully and said, "Enter, please."

Obeying as quickly as possible, Quincey closed the door behind him. He looked about the spacious dressing room. A neat stack of steamer trunks towered in one corner like a small fortress. Framed posters of Basarab's previous productions were hung symmetrically against the wall fabric. Opulent furniture decorated the room, which was far more lavish than the standard assortment of spare, unmatched chairs normally found in an actor's dressing room. An extravagant chaise longue that looked Egyptian was sitting next to a small, elegant pedestal table that was set for tea. Basarab kept reading. Quincey wondered if he was looking at the letter for the first time.

"Forgive me, Master Harker," Basarab said, his tone friendly. "I was quite taken by your letter. So honored, in fact, that I wanted to read it a second time very carefully."

It was as if Basarab could read his mind. Quincey said hastily, "I can't believe I'm standing in your presence. I can't explain it, but I see you and suddenly my entire life makes sense."

Quincey wondered if he could possibly have said anything more idiotic, but to his surprise, Basarab smiled warmly.

"Forgive my ill manners." Basarab laughed. "My father would disown me. Please, sit down and join me for some tea."

Quincey was almost afraid to sit on the delicate antique Egyptian chaise, but he didn't want to offend his host. He perched on its edge while Basarab poured tea into two elegant glass teacups. Quincey carefully picked one up to study its silver-covered base and handle, engraved with the initials *I. L.* The teapot, cream jug, and sugar bowl all bore the same monogram. Quincey wondered who I. L. was.

"Ivan Lebedkin," Basarab said.

Quincey gave him a startled look; once more the actor seemed to be reading his mind. Then he realized that he was unconsciously tracing the initials on his cup. Basarab wasn't clairvoyant; he was a keen observer of human behavior. No doubt one of the many reasons why he was such a magnificent performer.

Basarab continued, "He was the czar's assay master. His initials verify that it is, in fact, silver."

"The czar?"

"Yes. This tea set and the tea itself, Lapsang souchong, was a gift from Czar Nicholas. Enjoy. *Na zdarovia*," Basarab toasted. He was about to take a drink from his cup when he realized his nose or, to be exact, Richard III's nose, was in the way. He smiled, setting the cup down. "Excuse me for a moment."

As Basarab crossed back to his dressing table, Quincey couldn't help but contemplate the odd ways of the world. A day earlier, he had been imprisoned at the Sorbonne. Now he was sipping tea—chosen by the ruler of Russia—with the most celebrated actor in Europe.

"I've seen you before, Master Harker," Basarab said, pulling off the artificial nose, which had been fashioned from mortician's wax.

"Truly?" Quincey wondered if he remembered him hanging from the statue the previous night.

"It was at the London Hippodrome. You were performing a one-man production of *Faust*."

Quincey coughed so suddenly that the tea almost erupted from his nostrils. The great Basarab had been in that small, unassuming variety theatre over a year ago? "You have seen me perform?"

"Yes, I found you quite entertaining. Very original, and that is not an easy feat in this business. I proceeded backstage to congratulate you, but found you were in the midst of an intense argument with an older gentleman."

He knew exactly which night Basarab referred to. That night, his father, Jonathan Harker, had also been in the audience. Quincey had no idea he was there until it was too late. He had tried to sneak out after the show, but his father had already found his way backstage and was yelling at the house manager.

". . . and if you think you can stand in my way . . ."

"Father, please!"

"Get your things, Quincey!" Jonathan barked. "You will not be returning to this place."

"You cannot stop—"

"What I *cannot* do is to allow you to pursue this avenue. You draw too much attention . . . on the stage you're exposed . . . this is not safe."

"Exposed to what? I am not a child. I can choose what I do with my life."

"Very well. If that is your wish, fine. But, if you choose this course of action," Jonathan said, coldly lowering his voice, "you will have to survive like your fellow performers, without any financial assistance from me."

Quincey had wanted to stand his ground, but he was not yet in any financial position to meet his father's challenge. He was defeated. His silence answered his father's question.

"I thought as much," Jonathan barked. "While you're living off my money, you will comply with my wishes."

The elder Harker wasted no time in contacting old acquaintances and former colleagues to call in some outstanding favors. The following week, Quincey found himself whisked away to the Sorbonne.

Quincey frowned into the exotic tea. The evening had been going swimmingly until the memory of that encounter with his father tainted it.

"Forcing you to study law? I assume, then, that your father is a solicitor himself."

"Pardon? Oh, yes," Quincey said as he realized he must have been speaking his thoughts aloud.

"Now I understand why I have not seen or heard of you since. A father wishing his son to follow in his own footsteps is far from rare. Alas, the story is as old as man's dominion in this world. Perhaps you have a sibling who is more interested in the law, and can take your place?"

"I am an only child. No one else to share the burden."

"Consider yourself fortunate," Basarab replied. "You could have had a younger brother whom everyone favored. Comparisons between siblings always spark rivalry."

It had never occurred to Quincey that Basarab could have a brother. There was barely any information in the public arena surrounding Basarab's private life. He cleared his throat and delicately inquired, "I assume your brother is not an actor."

"You assume correctly. He and I are polar opposites," Basarab said. He gestured to the crown he had worn onstage. "I dare say that King Richard and his brother had a better relationship . . . nay, Cain and Abel."

Quincey laughed along with Basarab. The actor smiled. "Fate certainly has a strange way of bringing people with common bonds together." As he was about to take a sip of tea, a banshee wail rang from outside the door. Basarab sprang to his feet.

Someone pounded on the door, and a man's voice called out, "Mr. Basarab! Save yourself!"

With very few people left backstage to witness them, the two Women in White moved silently through the hallway, stopping at the door marked with the gold star. Faces bent in predatory grins, they licked their lips as they unsheathed their scimitars. Their eyes turned black; their fangs elongated. The dark one reached for the doorknob and the pale-haired harpy crouched like a cat waiting to pounce.

Suddenly, a sandbag fell from above and hit the blonde, sending her chin into the floor. In that same instant, Seward swung down on one of the many ropes from the catwalks above. As he swooped close, he flicked a cross-etched glass bottle, splattering holy water onto the Women in White. Their skin sizzled and blistered. Their terrible wails echoed through the corridor.

While the Women in White ran off, flailing in pain, Seward dived toward Basarab's door and pounded on it. "Mr. Basarab! Save yourself!"

Basarab turned to Quincey and pointed to the large steamer trunks. "For your safety, stay behind those."

Quincey swiftly did as he was commanded. Screams and commotion came from outside the door. Basarab grabbed a large steel broadsword from behind his desk. If Quincey hadn't known better, he would have sworn the blade was deadly real, not a dull prop weapon. Basarab swung the dressing room door open, raised his sword, and leapt out, ready for a fight. But, except for a few terrified stagehands, the hall seemed free of danger. The actor focused on the fallen sandbag, and snapped his head up to the rafters.

Looking left and right down the hall, he moved cautiously as if he expected another attack: Could the screams and banging on the door have been only a diversionary tactic?

Quincey wondered what secrets Basarab was hiding.

Seward chased the Women in White along the backstage corridor, and caught up to them on the stage behind the closed curtain. Seeing a shadow fall across the floor, he dropped down just as one she-devil's scimitar hummed past his head. The pale-haired demon rushed at him from the other direction.

Drawing his bone-handled bowie knife from its sheath, Seward cast it at her heart. With reflexes and speed far superior to any human, the Woman in White was able to dodge the blade's killer thrust so that it missed her heart and struck deep into her shoulder. The dark-haired vampire grabbed Seward about the throat, but she inadvertently touched the silver chain around his neck, which had an assortment of small religious icons dangling from its length. Hot steam leapt from her blistering hand where she touched the chain, and Seward felt a terrible glee. He wore the chain for situations such as this. The wounded pair fled, bursting through the main curtain, and Seward's pride swelled. For the moment, the weak old man had the advantage.

The Women in White tore through the red velvet theatre curtain and leapt from the stage into the seats, bounding like wild cats on all fours from seat top to seat top. Seward jumped from the stage, twisting his ankle as he landed. He continued the pursuit, hobbling up the theatre aisle.

The head usher, whom Seward had earlier followed into the backstage area, appeared at the top of the aisle and demanded in understandable bemusement, *"Qu'est-ce qui ce passe?"*

The pale-haired woman hurled him out of her way, smashing his body into a nearby column. As she fled, she pulled the bone-handled bowie knife out of her shoulder. Seward paused by the man for an instant, but when he had determined the fellow was not too badly injured, he continued his chase.

Seward stopped on the top step of the Théâtre de l'Odéon's entrance. Smoke escaped from his mouth as the cold air clashed with his hot breath. Through the thick blanket of fog that had rolled into the Paris night, he could barely make out the shadowy figures of the Women in White across the street; but he could see by the flickering reflection of their steel knives in the gas lamps that they were waiting for him in ambush behind a monument that held a stone bust upon its central pillar. This was Seward's moment at last. He caressed his beloved watch for courage. He would kill one of these demons in the name of Lucy and the other would die in memory of the poor girl slain in Marseilles. Seward drew his sword. He was God's madman again. God's soldier.

With a battle cry, Seward raised his sword over his head and raced down the stone steps with surprising agility, ignoring the pain in his ankle. The two vampires watched his charge, making no effort to move. They smiled as he reached the bottom step and raced onto the rue de Vaugirard.

A horse whinnied and Seward whirled in horror to see the error of his strategy. He had been so focused on attacking the two pawns that he had forgotten the black queen could attack from any direction. Out of the fog, the driverless carriage descended swiftly upon him. With no time to react, Seward was thrown down amidst trampling hooves and carriage wheels.

Lying battered and beaten, he instantly knew he had not only failed the Benefactor, but he had also failed God. The shame he felt was even greater than the pain in his broken body. Through stinging tears, he saw the Women in White deftly catch up to the racing carriage and bound effortlessly onto it. The dark-haired demon turned to laugh at him before climbing inside the coach.

Seward saw his watch lying on the ground nearby. He tried to retrieve it, but when he moved, the pain was too great. He coughed up blood, fighting to scream. A man loomed over him, and Seward tried to signal the man to give him his watch. The man followed Seward's eyes and picked up the cherished timepiece. He said softly in French, "You won't need this where you're going."

As life slowly ebbed away, Seward watched helplessly as the man ran away with his most prized possession.

CHAPTER VIII.

❖

Antoine hurried Quincey out through the front of the theatre, where the young man was shocked to see the mangled body of a man lying in a pool of blood on the cobblestones. Pedestrians ran, calling for police and a doctor.

"My God," Quincey said, "what happened?"

Whistles sounded from all directions as policemen headed for the scene. Antoine pulled Quincey down the front steps, attempting to usher him away as quickly as possible. "As I understand it, a crazed man attacked two women in the theatre."

Quincey saw a vagabond leaning down to talk with the injured man on the street and was alarmed to see him grab the victim's watch and run off. Without thinking, he yelled, "Thief!" and charged after the fellow, pushing past Antoine.

It was too late. The thief had run up the street, out of Quincey's range. Flustered at his lost chance at heroics, Quincey was forced to join the other mild-mannered pedestrians pointing the thief out to the arriving policemen. Within moments, two policemen had tackled and apprehended the vagabond and retrieved the silver watch.

Antoine grabbed Quincey by the arm, dragging him away. "Mr.

Basarab charged me with taking you safely back to the Sorbonne. Come with me right now, young man; this is no place for you."

Like Antoine, Quincey would not dare disobey Basarab's wishes. As they shuffled through the crowd, he whispered, "What about Mr. Basarab?"

"Surely you cannot expect a famous public man like Basarab to be seen around such a tragedy? Think of his reputation."

Quincey nodded, but he could not help but wonder what had really happened backstage, and why the great actor had remained behind when there could still be danger. The policemen were clearing the area now, allowing the injured man room to breathe. Quincey glanced back, finally able to glimpse the victim's face. The man seemed oddly familiar.

Looking up into the night sky, Seward realized that he felt no more pain. With his last gasp, he uttered a single word.
"Lucy."

The driverless black carriage raced across the Seine by way of the boulevard du Palais bridge. The City of Lights sparkled in the night. Poets have written that when those lights shine, "Paris is a city for lovers." But Bathory had lived long enough to know that the sparkle was just an illusion, like love itself.

Countess Elizabeth Bathory had become her aunt Karla's willing student, doing anything Karla asked for fear that the instruction might end. Yet, as the countess embraced who she was and found herself at last happy, safe, and content, she realized that she might find more bliss with someone her own age, in particular Ilka, the kitchen maid. Ilka was young, beautiful, innocent, and sweet. More importantly, Ilka always spoke of the future, unlike Karla, who often dwelled on the past. With Ilka, Bathory had someone with whom to share her youthful energy, to run in the fields and seek adventures. Bathory meant no harm to her aunt, and justified the dalliance by believing in her newfound philosophy that love could never be wrong.

Aunt Karla began to suspect her and confronted Ilka. Blinded by jealousy and rage, she had denounced Ilka as a thief and saw to it that she was swiftly hanged for her crimes. When Bathory retaliated by banning Karla from her bed, her aunt betrayed Bathory's whereabouts to her family.

Days later, an armed escort arrived. When Bathory resisted, she was bound, gagged, hooded, and thrown over the back of a horse. She was told that her family was sending her back to her husband to fulfill her marriage vows before God and produce an heir for Count Nádasdy.

It was then that Bathory came to believe that love was just a temporary illusion created by God to heap more suffering upon his children.

Looking out now upon this so-called City for Lovers, from the driverless black carriage that raced away from the Théâtre de l'Odéon, Bathory swore she would one day burn Paris to the ground and stamp her boots upon its ashes.

She turned from the small opening in the curtains shrouding the coach's windows. "We must expedite our plan more swiftly."

"Your trap was ingenious, mistress," her pale-haired companion said, with a hint of worry in her voice.

"The vampire hunter is now dead and can never reveal to anyone what he saw in Marseilles," the dark Woman in White added, her pretty brow puckered.

"I knew him," Bathory replied. "He was but one of many. Now the others will come. *We* shall strike first."

CHAPTER IX.

—◦—

Mina Harker stood on the small balcony and looked out into the night, longing for something, but for what, she couldn't say. She shivered at the sound of the chimes ringing from the nearby cathedral, though she was not cold. Above the cathedral, what looked like an unnatural crimson fog was descending from the clouds, as if the sky itself were bleeding. The fog moved swiftly toward her, against the wind. Her eyes widened as she stepped back into her husband's study and closed the shutter doors. In a wave of panic, she dashed from window to window, slamming them shut. Mere moments later, an angry wind pounded the glass so forcefully that Mina backed away for fear it would shatter.

The howling wind grew louder and louder. Then, in an instant, there was nothing, only a deafening silence. Mina strained to listen for any sound, any movement. Daring at last to peer through the shutters, she saw that the house was enveloped. She couldn't see an inch past the window.

A loud, hollow knock upon the front door echoed to the high rafters of the foyer and Mina jumped violently. Another knock came, and then another. The pounding grew louder, more forceful.

She did not move. She could not move. She wanted to run, but found herself frozen by the dark fear that it could be *him*, returned. She knew it was impossible. He was dead. They had all watched him die. There came the sound of glass breaking from the floor below. Mina could hear the front doors swing open and the sound of something being dragged along the marble floor. Jonathan had gone out, as usual. Manning, the butler, had been dismissed for the evening. But now someone else—or something—was in the house with her. Mina backed into a corner, cowering in fear. She was angry with herself for being so weak; she would not be a prisoner in her own home, to anyone or anything, least of all to herself. Her previous experiences with the supernatural had taught her that shrinking away like a frightened schoolgirl would not force evil to recede. Confronting it head-on was the only way to combat the darkness.

She snatched a ceremonial Japanese sword from the wall, a gift from one of Jonathan's clients. Ironically, she had always despised the prominent place Jonathan had given it in the room. Nearing the top of the grand staircase, Mina knelt to peer through the banister's ornate iron rails. The front door was wide open. A meandering trail of smeared blood stained the floor from the threshold, across the foyer, and into the drawing room. The frightful thought that Jonathan had returned home and was somehow injured banished all her fears, and she raced down the stairs and into the drawing room. Following the bloody path to a corner, she found a man huddled beneath the portrait that hid the family wall safe. A bolt of lightning ripped through the sky, illuminating the study. She gasped, shocked at the ghastly appearance of a man she knew.

"Jack?"

Not only was Jack Seward covered from head to foot in blood, but he looked so frail and ill, vastly different from the robust man she had once known. He looked up at her, opened his mouth, and tried to speak. Blood gurgled out instead of words. Dropping the sword, she knelt beside him. "Jack, don't try to speak. I'll fetch a physician."

As she rose, Seward grabbed her arm. He shook his head vigorously. He pointed to the floor, where he had written with his own blood: "B-E-W-A-R."

"Beware?" Mina implored. "Beware of what . . . of whom?"

Seward screamed, but it was abruptly silenced. He fell back, his face frozen in horror.

Jack Seward was dead.

Her own screams woke Mina from the nightmare.

She was safe in her own chambers, in her own bed, tangled in her sheets. In those few disorienting seconds between the dream state and reality, Mina was certain that she saw the crimson fog seep out of her bedroom window and into the night. Although she was sure that she felt a presence in her room, she dismissed it as the last dissipating fragment of her vision. She sighed and dropped back into her pillow, watching the curtains billowing in the wind.

She had shut the window before retiring to bed. She vividly remembered fastening the lock.

The cathedral bells rang, and Mina glanced at the clock resting on the mantelpiece. It was a quarter past twelve.

She ran to the window and reached to grab the latch handle. She froze. The crimson red fog was in her front courtyard, slithering around the hedges and trees as it retreated from the house.

After drawing the curtains, Mina raced down the hall to Jonathan's bedroom to find comfort in her husband's arms but was disheartened to find his room empty. The bedsheets had not even been turned back. He had not yet come home.

"Damn him," Mina cursed. He was supposed to have been on the 6:31 train from Paddington, arriving at St. David's station by 10:05. She looked back into the night, wondering if she should ring up Mark at the Half Moon down the lane to see if Jonathan had stumbled in from the station. Then she remembered the embarrassing incident from the last time when Jonathan had traded blows with a fellow drunkard over the favors of an aged consumptive whore. Mina had been forced to endure the shame of traveling into town to bail her husband out of the police station's cells.

Despite that dreadful incident, she still wished Jonathan were here. He was rarely home of late. Now that her son, Quincey, was away at the Sorbonne, Mina often found herself alone in this grand, empty house. Tonight her loneliness was poignant and the house was like a tomb.

She gazed at the row of framed photographs on the mantelpiece. What had happened to all those people? Some were deceased, but most had simply drifted away. *How did my whole life crash on the rocks?* Mina's eye fell upon one of her favorite photographs, and she picked it up, a portrait of Lucy and herself, taken before the darkness came into their lives. Before she made her fateful choice. The naïveté of youthful innocence in those smiles comforted her. She could still clearly remember that beautiful August day in 1885 when she had first met the love of her life, Jonathan Harker, at the Exeter Summer Fair.

Lucy had looked radiant in her new Parisian garden dress. She had waited for months to show it off. Mina was fortunate enough to fit into the dress that Lucy had worn two summers before, though she found it stifling. She did not quite have Lucy's eighteen-inch waist, and the corset made her feel as if her breasts were being pressed up to her chin. The revealing décolleté was much more Lucy's style. Though it made Mina feel uncomfortable, she couldn't help but enjoy the looks it was attracting from the young men as they passed by.

Lucy was trying to introduce Mina to some guests from London, most notably Arthur Fraser Walter, whose family had owned and operated the *Times* newspaper for the past century. As they were searching for the Walter family, Lucy had suddenly found herself swarmed upon by a bevy of dashing young suitors asking to be included on her dance card for the evening ball. With her silvery giggle and a false sincerity, Lucy certainly knew how to play the part well. If they only knew her the way Mina knew her. Mina believed God had marked Lucy with red flaming hair as a beacon warning men to beware of her insatiable nature. "Our society will perish if we do not make the necessary social improvements quickly," said a male voice nearby. She turned to see a young man with a mop of disheveled black hair, dressed in a rumpled woolen suit, shaking a handful of loose pages in front of Lord Henry Stafford Northcote. The staunch lord, Exeter's Member of Parliament to the House of Commons, seemed to be as wary of the energetic young man as he would a growling dog.

"Workhouses are not the answer," the young man continued. "Many destitute children live by stealing, or worse. Something has to be done about the education system to preserve both morality and law and order."

"Mr. Harker," Lord Northcote sniffed, "the Education Act has made it compulsory for children between the ages of five and thirteen to attend school."

"But it costs nine pence per week per child. Many families cannot afford such a sum."

"There are means for the children to earn money."

"Yes, by working in a factory, which is basically indentured slavery for eighteen-hour days, leaving precious little time for school or studies. Is it any wonder that our impoverished youth turn to thievery or prostitution?" Lord Northcote raised a shocked eyebrow at Harker, who pressed on: "They are not as fortunate as you, who have been born into wealth, and you would have them sell themselves to afford what was handed to you by God."

"How dare you!"

"Mr. Harker is obviously a man of passion," Mina interrupted. She squeezed young Harker's arm to ensure he didn't speak out of turn. "What I'm certain Mr. Harker meant to say was: Imagine if you had been unable to read or write. You would never have attended Oxford, never have been assigned to the Foreign Office, and could never have held your elected position. A free education for our children would be a great investment in the future, giving them all a chance to improve themselves and the world around them. Every parent wishes the best for his children; it is through them that we achieve immortality. Would you not agree, your lordship?"

"How could I disagree with such wisdom?" Lord Northcote said, chuckling. "But really, Miss Murray, a woman as attractive as yourself is wasting her time by filling her mind with such a weighty matter. You would do better following the fine example set by your friend Miss Westenra, and spend your time searching for a decent husband."

Without allowing young Harker a chance to say another word, Lord Northcote offered his elbow to his demure wife and the two drifted into the crowd. Harker turned to Mina with a look of bemused awe.

"I thank you for trying. I couldn't have said it any better myself, but these fools refuse to see the right of it. I was trying to impress upon Lord Northcote the imperative to introduce legislation in the House of Lords to follow the example that the United States of America began in 1839 with a free common education. If we fail in this challenge, our society will be left behind. We will not be able to compete in this new industrial age of scientific discovery. Mark my words."

Mina smiled. "With your knowledge of the law, I would wager that you are either an aspiring politician or a solicitor?"

"Actually, I'm merely a clerk at Mr. Peter Hawkins's firm. I've been trying to impress one of the associates, Mr. Renfield, to take the case of two thirteen-year-old girls arrested for prostitution. Pro bono, of course. Unless I can make it a bigger case, more newsworthy, perhaps backed by new legislation, I doubt I shall have much luck. And two more young souls will be lost."

Mina was impressed by this young man's passion. She remembered an old Jewish proverb that she had always held dear, even though she could not recall where she had come across it: *He who saves one soul, saves the world entire.* And here was a man trying to save two.

"Have you read the work of William Murray in the *Daily Telegraph*? He seems to think as you do. He could be a valuable ally in your cause."

"Miss Murray! Is it possible that you are related to William Murray? I have been trying to reach him for some weeks now, but no one seems to know him. Any time I have stopped by his office, he is never at his copy desk. He is a bit of a mystery man. If I could meet him, I would be only too glad to shake his hand in thanks for bringing these social issues to the printed page."

Mina extended her hand. Harker's confused look slowly transformed into a surprised smile. "You're William Murray?"

"Wilhelmina Murray. But my friends call me Mina."

"Jonathan Harker." He took Mina's gloved hand and pumped it like a man's, forgetting his manners in his astonishment. "It is certainly a pleasure to meet you, Miss Murray."

"Please, call me Mina."

He looked into her eyes, and the look of respect she found there made Mina believe that this was a man she could easily love. Years later, Jonathan told Mina that had been the moment he had fallen in love with her.

"Do you dance, Mr. Harker?"

"No," Jonathan said quickly, "I'm afraid that I'm not much of a dancer."

He's shy, Mina thought. "Good. I would much rather talk about saving two young girls from the horrors of the street. Would you care to join me for a cup of tea?"

"I would be delighted."

Most men would have refused Mina's bold offer. Jonathan's eagerness to join her had made her love him even more.

Mina was unable to fall back to sleep after her macabre vision of Jack Seward. She pulled on a matronly floor-length woolen dress and went to the sitting room to take an early breakfast.

The servants returned at sunrise and brought her a pot of tea. She stared at her reflection in the silver service tray. Bags of sleeplessness would not even form under her restless eyes. A philosopher Mina had once read, though she could not recall his name, said, "The shadows man casts in the morning return to haunt him in the evening." For Mina, the past seemed to shroud her life in eternal darkness. At soirées in recent years, Mina had heard countless remarks that she must possess a portrait of herself that was aging in the attic, just like Dorian Gray in Mr. Wilde's risqué story published in *Lippincott's Magazine*. To poor Jonathan, it was no laughing matter but rather a constant reminder of her betrayal. She could see how he loathed looking at her now, though she tried to please him by dressing more maturely than she appeared. Even in the most spinsterish of clothing, her youthful appearance glowed through. Jonathan was now fifty years of age but looked ten years older. She understood how he suffered and why he drank. She could never know the true extent of the horror he'd sustained while imprisoned in that castle all those years ago. On occasion, she had heard him cry out in his sleep, but he would not share his nightmares. Could it be that he still did not trust her?

Jonathan avoided being home with her whenever possible, but this absence was worse than usual. Never had he been away for so many days without leaving word of where he had gone.

Manning placed the morning editions of the *Daily Telegraph* and the *Times* before her, and she settled in to read. She was thankfully distracted from her horrific night as she read the headline news of a French aviator named Henri Salmet who had set a new world record by flying nonstop from London to Paris in just under three hours. Mina marveled at man's boundless ingenuity, and wondered how long it would be before a woman's accomplishments adorned the front page of any newspaper.

At a quarter past ten, Jonathan stumbled into the room, unshaven, nursing a hangover, and dressed in a gray tweed suit that was as wrinkled as his brow. With a great moan he collapsed into his chair.

"Good morning, Jonathan."

With bloodshot eyes, he tried to focus on his wife. "Good morning, Wilhelmina." He was as cordial as usual which, in its own way, was more heartbreaking than anger.

Manning returned to the room, unobtrusively placed a fresh pot of tea and a basket of fresh bread on the side table, and shut the door silently behind him. Over the years in which he'd worked for the Harkers, he'd grown accustomed to their troubled marriage, and could sense their subtle stresses.

The sound of the door closing made Jonathan wince. He tried to steady himself on the chair.

"Are you still inebriated?"

Jonathan looked up at Mina as if surprised that she was still there. He reached for the tea. "God, I hope so."

"Where did you spend these past nights? In an alley? Or with one of your . . . *companions*?"

"It was not in an alley, that I can assure you," he said, pouring unsteadily.

"Why have you become so cruel?"

Jonathan raised his cup as if in a toast. "The world is cruel, my dear. I am merely a *reflection* of it."

He was mocking her and the youthful reflection she cast in a mirror.

"Then reflect upon this," Mina said, gathering her resolve. "Our marriage may not be all we had hoped. We may even sleep in separate bedchambers. But sometimes I do still need you here!"

"You forget, Mrs. Harker, that I needed you once."

Mina bit her bottom lip. "I had visions again."

"Dreams of him?" He reached for the *Times*.

"These are not dreams. They're different."

"I believe you want to have these *dreams*, Mina, that deep inside, you still desire him. You hold for him a passion I could never fulfill."

Passion! Reeling with rage, Mina straightened her back like a cobra ready to strike. "Now, wait a moment . . ."

"Why?" he interrupted. "Why must he always come between us, Mina, invading our marriage like a cancer?"

"It is you, Jonathan, not I, who puts him between us. I chose you."

Jonathan slowly turned and looked at her with such longing that she thought for the first time he had actually listened to her words. "Oh, my dear, dear Mina, still as beautiful and young as the day I first met you. Is that why you still call his name in the night, because you love me so much?"

Mina's heart sank. "How long will you continue to punish me for my mistakes? I was only a foolish young girl. I could not see the monster behind the mask."

"What did he do to you? While I grow old, you . . ." He gestured to her youthful body, shook his head in despair, and gulped his tea.

The passion, the fire, the concern for others had all been drowned in gallons of whisky. The man she looked at now had killed her husband, the love of her life. She detested this wretch before her. There was no resemblance in him to the man she had fallen in love with.

If that was the game he would play, so be it. Locking her emotions behind a bland mask of politeness, Mina sat down and forced her attention back to her newspaper. A small headline in the *Daily Telegraph*'s society page caught her eye: "FORMER HEAD OF WHITBY ASYLUM DEAD IN PARIS."

Horrified, she scanned the first paragraph. "Jack Seward is dead!"

"What are you clamoring on about now?"

"My vision last night. Jack's death!" Mina cried. She slapped the newspaper onto the table in front of her husband. "This is no coincidence."

A light appeared in Jonathan's eyes as he struggled to repress his alcoholic daze. Seeming almost lucid, he said, "God rest his troubled soul." He bent his head to read the entire article. When he looked up again, an unspoken question hung between them.

Has he returned for revenge?

Jonathan sat for a moment in silence, as if making a decision. Then his shoulders slouched, and his mind fell back into the void. He handed the paper back to Mina. "Run over by a carriage. It says right here it was an accident." He tapped his finger on the line for emphasis.

Fury ignited Mina. "You've withered into a blind, drunken old fool, Jonathan!"

The moment she said it, she regretted it. She was trying to spark him to action. Her severity only wounded this fragile man.

"I envy Jack," Jonathan whispered, tears welling in his bleary eyes. "His pain is finally at an end." He rose and headed for the door.

Mina felt the chill again. Her visions were real. Something terrible was in their future. And this time she knew she would have to face it alone.

In a panic, Mina chased Jonathan, catching him outside. "I'm sorry, Jonathan. I love you. I always have. How many more times must I say it?"

Jonathan didn't look back as he climbed into his car and pulled the goggles over his eyes. "I need to contact Jack's ex-wife and daughter in New York. As far as I know, I am still executor of his estate, and there are arrangements to be seen to."

Jonathan depressed the accelerator, let off the brake, and sped off at a roaring ten miles per hour.

Mina watched Jonathan's motorcar disappear in the direction of the station. The finality of his departure caused tears to sting her eyes. She blinked them away, suddenly seized by the conviction that she was being watched. Someone was hiding in the nearby shrubbery.

CHAPTER X.

——◇——

Inspector Colin Cotford walked along Fenchurch Street, heading toward the heart of Whitechapel. It was the most loathsome place on earth. After thirty years of service with Scotland Yard, Cotford had seen the worst of mankind. He no longer believed in the notions of heaven and hell that he had been taught as a child. He had seen hell on earth, and Whitechapel was it. One of the poorest districts in London's East End, it attracted the dissolute to its factories in the hope of finding work, but there were more people than there were jobs, which resulted in extreme poverty and overcrowding. The whole district had a distinct odor, a mix of bodily waste, filth, and rotting flesh.

Walking along Commercial Street, Cotford tried not to breathe through his nose, in an attempt to avoid that foul stench. It was early in the morning; daylight was breaking, and vendors were starting to move their fruit, milk, and water wagons toward Covent Garden. A locksmith's cart clanged past him along the cobbled road. Cotford continued, pretending not to see the crawlers—old women reduced by poverty and vice to the depths of wretchedness. They no longer had the strength to beg for food. Instead, they huddled together for warmth and waited for starvation to end their miserable existence.

Cotford had received an early morning call from the chief

superintendent "requesting" that, as soon as possible, he look into the death of some vagabond who had died in Paris. Cotford had spoken to Lieutenant Jourdan, the French police officer assigned to the case, though he did not see the point in this investigation. Crazed, poverty-stricken men were run over by horse and carriages at least a dozen times a day in London. He would have to assume the statistic would be similar in Paris.

But Jourdan appeared to think there was more to the case. The victim had been carrying a silver-plated sword and, according to civic records, had at one time received grants from France for scientific studies. Unlike the Metropolitan Police in London, La Sûreté Nationale in Paris was not municipally operated but rather an agency of the government of France, and they wanted to be certain that Dr. Jack Seward's death was not the result of foul play.

Cotford had rolled his eyes as he listened to Jourdan prattle on in broken English. The man had seemed to be insinuating the existence of some odd conspiracy and, when Cotford had shown his contempt at such nonsense, had threatened to go over Cotford's head.

Now Cotford stopped in front of the lodging house opposite the massive warehouse on Wentworth Street. He took a swig from his silver flask for warmth before entering the dilapidated building.

When he'd first joined Scotland Yard, he thought of himself as an Irish bloodhound. In recent years, however, he had felt more like a retriever. By this point in his career, he had expected to be a superintendent, at the very least. He had been, after all, the youngest man to be assigned to work as a detective constable, handpicked twenty-five years ago by the great Inspector Frederick Abberline himself. But Cotford was still only an inspector and still stuck in H division. Instead of sitting in a warm, spacious office in the Norman Shaw buildings of New Scotland Yard, he was fetching facts for useless, dead-end cases.

He entered the stench-filled flat on the top floor. There were no electric lights, and the windows had been boarded up from the inside. Cotford retrieved an electric torch from his coat pocket. Its beam cut through the dusty air and revealed several books scattered about the room. He checked the titles: All were about the occult. Dried garlic cloves and holly leaves were draped around each window frame and door. Artifacts and symbols of dozens of religions hung from the ceiling. Yellowing clippings taken from the London press were stuck in the edges of a mirror, their ink so faded that Cotford, without his reading spectacles, could no longer discern the stories. A rather large insect scurried to escape his torchlight.

Within minutes, Sergeant Lee and two constables arrived to help pack everything up to send to La Sûreté Nationale, France's equivalent of Scotland Yard.

"Bloody hell," Lee said when he got his first look at the room. Cotford wasn't sure if the remark was in reference to the state of the room or the daunting task at hand. As a result of his extraordinary height, Lee kept hitting his head on the various artifacts hanging from the ceiling, causing them to sway like a ghastly parody of Christmas tinsel.

Sergeant Lee looked up to Cotford with a sort of hero worship because the old inspector had at one time worked on the most notorious case in Scotland Yard's history. The publicity surrounding the case had given Cotford some notoriety. Unfortunately, since the case was never solved, it was also Cotford's biggest failure and had tarnished his reputation within his profession as well as in the public's eye. He felt that Lee's admiration of him was unwarranted. He could see great promise in the sergeant, and hoped Lee would achieve the success that had eluded him. Unlike himself, Lee was a family man. Other than that, the inspector knew very little of Lee's personal life, and Cotford preferred it that way.

The beam from Cotford's torch illuminated walls that were wallpapered with torn pages of the Bible. The light caught a hint of red on the far wall. Cotford stepped closer. Scrawled in what appeared to be blood were the words *Vivus est*.

"Mad as a March hare," Lee said, shaking his head in disbelief. "What does it mean?"

"I'm not sure, lad," Cotford replied. "I think it's Latin."

Cotford picked up a leather-bound book, blew the dust off, and opened it. A photograph fell from beneath its cover. Lee picked it up as Cotford flipped through the hand-scrawled pages. Turning the picture over, Lee showed the inscription to Cotford: *Lucy Westenra, my love, June 1887.* Cotford shook his head. Nothing of interest. Lee tossed the picture into a box that one of the constables had started to pack for shipment to Paris.

Cotford closed the book and was about to follow suit, but something struck a familiar nerve. He couldn't believe what he had glanced at within the book's pages. He wondered if being back in Whitechapel was causing his mind to play tricks on him.

"What is it, sir?" Lee asked.

Cotford reopened the book, found the page again, and reread the passage. There it was in black and white. Could it be true? He tapped his finger on the page and, without looking down, recited the words already etched in his memory, "It was the professor who lifted his surgical saw and began severing Lucy's limbs from her body."

Cotford dashed back to the box and scooped out the picture of Lucy Westenra. He paused for a moment, mourning a girl he did not even know. Even after all this time, he still blamed himself and thought, as Karl Marx once said, *The past lies like a nightmare upon the present.*

A second more and he was racing for the door. "Finish packing the rest of those diaries and follow me with that crate straightaway, Sergeant Lee."

Within the hour, Cotford and Lee were back on the Victoria Embankment. They arrived at the Gothic red-and-white-bricked building of New Scotland Yard. Without saying a word, they made their way down to the Records Room, also known as "the other morgue," to search the files.

Hours later, they were losing steam.

"Where the blazes are those files?" Cotford swore.

"Some seem to be missing, sir."

"I can see that! Why are they missing? The entire case should be displayed in the lobby to remind us all of our folly."

"Begging your pardon, sir. But that case was at the Whitehall office."

"I know it was at the Whitehall office. I worked on the damned case."

"Well, when we moved from Scotland Yard to this building, the files . . . not all the files were moved. Some are unaccounted for."

Cotford growled, "That case was a blemish on this institution, and it's haunted me like the plague. If anyone hears we've misplaced the files, we'll never live it down."

"Here's something, sir." Lee pulled out a tall black cardboard file box. The edges were frayed, and the box itself was held together with a red ribbon. Cotford recognized it immediately. He took the box from Lee as if it were a priceless antique. The label, now yellowed with age, was still firmly gummed on. In typed lettering, it read, WHITECHAPEL MURDERS, 1888. Beneath, in Cotford's own handwriting, the file number: 57825.

Under that: JACK THE RIPPER.

From August 31, 1888, to November 9, 1888, London had been in the grip of terror as five women were brutally murdered in the Whitechapel district by an unknown assailant. The killer had never been caught. He would strike in the night and disappear without a trace. This was the infamous case on which Abberline, the lead investigator, promoted the promising young Constable Cotford so he might join the investigation. Cotford's beat was the H division—Whitechapel—and, with his many commendations, Cotford was the obvious choice. It was the greatest regret in Cotford's life that on one fateful night he had failed to apprehend the killer by mere inches. On September 30, Cotford had happened upon the scene in Dutfield's Yard where the third victim, Elizabeth Stride, was murdered. Cotford had seen a dark figure fleeing the scene, leaving a trail of blood for him to follow. He had blown his whistle to summon the other police officers and gave chase. But when he'd neared the fleeing suspect, Cotford had tripped on a curb he hadn't seen in the fog that rolled in each night off the river. When Cotford picked himself up, he had lost sight of his suspect and was unable to see anything past his nose. He had even found himself lost in the streets, unable to find his way back to the scene of Stride's death.

The night ended with another murder. The fourth victim was discovered in Mitre Square, a mere stone's throw from where Cotford had tripped. When he fell, so had his career. If only he had been more careful, he could have been known as the man who apprehended Jack the

Ripper. How different his life would have been! He would never admit to Abberline that he had fallen. Cotford idolized the great detective and was afraid of losing his respect. Something told him that Abberline knew, or at the very least suspected, that he was hiding something, but it didn't stop him from standing by Cotford and the rest of the investigating officers when the public wanted to lynch them all for their seeming incompetence. This selfless act by Abberline meant nothing to the public and probably even hastened the great man's fall within the Yard, but it meant the world to his men.

Cotford felt as if he were going back in time as he pulled out the file folders containing the transcripts of suspect interviews. Dr. Alexander Pedachenko, a Russian doctor, also used the alias Count Luiskovo. At the time of the murder of the fifth victim, Mary Jane Kelly, Dr. Pedachenko had been a patient in the Whitby Asylum, so Abberline had ruled him out as a suspect.

Cotford opened another file, marked CONFIDENTIAL. Upon opening it, he remembered why it was marked as such; the suspect was Dr. William Gull.

"Dr. Gull? The Queen's personal physician?" Lee asked, reading over his shoulder.

"The very same," Cotford said. "We were secretly investigating a lead that went dead. In 1888, Dr. Gull was seventy years old and had suffered a stroke. He was mostly paralyzed on the left side. Definitely not the one I was chasing that night."

"What night?"

Cotford ignored the question. He pulled out another file. *This is it!* His chance at redemption. Fate had dealt him a new hand. He was so thrilled that he started to laugh.

Lee was cautious of Cotford's uncharacteristically ebullient behavior. "I don't understand, sir."

Cotford didn't need Lee to understand. The dream of exposing the identity of Jack the Ripper and bringing him to justice was at last within his grasp. The professor Seward wrote of in his journal was indeed the same man who was one of Abberline's prime suspects. Though he had never discovered any evidence to place this suspect at any of the crime scenes, his gruesome biography did not allow for a complete dismissal of suspicion. The suspect in question was a disgraced professor and doctor. He possessed great surgical skills and had lost both his medical license and his university tenure due to performing experimental medical procedures on his patients and stealing university cadavers for heinous, ritual-inspired mutilations.

Cotford triumphantly handed this deranged suspect's folder to his second. "Mark my words. Every dog has his day."

Sergeant Lee looked at Cotford with confusion before reading aloud the name on the suspect's file folder: DR. ABRAHAM VAN HELSING.

CHAPTER XI.

—•—◇—•—

"How long did you plan to hide in those ridiculous shrubberies, my love?" Mina said. She stared right at him, as if she could see through the thicket.

Trying not to catch himself on a thorn, Quincey slowly emerged from the hedges. "I saw father's motorcar. I was waiting for him to leave," he replied, brushing dirt off his coat. "How did you know I was here?"

"I am your mother, foolish boy," Mina said, laughing. She gave him a warm embrace, then pulled away to take another look at him. "It's been so long. Let me have a proper look at you. I've missed you."

"I've missed you, too, Mother. . . ." Quincey paused. He saw that she had been crying. "What's wrong? What happened?"

"You needn't trouble yourself about me." She plucked leaves out of his hair.

"Is it Father? Has he been drinking again?"

"Please, Quincey, that is very disrespectful."

"Sorry, Mum."

"Come inside. It is good to see you, my handsome young man. You look as if you haven't had a decent meal in weeks."

.   .   .

In the three years in which Quincey had been away, he had gone all over the United Kingdom and Ireland with the traveling show, and then in the last year, he had been trapped in Paris. He had experienced completely opposite worlds.

Entering the home in which he had grown up was a surreal experience. The familiar foyer made him feel as if time had stood still. There was the banister on the grand staircase that he used to love to slide down as a child, against his father's warnings that he would be hurt. Quincey peered into the drawing room. Everything was exactly as he had last seen it, almost as if he had never left. There was his mother's favorite tea set, with the morning newspapers stacked close by. Quincey recognized his father's crystal decanter half filled with his preferred Scotch whisky. Quincey remembered the harsh scolding he had received when, as a child, he broke the original decanter. He wondered if his father was more upset about the loss of an expensive crystal or of the whisky it held.

While he was staring at the room, Mina crossed to the table and picked up one of the newspapers that lay open. Quincey thought he saw her hand tremble as she folded the newspaper and tucked it under her arm.

"Mother, are you sure you're all right?"

"I'm fine, Quincey," Mina said, offering a meek smile. "Now, why don't you clean yourself up, and I'll have the cook make a plate for you."

After the rigors of traveling nonstop from Paris, Quincey felt renewed as he dressed in clean clothes. He glanced around his old room. It was the bedroom of a young boy. He now felt out of place within it.

He passed the study and saw his mother lost in thought, staring again at that old photograph of herself and her childhood friend Lucy, who had passed away from disease at about the same age he was now. How awful it must be to lose one's life just as it was beginning. He always knew when his mother was troubled, for she always turned to that photograph. It was as if she were still turning to her dead friend for guidance.

As he stared at his mother, Quincey was struck by the realization that, just as this house had hardly changed at all, his mother looked exactly the same as she had three years earlier. He doubted the years would have been as kind to his sour, pickled father. He recalled a day a few years back when he had discovered that some of the blokes from school had made inappropriate remarks regarding his mother's youthful appearance and how he had been so outraged that he had taken on all three boys at once and given them all a beating. Despite earning himself a temporary suspension from school, Quincey was proud of his chivalry. He remembered how he and his mother used to trick strangers into believing they were brother and sister. He supposed one day she would grow old like his father but was glad that day was not yet. After being away for so long, if he had returned to find his mother aged and sickly, the guilt would have been far too great to bear, and the rage toward his father for chasing him away these last years would have been volcanic.

Quincey didn't realize how hungry he was until he started eating. He had not had a good kipper since leaving home. As soon as he polished off the plateful, Mary, the housemaid, appeared to clear away the dishes.

"Now that you've have had a proper meal," said Mina, "would you be good enough to explain why, after being away all this time, you choose to come now in the midst of a university term?"

"Promise you will not be angry?"

"You know I would never make such a promise."

"All too well. I suppose there is no easy way to say this." He took a deep breath and blurted out, "I have met someone. Someone wonderful."

Mina opened her mouth to speak, but seemed dumbfounded. Quincey was about to continue when Mary returned with freshly brewed tea and Garibaldi biscuits, Quincey's favorite.

The instant Mary left, Mina said, "So tell me, who is the fortunate young lady?"

"Young lady?"

"You said you met 'someone wonderful'?"

"I did, but . . . ," he said. "Mother, prepare yourself. I had a meeting with Basarab."

"Who?"

"Have you not heard of him? He is a brilliant man, Mother. The toast of all Paris. The greatest Shakespearean actor in the world."

"Oh, Quincey, not this again."

"Basarab advised me to stop following my father's broken dreams and to follow my own before I grow old."

"A tad presumptuous to assume he would know better than your parents what's best for you."

"I believe he saw potential in me."

"So do your father and I. What about your law degree?"

"Basarab's encouragement has convinced me to leave the Sorbonne and seek an acting apprenticeship at the Lyceum."

"I do not know what to say, Quincey. You made an agreement with your father. As you would have learned if you stayed at the Sorbonne, a verbal agreement is certainly as binding as a written contract."

"Please, Mother, that agreement was made under duress. I had saved no money. He paid off that theatre manager to fire me on the spot and toss me out into the street. It was either accept Father's agreement or be homeless and starve."

"I intervened on your behalf. I gave my word. Your father wanted you to go to Cambridge, and I, with the promise that you would graduate and take the bar, convinced him to allow you to go to Paris—"

"So I could at least be around the art world, I know," he interrupted. "I would have been better off in Cambridge. Do you have any idea what it's like to want something so badly, to see it all around you every day, and know that it is forbidden fruit? It's enough to drive one mad."

"I understand how you feel more than you know, but none of that changes the fact that you promised to finish your degree. A promise is a promise."

"If I am as talented as Basarab believes I am," Quincey proclaimed, "I will be hired for this apprenticeship. Then I will have my own means and the old fool can go to hell."

Mina leapt forward and slapped Quincey across his cheek. It was a shock to both of them. Never before had either of his parents raised a hand to him.

"Quincey Arthur John Abraham Harker!" Mina did her best to control her raging emotions. "Jonathan is still your father and he loves you very much."

"Then why does he not show it?"

"You are still too young and naïve to understand, but he shows it every day. I know his true heart, and there is purpose in all he does. There is more at stake here than your selfish desires. I cannot give you my blessing on this, Quincey. You must trust us that we know what's best for you."

Quincey was brokenhearted. He and his mother had always been close. She was the one who would listen to his hopes and dreams and encourage him. Now she was trying to stifle those same dreams, just as his father had. It would seem that some things had indeed changed here, after all. He had always known that his parents had many secrets that they chose not to share with him. Whatever they were, it no longer mattered. "*Ego sum qui sum.* 'I am what I am,' and it's time for me to be."

Tears welled in Mina's eyes, her face distorted with what Quincey could see only as irrational fear. She implored her son one last time, "Please, Quincey, do not do this."

The clock rang eleven. He coldly said, "I have a train to catch. I'll be taking lodgings in London. I shan't trouble you any further."

Not wanting to look her in the eye, Quincey turned and, for the first time in his life, left without kissing his mother good-bye.

CHAPTER XII.

---◆---

The tall figure of Count Dracula, wearing a well-worn dinner jacket and a black cape lined with red, filled the dusty English drawing room menacingly. His dark eyes stared out from under a furrowed brow. This grim expression slowly gave place to an ominous smile as he asked with a thick continental accent, "Would you repeat what you just said, professor?"

The older man sighed. "I said, 'Count, do you wish to know what I prescribed for our ailing Miss Westenra?'"

"Anything you do concerning my dear Lucy is of the utmost interest to me, professor."

Professor Van Helsing produced a massive wooden cross and spun to face the Count. Dracula hissed and recoiled, snapping his cape. Stepping on a corner of it, he tripped into the furniture, knocking over a lamp table. An explosion of smoke startled both men.

The count coughed uncontrollably. "Now that you . . . you and that solicitor . . . Jonathan Harker . . . have learned what you think it is . . . you have learned, Professor Van . . . Helstock . . ."

Van Helsing rolled his eyes.

Count Dracula continued, "It is time for you to depart these shores for . . ." He was at a momentary loss for words. ". . . the land of your little wooden shoes."

"The name is Van Helsing!" the other man shouted. "And could you be referring to my home of *Holland*, you idiot?"

"You insolent little fly speck!" Count Dracula screamed back, without any trace of an accent. "Do you have any idea of the awe-inspiring talent that stands before you?"

"All I see before me is a talentless drunkard who can't remember his bloody lines."

Outraged, Count Dracula turned toward the lights. "Stoker! Fire this arse immediately!"

Van Helsing grabbed Dracula's cape and pulled it over his head. Dracula, in turn, caught hold of Van Helsing's collar. The men struggled until the count was plagued by a second coughing fit.

"I've swallowed a goddamn fang!" he bellowed. He tore himself away from the cape and struck Van Helsing with a right hook. Van Helsing's nose exploded in a spray of blood.

In a blind rage, Van Helsing lowered his head and charged at Count Dracula.

"Keep away, you fool! You're getting blood all over my jacket!"

At the back of the opulent, Greek-inspired Lyceum Theatre, Quincey Harker shook his head. So this was the great actor John Barrymore from America, stumbling about the stage in a cheap magician's cape. He even expected more decorum from Tom Reynolds, the man playing Van Helsing, whom Quincey had once seen in *Madame Sans-Gêne* as Vinaigre. Now in a tremendous amount of pain, Mr. Reynolds had forgotten about respect for his fellow actor and was wildly trading blows with the staggering Barrymore.

It was a most unbecoming sight to behold. The theatre was not a boxing ring. There were very specific rules of decorum to be followed. To see actors behaving in such an uncouth manner gave truth to every negative opinion that the general public held about them. Even so, Quincey knew he had made the right choice in following Basarab's advice. Basarab was elegant and professional—just what Quincey wanted to be. But the sight of the sad circus on the stage was not the only thing that bothered Quincey.

Bram Stoker, a husky old Irishman with graying reddish hair and a beard, sat in the front row. He pounded his cane onto the floor, shouting, "Gentlemen! You are professionals!"

The younger man sitting beside him jumped up onto the stage to break up the fight, crying out, "Stop now! You are behaving like children!"

"He started it!" Reynolds snorted, bloodied hands cupped under his nose.

Barrymore tried to steady himself. "Mr. Stoker, I will not tolerate insubordination from such an inconsequential jackass! I demand he be dismissed immediately."

"Mr. Barrymore, please be reasonable."

"Reason? This is a point of honor."

"Let us not forget that I am the one who is producing this play," Hamilton Deane interjected. "I say who is to be fired and who is not. To recast would be an unnecessary expense. Mr. Reynolds stays."

"Then, Mr. Hamilton Deane, producer of garbage—you have lost your star!"

And with that, Barrymore marched off the stage.

Leaning heavily on his cane, Stoker rose. "I brought you here from America out of my high regard for your father, God rest his tortured soul. He made his theatrical debut on this very stage. Stop treating this play as one of your silly comedies. You have the potential to be a great dramatic actor here in London. Even greater than Henry Irving, but at least he ruined himself with the evils of alcohol *after* his fame was secured. You're well on your way to destroying yourself before the public has the chance to see your full potential."

"Are you going to fire this dolt or not?"

"I most certainly will not. Mr. Reynolds has been a loyal member of the Lyceum Company for over thirty years."

"Then I'm on the first tub back to America," Barrymore said. He turned and stumbled up the aisle.

"Mr. Barrymore, think of what you're doing," Stoker called after him. "You left New York because no one there would hire a drunken lead actor."

John Barrymore paused, swayed a little, turned back toward Stoker, and said, "You think yours is the only offer presented to a man of my talents? I'm going to California. I've been offered a role in a moving picture. Mark my words; you will regret this moment for the rest of your life."

Quincey had seen some of those motion pictures at the flicker house in Paris. It was cheap entertainment: He found it exceedingly odd that a serious actor would put any stock in it. Since there was no sound, performers had to overact to convey their intent.

On his way out the door, Barrymore crashed into Quincey. "Watch where you're going, boy," he slurred.

"Mr. Barrymore, I beg your pardon."

The theatre door slammed. With that, the great John Barrymore was gone. Quincey stood there, dumbfounded.

Deane and Stoker stared at him.

"Who the devil are you?" Deane demanded. "This is a private rehearsal."

"I'm sorry I'm early, but I have an appointment with a Mr. Hamilton Deane," Quincey said.

"Oh, yes. You're the chap applying for apprenticeship. What is your name?"

"Quincey Harker."

Stoker reacted as if he had swallowed a fly.

"Did I hear correctly?" Quincey continued. "Is one of the characters in your play a solicitor named Jonathan Harker?"

"Yes. What of it?" Stoker thundered.

"My father's name is Jonathan Harker . . . and he's a solicitor."

A few minutes later, Stoker, Deane, and Quincey were crammed into Stoker's tiny office. Framed posters from Henry Irving's reign at the Lyceum Theatre lined the wall. Stoker looked concerned as Deane handed Quincey a book with a bright yellow cover and red type:

DRACULA by Bram Stoker

"A character in a novel. My father never even told me," Quincey said, flipping through the pages. At last he held in his hands proof of his father's hypocrisy toward the arts. How fascinating. There were so many questions racing through Quincey's mind. And yet . . . Quincey bit his tongue. He did not want to start off on the wrong foot and show the same lack of respect for the theatrical rules of decorum as Barrymore. A lowly theatre apprentice never questions the producer or director of a play, not if he wishes to keep his job . . . and Quincey wasn't even hired yet.

Stoker snatched the book from Quincey. "This is ridiculous!" he barked. "I based the name on Joseph Harker, a scenic designer we had working for us in the eighties. Any connection with your father is mere coincidence."

"A rather large one, wouldn't you say, Bram?" Deane said.

"*Dracula* is my novel, and completely fictitious."

"No one has said otherwise," Deane said. "Though I seem to recall that you insisted upon staging a reading of it in order to prove your copyright. I still don't understand why."

"The only thing you need to understand is the copyright is entirely mine," Stoker snarled, who then turned his wrath upon Quincey. "I'm sorry, young man, but the Lyceum has no need for an apprentice at this time. Thank you."

"But, Mr. Stoker . . ."

Stoker turned to leave. Deane placed his hand on his arm and whispered, "Bram, we're behind schedule. Any assistance to this production would be very beneficial. We're over budget and understaffed as it is. And furthermore, we've lost our lead actor."

Quincey leapt up as an idea struck him. "Perhaps I can be of assistance with your dilemma." The two men looked at Quincey. This was his moment. "What if I could produce for you the greatest actor of our age? A man about whom the reviewers have said, 'When he performs Shakespeare, it's almost as if he actually lived the role, walked in the blood, fought in the battles.'"

"You're talking about Basarab," Deane said.

"He's a personal friend. And I'm sure his name on the boards would increase your box office potential, justifying any further expenditure you might incur."

Deane raised his eyebrow, contemplating the idea.

Stoker pounded the floor with his cane. "John Barrymore is the star of this play. He'll be back." He marched out of the office, grumbling, "Those motion pictures will never amount to anything."

When Stoker was out of earshot, Deane said, "What Mr. Stoker forgets is, it will be three weeks of traveling before Mr. Barrymore even reaches California. Even if he discovers he has made a terrible mistake and comes back to us hat in hand, we'll be bankrupt by then."

"Basarab is only a day away in Paris. To me, your choice is clear."

Deane searched Quincey's eyes for an uncomfortable moment. "Are you a man of your word, Mr. Harker? A man to be trusted?"

"I most certainly am, Mr. Deane."

"Good. Then perhaps you should join me for dinner," Deane said. "I think we have much to discuss."

CHAPTER XIII.

＊—◇—＊

Q*uid verum atque decens* was the Stoker family motto: "Whatever is true and honorable." Bram Stoker's father had imposed it upon all seven of his children, but it was a sentiment that Bram was finding exceedingly difficult to embrace these days.

"*T'anam an Diabhal,*" cursed Bram Stoker in his native Gaelic under his breath. He had been waiting for that whip of a boy, Quincey Harker, to leave before emerging from his office. Much to his dismay, he overheard the boy leaving with Hamilton Deane. Heading off to Ye Olde Cheshire Cheese, Deane's favorite watering hole, to discuss Basarab, no doubt. It would seem Deane was not going to drop this matter as Stoker had hoped. Stoker was always meticulous in life, even when it seemed to everyone that he was changing careers erratically. His every action was part of a bigger, well-thought-out plan. Having an unpredictable variable like Quincey Harker in the mix was unsettling.

Dracula was Bram Stoker's last chance. One last chance to prove himself as a writer; one last chance to live his dream; one last chance to keep his theatre. Now that his son was grown and had left the house, Stoker had nothing waiting at home. Even his beautiful wife made him feel quite unwelcome, and it no longer mattered to Bram if his bed was loveless. The Lyceum had been his true home for decades, and he would die before he allowed anyone like Hamilton Deane to take over.

Stoker hobbled onto the stage deck. So many shows, so many memories in this great auditorium, and yet so much had changed. Gone was that glorious domed ceiling that he had loved so much. Two extra rows of seats cramped the orchestra. He despised how Deane was turning his beloved classic theatre into some sort of playhouse. While Stoker was not opposed to the new industrial age, he believed that a theatre was hallowed ground. Would one modernize the great Gothic cathedrals of Venice? He laughed to himself. Perhaps Deane would. Deane was obsessed with the latest modern gadgetry and he had marred Stoker's theatre with it. He had installed Marconi's private wireless station with the excuse that it would prevent actors from constantly running off to retrieve messages. There was Edison's new "concentrated filament" spotlight. Deane even brought in famed theatre architect Bertie Crewe to redesign the interior of the theatre for "better acoustics." Though Stoker detested Deane's love for the "new and modern," Stoker understood that it was this same love that allowed Deane to see value in innovative ideas. Deane saw potential in Stoker's novel. He could see that horror stories, which had once been relegated to penny dreadfuls and pulp novellas, were finally finding a wider audience. Staging *Dracula* to compete with the successful adaptations of *Frankenstein* and *Jekyll and Hyde* could make a small fortune. Stoker had the theatre, and Deane had the money: a perfect combination. But Stoker had been in the entertainment business long enough to know the Golden Rule: He who has the gold crafts the rules. Deane refused to listen to Stoker. And why should he? If Stoker knew so much, why was his theatre failing?

Bram had always had aspirations of becoming an author. In order to honor his parents and stay true to himself, in his youth he had studied law in college, but he had never stopped writing. He had hoped his teachers would recognize his talent. Then he could persuade his parents to allow him to change his vocation. Unfortunately, this was not to be, for he had been overshadowed by his friend and classmate, Oscar Wilde. Bram's rivalry with Wilde even carried into romance. From afar, Bram loved Florence Balcombe, the most beautiful woman he had ever seen.

Yet it was Wilde, courting her with gilded poems of love, who swept her off her feet.

Perhaps Florence had an inkling that Oscar preferred the company of young men, for their relationship eventually ended, and she came to accept Bram's company. But as time passed, Bram realized that Florence's choice had been motivated more by financial security than by love. He had been hired to clerk in a law firm, and Florence did not want to eke out an existence with a vagabond artist. She yearned to be a part of London's high society. Stoker shook his head. Although Oscar might have lost the lady, Bram continued to covet Wilde's literary status. In order to keep his sanity, Bram kept one foot in the literary world. He wrote theatre reviews for the *Dublin Mail* for no pay. And after he had written a lustrous review of Henry Irving's *Hamlet*, he had been invited into that great Shakespearean actor's circle of high society friends in London.

Bram soon quit his job and became Irving's business partner and theatrical manager. This was a great gift, for it allowed Bram to live out his own dreams vicariously through Irving's stardom. Florence had felt sure that this would be another of Bram's failures but, as the money came rolling in, she had had a change of heart. The Stokers hobnobbed with the likes of the painter James McNeill Whistler, the poet Frances Featherstone, and Sir Arthur Conan Doyle. They found themselves in the company of greatness, but Bram knew it was only by association with Irving that he was allowed into this elite circle. No matter how much he pleaded, Irving would never produce any of Stoker's plays. Despite the fact that Stoker worked tirelessly to manage all of his affairs, even his trysts with women, Irving disparaged Bram's writing and would help him not one whit.

At last, a chance came for Stoker to step into center stage. In 1890, Oscar Wilde, straying from his usual style, penned a gothic tale, *The Picture of Dorian Gray*, and it was an instant success. Then suddenly, Bram's former friend and rival was arrested, and the result had been a highly publicized trial for charges of gross indecency. Hoping to cash in on the latest literary fashion, Stoker had drawn from Wilde's example and that of Mary Shelley and John Polidori. During the summer of 1816, the famed poet Lord Byron had challenged himself and his houseguests to write a horror story. It was assumed that the two established authors present, Lord Byron and Percy Shelley, would be triumphant. No one expected that Percy's wife, Mary Shelley, or Dr. John Polidori, would rise above the others. Both the novel *Frankenstein* and the short story *The Vampyre* were born that night, resulting in the two most inexperienced authors in the group writing two hugely successful books. Bram adored all of these gothic horror stories and began to search for the opportunity to match their accomplishment. That opportunity came when Wilde's imprisonment left a literary void. Bram decided this was the time to step out of the shadow of Irving and Wilde. Bram wasn't being opportunistic—he just believed that his hard work had to pay off sometime.

It came as no surprise to him that his editor and publisher did not share his newfound desire; after all, Bram had previously published successful biographical and reference titles. But he was taken aback by Florence's total lack of support. She thought Bram was wasting his time trying to write horror, and she considered this newest endeavor beneath them. Stoker solemnly realized he was quite alone in his quest to become a successful novelist.

Reflecting on this, Stoker understood that he should have sought a different editor and a new publisher for his novel. He was certain they had wanted him to fail, in the hope that he would "return to his senses" and pen only factual material. The cretins had not only changed the novel's title from *The Un-Dead* to *Dracula* but had also cut hundreds of vital pages from the book. Stoker wagered that Wilde had never been censored. Furthermore, his publisher had made no attempt to promote *Dracula* to Wilde's literary followers. Of course the publisher blamed Bram alone for the unsurprising poor sales.

After all these years, Bram still felt overshadowed by his former friend. Even from prison, and later in death, Wilde was the greater success. *Dorian Gray* sold faster than it could be printed. Stoker had hoped that Irving might publicly praise *Dracula*. Instead, he proclaimed it "dreadful" and, with one word, killed Stoker's hopes, for which Stoker never forgave Irving.

A few years later, Irving died before either man had a chance to apologize. To his surprise, Irving left the Lyceum Theatre to Stoker in his will. Stoker finally had full control of something in his life. But, without Henry Irving's name attached to the productions, the audiences stayed home. Slowly, the best and brightest of his staff went to neighboring theatres. The Lyceum was hemorrhaging money, and the pressure was almost too much to bear. Stoker had a stroke.

Bram was aware that he was in the last act of his life and had one last chance to make his novel a success. He needed the theatrical version of *Dracula* to be a hit in order to drive the sales of the novel. If the play failed, he was sure that his failing health would never give him the opportunity for an encore. He did not want to be remembered as a faded footnote in Irving's illustrious biography. He had to be the one to bring the successful ingredient to this production, not Hamilton Deane, or Quincey Harker.

Bram looked at the empty crimson seats of the Lyceum Theatre. *He* needed to be the one to fill them. He needed to bring Barrymore back and reestablish some modicum of control over his own play. He found it ironic that he could use Deane's infernal wireless station to send a telegram to Southampton and beg Barrymore not to journey on to America. Barrymore was the star Bram wanted. He no longer had the desire or the time to compromise.

CHAPTER XIV.

— ◇ —

T he distant bell from the Westertoren rang out a new hour. It chimed every fifteen minutes. The old man no longer noticed it each time it rang, since it now rang so often. Lately, though, the bell had seemed to grow louder, as if it were taunting him, counting down the minutes to the end of his life. He spent most days sitting in his apartment on Haar-lemmer Houttuinen looking out of his third-story window toward the Prinsengracht Canal, among his many books. His only connection to the outside world was the stack of newspapers that were delivered at the end of each week at the same time as his groceries.

The old man put on his spectacles and picked up the *Times*. Some Frenchman had set a new record in aviation. The old man shook his head. Man had no business flying. Even Greek mythology offered a warning in the story of Icarus, who flew too close to the sun. The moral of that story still held true to this day: *Pride comes before a fall.* This new industrial age had betrayed man's arrogance. The old man turned the paper over and saw the back listing for the society pages. Normally, he did not bother with the goings-on of the upper classes, but a headline caught his eye: "FORMER HEAD OF WHITBY ASYLUM DEAD IN PARIS."

The old man's hand trembled as his wrinkled finger followed the text. His heart beat rapidly, his suspicions confirmed, as he read the name of the victim: Dr. Jack Seward.

There were very few details surrounding his death, some accident with a carriage. What had Jack been doing in Paris? The old man reread the date. Jack had died almost a week ago. It had taken that long for the newspaper to reach him. *Damn!* He rifled through the other newspapers, finding the recent editions of *Le Temps*, and in one of these a companion article written the day after Jack's death. He read it as best as he could, though he had forgotten most of his French. It didn't really matter, for there were only minor new details to be found. A thick fog, the driver of the carriage failed to stop, and Jack, dead in front of the Théâtre de l'Odéon. A tragic accident.

The old man was about to shut the paper when the article caught his attention once more. A witness was quoted as saying he had seen two women climb into the carriage as it fled the scene, but that the police believed the witness was mistaken when he claimed that the carriage had been driverless.

It might have seemed an insignificant detail to the French authorities, but to the old man, it was a beacon of danger. He had always believed there were no such things as accidents.

"Hij leeft . . . He lives," he whispered to himself, his heart now racing in fear. He felt a sharp pain in his jaw, as if being impaled by a hot knife.

Within seconds, his chest tightened. The old man reached into his pocket for his brass pillbox. His left arm went numb. His fingers shook as he struggled one-handed to unhinge the tiny clasp. The Reaper squeezed tighter, causing him to drop the tablets onto the rug. The old man opened his mouth to scream in agony, but only a whimper emerged from his dry lips. He fell out of his chair, onto the floor. If he died here, his body would not be discovered until the delivery boy returned the next week. He would lie rotting, alone and forgotten. The old man grabbed a single nitroglycerine pill, placed it under his tongue, and waited for the tablet to take effect. The warm glow from the fire flickered, casting an eerie light into the glass eyes of the taxidermied birds and animals displayed about the room. Their dead stares taunted him.

In a few minutes, he felt warm blood coursing through his limbs again. Death loosened its grip. His rheumy eyes glanced back to the newspaper. The old man knew that death from something as mundane as a heart attack would not be his fate. There was a reason God had kept him alive. With all the strength he could muster, he pulled himself back up into his chair and rose with purpose.

CHAPTER XV.

Quincey had no memory of his trip from London to Harbor station in Dover Priory, or of waiting for the ferry to take him to Calais. For the entire twenty-four-hour journey, his nose was stuck in Bram Stoker's novel. He continued turning pages traveling from Calais-Fréthun station on the Chemin de Fer du Nord to the Gare du Nord in Paris.

He found Stoker's combination of a first-person narrative, journal entries, and letter correspondence unique, and despite the fact that a walking dead monster was completely unrealistic, he found himself intrigued by the character of Dracula, a creation full of contradictions: a tragic figure, a symbol of pure evil, the dark hunter who then becomes the hunted. But seeing his mother and father featured as the main characters was quite surreal. Even his home in Exeter and how his father had inherited the Hawkins law firm were mentioned. He found it offensive to read Stoker's suggestion that his mother would have been less than pure in her dealings with the vampire Dracula. But as Quincey read on, his anger subsided. In the end, Stoker had restored his mother's virtue by having her help the brave band of heroes hunt down and destroy Dracula. Funny, he had never thought of his father as much of a hero. But there had to be a reason that Stoker chose his parents as models for the lead characters in his novel, and he hoped Stoker would be more receptive to questions next time he met him.

Quincey became excited at the prospect of using this stage adaptation of *Dracula* not only as an opportunity to prove to himself that he could succeed in the theatrical business and as an actor, but also to prove his worth to Stoker as a member of the Lyceum Theatre Company.

"Welcome, Monsieur Harker!" Antoine, the manager of the Théâtre de l'Odéon, was waiting for Quincey when he arrived shortly after four o'clock. Quincey was taken aback by the warm reception, a far cry from the welcome he'd received only a week ago.

Antoine shook his hand. "How was your *voyage* to London?"

"Quite eventful," Quincey replied. "Is Monsieur Basarab here?"

"*Non*, I'm afraid none of the actors has arrived yet. Call time is not for another two hours."

Quincey had suspected as much. He took *Dracula* out of his satchel, along with a sealed envelope, which he placed inside the book's front cover. "Could you see that Mr. Basarab receives this for me?"

"I shall hand it to him personally."

After watching Antoine disappear into the theatre, Quincey set off to find a room for the night in the Latin Quarter. Quincey yawned as he dragged his feet along the cobbled street. He had not slept since leaving London and hoped to return to the theatre after the show, but he knew that the moment his head made contact with a pillow, he would be dead to the world.

He dreamed that night of a future when his name would appear on the boards beside Basarab's, and awoke the next morning feeling refreshed, and itching to know what Basarab thought of the letter and the book itself. Everything hinged on his reaction. Quincey could hardly wait to go to the theatre in the evening and meet his fate head-on. Dressing quickly, he went out in search of breakfast and passed the theatre. He knew Basarab would not be there yet, but he felt the need to stop and dream once again.

Over the next few hours, Quincey strolled through the streets of Paris, his mind rolling through Stoker's novel over and over again. He wondered if Stoker was a genius at creating the character, or if his depiction of Dracula was actually based on someone. Stoker had written that Dracula was a Romanian noble. It occurred to Quincey that if a real Dracula had ever existed, Basarab might be familiar with his history. A good producer would acquaint himself as best he could with the historical Dracula in order to impress his potential star. With that thought, Quincey took himself to boulevard du Montparnasse, where a number of good bookshops were to be found along the stretch near the university.

Two hours and three bookshops later, and he had not found a single copy of Stoker's *Dracula*. It could be that it had not been well received. Quincey was beginning to fear that he had backed the wrong horse. He came to a fourth bookshop, known for having titles from all over the world. There, Quincey was surprised to find two books about Dracula, both translated from German. The smaller of the two was actually a long poem entitled *The Story of a Bloodthirsty Madman Called Dracula of Wallachia*. The other, larger book was *The Frightening and Truly Extraordinary Story of a Wicked Blood-Drinking Tyrant Called Prince Dracula*.

Could the Germans make their titles any longer?

Quincey's speculations about Dracula's origins were correct; Stoker's vampire, Count Dracula, had links to a real historical personage. Although he was trying to be frugal with his money, Quincey purchased the books for character research. He would have to save money by forgoing some meals, but it was a necessary sacrifice. He wanted to know all he could about this mysterious figure.

Quincey stopped at the office of Compagnie Française des Câbles Télégraphiques, on the boulevard Saint-Germaine, to send a telegram telling Hamilton Deane of his wondrous discovery at the bookstore. He spent most of the day at his favorite carved-stone bench, near the man-made pond in the Luxembourg Gardens, reading the historical accounts of Prince Dracula. He became so engrossed in the brutal accounts of the diabolical prince that he did not realize the sun was setting until he could barely read the type on the page. Almost eight o'clock! He dashed off northward to the theatre and there quickly sought out Antoine.

"Monsieur Harker, Basarab was expecting you to come by tonight. He asked that I give you a complimentary ticket to view the show."

Quincey was ecstatic to be able to see this grand production of *Richard III* a second time, only a week later. This time, while he watched Basarab as the king, he could see how easily he could play Dracula. The characters were similar: proud warriors, cunning, ambitious, cruel, and charming at the same time. He could not help but imagine what it would have been like to be alive in the fifteenth century and come face-to-face with the brutal Dracula himself. The thought gave him shudders. Dracula was a man who could impale forty thousand people. Quincey could not imagine the unspeakable pain Dracula's poor victims must have suffered. Richard III's crimes seemed to pale in comparison. Prince Dracula must have been a sadistic madman like Jack the Ripper. But at least Jack had been "kind" enough to slit his victims' throats so that they would be dead before he tore them to pieces.

After the show, Quincey made his way backstage. There was a great deal of activity as crew members packed away the sets. Basarab's production company was in Paris for only one week, hence the exorbitant ticket price. The timing could prove fortuitous. Quincey found his way to Basarab's dressing room, drew a breath, and knocked.

"Mr. Basarab?"

From inside: "Enter."

Quincey found Basarab garbed in a black-and-red satin smoking jacket, clipping articles about himself from a stack of newspapers and carefully placing them in a scrapbook.

"I see you found your reviews."

Basarab smiled. "Always remember, Mr. Harker, shame is placed on arrogance by those who lack talent."

"Yes, sir."

Quincey became aware of the strong scent of food on the table where the tea set had been the previous week. Skipping meals was proving more difficult than he'd imagined. He hoped Basarab couldn't hear his stomach rumbling.

After pasting in a clipping, Basarab reached behind his wooden makeup case and held up the copy of *Dracula*.

"I've read the book that you left for me."

Quincey was amazed that he could have read it so quickly. "What did you think?"

"A rather odd title."

"I've done some research," Quincey said, proudly pulling the German books from his satchel. "The title makes sense when you know there actually was a fifteenth-century Romanian prince named Vlad Dracula. He was quite the villain."

"I would hardly refer to him as a villain," Basarab said. "He was the father of my nation."

Quincey smiled to himself. The money he'd invested in the bookstore, instead of in food, was about to pay dividends. Basarab crossed the room and slipped behind the changing screen adjacent to his wardrobe trunk. As if reading Quincey's mind, he gestured to the spread of food and said, "Please, enjoy."

"Thank you." Quincey tried not to sound too eager. Putting his embarrassment aside, he sat down. As Basarab removed his smoking jacket, Quincey took a bite out of a delicious-looking roast chicken. It was the best he had ever tasted.

"This is wonderful. What is it?"

Without warning, the strong spice hit and Quincey's mouth began to burn. He coughed, scrambling for a glass of water to quench the flames.

"No," Basarab said, "water will only serve to fuel the spice. Eat some rice."

Quincey obeyed and was surprised how quickly the rice seemed to counter the spicy chicken's heat. After a moment, Quincey tried again, taking a bite of chicken and rice at the same time.

"It is called paprika hendl, a popular dish in my homeland."

"Very good, actually," Quincey said between mouthfuls. "Might I guess that you will be taking some time off now that the Paris leg of your tour is complete? Will you be returning to Romania?"

"I have not decided what my next course of action will be. I have a standing offer to bring the production to a theatre in Madrid. As of yet, I have not accepted."

Quincey strained not to smile. He could not believe his good fortune.

"So Dracula is considered the father of your nation? From what I've read, he murdered thousands, and was known to drink their blood."

"An ancient pagan ritual. It is said that those who drink the blood of their enemies consume their power."

"And then there is the translation of his name," Quincey said. He riffled through the pages to find the passage and read it to Basarab. "'Son of the Devil.'"

"The true translation of Dracula's name is 'Son of the Dragon.' His father was a knight in the Catholic Order of the Dragon, sworn to protect Christendom from the Muslims. The symbol for the Devil in Christian Orthodox culture is a dragon. Hence the confusion."

Basarab struggled with his ascot in front of the mirror. Quincey knew how to tie them; he'd seen his mother helping his father. Without thinking, he crossed the room and helped Basarab adjust his tie.

"I suppose, as in all things, the truth is relative to one's point of view. All the same, this fellow Dracula is quite an interesting character, wouldn't you say?"

It seemed as if an eternity passed as Basarab looked at him, considering his next words. "Ah, now we come to it. You want me to play Dracula for the stage. And you would, no doubt, play your father, Jonathan Harker?"

"He always did want me to follow in his footsteps."

Basarab chuckled, and gently placed a hand on Quincey's shoulder. "I'm quite impressed by your ambition, young Quincey. From hopeful apprentice to producer and star inside a week. A man to be reckoned with."

"You read my letter? You'll come to England?"

Basarab grabbed his hat, gloves, and walking stick. Quincey cursed himself for being too eager. The lack of immediate response from Basarab was more than he could bear.

The great actor turned to him. "I make no promises. I prefer to play English characters. They have a knack for dying well. I have made my career superbly playing well-died Englishmen."

Quincey and Basarab shared another laugh. All the tension seemed to leave the room. Quincey couldn't help but think that this was what he had always wished he could do with his own father. "I am going to watch some late-night performances at Les Folies Bergère," Basarab said. "Would you care to join me?"

A good sign! Quincey had often wanted to visit this infamous Parisian music hall, known for its exotic performances. He agreed readily.

"We shall have a few drinks and discuss this proposition of yours," Basarab said.

It took immense self-restraint for Quincey not to jump for joy.

They walked northward toward the 18th arrondissement of Paris. Basarab questioned him about the production of *Dracula*, the theatre, timing, and even payment. Quincey finally felt comfortable enough to ask a question of his own.

"There is one thing I was wondering about. My books make frequent reference to what I believe is a Romanian word. Dracula is sometimes referred to as *tepes*. Would you know what it means?"

Basarab spun toward Quincey with a sudden, icy look of anger, and stabbed him in the chest with his walking stick to emphasize his point. "It is a vile word used by Dracula's political enemies to discredit him. Never speak it again!"

After a few more steps, Basarab stopped and turned back. Thankfully, the anger had washed away, and Basarab was his charming self once again, as if he had realized he had been too harsh with the naïve young man. In a tone of apology, he said, "*Tepes* means 'impaler.'"

CHAPTER XVI.

———◇———

The Fleet Street Dragon was watching him. From Jonathan's office window, he could see it sitting on the street in the middle of Temple Bar, taunting him, judging him. The Temple Bar had once had a stone archway, which marked where Fleet Street turned into the Strand. Due to its vicinity to the Temple, a complex once owned by the Knights Templar, it was now where the guilds of solicitors organized into an area that was known as "Legal London." During the eighteenth century, the heads of traitors on iron spikes had been displayed in Temple Bar protruding from the top of the stone archway. That archway had been removed in 1878. Two years later, the Temple Bar Monument had been erected in its place, a forty-foot-tall pedestal surmounted by a black dragon, which stood in the middle of Fleet Street. The Fleet Street Dragon. Of the many solicitors' offices in the vicinity, among them was Hawkins & Harker.

Jack Seward's death had sobered Jonathan enough that morning to send him back to London. He spent a couple of days at the office trying to organize the necessary paperwork regarding Jack's final wishes. It was no easy task. Jonathan's once-prosperous law firm with a dozen employees had slowly disintegrated to the point at which Jonathan could no longer afford to keep on anyone but himself. He would not even have been able to maintain an office on Fleet Street had Peter Hawkins not purchased the building back in the 1870s. It was ironic that the competing law firms renting space on other floors now provided the only reliable cash flow to Jonathan's business. To help him survive the daunting task of organizing Jack's scattered life, Jonathan took frequent breaks at Mooney & Son's public house a little east on Fleet Street.

He wondered if he was wasting his time settling Jack's affairs. After all, they hadn't spoken in many years. Jack had got it into his drug-soaked, raving brain that their demon might still be alive and had demanded to speak to Mina. Jonathan had thrown him out on his arse. That was the last thing Mina needed to hear. Jonathan had always assumed he would one day receive a letter from a new attorney stating that he was no longer executor of Jack's estate. Since no such letter ever appeared, he was duty bound as a member of the bar to carry out Jack's final wishes.

On the third day, Jonathan awoke from a drunken stupor to find that a telegram had been delivered to his office. Blearily, he opened it and read that there was a change in Jack Seward's postmortem wishes. The author of the telegram claimed to be a witness to a verbal amendment requesting a burial instead of donating his body to science. Jonathan was somewhat relieved, as he had never been comfortable with Jack's original request. The unknown benefactor had also wired money to Child & Co. Bankers, one of England's oldest private banks, situated at the foot of Fleet Street. The telegram further instructed Jonathan to use the money to ship Jack's body back to London, and to pay for the necessary burial arrangements. The remainder of the sum was payment for Jonathan's service. There was no proof that what this benefactor wrote was true, yet Jonathan believed this to be the right thing to do. The benefactor instructed that Jack be buried in Hampstead Cemetery next to the Westenra mausoleum. Jack would finally find eternal rest next to the woman he'd loved. Jonathan couldn't help but wonder who this benefactor was, and how Seward might have known him.

Jonathan had always felt guilty over how he had treated Jack the last time they met. He should have tried to get him help, but seeing his old friend disturbed him greatly and he had not acted completely rationally.

Jack was yet another reminder of that journey into hell, from which none of them had ever quite returned. Jonathan looked about his barren office, recalling the first time he met Jack Seward. It was the day his life changed forever.

"*Dr.* Jack Seward," corrected the short, muscular man as he stood up to shake young Jonathan Harker's hand.

"Dr. Seward is a friend of the Westenra family," added the portly barrister, Peter Hawkins, as he sat back down in his leather office chair. "He is here to treat Mr. Renfield."

"What exactly has happened to Renfield?" Jonathan asked.

"It's still a mystery," Hawkins said. "He was found half naked in the snow in a cemetery in Munich."

"*Munich?*"

"My guess is, he was passing through on his way back from meeting a client."

Dr. Seward added, "He was found screaming in a fit of hysterics, and chanting verses of scripture."

"Mr. Renfield did have a habit of quoting from the Bible," Jonathan said.

"Not like this," Hawkins replied. "He was screaming text from the Book of Revelations and babbling on about having looked into the eyes of the Devil."

"Good heavens, what caused such a sudden outburst?"

"We cannot be certain until I begin treating him at my clinic in Whitby," Dr. Seward answered. "Meanwhile, I can only assume that he witnessed a great horror and his mind manifested some kind of devil image as a coping mechanism to suppress the reality of what he saw. Don't worry; I have the best facility in all of England."

"In the meantime, Mr. Harker," Hawkins said, "I need you to complete Mr. Renfield's business."

"Me, sir? I'm only a clerk."

"Don't be modest; it's most unbecoming." Hawkins laughed. "You've been much more than a clerk at this company for some time. In the single year that you have been with us, you have been instrumental, invaluable even, on many cases. Most notably, that case with the two young girls. They owe you their lives, and the publicity surrounding the case has generated a great deal of business. Your partnership with that Mr. Murray from the *Daily Telegraph* was the work of a master legal mind. A great solicitor need understand not only the law, but politics and the fourth estate as well."

Jonathan smiled. "I don't know what to say. Thank you."

"I know the best way you can thank me. After you are called to the bar, when you pass your exam on Friday—"

"What if I should fail my bar exam?" Jonathan said.

"I have no doubt that you will pass. And, as soon as you do, I will need you at your best to assist Mr. Renfield's former client. He's an Eastern European prince, you know, and he has some property acquisitions to complete here in London. We can't afford to lose the business of a man such as he."

"A prince, you say, Mr. Hawkins?" Seward said. Then, to Jonathan, "I believe congratulations are in order, Mr. Harker."

This was more than Jonathan could hope. He couldn't wait to tell his fiancée, Mina. She was working across the street at the *Daily Telegraph* office. As soon as he could break away, he would rush over and take her out to dinner for celebration. This was a momentous occasion. Meeting this prince could change their lives forever.

"Here is the necessary paperwork that you should take with you," Hawkins said, handing Jonathan a leather folder. "The rest of it has already been posted to the prince."

With that, Hawkins patted Jonathan on the shoulder and went back to his desk for a cigar.

"I dare say, Mr. Harker," Seward said as they stepped out of the door to Fleet Street a minute later. "I would be honored if you would join me at my home tonight for dinner. It would be most helpful if I could impose upon you to tell me about Mr. Renfield as he was before his breakdown. And, since this is such a momentous occasion for you, I shall break out the finest champagne from my cellar and make it a celebration."

"Would you mind if my fiancée were to join us?"

"I would be delighted to meet her, and hope that we three shall become fast friends."

After Seward and Jonathan shook hands and parted from each other, Jonathan inquisitively opened the folder Mr. Hawkins had handed to him, and read the name of his royal client.

"Dracula."

Jonathan was shocked by the sound of his own voice in the empty office. He had not said the name in twenty-five years. It left a vile taste in his mouth. Dracula's memory had been ever-present, driving a wedge between Jonathan and his family. Jonathan's bloodshot eyes focused on a framed photograph upon his desk, of Mina and a very young Quincey.

Quincey. Jonathan hadn't wanted to give his son that name, but Mina insisted out of respect for their fallen friend. Jonathan only ever wanted to please his wife and consented without argument. It was not that Jonathan was so cold that he did not want Mr. Morris to have a namesake. But rather, he wanted his son to be free from any of the terrible past that Jonathan tried so hard to forget.

After Quincey was born, Jonathan felt that his life was complete and, for a time, was able to suppress the horrors he had experienced. Quincey was the most special gift in his life. He wanted the best for Quincey, and it drove him to work harder. What had happened to that little boy who had once loved him so dearly? The little boy who would wait quietly in the bushes outside the front door of their house as Jonathan strolled up the path. Quincey would jump out and tackle Jonathan, smothering him with hugs.

As time went on and Jonathan aged and Quincey began to grow up, it became painfully apparent that Mina did not seem to have grown a single day older in the last quarter of a century. Jonathan was surely the envy of most men who wished that their wives would remain young and beautiful forever. But the cost was too much for Jonathan to bear. Even though Mina's outward appearance had not changed, something inside her had. She became insatiable in the bedchamber. Again, not something most men would complain about, but Jonathan found it physically impossible to keep up with her. So much so that she started to remind him of the three vampire women in Dracula's castle. He felt such shame that they had been his first sexual experience, not his beloved wife. When he and Mina married shortly after his escape from Dracula's clutches, the overwhelming guilt made it difficult for him to consummate their marriage. Then came that fateful night, when his son was about thirteen years of age. While trying to make love to his wife, Jonathan discovered through a slip of his wife's tongue that it was Dracula who had taken Mina's virginity. Dracula, with centuries of experience, first introduced her to passion. He'd left such a profound impression on her that Jonathan, no matter how hard he tried, could never match it. He had also heard many times in the public houses, and believed it to be true, "The man with whom a woman shares her first sexual experience will always live closest to her heart." Jonathan's bitterness and guilt only intensified, and Mina's longings throughout the years grew, and her face remained as beautiful as ever. The bottle provided his only solace.

Jonathan blinked away a tear as he stared at the photograph. In his own way, he tried to protect his son. He had to keep Quincey safe. Yet, the more Jonathan tried to tighten his grip, the more his son slipped away. It was a bitter irony that Jonathan had hated his own father for his strict, puritanical upbringing, for in the last few years, he had recognized the same look of hatred in Quincey's eyes for him. Jonathan knew he was a failure. To his business. To his wife. To his son. To his friends.

Jonathan looked out of the window at the five-story building with the words DAILY TELEGRAPH engraved in its stone. How different their lives would have been had he been fortunate enough to fail his bar exam. He would have never gone to Transylvania.

Mina had given up her writing career when Jonathan inherited the law company from Peter Hawkins. Using the knowledge of society that she had learned from Lucy, Mina had been able to blend into the lifestyle seamlessly. She hosted parties, dressed and coached Jonathan, and became not only his mouthpiece but a dutiful wife working tirelessly so that he could raise his status. Mina's last words to him, three days ago, played back in his mind. *"I'm sorry, Jonathan. I love you. I always have. How many more times must I say it?"*

She had sacrificed her own dreams and goals for him. Without Mina, he had not the breeding or sophistication to rise above his middle-class birth. Was this not the very definition of true love, to sacrifice yourself for another? Mina had chosen to live her dreams vicariously through Jonathan. She became the proper Victorian wife, something she loathed, so that he could succeed. Moreover, what if in the moment of truth, Mina had chosen that demon and not him? If it weren't for Mina, they would never have been able to find and utterly destroy Dracula.

Jonathan threw the whisky bottle against the mahogany wall. "Damn! What a fool I am!"

Jonathan looked at his watch; if he hurried, he could still reach the 10:31 train back to Exeter, back to Mina, if she would take him. He wouldn't blame her if she didn't, but he had to try to make amends. Perhaps together they would go to Paris to see Quincey. He needed to see his son. With Mina's agreement, he would at last tell Quincey all their family secrets. Together they would lay all their truths bare so that, if forgiveness was still possible, they could all move forward. He owed this new understanding to his old, dear friend Jack. His death would not be in vain. Jonathan locked the front office and made his way along Fleet Street toward the Strand to find a cabbie to take him west to Charing Cross station. He needed to stay off the street, lest he be tempted. *Blast!* There was not a hansom cab in sight. It had not been twenty minutes since he had smashed his whisky bottle, and Jonathan was already thirsty. He thought of the half-empty bottle still in his desk drawer that he kept for "emergencies." How weak he had become. He needed to hail a cab quickly.

He noticed an ornate gold-trimmed black carriage—no coachman on the box—left completely unattended, which was an odd sight at this time of night.

Two young lovers stumbled from the tavern, kissing passionately. Jonathan could not help but notice how the girl swooned at the man's slightest touch. His thirst grew in strength. He could no longer count the times he had found himself in this very position. There had been many times over the years when he had reached the decision that he still loved Mina, beyond all else, and wanted to be with her, apologizing for all of his mistakes and forgiving all of hers. Then the reality took over. Sooner or later, they would find themselves alone in bed, and all of Jonathan's shortcomings would rise once again to the surface. He did not know if it was the logic of his addiction speaking to him or sober calculated reason. His inability to satisfy Mina, his jealousy over her involvement with Dracula, and his horror of Mina's eternal youth would always bring him back to depression. And back to the drink, which was always waiting for him, patient and forgiving.

"Would you like some warmth on a cold night, boss?" a silvery female voice called from behind Jonathan. He turned and saw a beautiful, voluptuous blond woman dressed in a flowing, virgin-white gown emerging from the fog. In her extended hand she held the temptation of a copper, apple-shaped flask.

It was so unfair. Jonathan had almost made it back to Mina. He was so close. The woman licked her red lips and tipped the flask back, taking a nip for herself. The liquid on those lips. It was more than his willpower could overcome. He knew how weak he was. He was not worthy of Mina.

Jonathan stepped forward with an outstretched hand. "Don't mind if I do."

It was only courtesy that kept him from consuming every last drop in one gulp.

"Shall we?" the woman said. She gestured to the labyrinth of alleyways that headed toward the Victoria Embankment.

"As if I ever had a choice." Jonathan offered his arm.

The woman laughed as she took hold of Jonathan's sleeve. They walked into the privacy of the alleyway and found themselves enveloped by a curtain of fog.

Jonathan and the woman kissed ravenously. He pressed her against the alleyway's filthy brick wall.

"Your name is Mina," Jonathan whispered as he lashed his tongue between those red lips.

"Call me anything you like, boss."

Jonathan ripped her bodice open, and kissed his way down her neck, massaging her ample breasts.

"Tell me your name."

"My name is Mina."

Jonathan hiked up her dress, snaking one hand between her thighs as he unfastened the braces holding up his trousers with the other. "Tell me how much I satisfy you, Mina."

"Let me show you," the blond Woman in White moaned. She spun Jonathan around savagely and slammed his back against the brick. She slid down to her knees, her face below his waist. Jonathan smiled in anticipation as she opened her mouth to accept him. He could feel her cold breath on his rising flesh.

To his horror, her eyes turned into solid black orbs. Her face grew wild as her incisor teeth elongated into fangs. Her mouth opened extraordinarily wide, as if her jaw had unhinged itself from its socket. With a hideous, inhuman growl, she threw her fanged mouth forward. She was about to bite off his manhood! Jonathan screamed. With all the strength that he could muster, he punched the Woman in White to the ground, yanked up his trousers, and tried to run.

Hissing with venom, the Woman in White snapped to her feet. She pounced like a cat, grabbed Jonathan, and tossed him into some wooden crates stored in the alley. The force of his impact splintered the wood. Jonathan lay immobile, his body racked with pain. Why had he not listened to his heart and gone home as planned?

With an animal growl, the vampire hauled him out of the debris. Jonathan tried to fight back, but she was too strong. He could not escape her iron grip. The Woman in White bent Jonathan's head back, exposing his neck to her fangs. He cried out, "Please God, no!"

Out of the corner of his eye, he saw a shadow moving swiftly toward them. Without any warning, the shadow shrouded the Woman in White, coiling around her. It tore the woman off Jonathan and hurled her through the air, smashing her against the wall. Jonathan was paralyzed with fear as he watched the dark shadow ominously rise over her.

The woman cried out in terror, "Mistress!"

Jonathan followed the track of her gaze. It seemed as if she was calling out to an unearthly crimson mist that was slithering toward them. Suddenly, something cold and wet struck Jonathan in the face. Jonathan turned back to where the Woman in White had been on her knees. From within the shadow, bloody organs fell to the ground in a heap, severed limbs flung about. The wetness that had hit his face was the woman's blood.

A male voice called on the wind: "Run, you fool! Run!"

Jonathan heeded the warning. He raced for Fleet Street. He glanced back once to see if the shadow was pursuing him. What he saw, he could not explain. The shadow had somehow blocked the advance of the crimson red mist that coiled and recoiled like a cobra and struck at the shadow, finally bursting through. The shadow flew apart and dissipated. It seemed now that the shadow had been his protector, and the crimson mist that sped quickly toward him must be his enemy. Whatever the shadow was, it was no match for the red mist. Jonathan turned his attention to the end of the alleyway where it joined Fleet Street. People were walking all around. Freedom was only yards away.

Jonathan heard a horse neigh. A driverless black carriage exploded out of the fog, almost running him over, blocking his path. The red mist was hot on his heels. He would not be able to reach the safety of Fleet Street this way. There was only one path left. He turned left and sprinted down another alleyway, screaming for help. He was out of shape, his body ruined by drink. He tumbled hard onto the cobbles, gasping for breath. The ominous crimson red mist encircled him.

"Who are you? What do you want?"

"My God!"

The red fog attacked him. The last thing Jonathan heard was his own scream. His last thought was of Mina.

One hundred and eighty miles away, in Exeter, Mina Harker awoke screaming.

CHAPTER XVII.

Inspector Cotford toiled away at his paperwork at the Red Lion. His favorite seat was recessed in the darkest corner of the public house. No one ever sat there, since it was the farthest removed from the action at the bar. Cotford imagined that if this pub were more well-to-do, this secluded seat would be the perfect place for young lovers to whisper sweet nothings to each other in privacy. But this was a man's bar. A drinker's bar. A policeman's bar. It was not the type of establishment frequented by young ladies. The only bonding that happened here involved stiff whiskies, back-slapping, and off-color jokes.

Since the pub was the closest to the House of Commons, New Scotland Yard, and the prime minister's residence at 10 Downing Street, the Red Lion was infested with politicians, policemen, and civil servants. All the lucky men who had families had returned home by this time of night. Only the solitary ones who had no other lives remained, drinking their loneliness away. Cotford fitted right in. He liked the grim, dark wood-paneled surroundings. The long shadows around his corner created a barrier between him and the rest of the pub-goers. He wanted his privacy, to be alone with the only thing that he had left in his life—his work.

He signaled to the barmaid to pour another beer as he compared the handwritten notes with the typed transcripts that were to be sent to the director of public prosecutions. Cotford's eyes were blurry with the reports of a recent bicycle-snatching ring. Cotford supposed there was some nobility in finding justice for the impoverished, hardworking men who had lost their only mode of transportation, but still he found it degrading. Working in that dead-end office year in and year out was not helping Cotford tip the scales.

The barmaid replaced Cotford's empty glass with a pint of stout. Cotford had been coming to this public house for thirty years and knew the barmaid well. Sadly, in all these years, he had formed no rapport with her. No words were ever exchanged.

Cotford was aware of his infamous celebrity. He wondered if the barmaid had purposely ignored him all these years to show her dissatisfaction for his part in not bringing justice to the Ripper. Then again, perhaps it was nothing more than Cotford's lack of an outgoing personality. With that unpleasant thought circling in his head, he glanced at the other regulars' stern faces frowning from the painted portraits on the wall. Scotland Yard's best and brightest. Crime was an ongoing, unwinnable war, but the more crimes one solved, the more a policemen felt his life was worth. These great men on the wall had done so much to tip the scales in justice's favor. There was the retired Chief Inspector Donald Swanson. There was Superintendent Thomas Arnold, who had resigned to fight in the Crimean War, then returned the moment that conflict had ended. Most prominent was Cotford's old mentor, Chief Inspector Frederick Abberline. Cotford chuckled as he looked at the portrait of his old friend. *Bollocks, he always did look more like a bank manager than a policeman.* Cotford raised his glass to these distinguished men.

When Cotford had been an idealistic young detective constable doing a job he loved, he always wondered why such a respected man as Abberline carried the weight of the world on his shoulders. It was only now, in his advanced years, that Cotford finally understood. Abberline felt it was his duty to bring justice to the victims of violent crimes. There was no nobler calling. After the debacle of the Ripper case, the public outcry over their failure to capture the killer had been so great that

Abberline was forced to retire, twenty-five years ago. Yet Abberline had solved so many crimes over his long, glorious career that his failure to bring justice for the five murdered prostitutes did nothing to sully his reputation among his peers.

This was not the same for Cotford. After Abberline's forced retirement, he was reassigned to his present post, effectively ending his career in the investigation of murders, and all hopes of advancement. He guessed they expected him to do the honorable thing and resign. But he was far too stubborn for that. Those five dead whores dragged behind Cotford. Until he in some way made up for his failures, he could not walk away with a clean conscience. He prayed that the revelations in Dr. Seward's journal would at last bring peace to his guilt.

The pub's door slammed open. Every drunken, bloodshot eye turned to the constable running inside. The eager young man's face was flushed and sweaty. He stood in the center of the room and called out, "Is there an Inspector Cotford here?"

The silence was broken as the patrons whispered among one another.

"I'm the one you're looking for," Cotford rumbled from the shadows.

With a salute, the out-of-breath constable handed him a folded note.

"Inspector Cotford? I was ordered by Sergeant Lee to bring this to your immediate attention! I assume this is pertaining to an important case."

Cotford liked this lad. He reminded him of his younger, idealistic self. He unfolded the note, read it. And reread it, his mind reeling. Cotford had already propelled himself to the door when the young constable called out to him, "Inspector Cotford? I'm off duty, I can help if you need me."

Cotford considered the lad's offer. *Why not encourage this fine young recruit?* He said: "My notes are on the table back there. See them delivered immediately to the Crown Prosecution Service. Don't fail me, young man. The prosecution of malevolent criminals depends on your swiftness."

"Yes, sir! You can depend on me, sir!"

With his good deed done for the day, Cotford was on his way to what he hoped would be a dark destiny, the first step on a new path that would lead to a confrontation with evil he had spent twenty-five years searching for.

Sergeant Lee was blinded by a brilliant flash of light. Blue dots danced in front of his eyes. His vision returned by degrees, his eyes readjusting to the macabre crime scene. The police photographer reloaded the camera's flash powder and snapped another picture. This time, Lee turned away. He yearned for the days when crime scenes were sketched instead of photographed.

Since joining Scotland Yard, Lee had wondered what it would have been like to work on the Ripper case. In fact, it was his fascination with the ghastly murders that had caused him to seek out and befriend Cotford when he joined the force. The old inspector was the last man still on active duty who had worked on the case. Lee had been only a small boy when the murders occurred, but he remembered them well. In fact, the famous murder case was also the reason he had left military service after the Second Boer War in 1902 to join the Metropolitan Police. Now, ten years later, Sergeant Lee stood in an alley, looking down at a young woman's mutilated corpse. He had seen many bloody and torn bodies during the war, but they had all been men. The sight of a butchered woman was, for him, much worse. A torn leg thrown here, an arm thrown there, the head severed, and the heart carved out, left in a pool of blood on the cobbles. The torso had been disemboweled and the organs and intestines left on display in the open air.

Lee's steely gray eyes tracked Inspector Huntley, the man assigned to this case. Hands clasped behind his back, Huntley supervised the two constables gathering and cataloguing evidence.

A hacking cough echoed off the alley's brick walls. Lee, Huntley, and the constables turned to the Temple Bar alleyway entrance. A portly drunk appeared out of the fog. Huntley aimed his torchlight at the slouching figure. Sergeant Lee immediately recognized Cotford. He'd hoped that Cotford would have shown more discretion than to show up at a crime scene four sheets to the wind. He had sent Price to the Red

Lion public house to fetch Cotford without authorization. If Cotford made a fool of himself in front of Inspector Huntley, he would also be making a fool of Lee. Huntley never missed a chance to flex his authoritative muscle and would surely have Lee reprimanded. With his mentor staggering into view, Lee prayed that he had not made a terrible mistake.

Huntley made no effort to remove the beam of light from Cotford's sweaty, red-nosed face. Cotford stared directly into the light as if challenging Huntley.

"Inspector Cotford?" Huntley asked. "I think you have lost your way. The pubs are farther up Fleet Street."

The constables chuckled. Knowing his mentor, Lee wondered if he'd soon have to break up a fight. Luckily, Cotford merely sidestepped Inspector Huntley and lurched toward the victim's body. Huntley and his colleagues traded looks. Was Cotford seriously planning to *investigate* the crime? Their chuckles became outright laughter. Cotford seemed oblivious, but Lee was embarrassed for him.

"You're just in time, Inspector Cotford," Huntley said. "I am about to give my summation of the case thus far. You're welcome to stay if you'd like. Perhaps you'll learn something."

Lee wanted to punch Huntley's arrogant face, but Cotford took it in stride, his attention fixed on the bloodied remains as he circled the crime scene.

Huntley said, "You can tell by the hand-stitched beads on our victim's dress that she was no Whitechapel whore. She was either dragged into the alley by our assailant or was due to meet him here by choice. Since there were people out and about on Temple Bar, if she had been grabbed, passersby would have surely heard her screams. Therefore, one must assume she was here to meet her lover. Something went wrong. Perhaps she refused his advances. They argued. Her lover tried to take what was not offered. They struggled, smashing into those crates at the back side of the alley. She must have tried to escape. Her lover drew his knife."

Lee could not help but be impressed by such astute interpretation of the crime scene evidence.

Huntley was surprised to find Cotford still ignoring him. Cotford held aloft the severed head of the Woman in White. The dead woman's face was frozen in horror, but he remained unaffected, turning the head upside down, poking his finger into the raw, bloodied flesh, picking at the edges of torn skin. Cotford flipped the head into the air, caught it, and stared into the dead woman's open eyes.

Lee no longer feared a reprimand. He feared for his job.

Huntley watched in amazement as Cotford replaced the severed head on the cobbles and staggered toward the smashed crates.

Shaking his head in disbelief, he loudly continued his summation. "Our assailant, in a rage of passion, fell upon our hapless victim. He brutally murdered and mutilated her. I am convinced, based upon the fine quality of his paramour's dress, that our suspect was a gentleman. The haphazard butchery was done to throw us off his scent, hoping that a dolt of an inspector would blame the bloody crime on a man of the street. Temple Bar is known for men of high quality, solicitors and bankers. It is within their gentlemanly ranks that we must hunt for our killer."

There was a crash at the back of the alley. Once again, all eyes turned to Cotford. It appeared that he had fallen into the crates. Lee realized with dread that this situation was even worse than he feared. Cotford picked himself up from the unbroken crates, took a few steps back and ran forward, launching his girth into the air. He fell against the unbroken crate again. As Cotford struggled to pull himself back up, he at last noticed all eyes were on him.

"I beg your pardon, Inspector. Don't mind me."

One of the constables offered, "Inspector Huntley, you're forgetting the bloody footprint we found on a splintered crate."

"I most certainly am not! Our assailant, after completing his ghastly deed, found himself covered in blood. He staggered back as he regained his senses. Realizing what he had done, our assailant ran toward Temple Bar. We know this because, as he ran, he stepped on that piece of wood, and the print points toward the Temple Bar exit."

"Well done, old man," Cotford said.

Huntley turned to graciously accept his accolade but was left speechless when he saw Cotford on his knees, spinning a piece of wood on the cobbles as if he were a child spinning a top.

Lee felt an urgency to jump to Cotford's rescue. "Inspector Huntley! The police surgeon has arrived."

Huntley beamed. "Ah, the sawbones is here, lads. Our work is done. First round at the Red Lion is on me."

Huntley led his little gang from the alleyway, laughing. The police surgeon came forward, trying to hold down his dinner as he stared at the victim's remains.

As a third-generation military man, Lee had been brought up by his father to strictly follow protocol and respect the chain of command. He'd gone against those instincts by summoning Cotford, and now Lee would have to deal with the man who had become a drunken embarrassment. He took a deep breath and turned. Cotford was nowhere to be seen. *Where the devil could he have gotten to?*

Lee walked farther into the alleyway, toward the Fleet Street exit. He found Cotford on his hands and knees hovering over a dark, oozing pile on the cobblestones. Cotford picked up a sample of the pile, brought it to his nose, and sniffed. Lee realized Cotford was holding a piece of manure.

With great compassion, Lee knelt beside his friend and placed his hand on Cotford's back. "Inspector, why don't you let me take you home?"

Cotford dropped the manure, wiped his hands on his trouser leg, and looked up at Lee. He was stone-cold sober. His were the eyes of a detective.

Cotford stood as he spoke. "Huntley may be a bloviating blowhole, but he's a damned fine detective. He just needs a little seasoning. Those crates were reinforced oak. They were built to carry a heavy load. As you may have noticed, I have the figure of a sperm whale. I ran full speed, throwing my weight against the crates. Despite my best effort, they didn't break."

"What are you implying, Inspector?"

"The man and woman did meet here for a passionate tryst as Huntley had surmised. Though I believe they were attacked by a third assailant."

"What makes you think that?"

"Mind where you're standing. See those bloodied palm prints on the ground? Those are from a man's hands."

Lee looked down at the prints on the cobbles. Huntley had missed them.

"Notice the thumbs," Cotford said. "Whoever was here instinctively fell backward, trying to break his fall, causing the thumbs to face outward. This person was in retreat."

"Retreat from what?"

"See the manure. There were horses here. Probably attached to a carriage. They blocked his path. He was running from someone to the safety of Fleet Street, and he was already covered in blood."

Lee felt sorry that he had ever doubted Cotford. "He was running from your third person."

"Exactly! He must have been a very strong man, because he threw our unknown second victim with great force against those crates. Those were not knife wounds that cut that woman's head from her body. The jagged flesh on her neck can indicate only one thing. Her head was torn from her body by a pair of very powerful hands."

Lee was shocked. "Come now, Inspector. You stated a moment ago that the crates could not be smashed by the force of a human body against them. As for tearing off a head, what man could perform such an act?"

"Evidence does not lie. What we cannot readily explain, we dare not dismiss. In my experience, Sergeant Lee, an enraged madman can have the strength of ten men. I once chased such a lunatic."

Cotford turned and walked down another alleyway toward the embankment. Lee followed. Cotford stopped and picked up a small, shiny object. He tossed it to Lee. It was a brass button, with the engraved monogram: *W&S.*

"Wallingham and Sons," Lee said.

"Aye, one of the finest tailors in London."

There was fresh blood on the button.

"Our second victim was a man of means," Cotford said.

Lee stared at the button. "How did you know to look down this part of the alley?"

"You saw me spinning the wood on the ground earlier. A running man stepping on that wood would cause it to spin like a top on the uneven cobbles. The bloody footprint led Huntley to surmise that his suspect headed toward Temple Bar. Huntley was misled. The footprint is pointing in the wrong direction—and it belongs to our second victim. He was not running from his crime. He was running from the third person in the alley, and the chase ended here."

Cotford knelt down again, dipped his finger into one of the many small droplets of blood on the cobbles, and displayed it for Lee. "I need you to do me another favor, Sergeant. I need you to report to me exactly what is written in the police surgeon's report."

Lee hesitated, another breach of protocol. But he knew the old bloodhound had found the true scent. "Whatever you need, sir."

Cotford nodded and headed back toward the fog.

Lee said, "There is not a great deal of blood here, Inspector. We might have a living witness."

"Highly unlikely," Cotford said. "There are no other bloody footprints past this point. Our second victim did not walk out of this alley." He bowed his head. "I fear, Sergeant, come morning light, you will be calling Inspector Huntley to a new murder scene. God help us all."

CHAPTER XVIII.

———◇———

Kate Reed loathed mornings in London. The streets were a chaotic mass of pedestrians hurrying to work. The idea of being stuffed like a sardine in a can into the Underground tube train was repulsive. She was uncomfortable with the thought of all those strange people pressing against her body. Kate woke up before her husband and roused her children while darkness still filled the sky. She was desperate to finish her errands and be home before the suffocating rush-hour started.

Dragging a perambulator and with her young son, Matthew, in tow, Kate struggled up the steps at Piccadilly tube station. A few people were out and about, but not one offered to assist her with the heavy pram. *Chivalry was dead.* Coming to Piccadilly Circus depressed her; in recent years, it had fallen from grace. Two years previously, a beer company had installed a large advertisement, illuminated by dozens of incandescent lightbulbs. The advertising marred the beautiful architecture of the buildings around it. Now that Kate had young, impressionable children, she had become something of an activist, one of thousands who had lobbied to have it removed. Many argued that a single sign was harmless, but Kate knew if one company was permitted to peddle its wares here, others would follow. This sign illuminated the street at night, attracting a depraved crowd. Piccadilly had originally been designed to resemble an elegant Parisian boulevard, but it was soon to become too closely associated with the theatre district. *The vulgar side of town.* The beer sign was just further proof of its slide.

Kate would not have come here at all, but the soles of her husband's shoes needed to be mended, and John Tuck, here in Piccadilly, was the best cobbler in London, second only to Lobb on St. James's, but Kate couldn't afford the latter.

Once Kate and her children had successfully ascended the mountain of stairs from the tube station, she steered the carriage and her son around the longer route of the roundabout to avoid the electric sign. She did not want her son to be enticed by the wicked wonders of the flashing advertisement. Unfortunately, the alternate longer path was marred as well, for it led them around the Shaftesbury Monument, adorned with a nude winged statue: even more inappropriate.

The statue was much too sensual to be honoring such a sober, philanthropic, and respectable earl as Lord Shaftesbury. The city fathers had tried to temper objections to the statue by naming it the Angel of Christian Charity. Many good Christians, including Kate, were not fooled. Rumors of the statue's intended name continued to spread: Eros, the Greek god of love. A false god erected in memory of a good Christian soul. Kate averted her eyes.

Matthew was drawn to the open space of Piccadilly Circus. He broke free of his mother's hand and launched the model aircraft his father had built for him out of spruce twigs and paper. A strong breeze carried it backward. Enthralled by the mystery of flight, Matthew didn't seem to mind.

"I'm Henri Salmet! I'm flying across the channel!" The boy ran to retrieve his model.

"Come along, Matthew!" Kate called. "We don't have time for this. After the cobbler, Mummy still needs to get to Covent Garden before the best fish are sold."

Kate was forced to wait while several hansoms passed before she could cross Regent Street. She stepped to the edge of the curb and reached for her son.

"Come along, Matthew."

Her hand found only empty air. Exasperated that she had missed her chance to cross the street, she turned back to see where her son had gone. She found him standing in the middle of the square, looking up into air.

"Matthew, chop-chop!"

The boy didn't move. His model aircraft was lying on the ground in front of him. Was he gawking at the indecent statue in the center of the circus? A rap across the knuckles with a wooden spoon was long overdue.

"Matthew! Come here this instant."

Kate maneuvered the perambulator around pedestrians milling about the street and marched over to the boy. "Did you hear me calling you, young man?"

Matthew still did not seem to be aware of her. He was shaking from head to toe. Alarmed, Kate dropped to one knee and grabbed him by the shoulders. "Matthew, are you all right?"

The boy raised a quivering arm. There was something in his eyes that she had never seen before. Terror. She turned her head to see what her son was pointing at: a nearby tree. *Wait a moment; there are no trees in Piccadilly Circus.*

Kate's reaction was a scream so horrifying, it stopped all the pedestrians in their tracks.

Kate snatched her son up and covered his eyes as she continued to scream and weep. People came running to her aid. A man asked, "Madam, what's wrong?"

Kate pointed up. Words trembling, she said, "The Devil has come to London."

They followed her gaze. Their eyes widened, their jaws hung slack. It started with a murmur and swelled to a crest of sound like a tidal wave, a scream of horror washing over all of Piccadilly Circus.

Constables blew their whistles as they ran toward the crowd that had formed at the base of the tree. Women fainted. Men stopped dead. Motorcars screeched to a halt. Fruit wagons and milk carts slammed into one another. Pandemonium.

In the center of Piccadilly Circus, a forty-foot-long wooden pole had been erected, towering above the Angel of Christian Charity. At the top of the shaft, a naked man had been impaled through the fundament. The man's jaw was broken from the pointed stake erupting from his mouth. Intestines and other internal organs, hooked by the spike as it passed through his body, spilled from his lips. Blood trickled from his eyes, ears, and nose. The body twitched, croaking a bloodcurdling moan. This poor man was still alive.

It was indeed the work of a devil.

CHAPTER XIX.

❖

Whi>W</whi>hen Quincey first met Basarab the previous evening, he had not been sure what to expect. Basarab had informed Quincey that he would not be traveling with the company back to Romania, but he made no mention of accompanying him back to London instead. Quincey panicked, thinking that the actor was trying to get rid of him.

But Basarab laughed when he produced a contract from his pocket. He asked Quincey to join his theatre company and to be his representative, seeing to all of Basarab's arrangements prior to his arrival in London.

Quincey was overjoyed. Not even the deluge assaulting Paris could dampen his mood.

Pedestrians sought shelter. Not Quincey. He strolled along the boulevard to the Gare du Nord, allowing the rain to run down his face, grinning as if he had not a care in the world. Growing up in England, Quincey was quite accustomed to rain. The rain made everything look gray in London, but in Paris, the rain created a golden hue. The City of Lights sparkled doubly, a mirror of Quincey's own sparkling, bright future. There was a bounce in his step he had not felt since his father had dragged him kicking and screaming away from the theatre. He bounded onto the Calais train that would begin his journey back to

London, and settled into a seat in the restaurant car. His life was back on track. As he placed his ticket and passport into his inside coat pocket for quick retrieval when the conductor arrived, he found the telegram. In all the excitement, he had forgotten about it.

Mina had not known where to reach Quincey so she had been forced to send the telegram in the hope of reaching him at the Théâtre de l'Odéon where, the day before, Antoine had given it to him. He had been carrying it around, unopened, since then. He knew what his mother would say. She would beg him to reconsider his course of action and to return to the Sorbonne, no doubt pressured by his immovable father. Quincey still felt bad for having left his mother after such a bitter argument, but was not yet ready to make amends. He wanted to be properly established with the production before another word was said to his parents. They would witness his newfound success on the opening night of Bram Stoker's *Dracula*. Quincey hoped they would be proud of him when they saw his billing as coproducer and costar, realizing he was not throwing away a great future but making one. Until then, Quincey planned to avoid any unnecessary confrontation. Although it pained him to avoid his mother, he knew he needed to stay strong.

Quincey ordered tea and settled in for the journey back to the French coast. His excitement over closing the deal with Deane at the Lyceum drew him back to his books and with them the history of the Romanian prince. Why did Stoker call Dracula a count instead of his true title, prince? Curious. Perhaps he had wanted to separate his fictional character from the historic Dracula's bloody legacy, hoping to earn his villain some sympathy.

When his tea arrived, Quincey laid his down his books and notepad. He glanced up at the passenger in front of him, who was reading the evening edition of *Le Temps*.

Quincey nearly dropped his cup.

He snatched the newspaper from the man's hands, who saw the look on Quincey's face and raised no protest. Quincey could feel the gritty paper in his fingers, but couldn't believe the headline before his eyes: HOMME EMPALÉ.

Beneath the headline was a crosshatched sketch of the victim.

Quincey's eyes flew to the woodcut drawing in his book. Prince Dracula dined while surrounded by impaled bodies of his condemned. Quincey's heart was racing faster than the locomotive's engine as he read the newspaper story. *"Un homme a été découvert empalé hier matin á Piccadilly Circus."*

"Man found impaled yesterday morning in Piccadilly Circus."

Quincey's hands shook, making the text difficult to read. He placed the paper on the table to steady it as he reread the article. His translation was sound. Quincey breathed faster. Upon reaching the last line, he thought he might pass out. He forced himself to read it again.

> The impaled victim was identified as Mr. Jonathan Harker, a prominent solicitor from Exeter, a city to the west of London.

CHAPTER XX.

—•—◇—•—

Inspector Cotford took hold of the white cotton sheet. It had an eerie, iridescent glow under the hydrogen spotlight hung directly above it. He turned toward Mina Harker and observed how she took a deep breath to steady her nerves.

Cotford had watched her very carefully upon her entrance into Scotland Yard's morgue. She did not shrink at the door like so many other widows who came to view their husbands' remains. From the way she carried herself, and how she looked straight ahead when she marched into the room, Cotford could see her quiet strength. She had a calm, stately elegance. She was dressed from her ankles to her neck in a black dress, her blond tresses pulled up into a bun in the same way Cotford's mother used to wear her hair. He also could not help but notice that, despite her matronly bearing, Mrs. Harker looked quite lovely for a woman of her age. Her face was strikingly beautiful, devoid of lines. Cotford thought Jonathan Harker was an idiot to be looking for the company of a tart in an alley when there was such a remarkable woman waiting for him at home.

He put on his poker face. Back in the alley, he'd developed his theory, which the evidence seemed to support but could not yet completely prove. Then Lee had showed him the murder book from the as-yet-unidentified woman wearing white. The bloody handprints found in the alley matched Jonathan Harker's, and it was his blood type in the droplets. Cotford had no doubt in his mind that Jonathan Harker was the second victim from the alley. There was nothing quite like the warm sensation of being correct. Upon reading Seward's journal, Cotford realized that what was contained therein was indeed a confession, for in it Seward plainly named his coconspirators. In an instant, it became clear to Cotford why he and Abberline had failed to catch the elusive serial killer. Jack the Ripper was not just one man; he was a cabal of mad occultists. Since Seward died with a sword in his hand, he must have been killed to be silenced. It stood to reason that the leader of the cabal would begin to fear his coconspirators. Cotford knew that Seward's death would start a wave of new murders. The death of the woman wearing white was not a surprise to Cotford, either. Once drawn out, his bloodlust reignited, it was inevitable that the leader of the cabal would kill more women. The murder of the tart in the alley was, unfortunately, sauce for the goose.

Dr. Seward wrote of Mina Harker in his journals as well, but in close to saintly terms. Cotford doubted she was directly involved in the murders, but he was sure she had knowledge of them. He hoped Mrs. Harker would be the key to redeeming his past.

When Cotford asked for this meeting with Mrs. Harker, and asked for all chairs to be removed from the morgue, Lee did so without question. If Cotford were to take Dr. Seward's journals at face value, rather than as the ranting of a madman, then he would have to accept that Mina Harker was a strong woman. So much so, that she would be a formidable opponent. His only chance to trap her into betraying what she knew about the cabal was to severely rattle her. Forcing her to identify her husband's remains would immediately place her at a disadvantage. He hoped it would be enough. The moment she walked in, Cotford could see that he was going to have to be harsher than he'd ever been with a widow before.

Still gripping the white sheet, Cotford said, "I should warn you, madam, your husband's body is not in a very presentable state."

"Believe me, Inspector," Mina whispered, "after the things I have witnessed in my life, there is very little that can make me squeamish."

Cotford yanked the sheet away with a dramatic flourish. Beneath it lay the ravaged body of Jonathan Harker sprawled on a white enameled cast-iron gurney. After the wooden spike, forty feet high and four inches in diameter, had been removed postmortem, the man's face had collapsed in on itself. Jonathan Harker's hollow, misshapen body had begun to decay as Cotford waited two days before contacting his widow. The corpse's skin had become a greenish blue, which looked even worse under the hydrogen lamplight. The stench billowed out into the morgue the moment Cotford pulled back the sheet.

Most women would have broken down or fainted at the mere sight of their dead husband's corpse, let alone one so mutilated. Cotford noted that Mina simply stared at the body for a moment. Then, as the shock wore off, her eyes widened with realization at what she was seeing and she turned away. Her eyes moistened, but tears did not flow. Mina summoned her resolve and straightened her back. It was as if she was willing her calculating mind to overrule her heart. Cotford was impressed by her steel. *She has the iron will of a man hidden in the delicate form of a woman.* Dr. Seward had been correct in his description of Mina Harker.

"Good God, Jonathan," she said. She glanced about the room as if looking for a place to sit. When there was none to be found, her eyes went to the door. She was uncomfortable and wanted to leave. Her reaction was just as Cotford had hoped. Now he needed to add more fuel to the fire.

From a dark corner, the graying police surgeon bolted forward with a glass of water in one hand and a handkerchief in the other. Mina gave him a grateful smile. Cotford resisted the impulse to box the doctor's ears. Cotford had gone to great lengths to make the situation as uncomfortable as possible, and this twit was ruining his strategy. The surgeon then pulled a bottle of smelling salts out of his lab coat. The fool. She was not likely to faint. Cotford shot a disapproving glare at Lee, who seemed uncertain what to do. He needed to compensate.

"Buggered like a shish kebab he was," Cotford remarked. Chuckles of laughter from Lee's three subordinates erupted from behind him.

The police surgeon stepped into the light. "I find this completely improper and highly irregular."

Cotford shot another glare at Lee, who intercepted the police surgeon, intimidating him simply by towering over the man. In a low voice, Lee said, "Your job is to follow our orders and keep your comments to yourself."

Damn Lee. Even his voice at a whisper seemed loud enough for Mina to hear.

"Your compassion, Inspector, warms my soul," she said.

Lee and the other constables stopped their chortles and cleared their throats with embarrassment. *Touché, Mrs. Harker.* Cotford needed to gain the upper hand before he lost his advantage. "Forgive me, but you did say only moments ago that there is very little that can make you squeamish."

Mina made no response.

Cotford leaned on the wooden desk and slapped his hand on Seward's stacked leather-bound journals. "Based on the writings of the late Dr. Seward, untimely death is nothing new to your family."

Mina's eyes widened in surprise. For a moment, Cotford thought he had broken her, but once again he watched as Mina willed herself not to betray emotion of any kind.

"Just what are you implying?" Mina replied, resolute.

"The Grim Reaper has been your constant companion. Your son's namesake, Quincey Morris. An American. A Texan, to be exact—"

"Died twenty-five years ago while on a hunting trip in Romania," Mina interrupted.

"Do you know who could have done something like this to your husband? Did your husband have any enemies?"

There was a spark in Mina's eyes. "My husband was a solicitor. In the legal profession, there are always negative associations."

Ah, now we're getting somewhere, Cotford thought. "A crime this violent would require a more passionate motive."

"To what are you referring, Inspector?"

He had the hunch that there was a name etched in her mind. All he had to do was get it out of her. "Someone took great effort to erect a vast stake in Piccadilly Circus and impale your husband upon it. That is not a spontaneous act; this took planning. This was the work of someone with more than a passing grudge. Come now, Mrs. Harker, if there was someone in your past capable of such a ferocious act, his name would not be foreign to you."

It couldn't be him, Mina thought. Her heart was beating so quickly, she thought it would burst from her chest. No matter how much or little Cotford knew, he already knew too much. Mina felt for a moment as if she would swoon. Her prince was long dead. He lived only in her nightmares. Even if he were, somehow, still alive, she refused to believe he would hurt her like this. It couldn't be *him*. But if it was, why now? Why wait twenty-five years? *But who else could be so brutal?*

Mina's thoughts swirled. Her emotions had been frayed even before she had set foot in the morgue. The guilt from her last conversation with Jonathan, a heated and hurtful argument, weighed on her heart. There would never be any reconciliation. She'd never have a chance to say all that she had felt. She vowed never to make that mistake with Quincey.

The room was devoid of heat, and the stark lighting did nothing to warm it up. Somewhere in the darkness, Mina could hear the ticking of a clock. Time was not on her side.

The inspector pulled something from a folder on the desk. She recognized the familiar cut edges of photographic paper and prepared herself for the worst.

"Do you know this woman?" Cotford asked.

Mina looked at the photo. It was of a severed head. To her surprise, she did not know the woman at all. "No. Should I know her?"

"Well, your husband certainly *knew* her, if you catch my meaning. We found evidence to prove he was present when she was slain."

This line of questioning would get the old fool nowhere. Mina felt her strength return. "Why should this concern me, Inspector?"

"Your husband's blood was found near the woman's severed head. As well as this button . . ."

He was holding a brass button bearing the initials *W&S*. Cotford strolled casually toward the gurney. Next to Jonathan's body were torn pieces of his gray suit, gathered unceremoniously in a small pile.

"We found Mr. Harker's clothing a few yards away from the murder scene. You will see that this missing button fits right here."

He restored the button to its rightful place on the remnants of Jonathan's jacket, forcing Mina to look at his corpse again. Cotford was undoubtedly attempting to manipulate the situation. She could feel her face flush. She could not stand to look at what they had done to her husband. The stench of death overwhelmed her. She could taste her last meal. Her resolve was beginning to crack. She needed to leave. She needed to run.

Cotford continued, "The blood on this button does not belong to your husband. It's the murdered woman's blood type."

"Are you accusing my husband of killing this woman?"

"That is what I intend to ascertain. Did you know your husband was having relations with other women?"

"My husband had many faults, but he was not capable of murder. May I go now?"

By way of response, he stared at her as if his bloodshot eyes were trying to burrow into her soul. So far, Mina had evaded his line of questioning. She had to be careful.

Cotford held up a small, bloodstained business card. "According to La Sûreté report, a calling card was found in Dr. Seward's pocket. The same person's card was found in your husband's wallet."

Arthur Holmwood.

"Is there a point to all this, Inspector?"

"Lord Godalming has not gone by the name of Arthur Holmwood since before your hunting trip to Romania."

In this very cold room, Mina felt very hot. Cotford obviously knew more than she could have imagined. Had Seward truly described their horrid experiences in his diaries? If she told the police what she knew to be true, she would find herself locked up in an asylum like the one Seward had owned. Mina realized there was no way she could defend herself. Her only hope was to escape.

Cotford's gruff voice interrupted her thoughts. "Romania is a rather odd place to hunt, if I may say so. What were you hunting?"

"Wolves," Mina answered hotly. She moved toward the door.

Cotford tossed the bloody card onto the gurney, leapt around the table, and blocked her way. He was swift for such a portly man.

"Do you regularly enjoying hunting, Mrs. Harker? Or are you just an observer of blood sports?"

At least she had moved away from Jonathan's body, which was now behind her and out of sight. It was only the smell that kept the ghastly image burned in her brain. "Inspector, I sense there is a question you want to ask me. I would prefer if you just—"

"Sergeant Lee paid a call on Lord Godalming this morning, who swears he never met the late Dr. Seward . . . or your husband, for that matter. Do you have any idea why he may have said that?"

"No," Mina said truthfully.

"I despise unanswered questions, Mrs. Harker. This case is plagued with them. Here we have two men who knew each other, both meeting a tragic end just a week apart. In my line of work, there is no such thing as coincidence. Both men had a connection to Lord Godalming and he denies knowing either. You, Mrs. Harker, are the last living connection to all of them."

Memories of her adventures flooded Mina's mind. Even though she was standing in the center of the room, she felt trapped. The ticking clock seemed to go faster.

"Please, Inspector. I need to find my son. I need to tell him his father is dead."

Cotford was like a lion circling his prey. Mina was starting to crack. "There is just one more thing," he continued. "We just received this from Paris. You wouldn't happen to recognize this piece of jewelry, would you?"

Mina took from his hand a photograph of a bloodstained silver pocket watch. Mina could not hide from Cotford the flood of emotions as she read to herself the inscription: *"Oceans of Love, Lucy."*

She caressed the photograph. With a shaking voice, she responded, "It belonged to Jack. It was a gift to him from an old friend . . . Lucy Westenra."

"Lord Godalming's former fiancée. Do you know where I might find Miss Westenra now?"

Mina's head snapped up. He was trying to catch her out in an inconsistency or a lie. Was this interrogation somehow about Lucy's death, or Jonathan's? She sensed he was just waiting to put the handcuffs on her. One wrong word and she could find herself under arrest. She could not let Quincey wander alone in the open, exposed to danger, while she dealt with legalities.

Carefully choosing her words, Mina said, "I believe you already know the answer, Inspector. Lucy died twenty-five years ago."

"Your friends seem to have a high mortality rate, Mrs. Harker."

"Misfortune is not a crime." Mina knew that what she said next would cast further suspicion over her, but she had to get out of this infernal place. "I ask you to step aside, Inspector. If you have any further questions, you can ask them through my legal representative. I have to see to my husband's funeral arrangements. Good day."

"As you wish, madam. We will speak again very soon, I can assure you."

Cotford stood aside. Mina was wary. But her only purpose now was to find Quincey. Mina ran for the exit. A few more steps and she would be free.

Cotford called out, "Send my regards to Abraham Van Helsing!"

His words struck Mina like venom, paralyzing her spine. Her legs buckled.

Cotford reveled at the sight of Mina falling against an empty gurney. She spun around and glared at him. This time it was not shock in her eyes from his knowledge of her private life, but palpable fear. She shoved the gurney aside and scrambled out the door. At last, she had betrayed herself. Even after death, she was protecting her estranged husband. If it was not love, what bond was it that had held their marriage together? Their son? Cotford was skeptical. His investigation of the Harkers had told him that Quincey had already left the nest. Jonathan and Mina Harker were bound together by something deeper. A dark secret. *Honor among thieves, villains, and conspirators.* Cotford now knew that what he had read in Dr. Seward's journal regarding Lucy Westenra was true. Mina Harker was hiding something. Something terrible. The evil of

Abraham Van Helsing. The look on Mina's face at the mention of the professor's name told Cotford everything he needed to know. He would request Lucy's death certificate from the old archives. Undoubtedly, the death certificate would state she'd died of natural causes. His detective's instinct told him that was a lie no doubt concocted, bought, and paid for by the wealthy Arthur Holmwood.

Lee interrupted Cotford's thoughts. "What now?"

Cotford pulled a fat cigar from his pocket, an imported Iwan Ries. He sniffed along its spine, the scent of a hot trail. "Now, Sergeant Lee, we let the vultures gather around the carcass."

Lee struck a match for him. Cotford took a long puff on the pleasant cigar. For the first time, he felt worthy of the sergeant's admiration.

CHAPTER XXI.

—◆—

Mina rushed home, shaken to the core, the slow, rhythmic rain-drops falling out of rhythm with the pace of her heart. With each mile from London to Exeter, her angst grew. This four-hour journey felt like an eternity: It was the most excruciating train ride Mina had ever experienced. She so urgently felt the need to get home, and no train could move fast enough for her liking.

Mina was deeply hurt that her son was avoiding her. As with most families, she and Quincey had had minor quarrels over the years, but they had been over petty issues. Mina was certain that once he learned of his father's death, all would be forgiven, and their squabble would be cast aside in a heartbeat. But what Mina could not overcome was her fear, which was nagging and relentless: What if Quincey was in danger? What if he had already fallen victim to foul play? He had no knowledge of how to protect himself, no idea of the evil he was up against.

Returning home to retrieve her passport for the journey to Paris was taking precious time.

Contrary to what she had told that infuriating Inspector Cotford, Mina had decided to forgo holding a funeral service for Jonathan. Finding Quincey was paramount. Jonathan would understand. In fact, she knew that Jonathan would have insisted upon it; and if the situation were reversed, she would have wanted Jonathan to do the same. Sadly, there was also little point to a funeral service. No one would be there. Quincey was missing, Jack was dead, Arthur was an arse, and Jonathan no longer had any clients who had respects to pay. The only one left was Abraham Van Helsing. No, Mina couldn't risk that. She knew that the vile Cotford was most likely counting on his arrival.

Give my regards to Abraham Van Helsing. The inspector's words played over and over in her mind like a scratched phonograph. She would not give that stuffed Irish pig the satisfaction of delivering Van Helsing up to him. The circumstances surrounding Jonathan's death were complicated enough without some old bloodhound trying to make a name for himself by digging up the past. Some things were better left dead and buried, like her dear sweet Lucy.

Mina instructed the undertaker to cremate Jonathan's remains. She would collect his ashes at a later date. At least burning his corpse would ensure his eternal rest. Mina said a silent prayer for her beloved, wishing she could take back all she had said and done that had brought disharmony between them.

Mina was rain-drenched by the time she trudged up the stone steps of the house. This big house they had inherited from Peter Hawkins. How could she live here now? It was too large. Too empty. Despite Jonathan's frequent absences of late, already it felt different. Final and cold. There was no time to dwell on that now. She had only an hour to dry herself, to change, and to pack a few things before making her way to Portsmouth, where she'd take a ferry across the channel to Cherbourg and then another train to Paris—a two-day journey in all. Two days more in which Quincey remained exposed, in peril. That fat oaf of an inspector would no doubt be on the prowl twenty-four hours a day; but at least she would be beyond Cotford's reach in Paris. Perhaps this was the last time she would be able to freely return to her house. If Cotford dug too deeply, she might soon be on the run as an accomplice to murder. She struggled with the thought of alerting Arthur to the dangers of Cotford, but thought better of it. He would surely slam the door in her face.

Mina placed the iron key into her front door and realized something was wrong. It was already unlocked. She paused. Had she left it unlocked in the hurry to catch the train to London? No, she distinctly remembered locking it before setting out. She had given the house servants a few days off. There should be no one inside, yet Mina could sense that someone was in her house.

Slowly, she opened the door, hoping it would not creak, every nerve afire, expecting some monster to leap out at her. There was no one there. Mina cautiously craned her neck through the door and peered in. The sight of Quincey's unmistakable rag of a wet coat on the marble foyer floor made her heart soar. *Quincey was home!* But just as she began to smile with relief, there came a crash from the adjoining drawing room. He was home, but that did not necessarily mean he was safe. Her feet couldn't move fast enough.

Quincey heard the door slam and spun around to see his mother, looking like a drowned rat, standing at the doorway to the drawing room. For a moment, she stood motionless, shocked by the ransacked condition of the room. "Quincey, are you safe? Are you all right?"

"Yes, I'm fine." Quincey tried to sound civil, but his anger was palpable.

"I have been looking for you everywhere." Her eyes drifted to the mess he had made. "What in God's name . . . ?"

Like a good solicitor sifting through his research, trying to discover the history of a case, Quincey had laid bare all his family secrets. He had used a sledgehammer to smash open the family safe, pried open each of the locked cabinets, and rifled through each and every drawer. The result was stacks of letters, journals, Mina's private diaries, and newspaper clippings that he had painstakingly placed in chronological order: the entire hidden history of his mother and father's life before he was born.

Quincey scooped up a crisp, white envelope with one hand and a stack of handwritten letters with the other. He displayed the writing on the envelope for Mina to see and recognize.

LETTER FROM MINA HARKER TO HER SON, QUINCEY HARKER, ESQ.
(To be opened upon the sudden or unnatural death of Wilhelmina Harker)

The look on Mina's face was somewhere between relief and despair. Quincey flung the letter at his mother, the many pages raining down in a blizzard of paper. "Even in death, your shame would drive you to hide what you really are from me. You thought me a fool. You thought, and you were right, that you could hide your unnatural youth by pretending to strangers that we were brother and sister, turning it into a private joke between mother and son."

Mina implored her Quincey, "Everything you need to know is in that letter. Everything Jonathan and I should have told you years ago, but were afraid to."

"Everything you say is a lie!" Quincey was too furious for further niceties. "How do you know Bram Stoker?"

"Who?"

She seemed genuinely earnest in her confusion. Up until the day before, he would have taken his beloved mother at her word. Much had changed in a single day. "When I first read it, I thought it was a coincidence, but now . . ."

Quincey tossed the bright yellow-covered book toward his mother and studied her face as she read the title aloud.

"*Dracula* . . . by Bram Stoker." Mina gasped. Her fingers trembled as she fumbled through the pages. She looked up at him, aghast. "Where did you get this?"

Her performance was better than any he had seen on the stage thus far. All his life he had loved her. Confided in her. Sided with her against his father. But now he realized that he hardly knew his own mother. "Do not play the innocent. Within those pages lies the one truth you left out of your letter, the answer to the great mystery that has torn this family apart."

"I swear to you. I know nothing of this book."

"I'm not surprised you'd say that. Stoker wrote the truth you so conveniently left out of your letter. He writes you had a 'connection' to that monster, Dracula. I fear Stoker put too polite a spin on it."

"You are too bold!"

His mother looked so young, her face like that of a wounded adolescent. Quincey thought of the three schoolboys he had thrashed for insulting his mother's honor. Suddenly, he felt ashamed of his actions all those years ago. He grabbed the novel out of her hand. "That murderous creature, Dracula, is the chasm that always came between you and Father. Tell me I lie."

"You know nothing about it!"

"You conspired with Dracula against Father. You drank his *blood*," Quincey cried. Reciting from memory, he said, "Chapter twenty-one . . . On the bed beside the window lay Jonathan Harker . . .'"

"Enough!" Tears streamed down her face.

Quincey would have normally been horrified by the notion of making his mother cry, but the thought of her drinking that monster's blood while his father, her husband, slept only inches away, repulsed him.

All these years, he had thought his father's drinking had been responsible for bringing ruin to his family. Now, Quincey knew the truth. It was his mother's betrayal that had driven him to drink. She was the wretch who had brought a plague upon their house, ruining his father. "Stoker's book is no work of fiction. That demon Dracula is the reason for your eternal youth."

"I knew you wouldn't understand. I could not at your age." Mina sobbed. "Evil comes in shades of gray, not black and white."

Quincey shook the book again. "Oh, but I do understand. I understand everything now. This is why Father was so tortured, why he wanted to keep me under his control. To keep the truth of who my mother really is from me."

"Your father wanted you in his world so that he could protect you."

Quincey now understood that when his father had talked of "safety," he was not talking of financial safety but of Quincey's personal safety. This was why his father intervened when Quincey had been about to gain notoriety in the spotlight. It was for his son's protection. Quincey slammed the book on the desk and grabbed the copy of *Le Temps* he had spread there to dry. He held up the front page for his mother to see the crosshatched illustration of the man impaled in Piccadilly Circus.

"*Tepes* . . . The Impaler. In the end, it seems it was not me but Father who needed protection . . . from your former lover!"

Mina took a deep breath. "I loved your father as much as I love you."

Love. Quincey sneered inwardly. Mina's actions did not illustrate any love for his father. "All my life, you let me unjustly denounce my father. All those things I've said to him and about him. All those terrible lies you led me to believe. I can never take it back. I can never make amends. I cannot believe anything you say to me anymore. But rest assured, I am no undecided Hamlet. I shall avenge my father. God help you!"

Quincey stormed out into the vestibule, grabbing his coat from the floor.

Mina called after him, "No! Quincey, please! Hate me if you must, but this family has sacrificed enough! If you love me, look no more into those wild and terrible days. Leave the truth dead and buried, or you could suffer a fate worse than your father's."

Quincey slammed the door behind him. He never looked back.

Mina could not imagine her heart enduring more pain this week. Seeing the look of disgust and anger in her son's eyes was more than she could bear. Now she understood how Jonathan had felt when Quincey's anger was directed at him. Her only crime was sheltering her son, and now that very act had driven him away, perhaps into the very danger she and Jonathan tried so hard to protect him from.

She gripped the small gold cross around her neck and wondered, *Could my dark prince know the secret I had hidden from him all these years? Is his anger with me so great that he finally decided to enact his revenge . . . on me and all whom I love?*

CHAPTER XXII.

―――◇―――

"*D*ixitque Deus fiat lux et facta est lux. And said God let there be light, and light was made." It was the beginning of God's creation of the universe.

The old man traveled in a hansom through the London night. He frowned at Liverpool Street. Gone were the beautiful gas lampposts with their romantic, flickering flames; in their place were the new arc-light columns, their illumination harsh and intense. No longer could a lonely traveler look up to the stars for guidance. The poison of electric light obliterated the stars from view. Man had created light and cut himself off from the heavens. The old man took small comfort from the fact that he would not be around much longer to witness the downfall of his species. He had only one task left in his life, and had almost exhausted his energy in merely making the journey from Amsterdam.

He had forgotten how much he hated the weather in England. The rain made his joints ache, and he could feel the cold dampness in his bones. The voyage from Amsterdam had taken longer than expected. There had been a time when he could embark on this journey several times a month. Now his inability to move at a quick pace caused him to miss his train in Antwerp and he had had to wait a full day before the

{ 139 }

next one departed for France. His spirit was still strong, but he cursed his frail body.

The hansom cab pulled up to the familiar, redbrick Great Eastern Hotel. As with many things, it, too, had been altered since he'd last set foot in London. The quaint, genteel hotel had taken over the adjoining building and expanded into it.

As he paid the carriage driver his sixpence, something strange caught his attention. Across the street, there was a bank of street lamps that had gone dark. It was a common occurrence now, but gas flames never used to go out. *So much for man's technological advancement.*

A suspicious-looking young fellow in a bowler hat lurked under the dark lamppost, pretending to read a newspaper as he stared at the newcomer.

Using his cane to steady himself, the old man trudged slowly to the front door, happy that at least the rain had stopped. He drank in the sights, smells, and sounds of his surroundings. He had history here.

While the porters carried his trunk and carpetbags, the doorman offered to take his arm. The old man refused. He would not let age hamper him any more than it already had. Carefully, he moved step by step across the rain-slicked marble-and-onyx-tiled floor toward the front desk. Once there, he wheezed, "I have a reservation for a room."

The concierge smiled and opened the large black ledger. "Certainly, and your name, sir?"

The old man made no reply, preoccupied by the sensation that he was still being watched. He turned toward the front doors and spied the young man in the bowler hat peering in at him through the glass. In the instant in which the two men made eye contact, a look of panic crossed the young man's face and he receded into the night.

Why was this young man following him? *No doubt he was one of the demon's minions.*

It had finally stopped raining by the time Cotford and Lee entered the Highgate Cemetery through the Swains Lane entrance. The London night fog was rolling in. Cotford's electric torch illuminated the map, looking for Egyptian Avenue. The torchlight swept over the path, dominated by two huge obelisks decorated with papyrus and lotus leaves. The two men continued through the gate. The leafless trees, reaching out to the crescent moon like skeletal fingers, showered them with raindrops set free by the wind. Graceful stone angels, weeping carved figures, and statues of women carrying torches glowed in the moonlight. Stone faces peered through clusters of overgrown grass, ivy, and bramble.

It all reminded Cotford of his childhood. His mother used to tell old Irish folktales of banshees, leprechauns, changelings, and Caoineadh, the Lady of Death.

When Cotford was not quite a man, tuberculosis and influenza had swept through Ireland. In Cotford's village, the elders said it was the work of the Devil. Patients couldn't breathe at night because, they claimed, it felt as if a great weight was on their chests. The superstitious physician stated it was evidence of a vampire sitting on their torso, sucking their blood. Rumors and panic spread faster than the plague itself. Cotford could vividly remember the night the townsfolk dug up his brother's grave. Cotford was horrified when the priest claimed that, since his brother was the first to die of the plague, he must be the vampire infecting the others in the village. The priest had rammed an iron stake through his brother's body. Cotford, young and naïve, became a believer when his brother's dead body audibly moaned. Blood poured from his brother's mouth, eyes, and ears. The priest proclaimed the village saved. But five more people died, and Cotford's faith wavered.

Years later, Cotford's experience as a police officer showed him the truth of what had happened that night. Fermenting gases in a body cause it to bloat as it decomposes. When punctured, as with an iron stake or a police surgeon's scalpel, these gases are forced up over the corpse's vocal cords and through the mouth, forcing the jaw to open and a "moan" to escape. Once the gases are released, the body collapses in on itself, forcing blood out of every orifice. Cotford's brother had never been a vampire, just a victim of superstition and ignorance, bless his poor soul.

It was fear that had stopped Cotford's parents from keeping his brother's grave sacred. Fear of the unknown. Uneducated people feared what they did not understand, allowing superstition to flourish. Of course, after the death of his brother, Cotford learned that all those tales of folklore had been rubbish. It was this revelation that had caused him to turn his back on his home and seek an education in London. He had taken comfort in science, for it could explain the mysteries that haunted men. The supernatural preyed on fears. Through science, he would never be fooled again.

Cotford stopped cold. He heard something move in the graveyard. The moon slid behind the clouds, plunging the cemetery into darkness. Cotford raised his hand to signal to Lee, who also froze. Cotford strained to listen. A rustling came from his left. He aimed his electric torchlight. The specter of a ghostly, white horse caught in the light glared back at him.

Cotford heard Lee betray himself with a sharp intake of air. He looked up at the towering sergeant. He did not expect a man of his stature to be so affected.

"It's only a statue," Cotford said.

"I didn't see it, is all. Could have knocked my head on that stone horseshoe."

Cotford frowned back at the colossal statue. The moss growing on the horse's stone face gave it a scowling look. Cotford recognized it as the tomb of the famous coachman James Selby. The statue loomed over the other headstones, holding a whip and an inverted set of horseshoes.

After walking through the labyrinth of catacombs and tombstones, Lee and Cotford sidestepped a freshly dug grave waiting for its headstone. Finally, they came upon a mausoleum nestled among glowing white yew trees. The tomb was overrun by ivy that covered it like a spiderweb. Lee brushed away the dead leaves and branches covering the engraved name.

WESTENRA.

Lee sighed. "Are you certain you wish to go through with this?"

Cotford nodded; there was no other way. He lacked sufficient evidence to obtain a proper court order from the magistrate. He took a sip from his flask for warmth.

"You're asking me to help you commit a crime."

"This is no whim, Sergeant Lee." Cotford drew one of Jack Seward's leather-bound journals from his overcoat. "I have found proof that the Ripper committed a murder twenty-five years ago that we were unaware of until now. The testimony of Dr. Jack Seward, written by his own hand."

From a premarked page, Cotford read aloud by the light of the electric torch:

> It was Arthur, her betrothed, who screamed in agony as he plunged the iron stake into her loving heart. With that first blow of the mallet, the creature that had once been the fair Lucy shrieked like a tortured Siren. My God the blood! The horror! How I wept. Arthur loved Lucy beyond all others, yet that did not prevent him from striking the deathblow! How oft I have played the scene again in my mind; if I supposedly loved Lucy more than he, why did I not stay Arthur's hand? Yet I fared no better, for it was I who cut her beautiful head from her body. . . . Over the years I've told myself again and again, we were cleansing her soul. If that were true, why can I not get the sounds of her screams out of my mind? Or forget the horrible sight as Professor Van Helsing lifted his surgical saw and began severing Lucy's limbs from her body . . . ?

"Enough!" Lee cried.

"Perhaps, but know my zeal is born of a terrible guilt from which I pray you are spared. Lucy Westenra's death certificate states that she died of a rare blood disease. The physician who signed her death certificate was a Dr. Langella, the same man who only weeks before had signed Holmwood's marriage license. Rather convenient, wouldn't you say? As the journal clearly indicates, Lucy did not die quietly in her bed."

"What if this journal contains merely the drug-induced ravings of a madman?"

"Don't be a fool, Lee. After everything we have learned, you know it to be true. If we turn our backs on what we know and allow another woman to fall under the Ripper's blade . . ." Cotford paused and set his jaw. "It will be our souls who must answer for it."

Lee looked at his mentor for a long moment. He could not deny the logic. Gesturing to the aging tomb, he said softly, "May God forgive us if we're wrong."

"And protect us if we're right."

It took the full effort of both men to force open the iron door. The hinges screeched like wailing banshees. When the door struck the stone wall, the bang was louder than thunder.

Rats squealed and scurried away from the electric torch's beam. Cotford and Sergeant Lee pushed the stone sarcophagus lid aside. The stench of death was far worse than anything they had experienced in the morgue.

Lee coughed, an arm bent across his face to ward off the odor. "How could these old remains still give off such a terrible stench?" A dreadful thought came to him. "Perhaps there's been a new addition."

"That tomb door hasn't been opened in decades," Cotford said.

The sergeant nodded; Cotford was right. But it didn't explain how the pall of death could still be so powerful. And *fresh*.

He hoped it was a dead animal.

Cotford aimed his light into the open tomb. Inside the sarcophagus were the mutilated, skeletal remains of a female. The skull, with flowing red hair, had clearly been severed from her body. The mouth was stuffed with dried flowers, the limbs severed and crossed. An iron stake was still embedded in her skeletal chest. Dried blood stains were still visible beside the corpse. Cotford looked upon the ravaged remains of Lucy Westenra, and his mind was instantly flooded by the memories of those five bloodied prostitutes found in Whitechapel. All had been mutilated in much the same way. Clearly, the Ripper had reached a new low with Lucy. He had moved beyond prostitutes to women of means, murdered her in a place where no one heard her scream, and dealt the final blow with an iron stake. That was pure Van Helsing. He felt at once justified and sickened to the core.

"Madmen!"

"Murderers!" Lee added.

Cotford could see on Lee's face the same hunger for justice that he himself had suffered all these years.

"Sergeant Lee, I want every inch of this crime scene photographed and the remains taken to the morgue. Use only the subordinates you trust. Our superiors cannot yet get wind of what we're about. Wake that old fart, the surgeon, and have him do a full autopsy. Make sure he's finished and gone before first light, so as not to arouse suspicion. See to it that his report finds its way to my desk the instant it is complete."

"Yes, sir."

Cotford cocked his head. He raised a finger to his lips, signaling Lee to silence.

From outside, they heard someone running toward the tomb.

Cotford, as usual, was without a pistol. Perhaps he should have put his pride aside this night and taken one with him. He turned off his light as the footsteps approached. With his billy club in hand, Lee positioned himself next to the open doorway. Cotford held the heavy electric torch at the ready.

The footsteps drew nearer. Just as the moon peered through the clouds, a dark figure appeared in the doorway. The silhouette indicated he was wearing a bowler hat. Cotford switched on his electric torch. The beam of light blinded the intruder, catching him off guard.

Before Cotford struck, Lee cried out, "Constable Price! What the hell are you doing here out of uniform?"

Price removed his bowler hat, placed it under his arm, and came to attention. "You told me to be inconspicuous. Did I do wrong, sir?"

Cotford recognized Constable Price as the eager youngster who had run into the Red Lion, looking for him.

"Sergeant Lee," Price said, flushed and out of breath. "You wanted me to inform you . . . when the man in the photo . . . checked into the Great Eastern Hotel."

"Did he?" Cotford asked, glad that Lee had taken Price into their confidence. Cotford liked this young man and his unquestioning earnestness.

"Yes, sir. I saw him check in with my own eyes. He's much older now, but I recognized him."

Cotford took a sip from his flask, his face broad with a triumphant smirk. "And so it begins."

CHAPTER XXIII.

———◇———

Through the thick blanket of fog, Countess Bathory waited for the two policemen and the young man in the bowler hat to exit the mausoleum inscribed with the name: WESTENRA.

She had been observing their actions for several nights. Her interest had been piqued a week earlier as she sat upon the rooftop of the alleyway near Temple Bar, while the pig-shaped inspector attempted to deduce the circumstances surrounding the demise of her beloved Woman in White. She listened with amusement when the other inspector, Huntley, blathered on with his ridiculous summation. It was an insult to her lady. The thought that this Harker, a weakling of a man, could have killed her golden-haired beloved was repulsive. She would have torn Harker to shreds, too, if she had had the chance.

This fat detective, by contrast, was no fool. Not only did he deduce the events that had occurred, but he actually surmised Bathory's presence at the scene. Since then, she had been watching that one with great interest.

The taller of the two officers addressed the fat one by the name Inspector Cotford. Bathory did not know the name, but she recognized his face. She had seen his portrait in the newspapers years ago, with that cretin, Abberline. *Yes, Cotford. I do remember the name.* He looked somewhat different now, certainly heavier, and much older. Bathory marveled at how drastically mortal men aged in a mere quarter of a century.

Cotford might have been more astute than others who had crossed her path, but he was far from enlightened. He had been able to find all the pieces of the puzzle, though his narrow mind would not allow him to see the full picture. Bathory had resisted the urge to pounce down on him and bash his skull against the wall. She imagined the look of shock on his face when he saw firsthand how a woman could be more powerful than a man. For centuries, Bathory had been confused by the notion that God created man in his own image. If it were so, then God was weak. Man was so fragile and limited. Without technology, man would be near the bottom of the food chain. Bathory had discovered the truth that even lowly beasts had known for millennia: Man was easy prey, and his blood was like a fine vintage. She wondered if the beasts that had tasted man's flesh felt the same satisfaction she did. The only human for whom Bathory held any respect was Charles Darwin. Survival of the fittest. Bathory was humanity perfected. Her powers of sight, hearing, smell, and taste were tenfold those of a human, as was her strength. She was blessed with an even more powerful sixth sense, that of the mind. For centuries, man had marveled at magicians who could manipulate objects, read and control minds. For Bathory, it involved no trick or illusion: She could enter a human's consciousness and force their mind's eye to see her as a wolf, gargoyle, rat, or mist. Her powers had grown to the point at which she could enter a person's mind even from hundreds of miles away and have them see what she wished. She had the ability to move at incredible speeds. She could even levitate and move through the skies, soaring on the winds. Man needed a machine to fly. Bathory was indeed the fittest, the next level of human evolution.

Bathory tried to determine whether she should kill Cotford for what he had learned, or make him an unwitting ally. Her first instinct was to kill the three men in the mausoleum now, before they spilled their bile to others. She had killed Jack Seward for less, and this lonely place was a perfect setting for murder. The cemetery was vast, and she was many yards away, but Bathory's preternatural eyes easily pierced the fog and darkness. The Westenra mausoleum. *So, they are digging up the past. Collecting more pieces of the puzzle.*

She considered the fate of the fat inspector. This was an obsessed, narrow-minded man. Perhaps his contemporaries thought him as mad as the criminals he pursued. She loved to gamble, but not with cards or money. Life and death were better prizes. It was all so arbitrary anyway, and in this game she had always been the winner. She was ready to wager that Cotford had sworn the policemen with him to secrecy. He was obviously bright, but failure to recognize Seward's grave next to Lucy's led her to believe that his thinking was pathetically linear. Could she use Cotford to her own ends? Yes. She would use Cotford to draw the rest of them out. He would bring them to her. Bathory smiled. England wasn't going to be as dull and dreary as she remembered.

Bathory deemed that Cotford and his subordinates should live at least a while longer. This was not because she felt pity, or compassion, for she did not possess the ability for such feelings: She was the perfect carnivore. But she would put aside her bloodlust, this night, in favor of the game. *Let's give my new pawns another piece of the puzzle.*

Bathory used her gold-tipped walking stick to tap the ceiling of the carriage after she climbed in. The driverless carriage dashed out of Hampstead Cemetery and headed south to Whitechapel.

Kristan was exhausted. Her feet were blistered from walking Commercial Street all night. The newspapers she had stuffed into her shoes for warmth had become soggy and were falling apart, carrying the odor of rotted fish. As Kristan hobbled her way to her dilapidated lodgings on Devonshire Square, she heard horses approaching. She wanted to ignore them, but her financial situation did not grant her such luxuries. She forced a smile and turned to see a black carriage appearing through the thick, night fog. Something was not right. Carriages did not simply drive themselves. She noticed that the black carriage was richly adorned with gold fixtures. A new thought crept into her head. This was the age of invention. The wealthy always had the best and newest toys. A driverless black carriage was probably a cross between a motorcar and a hansom. Focused on the approaching gold, Kristan became excited. She had already had five customers that night, but their small fees would hardly pay for her next day's meals. This carriage could be carrying a potential well-to-do customer. If she entertained correctly, she could charge enough to pay her rent for a month. This must be her lucky night.

The carriage slowed to a stop inches away from her tattered shoes. She waited for the carriage door to open and reveal a handsome gentleman. The upholstered carriage would serve her bottom much better than the cold cobblestones of an alleyway. After a few moments, Kristan realized this gent wanted her to work for it. She licked her lips in hopes of moistening them enough to hide the cracks caused by the March wind. She adjusted her blouse to prop up her large bosom, her *selling assets*, sashayed as flamboyantly as her disintegrating footwear would allow toward the coach, and gave the ornate carriage door a dainty knock.

"Looking for someone, guv'nor?"

No response. This one was playing hard-to-get. "'Allo? Anybody 'ome?"

Kristan took a step back as a black-gloved hand wearing a ruby ring pushed back the bloodred curtain, reached out, and offered a Spanish gold doubloon. Kristan smiled greedily and snatched the coin.

"Now you're talkin' me language, luv."

The coach door opened slowly. A black-gloved index finger gestured for Kristan to climb inside. At this price, the gentleman could do anything he wanted with her. Being a good businesswoman, Kristan knew a gentleman in this part of town willing to pay this much money was looking for something special. Even if it hurt, she'd play along. If she was lucky, perhaps he would become a regular.

Kristan deftly placed the coin down her blouse in the most alluring way she could and took the black-gloved hand in hers.

The gloved hand closed the door. Her customer's face was finally revealed. Kristan was shocked to see not a gentleman but a beautiful, blue-eyed, raven-haired woman elegantly wrapped in a man's coat and tails. Kristan was glad she would avoid another ravaging poke and still make a fee. She became aroused at the thought of this beautiful woman soothing her most private aches.

· · ·

Bathory's carriage raced along the Lower Thames near the Tower of London. The six black mares' nostrils flared with hot breath. The carriage bounced and rattled as it swept over the cobbles.

The mares braced to a quick stop, their heads snapping back and their knees locking as if an invisible rein had been pulled. It was the dead of night in the center of the city, an hour before dawn. There was no one on the street. There would be no witnesses. The carriage door swung slowly open. As if it were no heavier than a small sack of dirty rags, Bathory hurled Kristan's bloodied body into the River Thames.

Kristan's throat had been torn away and her face was locked, mouth agape, in an expression of abject horror. Her bodice had been torn open, revealing her breasts, and her knickers were down around her ankles. Bathory would spare this tasty child of God no humility in death. Bathory then booted Kristan's bag onto the street, spilling its contents: some coins, a handkerchief, and a rosary. She laughed at the sight. *Another hypocrite.* The prostitute's body floated away on the current of the river. Her dead eyes stared up to the heavens. Bathory could never understand how wretched people like this whore could still find any love for God. What had God done for them? Bathory's black-gloved hand tossed the gold coin into the water beside the body and smiled as Kristan and her gold sank below the black waves of the Thames.

Who said you can't take it with you?

"Yours for the finding, Inspector Cotford," Bathory mused.

CHAPTER XXIV.

———◇———

Quincey's blood boiled as he raced along Bonhay Road. Why had his parents kept their past from him? Why had his father not trusted him? Why did his father have to die? Why had his mother betrayed her friends? His mind swirled as he ran through the rain. He heard the familiar whistle of the train pulling out of St. David's station. There was no time to purchase a ticket. For his own sanity, he needed to get away from Exeter as quickly as possible, and the next train wasn't due for another three hours. Without thinking, Quincey dashed along the tracks as the train picked up speed, and jumped onto the back of the rear carriage. Rain made the metal slippery, and Quincey lost his footing. He fumbled for a dangling chain, and held on for dear life as the train picked up speed. Clenching his teeth, he pulled himself upright and stood there, heart thumping. When he was finally safe on the train, he turned to see Exeter fading in the distance, knowing this would be the last time he set foot in his hometown. With his father dead and all trust in his mother gone, there was nothing left for him there.

As the train continued up the line toward London, Quincey found a seat in one of the carriages where it was comfortable and tranquil; but his mind would not quiet. How much of Stoker's book was actually true? Could the un-dead really walk the earth? It seemed preposterous.

The letter from his mother claimed that monsters did exist; this monster had killed his father and torn his family apart. Quincey felt in himself a growing thirst for revenge. *But how could he fight such evil?* He was faced by an adversary who, centuries ago, had commanded vast armies. Remorseless and brutal, this monster had the power of devils on his side. Quincey was alone, and feeling overwhelmed. The only others who knew the truth about what Quincey was facing was the brave band of heroes. Their bond had been broken long ago; and now most of them were dead. But perhaps there was one he could still turn to. Mina had kept a complete dossier about his exploits. He was a hero who had served alongside Quincey P. Morris in the French Foreign Legion. The fighting skills of that elite unit were legendary. He had fought in the Siege of Tuyen Quang against the Empire of China; escaped from cannibals in the Marquesas; and guarded the empress of Korea from Japanese assassins. Moreover, he had faced Prince Dracula in battle and survived. *Yes,* thought Quincey. *I will go to see him. I will go to see Arthur Holmwood.*

The sun was setting by the time the hansom cab raced up to the front entrance gate of the home of Arthur Holmwood, also known as Lord Godalming. Quincey leapt out and tossed coins up to the driver.

He gaped up at the stately mansion. It was at least three times larger than the Harker house in Exeter. What a puzzle this Holmwood was. A man of such means could certainly have enjoyed the privileges of wealth. The fact that he had instead risked his life time and again made Quincey admire Holmwood before even meeting him. He was surely a man to be reckoned with, and just the help Quincey would need.

Stoker's novel made no mention of how the band of heroes had come together. Quincey had learned of their long bonds from Mina's carefully kept records and journals. Jack, Arthur, and his namesake, Quincey P. Morris, had all attended the elite Huguenot boarding school outside London as boys. Jack was a Catholic, but his father, a prominent physician, had not wanted his son to be limited by attending a parochial school. Instead, he had sent Jack to the Protestant private school to mingle with a higher class of British society. There, Jack had met Arthur, and they had become close friends.

Quincey P. Morris's father, Brutus, was a wealthy rancher in Texas. When America's Civil War broke out in 1861, Texas had reserved the right not to secede from the Union, as well as not to join the Confederacy. To that end, an embassy had been opened in London, and Brutus Morris had been named by Texas as the ambassador. As befitting a man of such stature, Brutus had sent his son to the same elite private school that Jack and Arthur attended. It was Quincey P. Morris's great regret that he had been too young to have fought in the American Civil War. This regret eventually sent him back home to fight in the wars against the Indians and to help tame the Wild West. Arthur had been inspired by Morris's heroics on America's Great Plains and had been moved to join him on his next adventure, enlisting in the Foreign Legion. Jack Seward could not be persuaded to join them, choosing instead to pursue his own glory in science, enrolling in the prestigious Vrije University of Holland as student and graduate assistant to Professor Abraham Van Helsing.

At the top of the mansion's front steps, Quincey Harker paused to catch his breath and compose himself. He did not want to meet the great Arthur Holmwood looking like a messenger boy. Standing on the doorstep, it occurred to him that this was where the band of heroes had often met. This is where the plan to rid the world of Dracula's evil had been hatched. And yet, even with a man like Arthur Holmwood in their midst, they'd failed. Quincey feared this foe he was facing was simply too strong.

He reached for the brass door knocker, but there was none to be found. He looked about, saw a pull rope adjacent to the door, and realized his mistake. Of course, this man would have the finest of luxuries, including a new doorbell.

Quincey pulled the rope and a somber tone rang out. There was no answer. He pulled the rope again; still no answer. He was about to pound on the door when it opened, slightly.

A butler peered out. "May I help you?"

"Quincey Harker here to see . . ." Quincey paused. A man like Arthur Holmwood should be addressed by his proper title. ". . . Lord Godalming. It is a matter of great urgency."

The butler opened the door another few inches and held up a small silver tray. Quincey was expected to supply a calling card. Fortunately, Basarab had provided some for his young protégé. Quincey searched his coat, eventually finding them stashed in a tattered pocket. The butler raised his eyebrow, as a proper gentleman always carried his cards in a case. "One moment, please," the man said, and closed the door in Quincey's face.

Quincey's leg twitched with apprehension as he waited. He had read so much about Holmwood in the last few days. The exploits in Transylvania were just the tip of the iceberg. Among Mina's things, Quincey had found information about Arthur's early life, and also newspaper clippings cut from society pages highlighting Arthur's life since their battles against Dracula. Though Arthur had become Lord Godalming upon the death of his father, he'd not commonly used the moniker until after returning from Transylvania. Quincey wondered if Arthur had changed his name because he knew Dracula was still alive; but Lord Godalming certainly did not cower in his mansion in fear. He had gone on to become a champion sail racer on the Thames, an expert polo player, and a master duelist. He had frequently defended his honor by pistols and by swords, killing three men and wounding twelve others who had insulted him. Quincey expected no less from the man who risked everything he had for the honor of his great love, Lucy Westenra. A man such as this would surely rise up to battle against the evils brought forth by Dracula's return.

Quincey had remembered meeting someone referred to as "Uncle Arthur" in his childhood and realized now that it must have been Arthur Holmwood. But this man hadn't had any contact with the Harkers in almost two decades, for reasons Quincey could only assume were connected to his mother's betrayal and his father's drinking. He only hoped that Holmwood would be able to look past their shame and bring himself to trust Quincey because he desperately needed Arthur's help.

Men such as Lord Godalming were a dying breed. Quincey had read that a friend of Arthur's father had lost his fortune due to bad investments. Rather than allow his friend to forfeit his lands and wealth,

Holmwood had married the man's daughter. If he had been willing to marry a stranger to help a friend, Quincey hoped Lord Godalming would be equally beneficent in his case.

Quincey was overcome with remorse as he thought of his father. Now he would never have the chance to apologize for the way he had behaved toward him. He now knew that his father had loved him. Jonathan Harker had sacrificed everything for his son, and Quincey was determined to prove he was worthy of that sacrifice.

At long last, the door opened again. The butler stepped out and pronounced, "Lord Godalming will see you now."

Quincey stepped forward to enter, but the butler stood in his way. Clearing his throat, the butler glanced down at Quincey's muddy shoes. Caught out once again, Quincey passed the sole of each shoe over the cast-iron boot scraper beside the door.

At last he was ushered into Arthur Holmwood's study. The butler took Quincey's coat and left, closing the doors behind him.

There was a familiar scent to the room. Quincey realized he had been here before and suddenly he was overcome by a flood of memories. He recognized the burgundy wall fabric, an authentic and very expensive William Morris design. Fine swords, rapiers, and daggers were displayed on the wall. During his years in the theatre, Quincey had held many wooden prop swords, but these were authentic blades. Although there were nicks in a few, none bore any traces of blood.

As a child, he remembered abruptly, he'd reached out to touch one of the swords. But his father had grabbed his hand. *You could have cut yourself.*

Quincey remembered the hand-carved oak furnishings, the stained glass in the windows, and shelves packed with more books than he could have hoped to read in a lifetime.

There was a portrait, too, he recalled, of a beautiful woman with red hair. Yes, even as a child he recognized the woman in the portrait was the same woman in the photograph that his mother held so dear.

Quincey turned to look above the fireplace, where he remembered the portrait had hung, but it was gone, replaced by a simple landscape painting. "The painting of Lucy . . . ," he mused aloud to himself.

"The painting you are referring to," said a voice behind Quincey, "was taken down ten years ago, out of respect for Beth, my wife."

Arthur Holmwood, Lord Godalming, sat behind a massive mahogany desk. Below a beautiful lamp rested the silver tray bearing Quincey's calling card.

Quincey was taken aback. Arthur Holmwood had barely changed. He was older than Jonathan, yet anyone who saw them together would have been hard-pressed to believe it. With his thick blond hair, square jaw, and steel blue eyes, it was easy to see why Lucy would have chosen this man above all other possible suitors. Poor Dr. Seward had never stood a chance.

Quincey straightened and cleared his throat. "Good day, Mr. . . . Lord Godalming. Forgive me, I didn't see you there."

"I'm sure you did not come here to discuss my décor."

Quincey was surprised by his brusque tone, but he forged ahead. "I'm Jonathan and Mina Harker's son. . . ."

"I know who you are, Master Harker. Cognac?"

"No, thank you." Quincey hoped his refusal to drink would be taken as a sign that he did not share his father's weakness.

Lord Godalming stood up and crossed the room to a fully stocked bar. He cut an impressive figure, standing at six foot, four inches; his suit was perfectly tailored to a trim, muscular frame. His midsection was as tight as a drum, and his neck was void of the sag most men had at his age. He moved so decorously, it was hard to believe all the adventurous stories Quincey had read about him. Only a few gray hairs at the temples betrayed Holmwood's fifty-plus years of life, and these gave him a distinguished air. Arthur took hold of the delicate crystal glass and decanter and turned so that the dim light in the room fell upon him. At once, Quincey noticed two slight flaws: a scar on his right cheek, and a tip of an ear was gone. Quincey wondered what battle had left its trace upon Lord Godalming.

Arthur poured cognac from the crystal carafe into a snifter. "What, pray tell, brings you here, Master Harker?"

"I'm sure you know."

"I haven't the faintest notion."

"My father was murdered last week."

"Yes, I read that," replied Arthur, his voice aloof. "Condolences." He cupped the snifter, letting the warmth of his hand heat the cognac.

Quincey tried to make sense of Holmwood's cool distance. "Did you also read that Jack Seward was murdered two weeks ago in Paris?" he asked.

Arthur frowned, his face darkening. He shut his eyes. Bringing the snifter to his nose to absorb the aroma, he said nothing.

Quincey raised his voice. "Did you hear me? Jack is—"

"I heard you the first time." Arthur snapped his eyes open and glared at Quincey, who had the distinct impression that he wanted to kill the messenger. "Jack was an old fool. Stuck his nose into . . . business that should have been left alone."

"Jack Seward was your friend!"

Arthur's eyes narrowed and he took a step toward him. "Jack Seward was a morphine addict who lost his fortune, his reputation, his home, and his family!"

Every survival instinct told Quincey to stop now. But he had to stand his ground if he was to earn this man's respect. He straightened his back and planted his feet. But, just as quickly as it had appeared, Arthur's anger passed, to be replaced by a deep sadness.

"Jack was an old fool who could not let go of the past," Holmwood said as he consumed the cognac in one swift gulp, as if to drown the unpleasant memory.

"My father and Dr. Seward were murdered within days of each other; it's more than coincidence, wouldn't you agree?" Quincey asked. "You and your wife are in danger."

Arthur laughed and refilled his glass. "Danger? Master Harker, you don't know the meaning of the word."

Quincey could not believe this was the same Arthur Holmwood who'd ridden a stallion into battle against the gypsies and Dracula. He of all people should have understood the threat. A fury came upon him, and before he knew it, he had run forward and grabbed Arthur's arm, stopping him in mid-pour.

"Dracula is coming for revenge, and you know it. Help me kill him, once and for all."

Arthur gave the hand upon his arm a steely glare. With a powerful reflex, he yanked his arm away. "Rash, Master Harker. Foolhardy and rash. So she finally told you, then."

"No. I discovered the truth myself," Quincey said, trying with little success to keep a tremor from invading his voice.

"Dracula is dead. I saw him die." Arthur put down the carafe and walked back behind his desk. "We all did."

Quincey couldn't believe such willful blindness. Did he have to spell it out for him? "My father was impaled. *Tepes*—who else could it be?"

"I've fought my battles, Master Harker. In my life, I've stood on hell's battlefields and crossed oceans of blood. All of that is over for me. I will not walk there again." He picked up a small bell to summon the butler.

Quincey pounded his fist on the desk. "Coward!" He was sure this insult would incite Arthur to react, but the man's blue eyes were empty of emotion.

"Go home, boy," Holmwood sighed. "Before you hurt yourself."

Quincey heard the butler enter the room behind him.

"I gather our meeting is over?"

"Good afternoon, Master Harker." Arthur picked up a small book, turned to a marked page, and began reading.

The butler came forward with Quincey's coat. "This way, sir."

Quincey stood unmoving, utterly shocked. Then he seized his coat from the butler and spun back to the desk, pulling away the book in Arthur's hands. Their eyes locked. "I won't pity you when I see you next on the slab," he declared, hoping that the man would rise to the bait at last. Instead of meeting the challenge, Arthur stared at the bland painting over the fireplace and said in a near-whisper, "I doubt anyone will."

As the butler ushered Quincey out of the house and into the now-dark street, he dwelled on what had just happened. Whatever force had driven Jack Seward to madness, corrupted his mother, and taken his father's soul had also smothered Arthur's spirit. Quincey now knew that Lord Godalming did not fight duels for honor. Lord Godalming fought duels in the hope of death. He used the name Lord Godalming because Arthur Holmwood was no more.

CHAPTER XXV.

—•—◇—•—

The moon was low in the sky, shining through the windows of New Scotland Yard. Cotford struggled to keep his eyes open as he worked at his desk. To his left was the police surgeon's report of the Lucy Westenra postmortem and the stark, black-and-white photos of Lucy's exhumation. To his right lay the crime scene photographs of the butchered body of the woman found in the alley five nights earlier. He compared the two sets of photographs. Lucy Westenra's body, twenty-five years ago, had been torn apart in the same fashion as the recently murdered woman in the alleyway. In Cotford's mind, the two murders were connected, but he still had no hard proof. He could not go to his superiors; they would see it all as conjecture. He ran through the pictures and notes, looking for a clue, some small, overlooked morsel of information that would confirm that both murders had been committed by the same hand. He shook his head to keep sleep at bay. He had not slept in days.

"Inspector Cotford!"

Sergeant Lee's voice jarred Cotford awake. "Yes, what is it?" Cotford asked. His neck was sore and stiff. He raised his arm to shield his eyes from the blinding morning sunlight coming through the window. *Damn! I've slept too long.*

"They've found another body!"

"Where?" The cobwebs cleared instantly from Cotford's mind.

"The Thames, sir. Near the Tower of London."

Cotford grabbed his coat from the back of his chair and bolted for the door.

On the cold banks of the Lower Thames, near St. Katharine Docks just east of the Tower of London, a small crowd had gathered. Inspector Huntley oversaw the extraction of the corpse from the water. A rope had been tied under the arms of the body, with the other end hitched to the saddle of a horse. Onlookers gasped at the sight of the dead woman's ripped bodice and exposed breasts. Once the body was pulled up over the railing and onto the street, Huntley gallantly removed his jacket and placed it over the dead woman's chest, preserving her last ounce of dignity. The police surgeon knelt beside the body to begin his preliminary examination, conferring quietly with Huntley.

Nearby, another woman dressed in ragged, revealing attire wept as she spoke to a detective constable, who took her statement on a notepad.

Cotford grabbed Lee by the arm. They moved through the crowd, angling themselves closer so that they could overhear the young woman's statement.

". . . After that, I saw Kristan walking alone and turning onto Devonshire Square. She lives there . . . rents a room at twelve pence a week . . . I mean . . . she used to live there. . . ."

The girl broke into uncontrollable sobs. Cotford noticed a handkerchief in the detective constable's pocket, but the man did not move to offer it to his witness. *She's still a woman, damn you.*

Cotford reached into his pocket for his own handkerchief as he pushed through the crowd. But he'd waited too long, and another man beat him to it. The young woman graciously accepted the handkerchief, and Cotford was surprised that the gentleman was Inspector Huntley. The inspector noticed Cotford and frowned. In a friendly way, which Cotford thought too familiar, Huntley looped his arms through Cotford's and Lee's elbows and led them aside.

"What are you doing here, Sergeant Lee?" Huntley asked, his words quick and firm. "I can see now that Inspector Cotford's appearance the other night in the alleyway was no coincidence. What gibberish has he seduced you with? Associating with a man of his reputation could jeopardize your career." Huntley turned to Cotford and continued, "I'm sure Inspector Cotford will agree with me."

"How could I not? But keep in mind, the ends justify the means."

Lee cleared his throat to respond, but Huntley held up his hand to silence him. "Please, don't say anything to ruin my good opinion of you any further." And before Lee could say anything, he turned his attention to Cotford. "Inspector, let me first start by thanking you for your observations the other night. Sergeant Lee informed me you'd found the second set of bloodstains and the handprints. The fact that you instructed him to bring it directly to my attention and not to our superiors demonstrates that you still uphold protocol and show professional courtesy to your fellow officers."

Cotford nodded. "My only duty is to bring the killer to justice."

"Very well, allow me to return your professional courtesy," Huntley said. "I will thank you to not jump to any further conclusions. I know you, so let me say this plainly. There is no correlation whatsoever between the woman in the alleyway and this victim here today. This dead woman was a poor prostitute murdered by a depraved client, a common occurrence on these streets. The decapitated woman from the alleyway was wealthy. I concede that she was probably murdered by a third party as you surmised, but I maintain it was a crime of passion. Most likely a jealous husband. Rest assured, I will find him."

"This is personal for me," Cotford replied. "I'm not looking for glory, and I have no desire to show you up. I will gladly turn over to you any evidence before I present it to the High Court. As I said, my only duty is to bring the killer to justice."

"Let me be perfectly clear, Inspector Cotford." Huntley's tone became more forceful and exasperated. "If I find you interfering with my investigation, or creating a public panic with claims that these latest murders are connected, you will leave me no choice but to protect my own standing by reporting you to our superiors. I beg you, do not put me in that position. Please, it would be best that you not endanger your reputation by chasing ghosts." Not waiting for a reply, he patted Cotford on the back, gave him an encouraging smile, and marched over to greet the awaiting press.

Lee stepped forward anxiously and said into Cotford's ear, "What was that about?"

"Sergeant Lee, Huntley was not wrong. You have a family to think about. If you wish to bow out from our investigation now, I won't blame you."

Lee looked him in the eye. "I'm with you so long as you're right, Inspector. So long as you're right."

Cotford smiled as the two men walked over to the body of the dead woman lying beside the river's iron railing. Her hair was soaked, but she was clearly a red-haired woman, as Lucy Westenra had been. The face would have been quite pretty if it were not locked in an expression of absolute horror. Her dead green eyes were frozen wide-open, staring blankly at Cotford. Her neck had been gouged away, nearly to the bone. The wound looked more like the bite of an animal than anything a human could inflict. Cotford believed he was indeed chasing a madman.

Had he wasted precious time searching for hard evidence? Had his slow and steady scientific method cost this woman her life? Cotford realized that time was of the essence. He had to shake things up. He turned back to Lee, his blood surging. Something consumed him, something the weeping young woman had said. This victim, Kristan, had last been seen walking to her rented room on Devonshire Square.

Devonshire Square? That's only a stone's throw from . . . from the hotel where Van Helsing was staying.

"Damn him. Damn his eyes!" The veins in Cotford's head pulsed with rage. "Stay here, Sergeant. Find out everything you can."

Without another word, he raced northward.

CHAPTER XXVI.

The old man used his cane to adjust his position in the overly plush velvet chair. He sat in the opulent restaurant that had once been the grand Victorian ballroom in the Great Eastern Hotel. The old man took comfort in the familiar setting, a setting long unaffected by time. He had already finished his cold tomato consommé and was greatly looking forward to the steak and kidney pie for which this restaurant was famous. The taste and smell of the dish had remained with him over the decades since he'd last stayed here. His mouth watered when a young man approached with a silver tray. To his extreme surprise, the old man realized it was the concierge and not the waiter he had expected.

"Can't you see, young man, I'm anticipating a meal?"

"I beg your pardon, sir," the concierge said as he lifted the polished lid and presented the tray to the old man. "A telegram just arrived for you. Forwarded from Amsterdam."

The old man looked down at the familiar yellow envelope with his name inscribed upon it. Telegrams usually contained bad news; he had a feeling the odds were not in his favor.

"Thank you," he said with a sigh. He took the envelope with one hand and placed a half crown on the silver tray with the other. The concierge bowed politely and departed, slipping the coin into his pocket with practiced decorum. Obviously, Maaijcke, the grocery store delivery boy, had found his note in Amsterdam and was accordingly forwarding his correspondence.

Using the steak knife, the old man tore open the envelope:

TELEGRAM—Mina Harker, Exeter,
to Prof. Abraham Van Helsing, Amsterdam
QUINCEY IS ASKING QUESTIONS.
COME AT ONCE. WE NEED YOU. MINA.

He had always admired Mina Harker's strength and will, traits that had made her an asset during their adventures. Although that very same strength and will made her unpredictable at times. A woman with a mind of her own was dangerous. A man, apart from his sexual urges, was ruled by mind and logic. A woman in all things was ruled by her emotions, and in his experience, all her decisions were born from them.

Mina had been tempted by the demon, had even given in at one point. It was due to her loyalty to her husband, Jonathan, that she had chosen the path of light. Now that her husband was dead, she no longer had to be loyal. If tempted again, would Mina give in to her desires?

A hot steak and kidney pie was set in front of him. The food smelled delicious, just as he had remembered. His stomach growled; but even so, he found himself rereading the telegram. Quincey Harker was asking questions. No surprise, as so much had been kept from the boy. But secrets are like flowers buried under snow: Eventually they rise up and push through into the light.

He wondered if Quincey could handle the dark secret their band harbored. With luck, he would have inherited the unwavering faith that Jonathan Harker had possessed in his youth . . . and perhaps also his mother's strong will? That would be unfortunate. In any case, if Quincey was confronted by the demon, like his mother before him, he would have to make a choice. Youth could be reckless, and rebellious. If it came to that, Quincey could become a greater threat.

The old man frowned as a disturbing thought entered his mind: It might fall upon him to destroy Quincey. Would God grant him the strength to kill the boy he had once loved as a son? He prayed it would never come to that. Deciding that the price for his telegram's bad news was to forfeit his meal, Van Helsing rose from the table. He grabbed his cane and hobbled toward the lobby. It dawned on him that, in the time he had left, he might never again have the opportunity to sample the Great Eastern Hotel's steak and kidney pie. As he reached the lift, he sighed. Life at its best was made up of only small, special moments. *How many do we have in a lifetime?* For him, so few were left. He cursed the Harkers for stealing one of these from him. How could Jonathan and Mina have been stupid enough to have kept the truth from their son for so long? Ignorance bred anger. In their misguided attempt to protect their son, the Harkers had put Quincey in grave danger. The demon was out there, and the old man had to find Quincey first.

"And now all the vultures have at last assembled," a man said, breaking into Van Helsing's thoughts.

He knew that voice, though he had not heard it for a very long time.

"Cotford!" Van Helsing pivoted on his cane.

Standing in the middle of the lobby was a ghost from his past. Cotford looked much older now, and had gained even more weight, but the bloodhound still growled. Cotford in his younger days had been a gruff sort who did not waste his time with conforming to the niceties of society. Time had obviously not mellowed him. He hadn't even had the decency to remove his hat upon stepping inside.

"Death follows you like stink on a pig, Van Helsing."

Cotford watched as Van Helsing stepped forward, supported by his cane. The walking stick was a nice touch, playing up the frail old man act to deflect suspicion.

He tried to hide the fact that he was still out of breath, having almost run from the Thames straight to the Great Eastern Hotel. Perhaps it was no irony that Van Helsing liked to be a guest in this place. Before becoming a grand hotel in 1884, this building had once been a lunatic asylum, much like the one his former pupil, Dr. Jack Seward, had operated in Whitby.

Cotford had learned in his years of service that predators liked to oper-
ate close to their home base. The Great Eastern Hotel was on Liverpool
Street, west of Bishopsgate. A stone's throw away, on the east side of Bishopsgate, was Devonshire Square, where Kristan had last been seen. The
mad doctor had not even waited a night after checking in before claiming
his next victim. Cotford didn't have the irrefutable proof he needed to arrest
Van Helsing, yet he dared not wait for him to take another innocent life.
As he had with Mrs. Harker, Cotford hoped this surprise confrontation
would trip Van Helsing up and force a confession. The look of shock on the
professor's face indicated he had not expected to ever see him again. So far,
so good. He had the upper hand, with the element of surprise on his side.

"Still on the case, Detective Constable?" Van Helsing asked.

"It's Inspector now."

"How very British to hide failure with promotion."

Cotford was stung by Van Helsing's wit, but allowed this remark to
roll off his back. He retorted with some bite, "Another two women
ripped apart in Whitechapel, and here you are. In 1888, you escaped
justice. This time, I will have you and your band of murderers."

"Open your eyes wider, Cotford. There is no justice *you* can bring to
the evil you seek." Van Helsing turned back toward the lift.

Cotford glared at the old man's back, enraged. He despised men like
Van Helsing, who claimed to be men of science but, when faced with a
question their minds could not answer, leapt immediately toward the
supernatural. He was a product of a bygone era.

The professor pressed the button to call the lift. Cotford's whisky-
scarred voice echoed through the marble lobby: "I opened Lucy Westenra's grave."

Van Helsing stopped dead in his tracks. He turned slowly. The look
of anger in the eyes behind his spectacles was exactly what Cotford had
hoped for.

He hissed through his teeth: "You travel down the path of your insignificant life in ultimate complacency. Safe in your modern world of
machines and oblivious enlightenment. Blind to the ancient pagan evils
that rot the ground beneath your feet because you refuse to pay them
heed."

Patrons in the lobby by now had all stopped and were staring at the two men. Cotford didn't care: Let them all hear. It was time Van Helsing's madness was exposed.

"You were dismissed from Vrije University for stealing bodies from their graves," Cotford said loudly. "Those exploratory autopsies consisted of nothing more than ramming iron stakes through their hearts and mutilating the bodies."

He could hear his voice filling the room, stirring fear in the onlookers, but he was too infuriated. He had seen at first hand how imprudent men desecrated bodies of the dead. The priest of his old village in Ireland, like Van Helsing, had thought he was doing the good work of God when he desecrated his brother's grave, too.

"It was you," he continued, "who lost his medical license for performing experimental blood transfusions that killed your patients. You did not know to match the blood types. You claimed they had been bitten by vampires. . . ."

"No doctor knew of blood types until 1901, you ignorant oaf. I acted in my patients' best interests. I did everything I could to save them."

Cotford glared at Van Helsing with contempt. If the professor had devoted his research to science instead of mythology, he could have saved lives instead of expediting deaths. He could see the look of panic in the old man's face as he felt the verdict of the lobby's patrons. His heart was racing. It was time to break Van Helsing.

"It was you and those poor souls you brainwashed into following you who killed those poor women twenty-five years ago. I do see evil before me, Van Helsing! I see you. I see Jack the Ripper!"

Every person in the lobby began to whisper and gossip. Gentlemen instinctively shielded their wives. Children were hurried away. They all stepped away from Van Helsing, giving the accused killer a wide berth. He stood alone, exposed, and vulnerable.

Cotford expected his pride would force Van Helsing to justify his criminal acts in front of the bystanders. Instead, the old man's shoulders slumped. He looked upon Cotford with great compassion and pity.

"You see nothing. And what you do not see *will* kill you."

There was something in the way Van Helsing spoke that chilled

Cotford, and he was not easily unnerved. Van Helsing had turned the tables; it was now Cotford who was rattled. *Was that a threat?*

The lift door opened. Van Helsing nodded to the operator to hold the door for him. Cotford struggled to say something, but his mind was still churning over Van Helsing's last words. Then the lift door closed and the old man was gone, leaving Cotford standing in the opulent lobby. Everyone stared at him.

"Poppycock!" Cotford exclaimed. This confrontation had been folly. He would never be able to force a confession from Van Helsing. He knew he would have to resort to other means if he was going to bring Abraham Van Helsing to justice.

CHAPTER XXVII.

✦

The past was like a prison from which no inmate could escape. Over the last few days, Mina had felt her own personal cell close in. Her beloved Jonathan was dead, Quincey had run off. Paranoia began to set in: She found herself constantly looking out of the windows. Her warden was a cruel overseer: her fear that Cotford, that tall policeman and his subordinate wolves could be at her door any moment. She was going to need a new plan if she was to keep them at bay.

In the hours since Quincey had stormed out, she'd gone though the pages that he had left spread across the study floor. Sitting within a Stonehenge-like circle, she sifted through the ruins of her past life. She should have stopped Quincey from leaving. Now she had to deduce his next step in order to find him. He needed her protection, whether he wanted it or not. Night had fallen upon England. She was at a disadvantage, for their predator held all the cards.

Mina opened the thick folder containing the dossiers she had compiled. Arthur Holmwood's was on top, with the address in plain sight. Going to Arthur made sense. If she were in Quincey's place, that was where she would go first. Unfortunately, Quincey would not be aware of how much Arthur Holmwood had changed. Even if he were able to get an audience with Lord Godalming, she was certain it would not be productive. Unlike Mina and Jonathan, who'd tried to reenter public life after Transylvania, Lord Godalming had receded into his home at the Ring. As time passed, he'd become more and more withdrawn, angry, and bitter, until the Arthur Holmwood she remembered was entirely gone. He'd twisted the facts in his mind, and had come to despise the others in the brave band.

He blamed us for the death of his beloved Lucy. Didn't he know she was beloved to me as well? More than any of the others, Mina had become the focal point of Holmwood's anger. If Quincey did call upon Lord Godalming, he'd be fortunate if he did not find a mortal enemy.

Where would Quincey go next? Would he retrace their steps to Transylvania? Seek out Van Helsing? Mina's mind spun around the possibilities. She couldn't think anymore. She'd barely slept in the days since Jonathan's death. She had lost track of time, and now time was against her.

Mina surveyed the past that surrounded her. She asked herself why she'd kept all these papers. If she had destroyed them, perhaps Quincey would be safe in her nest at this very moment. She wondered if destroying the information would have made it easier for her to also destroy the memory. Without another thought, Mina tossed the lot into the nearby fireplace and watched the pages curl in the flames.

Let Cotford come, let him bring his search warrant. He would find nothing here except bitter ash. Now no one could ever prove Stoker's novel was anything more than a demented work of fiction.

Damn it! Who the hell was this Bram Stoker? How did he know their story? The brave band was bound by a sacred oath never to divulge the horrors that had befallen them. Could it be Jack Seward who had betrayed them to Stoker? Sadly, he was the obvious choice.

Mina was tired. Questions piled up in her mind like bricks, and her thoughts were getting walled in. She needed to sleep, if only for a few moments, just to clear her mind. She remembered that when her nightmares had started again a few months ago, Jonathan had brought her home a bottle of laudanum. He'd told her at the time that he was concerned about her lack of sleep and that the sedative would help her. She'd refused to take it, and suspected Jonathan of trying to drug her to stop her nightly longing for her dark prince.

Mina took the bottle of laudanum from the cupboard. She was so tired that her eyes could barely focus enough to read the dosage on the bottle. As she poured the liquid into a thimble, she remembered it was her refusal to take the drug that had caused Jonathan to stop sharing their bed—the first step toward the final disintegration of their marriage. She drank the laudanum quickly in the hope of washing away the painful memory.

It took effect swiftly. She stumbled back to the study, regretting how the love she and Jonathan had shared had turned so bitter at the end. Right at that moment, she didn't care. Whether it was Jonathan in his youth, or the wretch of latter day, she just wanted to be in his arms one last time.

Mina found a framed photograph of Jonathan on the table beside the armchair, taken the day Jonathan had been called to the bar. She had been so proud of him. At last he had been his own man, full of hope and promise. A teardrop landed on the glass covering the image of Jonathan's smiling face and gently she wiped the tear away, caressing the image beneath. She felt herself falling back into the armchair.

"Jonathan, I need you. I can't do this alone."

Her eyelids became increasingly heavy. In her last seconds of consciousness, she thought she saw red mist oozing from under the French doors.

Mina wasn't sure how long she had been asleep when she felt breath blown softly on her ankle. She forced her eyelids open, but saw no one. She was in a delirium, somewhere between drug and dream. She grasped the photograph tightly against her bosom, feeling the hard edges of the picture frame and imagined herself holding Jonathan once more.

She felt the touch.

It was a caress, as if a gentle hand was sliding up from her ankle, along her calf, over her stocking. The hand turned inward, past the roll of her stocking, and touched the soft flesh of her inner thigh. Mina bit her lip, feeling her temperature rise. *Please God, let it be Jonathan.*

The hand on her inner thigh parted her legs. Mina's blood quickened. She longed to be desired, to be loved, to be a woman again. A moan passed her lips. Her breasts pulsated with the rhythm of her quickly beating heart.

The spectral hands pulled at her undergarments. Mina's back arched as the hands touched and probed her most private place. She was about to give in to her passion, when a terrifying thought crossed her reeling mind. *This couldn't be Jonathan. He never allowed himself to learn the secrets of her body.* Mina gasped. No one knew how to touch her this way. *No one . . . but he.* Mina cried out. She wept. *No, please don't do this. It's Jonathan I love.*

A voice came to Mina's mind: *"I have seen to Jonathan's death. Now you are mine."*

Mina tried to scream. The clouds in her mind parted. Her dark prince had killed Jonathan and, by doing so, had betrayed the love they'd once shared. In an instant, the hands converged, simultaneously touching her in a thousand places. Mina shuddered; she couldn't resist any longer. *For the love of God, don't do this to me! Don't make me choose, my love!* It was too late. Passionate sensations overwhelmed her. Mina's mouth fell open, her eyes closed, and her head fell back. The hands touched and probed. Mina swooned.

Suddenly, she felt a strong, icy wind against her skin. She knew her body was prone, but she had the sensation that she was standing. The wind howled in her ears, so loud Mina thought she would go deaf. She tried to cover her ears, but she couldn't move. It was as if her body were paralyzed but her senses electrified. She could smell the scent of evergreen, water, and mud. She felt cold.

Although she had not willed them to, her eyes sprang open. She wanted to scream at what she saw, but she had no control over her own body. She was standing upon a broken battlement, looking down at a snow-swept field. Snowflakes danced on the wind. She recognized the jagged peaks of the Carpathian Mountains.

Mina was standing in Transylvania, on top of Castle Dracula's highest turret.

She heard approaching hooves, splashing as they raced through the slushy snow. Two dozen mounted men charged toward the castle. Gypsies. In the midst of them was a horse-drawn cart, swaying from side to side like a serpent's tail, slithering with each bump of the icy road. The cart bore a coffin. As they neared the broken gate of the castle, the gypsies flanked the cart and drew their weapons.

This was all too familiar for Mina. She was reliving the darkest moment of her past, a moment she'd spent the last twenty-five years trying to forget.

But this was not how Mina remembered it. Again, with no control over her body, she glanced to the east and saw a woman with blond hair astride a white horse. A man riding a gray stallion raced alongside, holding her horse's reins.

The woman below was . . . herself.

The man upon the gray stallion leading hers was Professor Van Helsing. Seeing herself from a distance was an odd sensation. Mina began to understand that she was witnessing these past events from a different vantage point. She had never been inside Dracula's castle. *Was she dead?* Mina was horrified by the thought that God's judgment should be that she be forced to relive the most horrible moment of her life, over and over again in purgatory.

A military bugle blasted in her ears. Mina instinctively turned her head, as did the gypsies. Mina recognized the men charging from the west. It was that beloved rogue, their Texan Quincey P. Morris, with Dr. Jack Seward at his side. Seeing Quincey Morris and Jack put Mina at ease. Perhaps it was true: When you died, you were reunited with your loved ones. She could sense the fear rising within the gypsies. They had never seen the likes of the Texan gunfighter before. No sooner had Quincey Morris and Seward appeared over the horizon than gunfire rang out from the south. Astride their steeds, Jonathan and Arthur fired their rifles into the gypsy band.

Mina remembered their plan to split up and take different modes of transportation through Transylvania, their plan being to converge on the gypsies at the same time, surrounding them from all directions. The idea had come from Quincey Morris, who had learned the technique as a cavalry officer during the Indian Wars.

The brave band of heroes were all together again, alive and vibrant. Their horses were bathed in sweat, nostrils flaring, hooves pounding through the blanket of snow as they raced the setting sun.

Following Jonathan and Arthur's lead, Quincey Morris and Dr. Seward opened fire upon the gypsies. Horses leapt and wheeled as the rifle shots rang out. The gypsies returned fire.

The castle's gate was fortuitously ruined, blocked by fallen debris. Mina saw that the fallen rubble had come from the decaying battlement where she stood. Again without willing herself to do so, Mina looked down upon the ensuing battle. She still could not wrap her mind around the idea of seeing herself approaching with the others. Her breath was momentarily taken away as the young Jonathan drew near. She had forgotten how dashing he'd looked on horseback that day. Unlike Arthur and Quincey Morris, Jonathan had never sought adventure in his life. Over the years, he had told her how terrified he had been that day, his fear almost paralyzing. He had risked his life for one reason only: to fight, and to die if need be, for the woman he loved.

The brave band of heroes converged on the cart that held the coffin, and a group of gypsies rode out to meet them. They were undisciplined, their formation disorganized. The rest of the gypsies lagged behind, surrounding the cart.

Quincey P. Morris, his fighting experience evident, clutched the reins of his horse in his teeth as he fired his Winchester rifle into the advancing gypsies. First one, then a second gypsy's chest exploded with splashes of blood. A gypsy bullet ricocheted with a clang and there was an explosion of sparks off Dr. Seward's rifle. Seward cried out as the rifle flew from his hands. Arthur fired again, blowing off half of a gypsy's face. The remaining gypsies rode forward to hem in Quincey Morris and Seward. Morris, using the butt of his gun as a club, battered another gypsy to the ground as he screamed to the defenseless Seward, "Swing your goddamn sword, man!"

Watching from the battlements above, Mina was amazed at the meek Jack Seward. He wildly swung his blade, screaming like a madman as he hacked and slashed the gypsies. She could swear she could hear his galloping heart.

A gypsy's rifle butt smashed into Seward's face, shattering his nose into a torrent of blood. Mina could smell it.

Her head spun to see that Professor Van Helsing and her younger self had dismounted. Van Helsing raised his rifle with the aim of a hunter, calm, patient. He fired, killing the gypsy that had smashed Seward's face. The sound of Van Helsing's shot alerted the gypsies. A second group broke off from the cart and raced toward him. Watching from above, Mina understood Van Helsing's strategy; he was thinning the herd around the coffin. She watched her younger self jump behind Van Helsing for protection as he drew two six-shooters.

Van Helsing fired into the gypsies, shouting, "The sun is setting. We have no time. Jonathan, Arthur, charge!"

From the top of the castle ruins, Mina watched her younger self take up Van Helsing's discarded rifle and join the fight with him against the gypsies.

A new barrage of gunfire came to her ears. Jonathan and Arthur were upon the coffin's defenders. Every shot Jonathan fired missed its target, but the bounding horse did not affect Arthur's aim at all. He felled two more gypsies. The remaining defenders focused their fire on Arthur. Arthur's head suddenly snapped back, spouting a stream of blood as he fell off his mount.

Jack Seward drew his pistol and fired point-blank. Quincey Morris dug his spurs into his horse's sides, riding hard to collide with a gypsy's mount. With the force of the blow, the gypsy's horse wheeled, throwing the gypsy to the ground. Van Helsing emptied his six-shooters, then threw the pistols at the gypsies, drew a scimitar from his belt with his right hand, and brandished a short, curved blade in his left. He crossed the swords, masterfully dueling three gypsies at once.

Mina saw her younger self stiffen. Below, the commands of her dark prince entered Mina's mind. In the present, she remembered sensing his love, beckoning her to turn the rifle on Van Helsing's back and kill him. Mina recalled her internal struggle. She tossed the rifle away, clutching her head from the searing pain that came whenever Dracula invaded her thoughts.

Van Helsing stabbed a gypsy in the chest with his scimitar and slashed the throat of another with his short sword. Mina fell behind the professor, clasping the gold cross around her neck, delirious with brain fever.

Atop the battlement, Mina saw Jack Seward jump from his horse, the bodies of slain gypsies all around him. He retrieved one of the dead gypsy's rifles and fired across the field into those defending the crate.

Arthur staggered to his feet. Blood flowed from a deep gash where the bullet had grazed his cheek. The tip of his right ear was gone. He cocked his Winchester and joined Seward. Their covering fire cleared a path for Jonathan and Quincey Morris.

With a war cry, Quincey Morris drew his kukri knife and leapt from his steed onto the cart. For a moment, Jonathan froze, his fear evident. Mina saw him look back at her younger self, writhing in pain behind Van Helsing. From this new vantage point, she noticed something she could never have seen before. The sight of his wife suffering in pain had turned Jonathan's fear to rage. Glaring at the coffin, Jonathan drew his sword, slashed a gypsy, and jumped onto the cart beside Quincey Morris.

Together, they tore away the wooden coffin's lid to reveal its hideous cargo: a skeletal creature with pointed ears and razor teeth, dressed in well-tailored clothes.

"Goddamn, Harker!" Quincey Morris gasped. "What is it?"

"Pure evil."

A gypsy had his hands around the professor's throat. Van Helsing reached down to his boot, drew a hidden blade, and savagely stabbed the gypsy in his groin. The gypsy's hand sprang free from Van Helsing's neck as he cried out in pain. Van Helsing reared his head back and then butted his attacker's skull. The gypsy's eyes rolled back as he fell unconscious. Van Helsing turned to see Quincey Morris and Jonathan staring into the open crate.

"Do not look at him! Strike now!"

It was too late. The creature's eyelids sprang open. Two black, glowing orbs, empty of all but evil, stared up at Quincey Morris and Jonathan. The two champions were frozen. On the battlement, Mina saw herself regain her senses. She understood what had happened; her dark prince's attention had shifted from her to the now-hypnotized men.

Mina watched Van Helsing pluck up his rifle and run toward the crate, motioning for Jack and Arthur to join him. Arthur continued to fire in an attempt to keep the gypsies off his paralyzed friends. A single gypsy slipped through the barrage, and suddenly a blade erupted through Quincey's chest as the gypsy stabbed him in the back.

His friend's scream broke the hypnotic spell ensnaring Jonathan. "Quincey!" Jonathan turned to see the gypsy coldly yank the sword from Morris's back. Quincey Morris grabbed the side of the coffin for support as his blood streamed out. The gypsy raised his sword high, swinging at Jonathan's head. From above, Mina could hear the whirr of steal cutting through the air. Jonathan raised his sword to block the killing blow. The force of the gypsy's blade impacting against Jonathan's sword sent him crashing to the ground. Mina heard her younger self scream out, "Jonathan!"

Arthur, Jack, and Van Helsing all fired as one, all three bullets finding their mark. The gypsy was blown off the cart, saving Jonathan's life.

Mina saw Jonathan's and her younger self's eyes meet.

Van Helsing shouted over the gunfire to Jonathan, "Finish it, man. The sun is setting!"

The sun was almost at the horizon line, its bright orange glare blinding. Steam rose from the coffin as the creature within began to burn from the rays of the setting sun.

Jonathan's face was pained as Mina, confused and panicked, turned from her husband to the smoking coffin.

Quincey Morris, stained with his own blood, fell forward to plunge his kukri knife into the creature's chest. Mina screamed as the creature unleashed an unearthly howl.

His mighty strength sapped, Quincey Morris collapsed. The creature's blistered hand shoved him back. The Texan flew through the air, landing hard in the snow. Growling in pain, the creature forced itself onto its feet. Dark blood poured from his wound. The sun's deadly rays fell directly upon Dracula. Flames erupted from his body as he reached out a hand to Mina.

"Mina! Help me, my love!"

Jonathan looked to his wife. Mina looked from her dark prince to her loving husband. A choice had to be made. Jonathan's fury grew at her hesitation. He grabbed his sword and climbed onto the cart. The burning creature's soulless black eyes met his mad glare.

"Goddamn you to hell, Prince Dracula!"

Jonathan swung his sword, attempting to slice off the creature's head. Not strong enough, the blade lodged in the creature's neck. Dracula lashed out, his flaming fist searing Jonathan's face, sending him flying backward.

The vampire yanked the sword from his neck. Blood flowed like a waterfall. Flames engulfed his body as he fell to his knees, howling and thrashing in agony.

Jonathan picked himself up, unsheathed his bowie knife and ran forward, determined to finish this battle. In the same instant, Mina saw one of the wounded gypsies spring forward, a gun aimed at her husband.

Mina watched her younger self make a devastating choice. Two moments more and the sun would have set behind the Carpathian Mountains, and her prince would be saved. But, if she allowed those moments to pass, the man who had risked his life for her, her beloved husband, would be shot dead. Mina made the only choice she could, the choice that would haunt her for the rest of her life. She took up a fallen pistol, cocked it, and fired, hitting the wounded gypsy dead between the eyes.

Again, Jonathan raised his bowie knife. This time he would cut off the burning creature's head. But he never got the chance. The creature had seen Mina choose to save his rival instead of doing his bidding. It was more than he could bear. Jonathan stepped back in fear as the vampire wailed in anguish, charred flesh peeling away from his bones. Dracula was not bemoaning his demise but the betrayal of his beloved Mina.

The creature fell back as flames consumed him. His body caved in on itself. Then, with the kukri knife planted in his chest, he imploded into burning embers of ash.

It was over.

Mina watched the scene below, frozen. She found herself looking down at the coffin. Unsure if the emotion was her own, she felt anger, a bitter fury rise within her. From the ash, a thin white mist snaked its way around the debris and into the castle gate. Now Mina answered with a voice that was not her own, "Not this time."

In an instant, Mina was uncontrollably whisked through stone castle walls, past wood-paneled walls adorned with paintings, her view blurred by the velocity of her passing. She sped down a winding stairwell. Somehow her body seemed to know exactly where it was going. She heard the wind and felt its blast. The cold returned. She was outside in the snow.

Mina came to a jerking stop that left her queasy. She stood in the crumbling remains of a desecrated chapel. The ceiling had long ago collapsed, and the wood pews had rotted from centuries of neglect and weathering. The statue of Christ that had once hung over the altar had broken away and lay smashed on the stone floor.

She focused on the base of the altar. The white mist gathered there pooled and reconstituted. Mina watched in amazement as a body took shape. Dracula. He was charred black from the sun's fire, his throat was slit, his chest was still pierced by the kukri knife. His blood continued to pour. Yet somehow, he lived, screaming and writhing in torturous pain.

Dracula was alive. She marveled at her dark prince's tactical genius. He had made the band of heroes into a band of fools.

The creature's skeletal hands grasped the hilt of the kukri knife and attempted to extricate it from his chest. Mina wanted to run to help him, but whatever force was controlling her body allowed her only to calmly walk forward. She heard her boot heels click on the stone floor. With the moon now glowing behind her, Mina's shadow fell over her prince. Dracula sensed her presence. The sunken eyes in his charred, skull-like head turned to her as he reached out with a pleading hand.

"Sânge!"

Although Mina had never spoken Romanian, she knew he was asking for her blood. She heard herself laugh, a mocking, victorious peal. She watched as her long, black leather boot settled on the hilt of the kukri knife.

The creature's eyes flashed with rage. Mina heard herself speak, in a voice and tongue that was not hers. "You claim the moral high ground, yet you spurn me as an adulterous whore."

Mina's mind reeled. *What was she saying?*

She heard her voice bark out a guttural growl, "Sacrilege!"

Her boot pressed down harder. This time, the choice was being made for her. Mina wanted to scream, but instead a sound of joy passed her lips.

The creature roared in agony. His head fell back, eyes blank. A last gasp crossed the lips she had once kissed, and a moment later her beloved was truly dead. She was never again to be burdened with the dreadful choice.

For so many years, Mina had yearned to know the truth—she had seen him crumble to dust, but without seeing the body, there had always been a question in her mind. In some ways it had been better not to know. In not knowing, there had at least been the hope that he might have survived.

In one swift movement, Mina watched a black-gloved hand, adorned with a red ruby ring, grab the kukri knife's ivory handle. With great delight, the hand ripped the blade from the dead creature's corpse.

The blacked-gloved fingers wiped the knife on her right sleeve. For an instant, Mina saw a reflection in its steel. It was not her own face looking back at her, but the face of a stranger. And then she realized that the stranger's locks were a luscious raven black. Her eyes were ice blue and heartless, void of emotion. Her body vibrated with delight over the fresh kill, and the scent of the warm blood.

Mina was repulsed, but she felt every muscle in her body clench with rapture as a wave of frenzy cascaded over her.

She opened her eyes again and was shocked to find she was back in her Exeter home, in her drawing room chair. Her body was still vibrating, not in victory, but with rapture. The many hands were under her gown, caressing every inch of her skin at once. Her body convulsed in spastic waves and now she climaxed so violently that she screamed from the almost unbearable pleasure. Her orgasm was so powerful that it sent the framed photo of Jonathan, which she had been clasping to her chest, flying across the room, where it smashed against the bookcase. At last she lay back in overwhelming delight, heaving for breath. A smile curled her lips. In her heart she felt guilt, but her body felt unparalleled fulfillment. She had been right from the beginning; there was only one who could make her feel this way. *Was he a ghost now?* His name was about to cross her lips, when Mina was suddenly assaulted by the stench of the grave.

A crimson mist flowed out from under the bodice of her dress. It billowed upward and took the ghostly form of a woman. As the amorphous mist's features became more defined, Mina recognized the figure as the beauty she had seen reflected in the kukri knife's blade. This was the woman who had killed her prince. Mina felt sick.

She moved to escape her misty rapist, but her attacker forced her back down into the armchair, straddling her. Then she leaned forward, covering Mina's mouth with her own. As she forced her tongue into Mina's mouth, she ran it over her fangs, slicing it open. Blood dripped into Mina's mouth.

Mina screamed and spat and tried to turn her head, but the woman forced her lips apart, pulling Mina's tongue inside her mouth. Mina struggled as she felt the sting of the fangs and her mind filled with horrific, inexplicable visions. Young women hung upside down, stripped naked, their throats sliced open, their blood raining down in a shower of gore.

The woman pulled away, smiling. Her familiar voice broke the silence. "All that is left of your lover, your dark prince, is a weak shadow of his former self. You are alone. Your time has come, my sweet."

With that, she dissolved back into a red mist and left the house.

Mina fell from the armchair, clutching the small gold cross around her neck. Weak-kneed and trembling, she crawled to the bookshelf, where she found a bottle of whisky that had fallen to the floor but miraculously not broken. She ripped out the cork and desperately rinsed out her mouth with the burning liquid, moaning in pain as the alcohol found her wounded tongue. She coughed, whisky drooling from her mouth, and tried to gain control of herself. A scramble of memories that were not her own filled her mind. Mina and her attacker had shared blood; and now she realized that this she-monster's thoughts, her desires, her hatred, and her depravity were also hers. Her attacker had always been a hidden part of this terrible story. Her attacker was the killer of Dracula. Her attacker was the beast hunting the band of heroes down, murdering them one by one. Her attacker was Countess Elizabeth Bathory.

CHAPTER XXVIII.

Quincey stood on the vast, barren dock. A low-lying fog shrouded the water of the English Channel, but he could hear the waves gently lap against the wooden pilings. The peaceful setting belied his internal bitterness. He stamped his feet, hoping the friction would thaw his frigid toes. His coat, still damp from the earlier rain, did nothing to warm his body. Neither did his swirling, angry thoughts do anything to warm his soul.

Only a week before, his path had been clear and certain. He'd followed his heart. He had decided to become an actor and a producer, casting aside the wishes of his father once and for all. Yet now, his father murdered, his mother a liar, Quincey could focus on only one thing. Revenge. Quincey needed to seek out the beast that had taken his father and, with his own hand, destroy him. He stood at a crossroads of destiny. His dreams would have to wait.

He checked his watch; the schooner was late. He peered out to sea, knowing that he had to reach a decision by the time the ship arrived. He couldn't see anything through the ominous fog hugging the water's surface. Even the solitary beacon of light from the lighthouse couldn't penetrate the mist. Basarab had chartered a schooner to bring him to England under the cover of night, where no throngs of adoring fans or press would know he had arrived. The docks were void of all pedestrian traffic. Even the harbormaster had retired for the evening. Quincey stood alone.

He looked over his shoulder at the intimidating white cliffs of Dover, looming above the fog, moonlight reflecting eerily upon their chalk-scarred surface. The low gong of a ship's bell moaned across the water. The thick fog began to churn apart. Basarab's ship was approaching.

Quincey could see no movement in the mainmast's crow's nest. He strained, looking for any sign of life, but like himself, the ship seemed abandoned and adrift.

As the looming ship drew steadily closer, its silhouette became more clearly visible. Quincey couldn't help but think of Stoker's description of the *Demeter*, upon which Dracula had stowed away on his journey from Transylvania to England. Dracula had also wanted to keep his arrival in England a secret. The devil had then systematically killed everyone on board until only the captain remained. That pour soul had been found tied to the steering wheel on the bridge, clutching a rosary. Stoker described the gruesome discovery of the *Demeter* crashed aground on the rocky shores of Whitby, with a dead dog nearby. *"Its throat was torn away, and its belly was slit open as if with a savage claw."*

Basarab's ship showed no sign of slowing down. Quincey still could not see any human movement on the top deck.

Thud.

Quincey spun at the hollow sound of something on the dock behind him. He could see nothing in the darkness and remembered the last words his mother called out to him: *Leave the truth dead and buried, or you could suffer a fate worse than your father's.* An icy thought came to him. He'd read of tyrants who, throughout history, had killed not only their opponents but also their opponents' children, so they would not be able to grow up and exact revenge. Quincey knew that the creature that killed his father was just that sort of tyrant. Here he was, alone on this empty dock, with no good route of escape. The fog seemed to close in all around him. Did Stoker not write that the un-dead could take the forms of mist and fog?

Thud.

Quincey had the urge to run. He backed away from the edge of the dock, the pace of his feet quickening to match the beating of his heart.

A flame ignited off the shore of the water.

Thud.

A life buoy that had come loose was knocking against the dock. Quincey breathed a sigh of relief. He was out of immediate danger, but somehow he was not really comforted.

When he looked back at the ship, it was to see a solitary figure standing on the top deck of the schooner, holding a lantern aloft. He was a fool to think he stood a chance of battling a beast such as Dracula. If the mortal man was capable of such horrible carnage, the idea that this devil now possessed the powers of the un-dead made him surely invincible. Quincey had no idea if the methods of killing a vampire that Stoker described were efficacious. Like his father before him, Quincey had no experience of warfare. What his father had had were capable men at his side. Quincey did not.

But if his mother's words were true, Quincey couldn't simply run from the fight, either, for wherever he went, he knew that Dracula would find him.

A boatswain's whistle interrupted his thoughts. The schooner slowed and angled toward the dock. Quincey could see the familiar form of the well-tailored Basarab standing on the approaching bow. A bitter question leapt into his mind. What was he to tell Basarab? His mentor had traveled all this way at great expense on Quincey's behalf. What explanation could he give for his sudden decision to abandon the production? He couldn't possibly tell Basarab the truth. Basarab held the historic prince in high esteem—and would not accept that he was now an un-dead monster. For the first time, Quincey completely understood Shakespeare's *Hamlet*, a man facing two opposing paths of destiny. If he'd had the misfortune to play Hamlet before this day, he would have played him as an indecisive jellyfish; but given the opportunity in the future, Quincey knew he would play Hamlet weary with the weight of the world on his shoulders, brought to the brink of madness by the magnitude of the decision before him. He was utterly unsure of his next move.

There came the sound of grinding chains as the gangplank was lowered to the dock. The tall, dark figure of Basarab emerged from the mist, haloed by the moon. What a magnificent figure he struck, like a king parading through his court.

Quincey was out of time. He needed to make his next move. "Mr. Basarab, welcome to England," he said, extending his hand as the actor came down the gangplank.

"I received your telegram," Basarab said, his voice compassionate. "With the death of your father, I want you to feel no guilt whatsoever if you choose not to continue with the play."

Once again it was as if Basarab had read Quincey's mind. He was touched by the great actor's gesture. Perhaps he was not alone after all. Basarab was a man worthy of his trust. Perhaps he was the only person Quincey could count on.

The crewmen hoisted Basarab's luggage out of the cargo hold.

"I have been giving this matter a great deal of thought," Quincey said at last, which was a bit of an understatement. "I will be honest with you; I'm not sure what to do."

"What does your heart tell you?"

Being back in Basarab's presence put Quincey at ease. He could sense the actor's meaning; he was offering himself as an ally, no matter which path Quincey chose.

Quincey was not a warrior. He had no home. He could not run. He could not hide. But with Basarab by his side, perhaps he could become the warrior he needed to be. Basarab was strong, and brave. Quincey had already seen Basarab quickly take up arms when he was attacked at the theatre in Paris. Quincey made his decision. He would continue with the plans for the play, and use the time he had with Basarab to convince him of the evil of Dracula the Un-Dead. Then, with Basarab by his side, he would rise up and fight. In the meantime, he needed Basarab, and he needed time to make Basarab more than a mentor—but a fellow soldier in his fight.

Quincey happily realized that the decision didn't involve a choice at all. "I shall continue with the play as a tribute to my father," he said. "It's the least I can do. I shall show my father in death the love I so wrongly denied him in life."

Basarab smiled proudly. "Then we will make sure you are successful."

Quincey felt a great weight lift from his soul. The memories of all the arguments he had had with his father flooded his mind. He had been so full of rage and confusion that he had not yet given himself a chance to properly mourn his father. He didn't want to do so now. He turned away, not wanting Basarab to see the tears forming in his eyes.

Basarab placed his arm around his shoulder and spoke in a soothing baritone voice. "There is no shame in tears. I still recall the sad day I lost my own father."

"How did he die?"

"I was very young. My father was a warrior; he was assassinated by his own countrymen." There was an odd expression in Basarab's face. Without having to say it, Quincey understood that his mentor knew the meaning of the word *revenge*.

"You will do your father proud," Basarab said as he walked arm in arm with Quincey along the dock. "For better or worse, there are ties between a father and son that can never be broken."

For the first time in days, Quincey found himself smiling through his tears. Basarab offered him something his father never had: trust.

CHAPTER XXIX.

———◇———

Sergeant Lee looked up from the front door of the Red Lion to see the face of Big Ben illuminated by its new electric light. The sun was beginning to set behind the Parliament buildings as the clock tower cast its long shadow over the Thames. Cotford was supposed to have been here fifteen minutes ago, and Lee couldn't stand one more minute of waiting inside the pub. He didn't feel comfortable sitting there. He was getting thirsty and wanted to partake of the joviality, but was still on duty. To avoid temptation, he had stepped outside. It was for the best anyway. If his wife found out he was in a pub—especially this night, their wedding anniversary—she would have been more than a little cross.

Lee frowned as he glanced up to the clock again. He had not been home in time to tuck his children into bed for well over a week. He hoped his wife would understand that by having to work tonight of all nights, he was not purposely adding insult to injury. Clara knew, when she'd married him, that he was first and foremost a man of duty. Missing a candlelit dinner with his loving wife was a small price to pay for possibly saving another woman's life.

"Sergeant Lee?"

Lee spun around to see Cotford waddling toward him. "You're late, sir."

"Who did you leave watching our suspect?" Cotford asked anxiously. With a smile, he added, "That young Price chap?"

Lee laughed. He liked Price, too. "No, the poor lad was knackered. Hasn't slept all week. I've sent him home."

He could see the look of concern form on Cotford's face and thought it best that he clarify himself. "Don't worry yourself. Our suspect is hosting a dinner party. He'll be there for hours. You know that crowd, cigars and brandy till the sun comes up."

"Good. I want you to bring him in," Cotford said, voice laden with relish.

"Are you sure about that, sir? If I take him in front of his dinner guests, we'll be exposing our investigation."

"They only talk among themselves. We'll have to risk it, Sergeant. We need to rattle him."

Lee nodded and turned to carry out his orders, when Cotford grabbed his arm. "Be sure you bring him in by way of the Derby Gate entrance." He pointed to the alleyway running between Parliament Street and the Victoria Embankment. "No one will see you if you bring him in the side entrance."

Lee smiled. No one could ever say that Cotford wasn't thorough.

"Van Helsing is too sharp to incriminate himself," Cotford continued solemnly. "Our only option is to get one of his coconspirators to turn on him."

With that, Lee was on his way. He knew that Cotford felt as he did, that this suspect was going to be a hard nut to crack. Whatever the outcome, they were in for a long night.

With a sardonic expression, Arthur Holmwood watched as the fat inspector dropped Jack Seward's journals in front of him. He was certain Cotford was bluffing. They couldn't be written by Jack. But, when he read the selection the inspector had marked in the journal, he recognized Jack Seward's handwriting and was outraged that Jack had broken their oath and had re-created his own account of the events of that tragic night. Grimacing inwardly, he refused to indulge the Irish inspector with any sign of recognition.

Holmwood closed the book with a snap. "Who knows what drug-induced lunacy possessed Jack to write such drivel."

It was a publicly known fact that the once-esteemed scientist Jack Seward had not only gone mad, but was also addicted to morphine. No matter how incriminating they might appear, Jack's journals would not hold up in court. He studied the inspector. There was a great deal more to this man than his slovenly appearance suggested. He noted that Cotford had gone out of his way to make him uncomfortable. The interrogation room was barren, save for a table with a few stiff wooden chairs. Suspended only two feet above the table was a plain metal light fixture, which focused its harsh glare upon the table. The abnormally low placement of the light created a strain on the eyes. The room was hot. There was no coatrack, and no one had had the good manners to take his coat, thereby leaving him baking in his full evening best and a thick winter overcoat. Cotford had a glass of water for himself, but made no offer to him.

But none of this would have the effect Cotford desired. Arthur Holmwood had once been a prisoner in the Empire of China after the Tuyen Quang siege. The Chinese were masterful in their interrogation methods, inflicting both physical and mental anguish. By comparison, this Inspector Cotford was a rank amateur.

"Perhaps this will more readily spark your interest," Cotford said with a mischievous smirk, opening a pale green folder and holding it close for Holmwood to see.

Arthur's eyes drifted down to the handwritten scribbles on the open page. After a moment of reading, he looked up and said, "An autopsy report?"

"On Lucy Westenra."

This time, the man couldn't hide his shock. Cotford smiled.

Holmwood was confused. No autopsy had ever been performed. At the time it was determined that there was no need.

"Don't bother with all the clinical terms," Cotford said as he flipped to the last page in the folder. "It's the conclusion that matters."

He pointed to a handwritten line. Holmwood leaned forward to examine the word trapped under Cotford's finger.

"'Murder'?" he read aloud. "That's preposterous. Lucy died of a rare blood disorder."

The words stung his lips as they passed. The painful memories of Lucy's illness were ones he'd rather forget. Her inexplicable loss of blood, the desperate attempts to replenish her with blood transfusions, the money spent on specialists, none of whom could diagnose the cause. None except Dr. Van Helsing, and even he had been unable to prevent Lucy's death. *Death*. Ha. The image of Lucy lying un-dead in her coffin forever scarred his heart. Her true death that day was an event that had scarred him for life.

"Miss Westenra came from a wealthy family," Cotford said, his voice heavy with sarcastic mock-revelation. "Shortly before her death, on the eve of your impending marriage, she changed her will. You became the beneficiary."

"That gives you motive," Lee chimed in. He was standing by the back wall of the room, trying to look as imposing as possible. "Along with the testimony in Dr. Seward's journals, we have more than enough for an arrest warrant."

Holmwood's jaw clenched, his fist tightened. He felt his blood pressure starting to brew. He held his breath for a moment and cursed his rising anger. His first instinct was to bash both their skulls against the wall, but to give way to his fury would be playing into Cotford's perverse game. The malignant inspector was bluffing. Instead, he said, "This is a perverse joke. I had no need for the Westenra estate, as I am sure you know."

"I assure you, *this* is no laughing matter." Cotford produced a photograph from a pocket. He set it on the table.

The blood drained from Holmwood's heart.

It was a hideous, skeletal corpse. A mane of long hair flowed from the skull, which was severed from the body. An iron rod was impaled through the skeletal ribs. The ivory dress, which Lucy had made for their wedding, was rotted and stained with dirt and dried blood. Judging by the state of decomposition and the quality of the photo, the photograph had been taken recently. *That fat Irish bastard has opened Lucy's grave!* He wanted to look away from the horrid photograph, but could not. He wasn't even able to blink. He purposely did not pick up the photograph, as he knew Cotford would see his hands shake.

He was unnerved. Over the years, he had tried to pretend that night had never happened, but it plagued him nevertheless. How Van Helsing had forced him to go to the mausoleum where Lucy was laid to rest. How his heart had leapt for joy when he'd seen her walking, looking as alive and beautiful as she had only days before. At first, he had thought it was a hallucination, until he turned and saw the look of horror and shock on Jack Seward's face. Lucy had called to him, her voice as melodic and sweet as always. *Come to me, my husband. Kiss me. We can be together. Forever, as we promised.*

He had been given a second chance to be with his love. He could still remember how Lucy's smile had warmed him on that cold night. How he'd reached for her outstretched arms, longing to kiss her red lips. He knew that once he was in Lucy's embrace, all the pain he had felt since her funeral would melt away.

When his fingertips had been just inches away from hers, Van Helsing had bounded between them and held a crucifix up at Lucy. To Holmwood's unparalleled horror, Lucy had hissed, exposing her fangs, and spat blood at Van Helsing. Her eyes had become black orbs as she bent her body into her coffin. Holmwood had tried to seem grateful to Van Helsing for saving his life, but over the years, he had come to resent the professor for intervening in that fateful moment. Wouldn't an eternity of everlasting youth with his beloved Lucy be better than what his life had become? Van Helsing had tried to explain that it would have cost him his eternal soul, but what Van Helsing could never understand was the twenty-five intervening years without Lucy had cost him far more.

Cotford's voice jarred him back to the present. "Admit your crimes. Testify against Professor Van Helsing, and I'll save your worthless neck from the gallows."

Did the inspector actually think he was afraid of death? Holmwood had seen fates far worse. He had marched into the underworld: Death would be a blessing to him. For the first ten years after that hellish night, on every anniversary of Lucy's final death, he had locked himself away in his study and stared at Lucy's portrait as he polished his dueling pistols. He'd place the barrel of the gun to his temple, near where the tip of his ear had been, and tried to end his suffering by willing himself to shoot. He wanted to be with Lucy. But each time, the words of the Bible he had learned as a child had crept into his mind, reminding him that those who committed suicide were damned. He knew in his heart that Lucy's soul was in heaven. It had been his desire to free her soul that had allowed Van Helsing to persuade him to drive the iron stake into her un-dead heart. Even so, he found little comfort in the thought, remembering how his hands had trembled as Lucy screamed when the mallet had smashed the iron stake deep into her chest, splashing crimson blood over her beautiful ivory wedding dress. Fate was never so cruel as to ask a groom to kill his bride on the day that was to be their wedding. Lucy had never asked to be turned into a creature of the night. That devil, Dracula, had taken the deed upon himself.

Holmwood became aware of Cotford's watchful eyes upon him. It was time to force him to show his hand and find out how much the Irish bloodhound really knew. He pushed the journals and autopsy report back at Cotford, and reclined arrogantly in his chair. "A kind offer, but your evidence is purely circumstantial, Inspector. If you could have obtained an arrest warrant, I'd be in shackles now."

"You're playing a dangerous game," Cotford replied, gesturing to the journals. "Seward couldn't live with his guilt. He planned to expose Van Helsing, and the professor killed him."

"With all due respect to a representative of Scotland Yard, that is the most ludicrous thing I've ever heard. Jack Seward was Van Helsing's prize pupil, like the son he'd never had. That kind of bond does not end in murder. You are grasping at straws."

"When Jonathan Harker discovered the truth," Lee added, heedless of Holmwood's argument, "Van Helsing killed him as well."

"Van Helsing's covering his tracks," Cotford said. He leaned forward, taking a new tactic, trying to sound like a friend. "You're next on his list."

"I sincerely doubt that." Holmwood laughed as he called Cotford's bluff. "Van Helsing is a frail seventy-five years old."

"I'm not saying he acted alone. Van Helsing once played Svengali to you and your friends. He seduced you into committing murder."

Arthur Holmwood stopped laughing and fixed him with a battlefield glare. The abrupt silence was deafening, broken only by the ticking clock and their collective breath. Whoever spoke the next word would lose this battle of wills.

The inspector reminded him of a retired sea captain he had once met on holiday in Scotland. The captain had been hunting a monster believed to be lurking in the waters of Loch Ness. The old man spent all his time and resources trawling the waters for evidence of the creature. Cotford was doing the same and, like the sea captain, had no evidence, merely a theory based on fiction and myth, obviously hoping that under the guise of saving his life from an imagined threat, he could intimidate him into a confession to fit his wild theory.

Good Lord, the inspector had no idea to whom he was speaking!

The tension in the room continued to mount until Cotford finally blinked. "Who's to say Van Helsing hasn't found a new cabal of impressionable young men to murder for him?"

Arthur Holmwood shook his head at this useless prattling. Cotford was not the threat he'd at first taken him to be.

There was a look in Cotford's eyes. It was the same look Van Helsing had when he first spoke of the un-dead, the Nosferatu. The look of a zealot. Even though he had lost this hand, Holmwood knew that Cotford would never let this go. If it could end his bitter suffering, he would gladly confess to whatever trumped-up charge Cotford could concoct, and willingly accept a quick neck-snapping death at the end of a noose.

But he had to consider his wife Beth's place in society, and that of his family, all of whom would suffer if he allowed Cotford to besmirch the Holmwood name. Death at the gallows would allow him to join his Lucy in heaven, but he had already caused his family enough shame. He'd married Beth out of friendship, to save her family from crushing debt. Beth loved him, he knew, but he did not share her depth of emotion. She avoided dealing with the pain by consuming herself with the niceties of society. She had been planning tonight's dinner party for weeks, ensuring that all of the finest members of society would attend.

His arrest in front of all their guests had ruined her evening and would be shameful gossip among their peers for weeks to come. Although he did not love Beth the way a husband should, she was his best and only friend. The tears of embarrassment in her eyes as he was led away by Lee had nearly broken his frozen heart. He could not allow a conviction to damage Beth's place in society further. It was all she had.

He stood to face his accusers, calmly pulling his white gloves over his hands and challenged them: "I've heard quite enough. I am an English lord and you have no grounds for keeping me here. Harass me again, and I'll have both your badges."

Without another word, he started toward the door.

"You and Van Helsing may like to excuse your crimes by telling yourselves evil exists in an all-powerful devil," Cotford said. His words made Holmwood pause at the door. "I know the truth because I've seen it. True evil exits in the soul of man . . . and it's coming for you."

Arthur Holmwood exited with the last word: "It's coming for all of us."

Van Helsing had much to do. Upon reading Mina's telegram, he planned to immediately return to his room, grab his hat and coat, and rush out in search of Quincey. But after forgoing his meal, and exerting energy in the lobby confrontation with Cotford, he now felt too weak to begin his quest. He would start fresh in the morning. He'd wasted too much time trying to reason with Detective Constable . . . no, *Inspector* Cotford. After all the years he had spent doing God's work, fighting evil so that ignorant men like Cotford could sleep safely at night, this was the gratitude he received in the sunset of his years. *Accused of committing murder, indeed.* Cotford was as mad as a Spanish Inquisitor! Van Helsing had to put Cotford out of his mind. He had come back to London for a greater purpose, and Cotford was once again barking up the wrong tree. Van Helsing would not let the imbecile inspector interfere. He could only pray that Quincey was safe for one more night.

Pinned on the walls of Van Helsing's hotel room were portraits of the historical Dracula, the Romanian prince, Vlad the Impaler, and drawings depicting his bloody exploits. In the center of them all, prominently displayed, was the woodcut artwork depicting Dracula dining amidst thousands of his skewered enemies: the Forest of the Impaled.

Looking at these images, Van Helsing knew that a final confrontation with Dracula was his destiny and that destroying this evil creature utterly was his duty. He was doing God's will. If Cotford impeded him in any way, he would kill him as well.

"My time is almost done, devil," Van Helsing said as he stared into the painted eyes of Vlad Dracula. Arranged on a nearby table were crosses, wafers, holy water, a wooden stake, a bowie knife, and a crossbow armed and ready to fire. "Come to me and we shall die together. Not of old age, but in glorious battle."

Without warning, Van Helsing felt his chest tighten as if the Grim Reaper had come calling. He could feel the cold touch of death. *No! Not now! I just need a few more days!*

He leaned on the table for support. With trembling fingers, Van Helsing reached for the brass pillbox. Taking care not to drop one this time, he wobbled a lifesaving nitroglycerine pill under his tongue.

As death's grip melted, Van Helsing's strength returned. The good Lord was sending him a message: His time was even shorter than he thought. He looked once again upon the etched face of his mortal enemy, Prince Vlad Dracula. Van Helsing stood erect, his arms outstretched to the heavens as he cried out his challenge.

"DEMON, I AWAIT YOU!"

CHAPTER XXX.

❖

They journeyed northward toward London. Quincey sat opposite Basarab in the carriage. Basarab's warm demeanor had faded to a cool silence after Quincey had informed him of his last telephone conversation with Hamilton Deane. Bram Stoker had put his foot down. He did not approve of Basarab, and had gone so far as to wire Barrymore in America, trying to coax him to return. Quincey hoped that once Basarab arrived in person and put his considerable talents on display, Stoker would have a change of heart. As they drew closer to the theatre, Basarab became ever more contemplative. Outside, the weather worsened and the fog seemed to thicken. Quincey thought it best not to disturb him. Before the driver could pull the carriage to a full stop, Basarab was already leaning out of the door. He spoke to Quincey, but his eyes, like his mind, were trained on the theatre entrance.

"I will speak with Stoker alone," Basarab said, the layer of ice in his voice making Quincey uneasy. "Make sure we are not disturbed."

"What if Deane doesn't cooperate?" Quincey touched Basarab's arm to stay him. There was a flash of hot rage in Basarab's eyes, and Quincey snatched his hand away. He was reminded of Arthur Holmwood's reaction when he had done the same thing. He was not certain what Basarab wanted or expected of him.

Then, just as suddenly as it had flared, the anger was extinguished by a calm smile. The actor altered course and sat down next to Quincey. "Prince Vlad Dracula once led forty thousand men against a Turkish invasion of three hundred thousand, the greatest army ever amassed to kill one man. But, when Dracula rode out at the head of his army with a forest of thirty thousand impaled Muslim prisoners writhing on their bloody spikes at his back, his enemies on the battlefield rode off in terror."

Quincey shifted uncomfortably in the carriage seat, deeply disturbed by Basarab's praise of the man who had murdered his father. The memory of the hand-drawn illustration of his own father, dead and impaled in Piccadilly Circus, came to him. He reminded himself quickly that his mentor's adoration was for the living man, not the un-dead demon that Dracula became when he chose to forsake God. Now was not the time, but Quincey knew that Basarab would fight that evil with him when the hour came.

Basarab continued: "That great day, Dracula saved his country. He saved the Christian world. Dracula used the only weapon he had . . . *fear.* That's right. Fear can be a powerful tool, young Quincey. *Embrace it.*"

The cabbie opened the carriage. Basarab retrained his eyes on the theatre, and calmly stepped out. Quincey followed him up the front steps of the theatre, Basarab's words circling in his mind. Was Basarab insinuating that he should use intimidation to succeed? It was not the way he had been raised. But Basarab was a self-made man of proven success. It dawned on Quincey that maybe Basarab was trying to teach him a valuable lesson.

The night guard was waiting for them at the front door. Inside the dark lobby, Quincey took a moment to allow his eyes to adjust to the dim lighting. The comforting smell of greasepaint lingered. The night guard unlocked the door leading into the auditorium. Quincey moved quickly to follow Basarab's lead.

Once inside the auditorium, they marched down the dark aisle. The houselights were only on half power. Hamilton Deane stepped forward, draped in shadows, with his hand outstretched to greet them.

"Quincey! Mr. Basarab! Welcome."

Deane shook Basarab's hand first. He flinched slightly, as if Basarab had gripped too hard, but brushed it off and continued to smile. "Let's talk business, shall we?"

Quincey acquiesced to Deane's gesture to follow, but Basarab did not move. An ominous look in Basarab's eyes skewered Quincey. He was trusting him to act on his behalf, testing him to see how well he could follow his mentor's instructions.

"No disrespect of course," Quincey said, "but Mr. Basarab first wishes to speak privately with Mr. Stoker."

Deane seemed confused by Quincey's sudden boldness and answered sternly, "The decision to hire Mr. Basarab is mine. Mr. Stoker will just have to live with it."

There was a tone of finality in Deane's voice. Quincey was at a loss of what to say or do next. Deane had agreed to let Basarab play the role, but Quincey knew that his mentor wanted his time with Stoker. He had to help make that happen. He was an actor, so he decided to act. He stepped forward, far too close for comfort, and looked Deane straight in the eye. As if playing the part of a reprehensible villain, he confronted Deane by mimicking Basarab's icy imperiousness. He could tell by the look in Deane's eyes that the man was unsettled. *Basarab was right. Fear is powerful.*

Quincey was about to see how far this new tactic would take him when Basarab placed his hand on his shoulder and pulled him back.

"Please, Mr. Deane," Basarab interrupted, "I wish to avoid any unpleasantness. Allow me the opportunity to win over Mr. Stoker with my unique interpretation of his remarkable character, free from the unavoidably contentious eye of the money changers. With your permission?"

Quincey was baffled by Basarab's now-honey-laced words. Had Basarab intentionally manipulated him to look like the villain? No, he realized; Quincey was the stick and Basarab was the carrot. Once intimidated, Deane was more readily acceptable of Basarab's polite request. He was a genius. There was much Quincey could learn from him.

Deane smiled as he gestured to the door leading backstage. "With my blessing."

In a gentlemanly manner, Basarab bowed his head in thanks and disappeared.

Quincey looked back toward the stage. How fortunate he was. It was obvious the great actor knew how to achieve what he wanted. With every passing moment he spent with Basarab, Quincey was sure he would learn more of the tactics he would require if he was to exact the revenge he had in mind.

CHAPTER XXXI.

＋—◇—＋

Using his cane to steady himself, Bram Stoker sat at his desk in the sanctuary of his office. Stoker had precious little time to spare if he was going to coax John Barrymore back to London. Barrymore had responded to Stoker's last message, informing him it was simply too late for him to return. Ethel Barrymore, John's sister, had arranged for John to join her cast of James M. Barrie's *A Slice of Life*, playing at the Criterion Theatre on Broadway. The show had a limited run and would be closing at the end of the month, at which time Barrymore was to continue to California.

Thanks to his experience with Henry Irving, Stoker knew that the way for a writer to entice any actor was through great words. He was going to pen a soliloquy for the character of Dracula that any actor would kill to recite. Barrymore's tremendous ego would force him back to the Lyceum, not wanting any other actor to gain credit for the work. Stoker would quickly send the pages to his friend George Boldt, manager of both the Waldorf and Astoria in New York, the two closely connected hotels that John Barrymore always lodged at whenever he was working on Broadway. Mr. Boldt would personally give Barrymore the new version of the play.

Memories of Irving filled every corner of Stoker's cluttered office.

Lobby cards and posters adorned the walls, and a life-sized wooden mannequin stood in a corner, clad in Irving's Mephistopheles costume that he'd worn in their hugely successful production of *Faust*. Bram glanced up at Irving's portrait hanging on his wall—wearing the same diabolical attire. Irving should have played Dracula, not Barrymore or that Basarab fellow whom Deane had gone behind Stoker's back to acquire. Irving was a fool. If Irving had listened to him, he could have ended his life with one last great role instead of fading away ruined by drink. Then, as always, Stoker had put aside his own ambitions for the sake of another's wishes. This time, he would be true and honorable only to himself. By God, Bram Stoker would choose who would play his Dracula!

Stoker had stirred himself up into a frenzy. Now was the time to write. Fury would surely drive his pen to greatness. He sat at his desk and dipped his quill into the ink.

Moments after he had begun to write, he was interrupted by a knock on the door. Stoker slammed the quill down on the desk. After the row they'd had, Deane knew better than to disturb him while he was writing. Before he had the opportunity to dismiss his intruder, the door opened and in drifted a tall man with piercing dark eyes and coal black hair. Although the face was obscured by shadow, Bram was certain that the specter of Irving had come back to curse him for ruining his theatre. As the figure stepped farther into the room, Stoker realized that it was merely a man.

He was lean, with the long, imperial features of Eastern European royalty. His dark, deep-set eyes fixed on Stoker, who felt abruptly as if he were being watched by a bird of prey. There was something very strange about his face; the eyes were vicious but the mouth was smiling. Stoker recognized the man from the promotional pictures that had been left for him. Basarab. He remembered something that Ellen Terry, one of Irving's leading ladies, had once said: *Never trust a smiling actor, it's just a mask they wear.*

"Last-minute rewrites?" Basarab asked.

"I've been expecting you." Stoker covered the page he was writing. He had been dreading this moment since meeting the Harker lad. How much did the boy know? Stoker knew this visit was more than happenstance. The longer Deane associated with Quincey and Basarab, the greater was the risk of exposing the true origins of Stoker's book. He'd tried to banish the feelings of guilt. After all, he had not committed any wrongdoing. All Stoker had done was merge his own story with the fantastical tale that had been told to him in a pub.

He had been working on his own vampire novel with little success. Stoker cursed his years in the legal world for killing his imagination. Then, one night, he'd met a strange man in a pub who was more than willing to talk so long as Stoker supplied drink. The madman's implausible ravings had inspired him, persuaded him to change the name of his villain from Count Wampyre to Count Dracula. The name reminded Stoker of *droch-fhoula*, the Gaelic word for "bad blood," and sent a chill through his veins. How could Bram have known that some of the people in the madman's tale were real? But he also knew that the theatre could not afford any sort of controversial gossip now. *Damn Quincey Harker, why did he have to appear now?*

Basarab's smile dissolved. He turned and closed the door behind him. "I see pleasantries are out of the question, so I'll get right to the point."

"If you must."

"Your book is a financial failure. You need this play to be a success. Why challenge me? I can help you."

The words were like a wooden stake piercing Stoker's heart. He did not need this patronizing, pompous *actor* to inform him of his novel's lackluster sales.

"If Deane wants a war, he'll have it," Stoker said, trying to subdue his simmering blood. "I'm the manager of this theatre. I'll close it down before I give you the lead. The role is already cast."

Basarab laughed and shook his head as he removed his gloves and coat. Stoker frowned at the way this unwelcome guest was making himself at home.

"Of course, if I was to take the part, there would have to be some changes made to the play, and a new edition of your book to reflect these changes."

"You really are as arrogant as they say!" Stoker roared. He could see through Basarab's act. The actor was auditioning for the role of Dracula by behaving like the count to win him over. It wasn't working. Stoker's Dracula would have tried to ensnare with fear, not arrogance. Stoker was more certain than ever that Basarab was wrong for the role.

"Your book is ripe with inconsistencies, false presumptions, and bad imagination," Basarab snapped. He picked up Stoker's yellow-covered book from the lamp stand.

"I have heard of the great Basarab's legendary arrogance, but now I think you may also be mad," Stoker said as he stood to confront his guest. He had thought he would find anger in Basarab's hawklike eyes, but instead there was nothing but exasperation and sadness. Basarab seemed almost earnest. Or perhaps this Romanian was a better actor than he thought.

"Why do you provoke me?" Basarab asked. "My intention is not to do battle with you."

"That's unfortunate. Because my intention is for you to get the hell out of here!" Stoker sat back down and spun the chair, turning his back on the actor. He had wasted enough time with this fool.

Basarab slid up behind Stoker. His hands gently cupped Stoker's shoulders as he leaned to his ear and spoke in a whisper. "I warn you to take care. You are making a dreadful mistake."

Stoker struggled not to let his face show his fear, but the chill running up his spine caused him to tremble. Basarab could surely feel the shudder. Stoker had betrayed himself.

Quincey could sense that Deane was still a little apprehensive of him after their earlier encounter. He kept his distance while standing onstage, giving Quincey a tour of his newly installed facilities. Deane killed the houselights, plunging the theatre into darkness. Quincey thought it odd that he could still see Deane on the stage, fumbling about for another switch. There might have been a dim houselight for the crew, but he could not see where it was coming from.

There was a spark and a loud electric hum as Deane pulled the second switch. "Behold the marvel of the twentieth century," he said.

Electric footlights illuminated the stage. Quincey was enthralled to see a magnificent three-color lighting system using white, red, and green stage lights.

"Now observe this." Deane dimmed each of the colored lights to different levels.

Quincey was in awe. This was something that could never be accomplished with gaslight. It would enable them to add a malevolent mood never before seen on the stage. He found himself laughing like a child in a sweetshop.

Bram Stoker's Irish-accented voice resonated through the backstage catacombs. He was yelling, heated and angry.

"That's my cue," Deane exclaimed. "I had better get in there."

Make sure we are not disturbed. Basarab's words echoed in Quincey's memory as clearly as if he were standing beside him. Quincey could not fail him. As Deane started to move toward the backstage door, he leapt onto the stage and blocked his path. Deane started back, surprised by Quincey's speed.

"I'm sorry, but Mr. Basarab does not wish to be disturbed."

"I have a lot riding on this," Deane said. "I'm not going to let Stoker ruin it." He put his hand out to push Quincey aside, but the younger man stood firm. Deane was taken aback. The argument backstage intensified.

"Out of my way!" Deane cried. In his fury, his gentlemanly demeanor had vanished. He moved to force his way past Quincey.

"I'm sorry, but I must insist," Quincey said. He put out a hand to stop Deane.

Although the touch was light, Deane was thrown completely off balance. He flew back, and fell flat on his back in the middle of the stage. Quincey saw a flash of surprise and fear on Deane's face. He scuttled back along the floor and picked himself up. Deane flashed Quincey a glare and retreated off the stage.

Quincey could only watch, bewildered. *I barely touched him.* He looked at his hands, disgusted by his own actions. It was now Quincey who was afraid . . . of himself. Was this the man that Basarab wanted him to become?

. . .

Stoker kicked the desk, shoving the chair back and throwing Basarab's hand off his shoulders. He swung the chair around. "I don't care who you are. Do you think you can intimidate me into granting you this role?"

Basarab ignored the question. "You are a fool and your writing is reprehensible. Your Dracula walks about in daylight. You falsely accuse him of murdering Lucy Westenra's sick and elderly mother and feeding a live infant to his brides. You call him a count when he was a prince. This is an insult to my nation."

"Your nation is still in the Dark Ages. I'm not sure if the average Romanian can even read."

Basarab's eyes flashed. He slammed the yellow-jacketed book on the desk. The whole room seemed to shake. "You write casually of things you do not understand or believe, of people you have never met. You are a talentless oaf."

Stoker stammered, "I will not defend myself to you. Dracula is merely a character in a story born out of my own head."

"If Prince Dracula is such a villain, why did he allow Harker to live when he had him captive at his castle?"

"You speak of these things as if they were true events," Stoker said.

"If you had bothered to check with the harbormaster at Whitby, you would have discovered that a ship named the *Demeter* crashed upon the rocks during a storm in 1888, not 1897, as you claim in your book."

Stoker needed to end this, and end this now. He rose up into Basarab's face. "I demand you leave—"

"The crew of that ship died of plague brought on by rats," Basarab interrupted. "They went mad, killing one another. There was no hapless dog, and not a single throat was torn out, as you had written, by a savage claw."

Stoker's left eye twitched in anger. He prayed it would go unnoticed as he pointed at the door. "Immediately."

Basarab seemed to grow larger as he loomed over Stoker. The author retreated along the desk's edge.

"It was Van Helsing who murdered Lucy Westenra, not Dracula.

Van Helsing botched the blood transfusion and poisoned Lucy's blood. Dracula turned her into a vampire to save her."

"What do you know of Professor Van Helsing?" Stoker asked, retreating farther into the room. He felt as if all the warmth had run out of his body.

The candlelight threw living shadows across Basarab's face. "Van Helsing's arrogance is matched only by his ignorance."

Stoker's courage waned under Basarab's withering gaze. His breath ran short. The weakness in his threats were obvious. "If you are here as an advocate for Quincey Harker in some libelous lawsuit, I warn you . . ."

"You're just like the pompous hypocrites in your novel," Basarab said. "You really believe that by merely standing up to perceived evil, that evil will fall?"

Stoker could retreat no more. He was backed into a corner. The room seemed to grow darker. Basarab was so close that he completely filled Stoker's vision. *Those eyes! Those black eyes!* Stoker could feel his left arm growing numb and cold. He was on the verge of tears.

"Dracula was a monster of my own imagination!"

"No! He was a hero who did what he must to survive." Basarab's voice filled with pride as his speech rose to a crescendo. "Prince Dracula was ordained by the Pope himself as Captain of the Crusades. He stood alone in the name of God against the entire Ottoman Empire. Dracula would *never* shrink in fear of a ridiculous ass like Van Helsing and run back to Transylvania. You are, in fact, guilty of slander!"

Sweat poured down Stoker's face. He leaned against the wall for support, rubbing his dead arm. The room seemed to spin and tilt. Stoker averted his eyes to avoid Basarab's soul-piercing stare. Pain seared through his arm and into his neck as he struggled to breathe. Stoker forced himself to meet Basarab's gaze, even as he sensed himself sliding to the floor. "Who are you?" he gasped.

Basarab snapped his hand around Stoker's neck and squeezed. His face appeared to contort into that of a wolf, snapping at Stoker. "I am a gauntlet thrown before you," he said in an eerily calm whisper. "I am your judgment before God!" He released Stoker, his face curdled in disgust.

It was as if Basarab's grip had been the dam holding back the flood of pain. Searing agony shot up Stoker's neck, along the side of his jaw and into his brain. He grabbed his skull. It felt as if a hot poker had been thrust into his eye. Stoker collapsed to the floor. Basarab turned away from him. Stoker reached out for help, but was paralyzed. His pleas came out as dry wheezes.

He could only watch helplessly as Basarab took hold of his most prized possession: the *Dracula* playbook.

Then, blackness.

Quincey could feel Deane's eyes upon him as he sat in the aisle seat of the first row. They had not exchanged a single word. Quincey was still looking at his hands on the stage, contemplating the ramifications of his rash actions. He had pushed too hard.

Footsteps stage left. It was judgment time.

Basarab emerged from the backstage shadows, holding a booklet under his arm. He looked downstage at Deane and said simply, "Fetch a doctor. I fear Mr. Stoker has suffered a stroke."

It was not until Deane pounded up the steps to the stage that he was certain he had heard correctly.

"What are you waiting for? Fetch a doctor!" Deane shouted as he ran past Quincey. He shot Basarab a glare before disappearing backstage. The actor gave no reaction. Quincey turned to Basarab, and his mentor gave him a nod. Once again, he had his charge and he was off to carry out his orders. He leapt down to the house floor and started up the aisle. If Stoker died now, Quincey would never have the opportunity to question him about his book, his parents' secrets, or Dracula. He had to move fast.

"Fools, fools!" Basarab's baritone voice boomed from the stage. Quincey stopped and turned back to see Basarab, center stage, reading from the playbook.

"What devil or witch was ever so great as Attila, whose blood flows in these veins?"

Quincey knew time was of the essence, but he found himself riveted. Basarab had *become* the character of Count Dracula. His voice was haunted and hollow, his Eastern European accent more pronounced. The regal elegance fell away from his posture. His entire body seemed almost wolflike as he stalked the stage. The transformation was so quick and remarkable that it was almost supernatural. It was a drastic contrast to John Barrymore's farcical interpretation.

"But the warlike days are over," Basarab growled. "Blood is too precious a thing in these years of dishonorable peace, and the glories of the great Dracula are no more than a tale that is told."

Basarab stood downstage center; the footlights cast a chilling glow upon his face. In his eyes were centuries of torment. He was all blood and rage.

No longer reading from the book, but reciting as if from memory, Basarab allowed it to slip from his fingers. The angry wolf transformed again. Tears welled in his haunted eyes, his muscles strained and his head arched into the spotlight. So much pain. So much despair. Quincey stood in awe, frozen. Basarab continued to speak as if the lines were born in the depths of his own soul.

"Time has finally caught me," Basarab said, his eyes staring directly at Quincey, burning into his flesh. "There is no place in this age of machines and politicians and intellect for monsters roaming the countryside. Choose to evolve, or choose to die."

Quincey felt as if his feet were bolted to the ground. Basarab had transformed Dracula into a tragic hero, and in some distress, Quincey thought that if Basarab could so easily find sympathy in Dracula, how would he ever persuade his mentor to raise up arms against the monster?

The urgency of finding a doctor for Stoker jarred him back to reality. Quincey burst out through the theatre doors and ran up the street, calling for help. A man came forward, claiming to be a doctor, and Quincey raced with him back to the theatre.

Perhaps Basarab was not the ally Quincey needed. The loss of Stoker as a source of information was just the start of it. The demon had won the first battle and he had not even raised a single finger.

CHAPTER XXXII.

＊—◇—＊

Arthur Holmwood stepped into the front hall of his house and was surprised to find no one waiting for him. The staff had cleared up after the dinner party. The house was immaculate. It was quiet, like walking through a graveyard.

After the ruination of her perfectly planned dinner party, Arthur had expected Beth to be in the front room with a stern expression. Her absence spoke volumes. He supposed she wanted nothing to do with him at present. Wentworth, his butler, was meant to wait for his master until relieved and should have been at the door to take his coat, hat, and walking stick, but he was also nowhere to be found. It dawned on him that Beth might have dismissed Wentworth for the night, leaving him to fend for himself; another attempt to strike back at him for the humiliation she had suffered.

The horrifying memory of Lucy's crime scene photograph flashed across his mind. Thus it had been all evening. Like a bad meal, the images came up again and again. He needed to wash them away. Dropping his coat and hat onto his deacon's bench, he marched into his study and poured himself a drink. Then he opened his eyes wide and dropped the crystal goblet in utter disbelief.

The portrait of Lucy was back over the fireplace.

Holmwood's temper was ready to erupt. It had to be Beth. Whatever injustice his wife felt she'd suffered, this was a horrifying retaliation.

The sound of a footfall in the outer foyer caught his attention. "Beth?" There was no answer. "Wentworth?"

Again, there was no answer. A shadow moved across the marble floor. Someone was out there.

He called out, "Hello?"

More footsteps were the only response.

Holmwood sprang out from behind the study doorway. "Who's there, I say?"

The hall was still. He was alone. The temperature dropped ten degrees. He heard the faint sound of breathing. He looked around and, once again, found no one. That was when he saw that the window was open. Mystery solved. He laughed at his own paranoia and went to close the window. He imagined his old legionnaire comrades laughing at him. He closed the latch and turned to head back to the study to resume his drinking when he caught a familiar scent. *Lilac?* Surely not at this time of year. He felt the hairs on his arm stand at attention as he remembered that lilac was the scent Lucy used to wear. He had imported it directly from Paris for her.

A soft female voice broke the silence: *"Ar-thur."*

Holmwood spun around. He was alone.

"Beth?" The sound of his voice seemed unnaturally loud as it echoed in the vaulted ceiling. A silvery laugh chimed, as if coming from all directions at once. He recognized that laugh. But it couldn't be. His senses were deceiving him.

"Arthur," the voice said again.

Now it was directly above him. He glanced up the main staircase. What he saw there made his blood run cold. A luminescent figure slowly descended toward him, her body swaying like a cat as she drew near. A thick mane of flaming red hair cascaded down her shoulders; her porcelain white skin reflected the moonlight from the window. Her breasts rose and fell with each step; her eyes were soulless and black, her luscious, bloodred lips pouting. Her shroudlike white gown was torn, tattered, sheer, and revealing.

"Lucy?!" Holmwood gasped, still unable to believe his eyes.

She replied with that silvery harp laugh, revealing her sharp, glimmering teeth, and glided down the winding staircase.

He fought to breathe. Every instinct, every fiber of his body wanted to take her into his arms. But Lucy was dead. His love was dead.

As if she could read his innermost desires, she looked at him with sad compassion and said, "I know you wish to be with me, my beloved."

Lucy's voice swept over him like a cleansing wave. It was as if time had stopped, and all the pain of the last twenty-five years had been washed away. Lucy opened her hands. A white mist emanated from her palms, drifting to the floor. As the mist gathered at her feet, she rose into the air, held aloft by its cushion.

"Death is only the beginning, my love. There is so much more to life than the boundaries of the flesh." She floated toward him.

"No! This cannot be!" He had just seen the photographs of Lucy's remains in her tomb. The shock of it was undoubtedly affecting his senses.

"It's dark here, Arthur. I'm so lonely. My arms ache to hold you."

No! Lucy was supposed to be in the light. Van Helsing had promised that plunging the stake into her heart would release her soul to heaven. . . .

Lucy neared him, her arms outstretched. He felt torn in two. He so desperately wanted to embrace her once again. It was the same longing he had felt outside her mausoleum that fateful night. This time, there would be no Van Helsing to interfere.

She was on top of him. He closed his eyes as he felt those gentle lips kiss him. Her touch was so electrifying, it felt as if his heart beat for the first time in a quarter-century. Her lips pulled suddenly away. *No, he wanted the kiss to last for eternity.*

"Lucy, you don't have to be alone. Let me be with you in the dark."

He opened his eyes and his heart stopped again. Lucy's beautiful face exploded with horrific putrescence. Her face cracked and decomposed. Her pale skin turned purple. The scent of lilac soured into the stench of the grave. Lucy's eyes sank back into her skull-like head, and her lips receded and tightened, revealing the extent of her fangs. Worms erupted from the arms encircling his neck, crawling through her rotted flesh. She opened her mouth to speak, only to vomit forth a waterfall of wriggling maggots.

Holmwood stumbled back against the wall, frozen in fear. His love had become a nightmare. "Have pity on me!" he cried.

Lucy's muscles and sinews liquefied into black ooze, dripping off her bones. Her beautiful, harplike voice was gone. A hollow bell rang in her mouth. "Pity? The same pity you had for me when you drove the stake into my heart . . . my love!"

Growling like a rabid animal, she pounced upon him, slamming him against the wall. Her bony talons pierced his wrists as she spread his arms, nailing them into the rosewood paneling, crucifying him. Holmwood screamed in agony.

Lucy's jaw unhinged, opening impossibly wide. Her fangs positioned themselves over his throat. His shrieks were silenced as she tore the larynx from his throat. In his last horrifying seconds, Arthur Holmwood witnessed his beloved Lucy tilt her head back in ecstasy, bathing in his blood.

"Lucy!" he screamed as he sat up in the darkness, bewildered and lost. Was he dead? As his eyes focused, he realized he was in his bed. He reached to touch his neck. No wound, no blood. Merely a nightmare. He was breathing so quickly, his heart beating so fast, he thought he would have a heart attack.

Holmwood heard a muffled sob beside him. With great trepidation he looked across.

It was Beth. She was crying. There was agony in her eyes, such agony as he had never seen before. He knew what had happened. He had called out Lucy's name in his sleep. He could only imagine the hurt Beth must have felt. Without a word, his wife ran out of the room. Though muffled from behind the wooden door of the closet, her sobs were no less painful to hear.

He knew there were no words of comfort that would take away her pain. He despised himself. Beth's love for him was deep and real. Yet, the more she loved him, the more he pushed her away. Even in death, he could not betray Lucy.

He'd loved Lucy from the moment he saw her. They all had. Jonathan and Mina Harker, Jack Seward, Quincey P. Morris, and himself. After Jonathan passed his bar exam and left for Transylvania for his fateful meeting with Prince Dracula, Mina had searched for a way to fill the void in her life. Her best friend, Lucy, found the perfect way to ease Mina's loneliness. She'd hosted a charity soirée at her home in Whitby to benefit the poor and homeless of Whitechapel. It was at this soirée that Jack, Quincey Morris, and Arthur had all found themselves on Lucy's dance card. All three had instantly fallen in love with her. Arthur Holmwood and his two best friends had formed a gentleman's agreement; they would woo and court Lucy to the utmost of their abilities, and let the best man win. Holmwood had never known such joy as the day Lucy chose him above all others. His friends toasted their happy union and their future of a long, loving life together, which had made him feel proud to call Jack and Quincey Morris his best men at his forthcoming wedding. A wedding that never happened.

He dragged himself to Beth's dressing table and stared at his wretched reflection in the vanity mirror. For so long, he had only wanted to die, to feel nothing, to be with Lucy in heaven. Perhaps it was just his guilt, but as much as he yearned for death, he feared it. The lives he had taken in war, he felt, were justified. God would forgive him for doing righteous work against evil men. The three men he had killed in duels were a different story. Unable to take his own life for fear of an eternity in hell, he had sought out others to do what he could not. He had provoked those men into action, insulted their honor so severely that he had left them no choice. They were fair duels, but his opponents were still dead for no other reason than his own cowardice.

He touched the scar on his right cheek. His fingers traced up to where the tip of his ear had once been. Quincey Harker's words echoed. *Dracula is coming for revenge and you know it. Help me kill him once and for all.*

Holmwood thought back to the morning after driving the stake into

Lucy's heart. He'd stood before a statue of Christ in his family chapel and sworn an oath on Lucy's grave that he would not rest until he'd destroyed the demon that had claimed her life.

God had sent Lucy into his dream to remind him of his oath. After twenty-five wasted years, He was calling in His marker, and Arthur Holmwood was obliged to answer. It was the only way he could be assured of salvation and eternity with Lucy. In the morning, he would go to London in God's name and seek out the demon.

CHAPTER XXXIII.

A fter Mr. Stoker was taken to the hospital, Quincey had returned to his rented lodgings. Then grim reality sank in. Stoker's sudden incapacitation had removed him as the only obstacle in Basarab's acceptance of the role of Dracula. Deane was deeply in debt. He wouldn't be foolish enough to cancel the play, so it would fall upon Deane to take over directing duties. What would that mean for Quincey?

Although awed by Basarab's powerful portrayal of Dracula's soliloquy, it left Quincey uneasy. He could not allow Basarab to humanize Dracula. Quincey's first thought was to tell Basarab the truth, but what could he say? *Your national hero is a monster who destroyed my family, killed my father, and I am bound by honor to hunt and kill him?* Quincey didn't need to speak the words aloud to know how insane they sounded. What proof did he have? He paced about his room.

First order of business was to return to the Lyceum and apologize to Deane for his boorish behavior. For his scheme to work, he had to win Deane back to his side.

Quincey arrived at the Lyceum Theatre midmorning. There had been no mention in the newspaper of the events of the previous night, or of Mr. Stoker's current condition. This did not surprise Quincey, since the unfortunate incident had happened too late in the evening to make the morning edition. Quincey was disturbed that Deane was not at the theatre, and none of the workers had any knowledge of Stoker's health. He was just settling in to await Deane's arrival when he was approached by Mr. Edwards, the house manager.

Edwards was usually a sprightly fellow with a large smile. Quincey sensed trouble as Edwards approached, looking sombre. With pangs of panic in his stomach, Quincey's mind immediately went to the worst: *Deane was so enraged that he had canceled the production.*

As fate would have it, the horrors of Quincey's imagination paled in comparison with the reality. Edwards presented him with a note that had been left for him at the stage door. Quincey frowned. He had left strict instructions with all Lyceum Theatre workers to beware a youthful-looking woman who might claim to be his mother. No one, under any circumstances, was to allow her entry to the theatre or divulge Quincey's whereabouts. After all, he did not yet know whose side Mina was on.

With a note of apology in his voice, Edwards said, "An elderly gentleman came to call earlier this morning, claiming to be your grandfather. He said there was a family emergency and needed to locate you immediately. He left this note for you. I pray I did nothing wrong, but under the circumstances, I thought it best to give the old gentleman your address off the stage manager's contact list. Did I do wrong?"

Quincey reassured Edwards that everything was well and thanked him for his concern. The truth was, everything was far from well. The only family Quincey had left was his mother. This "grandfather" was an impostor.

Quincey opened the note and found there was no writing on the page. It had all been a ploy to gain his address. The pangs he felt now erupted into a wave of fear.

Night fell.

Quincey found himself standing before the Fleet Street Dragon. *How ironic.* Quincey had spent the day wandering the streets, afraid to return to the theatre or his flat. Thanks to Edwards, the mysterious stranger knew his home address and could be lying in wait. If the stranger grew tired of waiting, it was quite possible he would return to the theatre. Quincey sensed he should give this old man a wide berth.

He reasoned there could be three possibilities as to the elderly stranger's identity.

First: Since Mina would get no information as to Quincey's whereabouts if she came to the theatre herself, the elderly stranger might have been sent by his mother as a surrogate.

Second: He could be working with Scotland Yard. Perhaps the police wanted to question Quincey regarding Stoker's collapse. Scotland Yard could also be searching for him for one other reason: Something terrible might have happened to Mina. Quincey knew deep down that he still loved his mother, but he could not trust her. His instinct told him to send a telegram to ascertain whether his mother was alive and well, then rush home to his flat and wait for a reply.

It was only fear of the third possibility of the stranger's identity that kept Quincey's feet in limbo. Stoker had written in his novel that, when his father first met Dracula at his Transylvanian castle, the demon appeared as an old man. But this was not Stoker's novel. Quincey could not take that chance. He stared up at the Fleet Street Dragon, lamplight flickering eerily on its face.

He was tremendously tired. He could not think logically. He couldn't stay on the street all night. Basarab was at his hotel. He was the wisest man Quincey knew. He was his friend. Surely, he would help him. Yet Quincey could not risk exposing Basarab to the danger that hunted him. He gazed up at the window of his father's dark office. There was nothing for him there any longer. There was only one safe harbor he could think of.

Quincey turned on his heels and decided to head to Mooney & Son's, his father's favorite drinking hole. There, he would blend into the crowd. Become anonymous. Whether the elderly stranger was a policeman or his mother's surrogate, he would not think to look for him there. If Quincey's worst fear was realized, and the elderly stranger was indeed Dracula, he would be safe in public. The one thing Quincey knew for certain, Dracula needed to keep to the shadows. He could not risk exposing himself.

Fog rolled in. Two more blocks and he would find warmth, respite, and a hot meal. Approaching the Fleet Street alleyway, he was stung by the thought that if something so small as a false note from a stranger could send him into a fearful panic, how could he ever hope to defeat a demon like Dracula?

A hand reached from the fog, grabbed Quincey's coat, and propelled him into the alley's darkness.

The demon has found me. Quincey knew death had not come quickly for his father. Dracula would not be kinder with him. His death would be torturous. He prayed for strength.

Quincey watched as a man emerged from the swirling fog. He carried a cane. Before Quincey could react, there was a glinting flash of steel, a whisk through the air. He opened his mouth to scream for help but was quickly silenced by the razor point of a rapier at his neck.

"Do you know who I am?" asked an accented voice from the darkness.

The man with the blade leaned forward into the light. Quincey was both relieved and frightened at the same time. The man was gaunt and frail. Wavy white hair flopped against his face. His clothes were well tailored, yet hung on his skeletal frame like sacks. Quincey's attacker was an old, sick man. He should have felt secure with the knowledge that he could overpower the old man with the blade, but there was something in his eyes, a determined strength. Perhaps even a touch of madness. This old man was not Dracula, but he could be just as deadly.

"You must be Van Helsing."

"If you know my name, then you know what I'm capable of," Van Helsing said. "Stop looking into your father's death."

After the cold reception from Arthur Holmwood, Quincey should not have been surprised to find another member of the band of heroes trying to dissuade him from his path of revenge. Yet he did not expect to see the old professor out roaming the night streets, let alone in London. It hadn't even occurred to him that Van Helsing might be the mysterious stranger. Surely he was being ruled by fear. Van Helsing must have grown tired of waiting for Quincey at his lodgings and set out to search for him. Quincey pushed the rapier away from his neck. "My mother sent you."

Van Helsing whipped the sword point back onto Quincey's neck, forcing him against the brick wall. The look of desperate rage on his face made Quincey understand this was not a man who had time to waste with petty arguments. To make his point clear, Van Helsing twisted the blade, scoring the flesh. Warm blood trickled down Quincey's neck. The old man was not as weak as he appeared.

"There are no answers for you," he said, "only darkness."

"What secrets are you all so desperate to hide from me?" Quincey asked, hoping the old man wouldn't hear the tremble in his voice.

A look of madness came to Van Helsing's eyes. Quincey held his breath, not sure if he was going to leave this alley alive. But the old man's face softened. His eyes remained stern, but now he looked more like a loving grandparent than an assassin.

"Most of us walk through life sure in our faith," Van Helsing said in earnest, an old professor giving one last lecture to a student in whom he saw no potential. "Others who are not so lucky face a moment when that faith is tested. That is the moment when one must choose between the light and the dark. Not all have the strength or wisdom to make the right choice."

Van Helsing pulled back the blade and sheathed it in his cane. "Go back to the Sorbonne," he pleaded. "For your mother's sake, live on in oblivious bliss and remain a child of God."

Then, his point made and the lesson over, the old man stepped back into the shadowy fog and hobbled away on his cane without looking back.

Quincey was outraged. His mother had obviously sent Van Helsing to tell her son he was weak and in need of protection. But he would show her. He would show them all.

CHAPTER XXXIV.

Dracula was dead. Mina knew that now. Through Bathory's eyes, she had witnessed his final demise. She wanted to grieve for both of them, Dracula and Jonathan, but there was no time for that. She was being hunted. If she survived, there would be many lonely days and nights ahead to weep for all those she had lost. If she did not survive, it would not matter. She had so little to live for now, with her husband in the grave, and her son full of rage about things he did not understand. She needed to arm herself not only with weapons but with something even more powerful: knowledge. Even if she did not survive, she wanted her son to know of all the evil in the world.

Mina decided that she had to find out everything she could about Countess Elizabeth Bathory. Professor Van Helsing always used to say, "In order to battle your enemy, you must first learn everything about them." Bathory was Mina's new enemy.

Mina and Bathory had exchanged blood, and now her mind was connected to Bathory's, just as it had been to Dracula's, twenty-five years ago, which meant that Bathory would be privy to Mina's thoughts, desires, and secrets. But it also meant that Mina was given a glimpse into what Bathory was thinking, and her head was throbbing as centuries of memories came to her. At the local bookshop, Mina searched through the piles of information, compiling an account of the countess's storied life. She had been prepared to behold a horror story, but what she found was surprising, and sadly compelling. Like many of the evildoers in this world, Bathory had not been born a monster, but had become one. As constraining as the bonds of her own time were, the oppression of women in the sixteenth century was ten times worse: Bathory had been compelled into an arranged marriage to someone twice her age. Mina's eyes drifted to the name, Ferenc Nádasdy, and was suddenly overwhelmed by feelings of deep hatred. Her mind was assaulted by images of physical abuse and violation, and a horrible stench. She slammed the book shut as if it would help shut out the images.

And yet, like small pinpricks of light in the darkness, a set of impressions began to form in Mina's mind. The amount of blood she and Bathory had exchanged could not have been more than a thimbleful, giving Mina access to only scattered images, but it was enough to help her piece together a painful tale. Mina was not surprised to learn that Bathory was fluent in Hungarian, Latin, and German, an uncommon accomplishment. Mina, always one for meticulous notes, wrote and then circled *highly educated*. This alone made Bathory a dangerous foe. She then found references to Bathory's expert equestrian and sword skills, which were equally alarming.

One passage that Mina found gave her pause for thought. She read that while her husband was at war, Bathory had been left at home with her aunt, Countess Karla. Mina "saw" the face of Aunt Karla in her mind . . . along with another image, a young blond maid . . . hanging dead by her neck. *What did that mean? Who was this girl? Why had she been executed?* She tried to focus on the memories, but the images faded like steam upon a mirror. She read that Bathory's relationship with her aunt Karla had ended abruptly when Bathory's family sent an armed guard to retrieve the countess.

According to historians, Bathory had children shortly after her return. They were cared for by governesses as was then the custom, but Bathory was a devoted mother. Mina found this difficult to imagine, but then she read that Bathory's daughter, Ursula, and her son, Andráshad, both died of disease at an early age.

Feelings of rage and sorrow overcame her. She could see the terrible sneer of Ferenc screaming as he first struck Bathory with his fist and then kicked her while she lay helpless on the ground. "I have no heir. God is punishing me for your sins!"

Mina could feel Bathory's mind unhinge and her heart turn cold. Though Bathory's jaw was broken, she spat out her own blood and spoke under her breath, not to her husband, but to God. "You have taken from me everything that I ever loved. Now I will make your most hated enemies my friends. Now I will take from you what you hold most dear. 'Suffer the little children to come unto me.' Isn't that what you said?" Mina could understand a mother's anguish at the loss of her children. But she herself had never felt as much rage as Bathory at that moment. Bathory's rage against God and man was a fiery wrath that would consume her.

It is no wonder, given this turn of events, that Bathory's rage had turned toward her nearest bane. In January 1604, Ferenc Nádasdy had received a deep wound, supposedly inflicted by a whore whom he refused to pay. A brief image of Ferenc sleeping in his bedchamber pierced Mina's mind. She could see Bathory's delicate hands pulling back the cloth bandages from her husband's torso. Again, a horrible stench came to Mina. Using a silver spoon, a delicate hand carefully sprinkled rancid manure into Ferenc's wound as her other hand gingerly replaced the bandage.

He had apparently died some days later, in excruciating pain. Cause of death: an infected wound. Mina found herself disgusted. What a cruel and calculating way to kill another human being, even someone as vile as Ferenc.

Once freed from the constraints of her marriage, and believing she was above the laws of God and his bible, it appeared that Bathory had begun to embrace her true nature. She openly flaunted her tendencies by engaging in relations with local women. Where they had once embraced and welcomed her leadership, the villagers feared that Bathory's ungodly behavior would bring a curse down upon them and their lands, and began to shun her. Seeking aid from higher authorities, they asked that Bathory be removed and imprisoned. Instead, a plea was sent to Bathory's family to intervene. Bathory's family sent priests. She spurned them all. Her family, fearing their name would be ruined, imprisoned her in their castle, where she remained for four years. Mina now had an image of a "dark stranger" coming to Bathory while her family held her captive, but could not discern why the dark stranger had come, whether to rescue her or to save her soul. Mina strained her mind to find a face for the dark stranger, but could find only an empty void. Mina closed her eyes, and for an instant, the image of Dracula slipped into her mind. Was it Bathory's memory or her own experience coming back to her? Mina could not be certain.

She continued to read. The historical texts held no information about the next three years in Bathory's life. It was as if she had disappeared off the face of the earth. Then, when Bathory was nearing her fortieth year, she had miraculously returned to her castle in Hungary, by all accounts a changed woman.

Almost immediately, a series of violent murders befell both the Bathory and Nádasdy families, and young peasant girls from the villages disappeared. Fear fell like a shadow over the countryside, and Elizabeth Bathory was named the cause. The images now flashing in Mina's mind became obscene. What she saw now were debauched images of orgies, perverse practices, even heretical pagan rituals and elements of Devil worship. Bathory had completely broken with God— and Mina was seeing the result.

In fearful whispers, townsfolk said that the dark stranger who had taken Bathory away was a warlock who had instructed her in the dark arts. Bathory's male servants fled the castle. The tales of evil and debauchery they told were unprecedented. Bathory now appointed only women to attend her. The number of murders mounted, and more blood was spilled. Bathory had become a butcher who had sworn war against all Christians.

The authorities raided Bathory's castle, arresting her in the midst of an orgy with three young women—her servants—bathing in and drinking another young woman's blood. Mina knew then that Bathory had been made a vampire.

In Bathory's castle dungeon, the authorities discovered the most heinous torture devices ever conceived. Numerous peasant girls were found naked, horribly wounded, raped, and in some cases lifeless. Upon digging up the ground around her castle, dozens more skeletons were found.

For their crimes, Bathory's female servants were put to death, their bodies burned, their ashes scattered. Bathory was tried and convicted. Only her family's influence kept her from being burnt at the stake. A compromise was made: life in prison.

Bathory's family wept for her. She had been born into privilege, blessed by God, considered to be the most beautiful woman of her age, yet she had cast it all away and would pay for her crimes with an eternity in hell.

Once again, Bathory's disjointed memories invaded Mina's mind. She now sensed the presence of another man who had come to Bathory's aid. This stranger instigated a plan for her escape. Bathory had been walled up in her bedchamber, with only an open hole in the brick wall close to the floor through which she received her meals. It was through this hole that a letter by this stranger was passed to her. As Mina concentrated her thoughts, she saw that the text had been written in Hungarian. With Bathory's blood coursing through her veins, Mina was able to read the words.

The letter told Bathory that her blood had been transmuted. If a human body was invaded by vampire blood, the body resisted the venom. But, when the human body died and could no longer fight, the vampire venom took over, transforming the body into something new and greater. Vampire blood swam through the veins and arteries, making the once-dead human into the un-dead. The once-human heart began to pump vampire venom, and the body was reborn to a second life of immense power. Only piercing the heart could destroy the wellspring of venom and kill the vampire. In conclusion, the letter pointed out to Bathory that a vampire's heart beat so slowly that its rhythm was imperceptible to mortals.

At last, Mina understood what was happening to her own body. While Dracula's vampire blood resided within her, her living body kept the venom from taking complete control. Yet the venom had in one way already taken effect: It had given Mina eternal youth. Now both worried and curious, Mina wondered what other effects Dracula's blood, and now Bathory's, would have on her body. At least there was comfort in the thought that, as long as she lived and her human heart continued to beat, she would never be a true vampire.

She continued to read. After Bathory had not eaten for several days, a physician had been summoned to her prison. Prostrating himself on the floor, he looked through the hole in the brick wall and saw Bathory lying motionless. The wall was hammered down. Bathory was found to have no discernible heartbeat or breath. To all appearances, Bathory was dead. She was quickly carted off under the cover of darkness to avoid prying eyes, sealed in a coffin, buried, and forgotten.

But Mina could sense Bathory clawing at her coffin, digging through earth, ripping herself from her own grave. Once she was released, centuries of horrific evil had been unleashed upon the world. Mina had faced evil before, but Bathory was not like Dracula. Dracula had always had a purpose, a reason. This demon killed for sport. She lacked the slightest touch of human compassion. Mina was more afraid than she had ever been.

Mina was about to close the books and plan her next move when an image caught her eye: an illustration of Bathory's family tree. She scanned the genealogy. Bathory's grandfather was Stephan Bathory, a famous Hungarian nobleman. *Where did she know that name from?* Her finger traced back across several branches of Stephan Bathory's family tree to the name Helen Szilagy. Mina's hand trembled; a shiver ran through her body. Now she began to see that Dracula and Bathory had a deeper bond than their need for blood.

Helen Szilagy's husband was Vlad Dracula III.

Stephan Bathory had fought beside Prince Dracula, helping him reclaim his throne after the death of his father. Dracula, Mina's dark prince, had taken Stephan's cousin as his wife to secure an alliance with the Holy Roman Emperor. Dracula believed he was Christ's holy warrior and that his marriage would help him join the two facets of Christianity into one force against the Ottomans.

The dark stranger. Mina now knew that she had seen Dracula's face for a reason. It had been Elizabeth Bathory's distant cousin, Dracula, who had come to rescue her. The dark art in which she'd been "instructed" was no doubt the kiss of the vampire. How could Dracula, who claimed to be a warrior for God, be a part of unleashing a murderous she-devil like his cousin Elizabeth Bathory upon the world for all eternity? Mina was confused.

No matter what Dracula's relationship was to Bathory, or to the second man who had delivered the note, one thing was certain: Dracula had saved Bathory from a hellish life—she had created her own hell after life.

From her dream, Mina knew that Bathory was the one who had delivered the deathblow to Dracula. But why? Memories flooded back into Mina, and she heard the words Bathory had spoken before she plunged the knife into Dracula's heart. *"You spurned me for an adulterous whore."*

With shock, Mina realized that she had been the catalyst for Dracula and Bathory's enmity. This puzzled her. Dracula and Bathory could not have been lovers, but clearly their bonds ran deep. Dracula had planned to run away with Mina. Bathory must have felt betrayed and have harbored a deep jealousy toward Mina all these years.

Now Mina understood. Bathory was set on destroying her and the entire band of heroes who had, in her mind, turned Dracula away from her. But Mina was plagued by one question: What had spurred Bathory into action after all these years? Mina could only surmise that it had something to do with Jack Seward. Seward must have learned of Bathory's existence. That was the only answer. And since his friends ignored his warnings, Seward must have sought out Bathory himself. Alone, he was no match for the countess. His attack on Bathory must have set her on her new path of revenge. Bathory was nothing if not an opportunist. The brave band of heroes, now separated by years and the hardships of life, were low-hanging fruit, ripe for the picking. Now she understood what Bathory had meant when she said: *"Your time has come. . . . I will take from you what you hold most dear. 'Suffer the little children to come unto me.'"*

Mina felt the room spin as she realized the depth of Bathory's madness. She intended to extract revenge like a biblical plague.

Mina had to find her son before Bathory did.

CHAPTER XXXV.

◆

Quincey trudged up three flights of stairs to his room on Archer Street in Soho. The flat was reasonably priced, and the area was filled with actors, painters, and other artists.

Quincey made the long walk down the hall to his own room, next to the shared water closet. Van Helsing's words continued to plague him. He wondered why no one ever trusted him—not his parents, not Arthur Holmwood. Perhaps that confrontation itself was a test, and Quincey had failed. A weak old man with a cane had bested him.

Quincey inserted the key into his lock and realized that the door was ajar, though he distinctly remembered locking it. *Someone was inside.* Running was futile. If Dracula was waiting for him inside, he would have heard the key in the lock. There was no way Quincey could outrun Dracula. It was now time for Quincey to prove to himself and the band of heroes that he was a man worthy of respect.

The door creaked as Quincey nudged it open and peered into the darkness. Across the room, the long, lean figure of a man was silhouetted against the window.

Summoning all of his courage, Quincey cried, "Who are you? What are you doing here?"

A flame ignited with the crack of a match. Quincey could make out the illuminated tip of a cigar and then billowing smoke. His first instinct was to run, but that was exactly what his mother and Van Helsing would have expected him to do. Quincey swallowed his fear and, stepping forward, reached for the light switch. The bulb flicked on with a hum and flooded the room. The tall man at the far end of the room stood with his back to Quincey, staring out the window at the street below.

Without turning, the tall man said, "Good evening, Master Harker."

Quincey recognized both the voice and thick, blond hair. "Lord Godalming?"

Arthur Holmwood turned to face him and pointed to the steamer trunk in the center of the room, upon which lay the business card Quincey had given him containing his address. The man seemed pale and worn, and there was a hollow look in his piercing blue eyes. Quincey wondered what could have unsettled him so. He was not the type to frighten easily.

Holmwood tossed the used match into the fireplace and ran his white-gloved finger through the dust on the mantelpiece. It came away smudged. His disapproval of Quincey's living conditions was evident.

"Have you also come at my mother's behest to threaten my life?" Quincey asked sharply.

Holmwood looked surprised.

"Van Helsing made his point very clear," Quincey said. He pulled down his scarf and indicated the bloody scratch on his throat.

"I have long considered Van Helsing's character above reproach. But now, I am no longer sure." He sighed.

This was a very different Arthur Holmwood from the man Quincey had met a few days ago. He was ready to hazard a guess: "Are you here to help me?"

Holmwood's face became stony. Then he turned away. "Lucy came to me in a dream and opened my eyes."

Although it sounded like madness, Quincey did not doubt for a moment the truth of what the man was telling him.

Holmwood stared out at Piccadilly Circus. "One way or another, it's time to finish what I began twenty-five years ago." His back straightened and his head came up. He inhaled deeply, stretching the silken material of his coat as his muscular back expanded. Then he pivoted on his heel like a soldier. When he faced Quincey again, his eyes were fierce and determined. "If you're right, Master Harker, and Dracula is somehow still alive, then at this very moment, you and I must swear an oath before God: that no matter what the cost, we shall once and for all destroy him." There was finality in his tone.

For the first time, Quincey had a clear ally in his battle against Dracula. Now was the time for action. Without hesitation, he said, "I swear before God to avenge my father and see, by my own hand, Dracula dead."

The door smashed open with one swift kick from Arthur Holmwood's boot. Rats squealed in the darkness. Holmwood ignited an electric torch. Quincey felt along the wall for the electric lights, but his companion placed his hand on his shoulder as they stepped into the decrepit room.

"This is Whitechapel. There are no electric lights here."

Holmwood's torchlight fell upon a rusted kerosene lamp on the floor. He tossed Quincey his box of matches and gestured for him to ignite the lamp. When he did, a wave of rats scurried out of the light, seeking the dark corners.

Quincey was unable to suppress his shock. "How could Dr. Jack Seward reside in such a place?"

"As I mentioned earlier, he was quite mad." Holmwood pointed to the ceiling, where symbols of every religion known to mankind were suspended. Quincey recognized the icon directly above him as the cross of the Rosicrucians. The ceiling was pasted with torn pages from both the Old and New Testaments, the Torah, and the Koran. Quincey guessed that Dr. Seward was covering his bets; he'd undoubtedly wanted them all on his side.

Quincey examined the walls. He discovered that the Bible pages were torn from different editions and various languages. His eyes were drawn to the words scribbled in . . . *was that blood?*

Vivus est.

"'He lives,'" Quincey translated. "You say he was mad. *Terrified* seems more the case."

Holmwood betrayed no emotion. He made his way to Seward's straw mattress and tapped the floorboards with his walking stick. One responded with a hollow thud.

"What are you doing?" Quincey asked.

"Would you be good enough to hand me the lancet from the wall there?"

Quincey glanced to where Arthur was pointing. Jack's surgical knife held a yellow, aged newspaper clipping to the wall. He withdrew the knife, reading the faded headline: "JACK THE RIPPER STRIKES AGAIN."

Perhaps Seward was mad. But as he scanned the walls, a pattern emerged, recurring themes among the chaos: Dracula, Jack the Ripper, vampires, religion, and productions of *Richard III* . . .

A loud creak drew Quincey's attention back to Holmwood. His companion had placed the tip of the lancet into the seam of the floorboard and was prying up the wood. When he had removed the floorboard, he reached down beneath the floor. Quincey stepped closer. *A secret compartment?*

Holmwood pulled out a rusted metal safe.

"How did you know that was there?"

Holmwood slammed the box against the wall, snapping the lock, and it sprang open with a loud pop. Morphine and chloral vials, a leather belt, and syringes fell out and rolled onto the mattress.

"Even if he had gone mad, you do not forsake a man who fought beside you in battle. Who do you think paid for his habit? For this room?" Holmwood asked.

He examined the interior of the box, walking his fingertips along the seams. Frustration creased his face. At last he threw the box across the room, and it clanged to the floor. "Blast! If Cotford missed anything, I thought for sure it would be in there."

He began to ransack the room, overturning furniture and pulling open empty bureau drawers. Quincey was not surprised by Holmwood's revelation: He was a man of duty and honor—his marriage showed that.

Wanting to help, Quincey raised his lantern and examined the secret compartment for himself. A herd of cockroaches swarmed over something white that was hidden below the floor.

"Wait! There's something else down here."

Quincey stamped on the boards to scatter the insects. With some trepidation, he reached down and pulled out a parcel of bound papers. Anxious to impress, he passed the bundle to Holmwood, who went to the desk and untied the string holding it together. Quincey held up the lantern to see what he had discovered.

It was a stack of postmarked envelopes—letters—which rested upon something thick, rectangular, and wrapped in white paper. Holmwood cast aside the envelopes and tore away the white wrapping, revealing a yellow, hard-covered book. Quincey knew what it was even before his companion turned the book over to reveal the cover.

Holmwood blanched visibly as he read the book's cover: *DRACULA*.

Holmwood's home, the Ring, was in East Finchley, but if they went there, they could be vulnerable. Quincey suggested that they seek refuge in the office of Hawkins & Harker. He had avoided his father's office as much as he could in recent years, but what better place was there to hide than the last place anyone would expect to find you?

He remembered the day his father had presented him with the office key. With pride in his voice, Jonathan had said, "Someday, it will be yours."

And Quincey repaid him with hate.

A loud bang drew his attention away from the envelopes he was sorting. Holmwood had slammed Stoker's novel onto the table, shoving it away with disgust. He could read no more.

"How could Jack have done this? After all I did for him, We all swore an oath of secrecy. It was not just because of our bond that I paid for his rent and his morphine. It was also to ensure that he kept his oath." Holmwood pounded the desk with a furious fist, remembering the moment when, after the battle with the gypsies, the surviving friends had placed their hands upon a Bible and sworn never to tell anyone what had transpired in their mad, bloody hunt for Dracula.

"How can you be sure it was Jack Seward who betrayed you to Stoker?"

Holmwood gestured to the book and envelopes. "Jack obviously needed someone to talk to, and we refused to listen."

Quincey wanted to say something poignant but decided it was best to focus on the letters. He paused for a moment, uncovering a tattered sheet, which looked different from the rest. The cursive handwriting was elegant and feminine. It was addressed to Seward from his ex-wife. Cold and to the point, it read: "Do not come to America. Stay away from our daughter."

Part of the signature was smeared. Seward's tears had marred the ink. Quincey wondered if the girl would ever even know her father was dead.

Holmwood crossed to the desk and pulled open the drawers one by one until he found a whisky bottle. He laughed out loud. "One thing was assured. You could always count on old Jonathan to have a drink handy." He blew the dust from a glass and poured himself a double shot.

Time seemed to stop as Quincey stared at the signature on the next letter. He blinked as if it would somehow clarify what he saw before him.

Holmwood looked up to see the blood draining from Quincey's face. "What is it?"

"This one is from . . ." Quincey nearly choked on the name. "Basarab."

"The man you told me about, the Romanian actor? Let me see." Holmwood took the letter from Quincey's trembling hand and read.

Quincey scrabbled through the rest of the stack. "And this one is as well," he said, holding up another.

He could see that Holmwood was just as disturbed as he was. Now he strode to Quincey's side and joined him in ransacking the letters, searching through the signatures.

At last he grabbed one up: "Here's another."

Quincey compared the letter he held with the one in Holmwood's hand. "This one, too. Seward and Basarab were obviously carrying on a correspondence."

Holmwood began sorting them by date. "How could Basarab have known Seward?"

Quincey was dumbfounded. He recalled the voice he had heard through the door the night when he'd first met Basarab in his dressing room. *Mr. Basarab! Save yourself!* It must have been Seward in the hall. The carriage that ran him down was no accident. How much did Basarab know? Had Basarab used Quincey from the very beginning? Whatever the truth was, the answers surely lay in Seward's letters.

By the time the sun set, Holmwood and Quincey had pieced together the jigsaw of correspondence between Basarab and Seward. Quincey pinned one of Seward's letters onto a corkboard.

"According to this letter, Basarab claims he learned of your exploits in Transylvania from the gypsies who survived the battle at Dracula's castle gates. But why contact Seward and no one else?"

Holmwood pinned a second letter to the wall. "By date, this is the next letter. Basarab asks for Seward's help in hunting someone he believed to be Jack the Ripper."

Quincey remembered the old newspaper article pinned to Seward's wall. He searched for the next letter by its corresponding date. Within the envelopes, they had also discovered a number of newspaper clippings in various languages from different countries, all concerning the gruesome murders of women. The dates on these clippings fell within the last ten years. Holmwood spread them out on the table, sorting them, trying to find a pattern. Each illustration depicted gory crime scenes, with women savagely wounded. The similarities to the Ripper murders were obvious.

Holmwood stood up suddenly, as if struck by an epiphany. "It is so clear." He dragged Quincey back to the table, pointing as he explained. "These clippings imply the Ripper murders did not end in 1888. They portray very similar crimes throughout Europe. The Ripper merely left London. For the past twenty-five years, he's been at work in other countries. As long as the Ripper kept moving from city to city, country to country, the different police jurisdictions and language barriers prevented the authorities from putting the pieces together. In each city, from what I am able to translate, there was a series of five or six slayings. In each case, all the victims were prostitutes, and in each instance, the killings would stop suddenly without explanation. Because the Ripper moved on."

Quincey yanked a letter from the corkboard, remembering its particular letterhead: The Moscow Art Theatre. He showed the letter to Holmwood. "This was the first letter from Basarab to Seward, sent when Basarab was in Moscow on the first leg of his tour of *Richard III*." Quincey took another letter from the stack adorned with the Théâtre de L'Odéon letterhead and found the corresponding newspaper clippings. "This one Basarab sent while he was in Paris. Again look. More clippings, more murders. In Paris!"

Quincey looked up at Holmwood, feeling like an eager schoolboy again. "Don't you see? The Ripper has been hacking his way west. Back to England."

"Basarab was using his touring company as cover while he chased the Ripper across Europe."

Quincey was about to say what was on both their minds when Holmwood stopped him: "Don't! We have no proof yet."

"Why else would Basarab contact Seward? Why else would Basarab ask for Seward's help in hunting the Ripper? The Ripper is a vampire. He has to be."

Holmwood went back to the stack of letters and examined them again. "Quincey, we have to be sure. There's no definitive proof in these letters. We need more evidence. The only thing we can be certain of is that Seward was trying to warn us about Jack the Ripper. He died trying to open our deaf ears."

Quincey knew Holmwood was trying to be logical, trying not to jump to conclusions. But to him the answer was clear. "If you refuse to say it, then I will. Jack the Ripper is Dracula. He has to be. '*Vivus est!*' It was written in Seward's blood. Who else could he have been referring to?"

"You're leaping ahead. We still have to ascertain proof of the identity of the Ripper," Holmwood said. "Only then can we be sure that our theory is correct, and only then can we connect all of this to us."

Quincey thought it a waste of valuable time. If Basarab knew Seward and had initiated Seward's quest for Jack the Ripper, then it stood to reason that the Ripper had to be Dracula, and that Basarab knew that, too. Quincey's blood boiled, remembering how Basarab had defended Dracula, going so far as to play the character sympathetically on the stage. But then he had reached out to Seward to hunt Dracula down. Whose side was Basarab on?

Quincey checked the time, then ran to retrieve his coat from the rack, calling back to Holmwood over his shoulder, "You said you were in need of more evidence. Then follow me and let's acquire some."

"From where?"

"I'm late for rehearsal. It's time I confronted my dear mentor. He's done nothing but confuse me, and I will have the truth from him at last."

Holmwood followed Quincey swiftly out the door.

They ran westward. A *Daily Telegraph* newspaper seller barked from the corner of Wellington Street: "France establishes a protectorate over Morocco! Explorers missing in the South Pole! Bram Stoker, manager of the Lyceum Theatre, near death!"

Quincey grabbed a copy of the late edition. He skimmed through the article about Bram Stoker, which merely confirmed that Stoker had suffered a stroke. He crumpled the paper and tossed it away. Useless.

They continued to the Lyceum and were admitted into the theatre by the box office manager, Joseph Hurst. Quincey was about to enter the auditorium when Holmwood stopped him, pointing out the show's lobby card mounted on an easel: NOW IN REHEARSAL: *A TALE OF TERROR—THE GREAT ROMANIAN ACTOR BASARAB—A NEW PLAY BY BRAM STOKER—PRODUCED BY HAMILTON DEANE AND QUINCEY HARKER.* Holmwood looked appalled. "How could you do this to us, knowing what you know? I cannot allow you to make a mockery of Lucy's death and tarnish my name in the process."

"Your name is not in the play."

"What do you mean?"

"Deane felt that, rather than pay three separate actors, it was more economical to merge you, Mr. Morris, and Dr. Seward into one character."

"That is an outrage!"

Quincey shook his head. The aristocracy was certainly eccentric. "Did you not just say you didn't want your name to be tarnished?"

"Quite right," Holmwood sighed.

As if on cue, Deane stepped into the lobby. Surprised to see Quincey, he kept his distance. "Rehearsals were canceled out of respect for Mr. Stoker."

"Why wasn't I aware of this?"

"I wasn't certain I wanted you there."

Quincey shrugged. "Fair enough." He paused, then asked, "Where's Basarab?"

Mention of the actor's name curdled Deane's face. "I told him Mr. Stoker had been sent home from the hospital, and I wanted to visit him to check on his condition. Basarab had the audacity to deny my request and left me with script changes that require me to build part of the set to his exact specifications. My crew will be working around the clock to carry out the reconstruction in time for tomorrow night's rehearsal. Meanwhile, to answer your question, I have no idea where the arrogant bastard is."

Quincey took a step toward him, Deane took a fearful step back, and Quincey felt embarrassed. "I beg your forgiveness, Mr. Deane . . . for everything. I was misled and am ashamed of my earlier behavior toward you. Now, please, I need to speak with Basarab immediately. It's urgent."

Although Deane was visibly relieved by Quincey's apology and polite request, Holmwood could easily detect the tension just under the surface of their exchange. He glanced at Quincey, the question obvious on his face.

Deane said, "Basarab said he wanted to call time for half past six tomorrow night. I can only assume he will return by then."

Quincey extended his hand to Deane, who took it warily. They shook hands and then Quincey and Holmwood departed.

"What the hell was that all about?" Holmwood said. "He seemed frightened of you."

Quincey noted that there was a shading of respect in Arthur's voice. He hated to admit it, but once again Basarab's teachings had proven valuable. He wished he had asked Basarab where he was staying, but it had never occurred to him. Now he would have to pay for his lack of attention to detail. "As frightened as Deane may be of me, he's terrified of Basarab. And now we'll have to wait until tomorrow to see if that fear is justified."

Holmwood was no longer listening, his mind shifting to another thought. "Deane does not concern me or Basarab at the moment. We have a greater problem. We need to discover why Van Helsing attacked you. We need to ascertain what game he's playing at."

Nestled in his hotel room bed, Van Helsing thought of Quincey. Mina Harker's son was a child playing with matches, and he had to ensure the boy would not set the world ablaze. Van Helsing hoped that he had been firm enough to scare the lad back to the Sorbonne. Dracula's blood had flowed through Mina's womb into her son. If Quincey succumbed to the darkness, he could become a powerful enemy. Van Helsing was determined to prevent this from happening: If necessary, he would make good on his threat and kill the boy before allowing him to fall into Dracula's hands.

It was not old age that kept Van Helsing from sleep; it was the endless waiting. He was certain that Dracula knew he was in London. He was an old man and an easy target. Dracula had killed Jack and Jonathan. He wondered when his turn would come.

Van Helsing looked at the weapons displayed on the table across the room. Dracula was not a fool. He had to know Van Helsing would be prepared to do battle with him. His greatest fear, next to death, was Dracula dismissing him as a weak, crazy old man, not worth the effort.

Something brushed against his leg under the covers. A bump appeared under the blanket, slithering across the mattress. Then another. Another. He stared at them, disbelieving. Had his time finally come? When the first bite came, he screamed, but could not move his aching joints quickly enough to leap from the bed. He thrashed in pain as the vicious bites came one after the other. Whatever it was under the blankets converged on him, tearing at his flesh.

Van Helsing threw back the covers to find a swarm of squealing, filthy rats tearing at his skin, gouging out bloody chunks. They crawled all over his body. He kicked and howled, slapping the rats away. A white rat, its red eyes glowing, teeth bared, ran up his chest, aiming for his neck. He grabbed the verminous creature and flung it across the room, where it smashed against the wall, exploding in a spray of blood.

At last the old man found the strength to lunge off the bed, but the fright and adrenaline were too much for him. His heart seized. He gripped his chest and fell to the floor. The pain was so immense that his jaw clenched. He could no longer even scream. Van Helsing reached for his pillbox on the nightstand. A new wave of torment overwhelmed him and he fell back. The Reaper's grip was strong this time.

After untold minutes, the old man noticed that the rats had disappeared. That there were no bites on his legs. But the shadows in his room were still moving; and now he knew that the rats had been merely a prelude.

For a moment, through his pain, Van Helsing felt a dark joy. At last, the final battle had come. Marshaling his strength, he lurched toward the nightstand, knocking over his spectacles as he reached out again for his pillbox. The shadows now coalesced and rose up in a spiraling tornado and splintered the nightstand. The pillbox fell to the floor. The deafening howls of wolves emanated from all around Van Helsing, seeming to come from everywhere and nowhere at the same time.

Van Helsing faced what might well become the final decision of his life: *The pillbox or the weapons, which to retrieve first?*

The dark shadow had almost reached the ceiling as it began to fill out into a three-dimensional form, a figure slowly becoming clear within the shadow's opaque envelope. Van Helsing was running out of time. With the last of his strength, he made his decision. Bracing his hands against the bed behind him, he pushed himself forward, flinging himself toward the weapon-covered table. If he was going to die, he would take his demon with him.

The figure in the shadow had taken on human form. Van Helsing's hand was inches away from the loaded and ready crossbow on the table. Before he could grasp the handle, a shadowy arm lashed out and flipped the table into the air. The weapons scattered out of Van Helsing's reach.

It was over. The old man rolled onto his back, awaiting the end. He had nothing left. His once-mighty heart had surrendered long before his will.

The howling grew louder as the shadow fell across Van Helsing.

"Forgive me, my friends," he whispered. "I have failed you."

The howls came to a crescendo, as if saluting their master's victory. The shadowy attacker lunged forward and Van Helsing screamed. He hoped his heart would stop in time to spare him the pain, but in the end, the Reaper was as sadistic as he was cruel. Van Helsing was still alive as he felt the fangs tear into his neck.

CHAPTER XXXVI.

—◆—

Mina desperately needed to find Quincey. All of her telegrams to Professor Van Helsing had gone unanswered. It was now very possible that she was alone in her quest. Quincey was out there somewhere exposed, vulnerable. And Bathory was far more sinister a force than she had ever faced.

Taking the iron key that she had kept hidden in her dressing table, she hurried down to the cellar to the room adjacent to the cold storage. Mina inserted the key into the rusted lock and tried to turn it. Because she had not wanted Quincey to find the contents of this room, the lock had not been opened in twenty-five years and it resisted her attentions stubbornly. Mina tried again with more determination. Still the key would not turn. *Damn it to hell!* With that outburst of frustration came a loud crack. The door came open. Mina was taken aback to see that the door frame surrounding the lock was now broken. At first frightened by her apparent strength, she quickly realized that the wood had been rotted away by damp.

Picking up the lantern she had brought down with her, Mina ventured into the dark room. On the shelf, alongside moldy, forgotten keepsakes, was the old box that she and Jonathan had once carried into battle in Transylvania. After witnessing the decay of the door frame, she should not have been surprised to see the sad state of the old wooden box. Her heart sank as she pried the lid open. The Bible was water-logged; the garlic and wolfbane were rotted and putrid; the contents of the bottles had long evaporated; the knives had rusted; the mallet and wooden stakes adorned with golden crosses were cracked or crumbling. They had once entrusted their lives to the contents of this box. It was now as close to extinction as the brave band of heroes.

Mina rushed back up to the study to retrieve the only remaining weapon of any use left in the house. Physically, she was no match for Bathory. She would need a sturdy weapon if she and Quincey were to have any chance against her at all. Her hand clasped the katana, the engraved, ceremonial Japanese sword that Jonathan had received as a gift from his clients.

JONATHAN HARKER
The Anglo-Japanese Alliance
January 30, 1902

In her rush, Mina unsheathed the katana carelessly, yanking her hand back and hitting her elbow on the mahogany bookshelves behind her. Wincing in pain, she dropped the blade instinctively.

Crack.

Mina turned to see that her elbow had smashed through the edge of the hardwood shelves. She rolled up her sleeve and examined her arm. There was very little pain, but the wound was already swelling, black and blue. She looked down at the cut in her hand. Her skin was sliced open and there was a steady stream of blood. But again, there was very little pain.

Strength. Could Dracula's blood be empowering her? After all these years? Was this Bathory's blood at work? What irony that Bathory would give Mina the power to make the inevitable fight between them more interesting.

She looked about and saw the decorative glass paperweight on the corner of the desk. She picked it up and squeezed. Nothing.

She tried again with all her might. Still nothing. Could the shelf have been a fluke? *Blast!*

Mina slammed the globe onto the desk, once again in frustration. To her amazement, the globe smashed into pieces. Mina opened her hand. There were blood-covered shards of glass protruding from the flesh of her palm. But again she felt very little pain.

For the first time in weeks, Mina smiled.

Why had this power never revealed itself before? It occurred to Mina that she had never before been prone to extreme outbursts of anger. Yet, now when she needed strength most, it was here. Whatever the reason, she had to be certain how to call on her newfound strength if it was to be an effective weapon against Bathory.

Mina positioned her hands on either side of the great oak desk, recalling the two bull-sized moving men who had strained to carry it into the house. She took a deep breath and tried to lift it. Her arms shook, but the mammoth desk would not budge.

Closing her eyes, she pictured Bathory, thinking of how the vile creature had entered her home and violated her. Her anger grew, but the desk refused to move. *Suffer the little children to come unto me.* Mina pushed off the desk to turn away. There was a loud screech as the desk slid away from her on the hardwood floor. She stared after it, puzzled. She needed to work out how to summon this strength quickly. She needed to be able to command it.

Mina's thoughts were interrupted by a sharp knock on the study door.

"Begging your pardon, madam," Manning said from outside the study, "but there is a gentleman at the front door who wishes to speak with you."

Mina had to be on the next train to London to find Quincey: He couldn't go unprotected for one more night. She had no time for empty condolence visits. "I'm dreadfully sorry, Manning, but I'll have to ask you to send him away. Tell him I'm not up to company as yet. I'm certain he'll understand."

"I had told him that you did not wish to be disturbed, but he gave me his card and insisted that you would make an allowance for him."

Not wanting Manning to see the mess she had made in the study, Mina cracked opened the door and took the small, ivory card. She nearly dropped it at the sight of the name inscribed upon it.

"Shall I send him away?" Manning asked.

"No." Mina knew if he was here, this visit was of the utmost importance. Her eyes darted to her bloody hand. *He can't know about any of this.* "Show him to the sitting room. Have him wait for me while I make myself presentable. I shall meet with him there."

Lord Godalming, Arthur Holmwood, had watched Quincey walk away. It was just as well that the young man had asked to be alone. He needed some time to digest the information they'd obtained from Seward's flat. Could Dracula really have been Jack the Ripper? Holmwood barely recalled the autumn of 1888, when London had been in the grip of terror. He had been immersed in his own fears, with his father and Lucy both struggling with failing health. He could not bring himself to believe that their enemy was still somehow alive. How could it be? Then there were the present-day Ripper-style murders throughout Eastern Europe, which could not be so easily dismissed as coincidence. He could not argue with Quincey's theory, nor think of anyone else but Dracula who could have killed Jonathan by impalement in the middle of Piccadilly without effort or witness. If Dracula had indeed returned to England, they were all in grave danger. Everyone had to be warned. Even so, he was reluctant to contact Mina Harker. Dracula might have come to take his revenge on her; or Mina might finally have succumbed to his charms now that she was no longer bound by her matrimonial oath. Her mind had always been a puzzle of contradictions. Holmwood could not hazard a guess at what her reaction would be to the news that Dracula was still alive. Despite his concerns, he decided to do the most honorable thing. Mina had to be given all the facts, and what she chose to do with that information was up to her. Unfortunately, he would have to share the consequences of Mina's choice.

The manservant took Arthur Holmwood's coat and led him into the sitting room.

"Would his lordship care for a drink?" asked the elderly butler.

"No, thank you."

Holmwood was distracted by the photographs on the mantelpiece,

most notably the picture of the Harker family taken during some distant
Christmas when Quincey was a small boy. His rage began to boil again
as he compared his losses. He had lost Lucy, and any chance of happiness in his life. In contrast, after their ordeal in Transylvania, Mina had
been able to resume some semblance of normalcy, to live with the man
she loved, raise a child, have a family. His eyes drifted to a framed photograph of Lucy and Mina. It was sacrilege for it to be there. After all,
Jonathan and his law firm had arranged to bring Dracula to England.
And, inadvertently or not, Mina had led the demon to his Lucy. He'd
driven a stake through his own beloved's heart. Mina had bedded the
demon that destroyed Lucy. How dare she display that portrait! He was
full of resentment, and the rage threatened to boil over. When the door
opened behind him, he spun around, ready to unleash his anger upon
Mina when she walked into the room. But when he saw her, he was
frozen speechless. It was as if he had stepped back in time. Despite the
years that had passed, Mina looked exactly as she had when he last had
seen her. For a brief moment, Holmwood half expected Lucy to trail
into the room behind Mina as she always had before. . . . The memory
of a skeletal Lucy in the crime scene photograph returned to him shockingly. Lucy was dead: She had rotted away like his heart. It was little
wonder Jonathan Harker had fallen to drink, having to live with a
woman who was a constant reminder of their shared tragedy.

Jolted back into the present, he noticed Mina Harker's black mourning dress, an old woman's finery. At least she had the good sense to be
ashamed of herself.

"Time has been good to you, Mrs. Harker," he said, making little
attempt to hide the sarcasm in his voice.

"I see you have not changed, either, Lord Godalming," Mina replied
in kind.

"Believe me, it is with little joy that I return here."

"If you've come out of obligation of duty to express your condolences,
consider it done and you are free to take your leave." Mina turned to
walk right back out the door.

"Wait."

She hesitated.

Knowing that challenging Mina head-on was a sure way of alienating such a stubborn woman, he moderated his tone. "I have come here to warn you. As unbelievable as it may sound, I have reason to believe that that which we once thought dead and buried may yet be undead."

Mina merely cocked her head to one side, without a trace of the shock he expected.

"Dear Arthur, always struggling to do what's right, even though your stomach may turn at the action."

What game was she playing? "Do not treat me like Jack Seward. You know I'm not given to wild theories," he said.

"I know you still hate me. I hear it in your voice. That is your right. But do not distrust me. Remember, it was I who led you to Dracula. I upheld my oath."

"That is the only reason I am here. I am guilty of many things, Mina. But the guilt of dismissing Jack's warnings as the ravings of a madman is what I am most ashamed of now." He produced a clipping he had taken from the collection of letters and thrust it toward Mina, only now noticing the bandage on her hand as she took the piece of paper. "What happened?"

"I broke a glass," she said quickly, turning her attention to the newspaper clipping. After a moment she looked up, puzzled. "This is about Jack the Ripper."

"Look at the details of the murders. The first in London took place on August thirty-first, 1888. Only a week after the *Demeter* foundered upon the shores of Whitby. The last recorded murder took place on November ninth, 1888, the day before Dracula eluded our capture by retreating back to Transylvania."

Mina listened, unmoving.

Holmwood brought out Seward's letters. "Jack believed the Ripper was a vampire," he said. "He was willing to risk his life to prove it to us, and the Ripper killed him for it. That is the mystery of his death. Forget what your eyes told you. Leave out emotion. Cold logic tells us the evidence clearly points to Dracula and Jack the Ripper being one and the same."

Mina laughed. "Oh, Arthur, you were always the bravest of us all. But you were wise to leave the thinking to Van Helsing."

His fists clenched, crushing the letters. "I come here to warn you that your life may be in danger, and you mock me?" Even as he said it, it occurred to him that this might be her ploy to throw him off the scent and protect Dracula. For all he knew, she might have been preparing to join her lover at this very moment.

As if Mina could read his thoughts, her mirth vanished, and she became deadly serious. "There is a vampire here in London. But it is not Dracula."

Holmwood rocked back on his heels. *Another vampire?* "There is no time for games. Lives are in danger."

"I was attacked in my house. I could have been killed."

"I see that you survived and the house seems to be in perfect order. What did this vicious vampire do? Throw a glass at you and leave?"

Mina's eyes narrowed. "I've listened to your theories. Now listen to mine. Have you ever heard of the Hungarian countess Elizabeth Bathory?"

"No, should I have?"

"Three hundred years ago, Elizabeth Bathory raped and butchered six hundred and fifty peasant girls and bathed in their blood. She believed it preserved her youth. Does that not describe a vampire in a cold historical analysis? And if Jack's assumptions were correct, does this not describe the crimes of Jack the Ripper as well?"

"Preposterous. Everyone knows that Jack the Ripper must have been a man. You cannot convince me that a member of the fairer sex is capable of such horrific crimes."

"Your prejudices blind you. The Ripper was never caught. Why should it not be a woman?"

"A black widow. How interesting," Holmwood mused aloud. Still, he wondered if Mina was hiding something. "Jonathan was impaled. Unless this countess was also called Impaler, I don't see the connection."

"It could be a clever ruse by Bathory to deceive us into thinking that Dracula is still alive."

He was not convinced. "Let us assume, for argument's sake, that you are correct and that there was a Countess Bathory, and she was indeed Jack the Ripper. Again, what is her connection to us? Why would she want us dead? It makes no sense."

Mina opened a leather-bound book to the illustrated family tree and handed it to him. She traced her finger from Elizabeth Bathory's name to Vlad Dracula III.

She saw no point in telling him the whole truth, wagering that this one point would be sufficient. "Dracula and Bathory were related by familial blood. They were cousins."

Arthur Holmwood felt the lightning strike of understanding hit him between the eyes. "She has come to avenge his death."

It was as if the universe had fallen into perfect order. Everything made sense. It didn't matter what Mina thought of Dracula, or what her desires were toward him. Bathory would blame them all equally for her cousin's death. This fact, in conjunction with what he had learned from Seward's letters to Basarab, convinced him that he and Mina were sinking in the same boat. He no longer had any choice but to trust her, with great caution, of course. "We must contact Van Helsing at once," he said.

"I have already tried. He hasn't responded to any of my telegrams."

Holmwood was about to tell Mina that Van Helsing had confronted Quincey, when a new, sickening revelation sprang into his mind. "Basarab!"

Mina's face went ashen. "What did you say?"

He thrust the letters into her hand, pointing out the signatures. "Jack Seward was working with Basarab to find the Ripper."

"If Bathory knew about Seward and killed him," Mina exclaimed as she read the signature on the letter, "then she would know about Basarab as well!"

The look of panic on her face almost made him feel sympathy for her. Once again, his sense of honor pushed him into action. "Quincey is planning to confront Basarab during his rehearsal at half past six tonight, at the Lyceum."

Mina gasped audibly as she turned to look at the clock on the mantel. "There is a train leaving Exeter in twenty minutes. It would get us to Waterloo station at ten past six. We have no time to waste: Quincey is in great danger."

She ran up the stairs as Holmwood walked into the hall to retrieve his hat, coat, and walking stick.

Mina returned carrying her handbag while wrapping something in her shawl that looked like a sheathed sword. "What are you gawking at? As you well know, I can fight my own battles."

Arthur Holmwood found this last remark to be most unbecoming. Mina had never quite conformed to the proper womanly role: She was in no way what he would describe as "delicately feminine." Never was there a woman more damned confounding. Who knew what was going on inside her head? He believed Mina up to a point. She sounded convincing; yet, other than her bandaged hand, there was not a mark on her. If this Countess Bathory had attacked her, how much of a fight could there have truly been? The alternative was too terrible to believe, that this might all be an elaborate plan: Dracula and Mina conspiring together in order to lure him into a trap.

He would ensure he never turned his back on Mina Harker. In any case, he wanted to talk to this Basarab fellow himself.

As they opened the front door, Manning tried to intercept Mina. "Madam, I'm glad I caught you. This telegram just arrived. More condolences . . ."

"Thank you, Manning," Mina said, taking the telegram in midstride. Shoving it into her handbag, she sailed out the door.

CHAPTER XXXVII.

A gaseous wave formed in the pit of Hamilton Deane's stomach, exploding out of his mouth as an echoing belch. A nearby crew member arched an eyebrow.

Deane had been experiencing abdominal distress since Stoker's stroke, and his attempts to deal with the ongoing issues with the production left him precious little time to seek out something to quell his stress-induced discomfort. The more precarious the situation, the more his gut churned.

Deane knew entirely too well that he stood upon shaky ground. He did not actually have the rights to produce *Dracula*. Should Stoker succumb to his illness, Deane would have to negotiate the rights from the sour Mrs. Stoker. He shuddered at the very thought. Deane had investors to please, and there were already plenty of other problems, too.

Basarab had made further demands to demolish the traditional drawing room set in favor of a movable, multilevel structure that could be transformed from the castle in Transylvania to the Whitby Asylum and then to Carfax Abbey. Because of this, the master carpenter had resigned in disgust. Deane had been left to oversee the workers himself. With Stoker bedridden, the play had no director, and Deane assumed that he would have to act in Stoker's stead. Basarab had other plans, however, taking over the directing without even consulting him. Deane was furious, but he dared not confront the eccentric Romanian. He did not care to end up like Stoker.

Disheveled, tired, and hungry, Deane's head and stomach swirled from the stress. He was less than an hour from the first rehearsal and there was still so much yet to do. With every turn, someone wanted his attention. The wardrobe mistress emerged from Basarab's dressing room in tears, investors clamored for hourly updates, journalists were looking for interviews, and there was an infestation of fans sneaking past the guard in the hope of glimpsing Basarab. Working in the theatre was not as glamorous as Deane had thought it would be when he'd made his ill-fated investment with Stoker.

By six o'clock, most of the cast were already at the theatre, half an hour before their required call time. This was not unusual for the first rehearsal, as the novelty of a fresh production was very exciting. The actors fell into noisy groups, chatting and gossiping while they waited to take their places on the stage.

Meanwhile, Deane was trying to carry on a conversation with the lighting designer. Deane could barely hear himself speak, let alone understand a word from the Scottish designer up in the booth at the back of the theatre, playing with his new electric toys. The Scot was trying to use his new Kliegl No. 5 to simulate moonlight in Transylvania, a scene from Act One. Deane felt that there was entirely too much illumination for a gothic nighttime scene and was trying to persuade the designer to dim the lights. The designer nodded; but as Deane watched from center stage, the light grew in intensity. So did the smoldering in his gut.

"Not brighter, you half-wit!" he bellowed over the actors' conversation. All eyes turned to him. He felt the rumblings in the pit of his stomach again as he realized he had just cast himself as the production's villain. His brain scrambled for a way to turn his outburst into a light-hearted joke, but he thought better of it. He had learned from the incident with Quincey Harker that fear was better than respect. The designer hurried to carry out Deane's orders, but in his haste, he mistakenly turned the set blue.

"Blue?! No, no, no! More red! How many times do I have to tell you? This is where Prince Dracula tells of his heroic days of war!"

A collective gasp went up from the actors behind him.

A voice asked: "And what do you know of the war, Mr. Deane?"

Deane was startled. He realized the gasp was not a result of the actors' fear of his wrath, but of Basarab's appearance.

All voices were silenced; all eyes and ears focused on Basarab. The entire cast and crew was rapt, waiting for his next word, like disciples listening to Christ's sermon on the mount. Basarab indeed cut an impressive figure. He was dressed in a black-and-gold satin robe with a flowing train, and he brandished a broadsword, holding the heavy steel weapon easily, as if it were an extension of his arm. The blade glinted in the spotlights.

Deane was the acting manager, producer, and—for the time being—director of the production, Basarab was an unwelcome guest on the stage at this point and time. He answered with new hatred, "What do I know of war? Obviously, not as much as you."

The tip of Basarab's sword was suddenly at his throat, silencing him. For safety, actors traditionally carried dull wooden swords on stage. But this blade was real: Its sharpened steel pressed against Deane's neck.

"Battle, Mr. Deane, cannot be re-created on a stage by changing the color of the lights," Basarab said. His cool words belied an undercurrent of fury. "A naked blade clenched in your fist, the bloodlust welling up within you as you take your enemy's life. *That* is combat. Battle is an art form unto itself. One that is sorely missed in these modern days."

His anger subsided, to be replaced with a look of melancholy, and it occurred to Deane that Basarab truly believed the rubbish he was spewing.

Basarab let the sword drop to his side. Deane's hands came up instinctively to his throat, checking for blood, finding none. Had Deane been lucky, or was Basarab really so skillful with a blade? Either way, the actor was clearly insane.

The doors to the theatre's Grand Circle exploded open, their boom echoing up to the cathedral-like ceiling. Everyone in the auditorium turned to see who had entered with such force. Deane shielded his eyes from the harsh stage lights to get a better look at the intruder. *How dare this man so brazenly interrupt my rehearsal!* he thought furiously.

But as the intruder emerged into the glow of the houselights, Deane realized it wasn't a man, but a woman. She was striking. Her coal black hair contrasted with her lily-white complexion. Her svelte body was clad in a perfectly tailored suit. Deane was flabbergasted by the vulgarity of a woman wearing trousers.

The woman clapped as she strolled down the aisle, mocking them. "Bravo! Oh, bravo! The power of your performances has grown Shakespearean in its mightiness."

The intruder tipped her top hat to a group of young actresses, smiling with a suggestive wink. "Good evening, ladies."

Deane had reached his limits. He may have been too weak to subdue Basarab, but he would be damned if he was going to let this woman's insolence go unchecked. He stalked toward the intruder. "Excuse me, I don't know who the hell you think you are, but this is a private rehearsal—"

Lightning fast, Basarab thrust his sword to block Deane from advancing farther. He whispered, "For your own safety, Mr. Deane, I caution you not to speak another word."

Deane met the woman's eyes. She leered at him, turning his blood to ice. He turned back to Basarab. There was a sincerity in Basarab's countenance that Deane had never seen before, confusing him even more.

Basarab faced the woman, his face like stone. She gave him a vicious sneer.

Deane sensed these two had a history, and a very unpleasant one at that.

"Countess, I have been expecting you," Basarab said.

"The old adage seems to be true," she said coyly, advancing toward the stage, her walking stick striking the floor like a dagger. She shook her head at Basarab as if she could not believe what she was seeing. "Time truly does seem to heal all wounds."

"Some wounds are much too deep to heal." Deane heard a deep anger in Basarab's voice.

The woman broke into a fit of laughter. No mockery, this, but true amusement. "Do you never grow weary of your simplistic little wordplay?"

Basarab brandished his sword. "Perhaps you would prefer something more sportive?"

The woman went rigid, like a viper ready to strike. "Why not?" she purred. Her eyes widened, gleaming in anticipation of the contest that was about to begin. "Swordplay is so much more . . . interesting."

At a brief stop in Salisbury, Arthur Holmwood dashed off the train onto the platform to one of the new telephone kiosks and paid the attendant to dial his home number in London. The first train whistle blew. Once connected, the attendant handed the receiver to him, allowing him to seek his privacy in the wooden telephone cabinet.

"All aboard!" the conductor cried.

Holmwood quickly told his butler, Wentworth, to make sure that his coach be waiting for him at Waterloo station at ten past six, the scheduled arrival time. "Do not be late!"

The final train whistle sounded. Not bothering to tip the attendant or replace the receiver in its cradle, Holmwood raced to the train as it lurched forward, bound for London. He got aboard just as it pulled away.

Unfortunately, due to a slow herd of sheep outside Basingstoke, the locomotive pulled into Waterloo station at a quarter past six. To add further frustration, over the last twelve years, the station had been in a never-ending state of remodeling, and the grand entrance on the northeast corner was barricaded. Arthur and Mina were forced to detour to the south, backtracking to where the Holmwood coach stood waiting. Time was not on their side. Quincey would be arriving at the Lyceum Theatre in five minutes for his rehearsal, and they were still at least ten minutes away.

Despite the urgency, Holmwood's manners were impeccable. He held the door to the coach open for Mina, offering her his hand. She refused his assistance and attempted to climb into the carriage on her own. He should have remembered that she perceived chivalry as an insult to her independence. Stepping on the hem of her skirt, Mina stumbled and the shawl-wrapped item and her handbag slipped off her shoulder and dropped to the ground with a clatter. Her purse, keys, and the unopened telegram she had taken from her servant spilled out of the bag. Holmwood allowed himself a tiny smile. *Serves her right.* Mina turned back to retrieve her things, but Holmwood, annoyed, took her by the waist and shoved her into the coach. Time was passing. He retrieved the handbag and fallen items, puzzling over the thing wrapped in the shawl, and hurried into the coach.

"Driver! At a gallop, if you please," Arthur bellowed.

To his dismay, he found Mina sitting in the rear seat of the carriage, forcing him to take the front. *Damn this woman!* It was common knowledge in polite society that a woman should never take the rear seat. Furthermore, he loathed sitting backward while the carriage was in motion.

The coach sped away, but not quickly enough to sate his impatience. He leaned out of the window and banged on the roof of the carriage with his walking stick. "Faster, man! Faster!"

"Arthur, relax. We need our wits."

He was offended at her tone. Mina sounded as if she were talking to a child who'd eaten too many sweets. As a show of his anger, Holmwood thrust the items he had retrieved at her.

Mina, perhaps for the first time in her life, thought better of opening her mouth. Instead, she chose avoidance. She took the things from him and placed them on the seat beside her; then, turning away from him, she tore open the telegram as an excuse to ignore him.

She gasped and looked up at him, sheer panic on her face, tears in her eyes. Her mouth opened, but no sound emerged.

In all the years he had known Mina, this was first time Holmwood had seen her at a complete loss for words.

At last, she said softly, "Van Helsing is here in London. He claims he was attacked in his hotel room by . . ." She stopped, struggling with the words.

"Who, damn you?"

"*Dracula.*"

"I knew it!" Holmwood snatched the telegram from Mina, needing to read the words with his own eyes. He had wanted proof. Now he had it.

"Van Helsing requests we come at once," Mina muttered, her face blank. Her hands were frozen in place as if she still held the telegram.

Time had stopped for Arthur Holmwood. In an instant, everything he knew or thought he knew had melted away as he experienced true fear for the first time in twenty-five years. But he also felt elation. Lucy was no longer so far away. Blood and death were in the offing, and he welcomed it. In war, the world was simple. Right or wrong, black or white. Live or die. In peace, he was lost in a sea of gray. Now it was time for war. Arthur Holmwood thrust his head out of the carriage window and growled at the driver, "Faster!"

He fell back into his seat with a wild smile of satisfaction. It was obvious that Mina did not share his enthusiasm but was lost in deep thought, clearly troubled. He tried to understand what must be swirling in Mina's mind. Dracula was alive. It was more than likely that he was the one who had impaled Jonathan. She had once been seduced by Dracula's charms, and now she was faced with the knowledge that he must have murdered her husband. Then there was Bathory, whom Mina claimed to be the true enemy. Were Dracula and Bathory working together? Did Bathory even exist? There were only questions, and only one certainty—that death was waiting for them.

With Seward's journals and a bundle of evidence in his arms, Inspector Cotford stormed past the rows of bored inspectors and constables at their desks. Cotford knew he was huffing and puffing, stamping his feet down like an angry child. He did not care. He had a right to be angry. His theories had been summarily dismissed and his integrity had been challenged, as well as his sanity. No one bothered to glance his way. None of them cared about old cases, or his need to challenge the system.

Cotford slammed the stack onto his desk. *He* cared, and thus was cursed. "Damned, gutless, spineless potato heads. 'Why dredge up the past, especially because of some outlandish theories?' they say!"

Popping the top off of his silver flask, Cotford cooled his fury with several gulps of whisky. Only then did the others notice him. There was old, fat, mad Cotford, breaking yet another rule by drinking on duty.

Lee came to his side and rested a hand on the flask, preventing Cotford from taking another swig. "Inspector, a little discretion, if you please."

"The Crown Prosecution Service refused to issue an arrest warrant for Van Helsing or Godalming!" Cotford fumed. "'The writings of a morphine-addicted lunatic are not sufficient evidence,' they say."

Lee stared at him for a long moment. He had said he would follow Cotford so long as he was right. The Scotland Yard brass had made it clear that they did not think Cotford was right. Undoubtedly, Huntley would be making an official statement. Not only had Cotford further ruined his own career, but he likely also hampered Lee's potential.

"I'm going home, sir," Lee bluntly replied. "I must speak with my wife. I have the feeling that the repercussions of our misadventure will be swift and harsh."

Cotford slumped into his chair, trying to assess the ruin surrounding him. He could see the writing on the wall. This latest folly would dredge up the past and no doubt make the newspapers. His superiors would berate him for soiling the reputation of the Yard, yet again. Forced retirement was inevitable.

"Bugger them!" Cotford said, reaching again for his silver flask.

"I almost forgot," Lee said, voice cold. He withdrew an envelope from his pocket. It was inscribed with red ink. "This arrived for you in the morning post."

He handed Cotford the envelope and left the office.

"A love letter from a secret admirer, no doubt," Cotford said sarcastically.

The constables and inspectors turned away and went back to their work. Cotford tore open the envelope and unfolded the letter inside. Even before reading a single word, he recognized the bloody scrawl, and suddenly he was plummeting twenty-five years into the past. His heart raced. *By God, he was right!*

Cotford leapt from his chair and ran out of the room, screaming

Lee's name. He caught the sergeant halfway down the stairs, so excited he could barely draw a breath to get the words out.

"It's from him! Twenty-five years ago, he wrote letters. Taunting Abberline. Taunting me. He even sent a letter once smeared with blood from one of his victim's kidneys." Cotford held up the envelope. "It's the same handwriting, signed and addressed the same way. It's him! We've done it, Sergeant! We've drawn the bastard out!"

Lee responded by giving him a strange look.

Cotford was smiling so widely that his grin almost split his face in two. He shoved the letter at Lee. "Don't just stare at me! Read it!"

Lee obliged carefully. "It's probably a prankster who knew of the Ripper's original letters," he said. "A copycat."

Lee was performing his due diligence, but Cotford was prepared. "Not possible. Our current investigation has not yet made it to the press. I only revealed it to the Crown Prosecution Service this morning. This letter was sent days ago, according to the postmark."

Lee's skeptical demeanor changed slightly. The inspector had a point.

He read the letter:

> Dear Boss,
>
> The Answers You Seek Are Held By Quincey Harker. Find Him Wednesday Night At The Lyceum Theatre And All Shall Be Revealed.
>
> Yours Truly,
> From Hell

Lee looked from the letter to Cotford. "That's tonight!"

Cotford smiled again. His partner was back. He wasn't sure what game the Ripper was playing at, but he was making contact for the first time in a quarter of a century. This time, Cotford was not going to trip up. The Ripper would not outrun him. One way or another, he was going to end this tonight.

"Sergeant Lee, gather your men."

CHAPTER XXXVIII.

T he backstage storage space was the perfect setting for an endgame. It was a dimly lit labyrinth of costumes, set pieces, and backdrops. There were no electric lights in that part of the theatre—the crew had no need for such luxuries. Gas lamps hissed in the four corners, casting long and wavering shadows.

Bathory laughed to herself as she waited in the dark for Basarab. He was so predicable; he still thought God was on his side. She watched as he moved straight ahead, the broadsword held before him. He was not afraid, which was his folly. Basarab didn't seem to understand that God never rewarded loyalty. *Yes, come to me and die.*

Bathory enjoyed the cat-and-mouse game. She could see Basarab's eyes seeking her out through the costumes hanging on the rack. He was no match for her. No man ever was. Even God couldn't destroy her, so how could Basarab?

Basarab lashed out, knocking down one of the costume racks. He thrust out the sword, but Bathory, with her preternatural speed, had already moved on.

"If you are so powerful, come out and face me, you witch!" Basarab roared.

Bathory wanted to savor the moment. It was not time yet. There were many debts to be repaid before this game was over. "It was you who sought me out," she taunted, unseen in the shadows. "Everything you do is so predictable. You're led by your vanity, your arrogance. You honestly believe after all you've done that God is still on your side."

Basarab stalked Bathory through the maze, biding his time, waiting for the opportune moment to corner her and strike.

"I thought I could save you. To bring you back from the darkness of your own making."

Bathory stopped. She raised her head so that she could be seen through one of the shelves. "You vowed to be my companion. To stand by my side."

She watched Basarab flinch. The pain of the past was still throbbing in the present. Basarab spoke with such morose sincerity that Bathory almost believed him when he said, "Yes, there was a time I was foolish enough to think we could join forces as companions. I even felt love for you once."

"You knew we could never be."

"It was your choice to sin against the laws of God and man," Basarab said.

"Ah, that's why you tried to kill me." With that, Bathory crept back into the shadows. Her game entered the final round.

Basarab raised his sword and splintered the wooden shelf where her head had been just seconds before. He raged forward, knocking down shelves, spilling the props as he advanced. "When I saw the evil that rots your soul, you left me no choice!"

Bathory stepped from behind one of the costume racks, facing Basarab from the opposite side of the room. Basarab spun, broadsword at the ready. He expected her to attack, but she was not ready to make her move yet. This game was too delicious to end before its time.

"Your God took away all that I held dear. His followers persecuted me for feelings I could not control. I have no choice but to take revenge on God and his children. Step aside."

Basarab let the sword drop to his side, an offering of peace. "Leave this place. Bother Quincey and his family and friends no more." He drew close to her.

Bathory stepped back and whispered from the shadows, "When you seduced Seward and his friends into crossing my path, you should have known the way would be paved in their blood." Ever the gamesman, Bathory backed into a corner lit by a lantern. She sucked in her breath, contracting her inner organs, forcing blood to ooze from her pores. She could see Basarab was confused. Why had she backed herself into a corner? Why was she showing fear? Basarab decided to take a chance. He puffed himself up and cried out, "End your mindless killing or I will destroy you!"

"You once faked your own death to escape my wrath!" Bathory smiled. It was time to pay her debt in full. The game was over. "Now your folly will become fact."

Basarab's compassion for her was the trap; she saw the panic in his eyes as he realized he had been ensnared. She might have been backed into a corner, but he was the one who would die.

It took only an instant, but for Basarab it must have been an eternity. Bathory's eyes went black. She snarled like a beast as she curled her lips, revealing her fangs. Basarab swung his sword, but he was far too slow. Bathory was already flying through the air, her hand reaching out for the burning lantern as she leapt upward. As she soared over Basarab's head, the lantern smashed onto the floor. She landed in safety behind Basarab as flames ignited at his feet. The train of the satin robe Basarab wore became a flaming torch. He thrashed and screamed as the robe was engulfed in fire, his struggles sending sparks flying about the room. The hanging costumes caught fire and began to burn. Within seconds, the entire room was ablaze. Basarab fell to the floor, screaming and desperately trying to quell the flames.

Bathory laughed. Then she calmly opened the door and left her past behind to burn.

Arthur Holmwood sighed. His associates on the London City Council had approached him years ago for a private donation to rebuild the Waterloo Bridge. Its Cornish granite was deteriorating, and it was plagued with several structural flaws. At the time, he could see no profit in financing such an endeavor. He'd dismissed the council's request, recommending that the bridge repair be financed through public funds. But with an already overtaxed population and a poorly funded Metropolitan Board of Works, there was no choice but to close down the bridge from time to time to make stopgap repairs. Today was one of those times. As Arthur inched along in the carriage with Mina, it was infuriating to know that the Lyceum Theatre was a mere pace away from the opposite end of Waterloo Bridge, and that their carriage, along with the throngs of others and hundreds of people, were forced to reroute over the Westminster Bridge.

Once they crossed the Westminster Bridge, the driver diverted along Victoria Embankment and veered back toward the Lyceum Theatre. Savoy Street, the adjoining street that would take them closest to their destination, had recently become a one-way going in the opposite direction. The carriage now had to continue eastward under the Waterloo Bridge, past King's College, to find a side street to take them northward to the Strand. What should have been a ten-minute drive from Waterloo became a desperate half-hour frustration. Even Mina's calm demeanor cracked under the pressure. Quincey would arrive for rehearsal, and they would be too late.

As the carriage raced toward the Lyceum, a low, distant din grew to a roar. Something was afoot. The street appeared empty, yet both Mina and Arthur could hear a commotion close by. It was probably another traffic snarl-up, but they had no choice but to plow ahead. Holmwood again slammed the walking stick into the ceiling of the carriage. In response, the driver slapped the reins on the horses' backs. The increase in speed did nothing to relieve the tension in Mina's face.

They reached the corner of Wellington Street, when a driverless black carriage bolted across their path.

Their driver pulled back on the reins with all his strength, and the stallions screamed. The carriages collided. Holmwood's driver was thrown through the air as the carriage tumbled end over end.

Inside the carriage, the last thing Arthur Holmwood remembered was hearing something crack. Then blackness.

· · ·

Pedestrians on Wellington Street carried water back and forth. Bells clanged in the distance. Carriages tried to race through the street, clambering to escape, held back by the throngs. Screams and black ash filled the sky.

Quincey burst through the crowd of onlookers and saw the Lyceum Theatre belching black smoke. Flames whipped from its windows. A section of the roof collapsed with a sickening crash. The huge fire illuminated the London nighttime sky with a devilish, red-and-orange hue. Actors and crew crawled from the smoking theatre, coughing and gasping for air, black soot covering their faces, their clothes singed. Some were badly burned, their reddened skin already peeling back like pages in a book. One woman's hair had caught fire, leaving the top of her head bald and blistered. The air had become tinged with the nauseating smell of ash and burned flesh. Quincey was dumbfounded. Then he saw the lanky figure of Hamilton Deane stumble out of the curtain of smoke. Quincey rushed to his side and took hold of him roughly. "Deane! What happened?"

Deane hacked in answer: "A woman arrived, some countess . . . Basarab left the stage with her . . . then . . . flames . . . everywhere."

"Basarab?!" He shook Deane by the shoulders. "Listen, man! Did he escape?"

"I'm not sure. I don't think so."

Quincey shoved him aside and ran toward the theatre's column-flanked entrance.

Deane screamed from behind him: "Quincey! No! It's suicide!"

The fire's searing heat held Quincey at bay. One half of him was desperate to save the man he trusted, his friend and mentor. The other half of him was desperate to find the man who had lied to him and betrayed that trust. Either way, Quincey had to save Basarab—how else would all of his questions be answered? Quincey shielded his face from the flames with his coat, took a deep breath, ran up the steps, and leapt inside the burning Lyceum Theatre.

The last thing Mina heard before she fell into unconsciousness was a loud crack as Arthur Holmwood fell on top of her. How long she lay there in a faint, she did not know, but when at last she swam through the darkness back to lucidity, it was to find him standing over her.

"Are you all right?"

"I believe I've survived," she said, amazed that this was the case.

Holmwood offered his hand. This time, she took it and allowed him to help her up. He helped Mina through the window to the top of the fallen carriage. Her long skirt made the maneuver difficult. "I heard a crack. Did you break something?"

Holmwood gestured to his walking stick. It lay on the cobbles, broken into two pieces. Mina reached back into the carriage and withdrew her concealed sword.

A moan from their driver caught their attention. He was lying in a twisted heap in the middle of the road. Mina and Holmwood, still dazed, hobbled to his aid. The bone in his broken leg had ruptured his skin. Blood poured from the gaping wound.

"There's too much blood," Mina said. "He may have torn an artery."

She unwrapped the shawl from the sword and tightly tied it around the driver's leg, above the wound, hoping to stem the flow of blood and save the poor man's life. When she noticed that Holmwood wasn't helping, she immediately assumed that it was because he wouldn't get his hands dirty to aid a lowly servant. But as she looked up to rebuke him, she saw that he had run for help, and to investigate the clamor coming from Wellington Street.

"Fire!" Holmwood cried. "It looks like the Lyceum!"

They shared the same thought: *This fire was no coincidence.*

Mina said, "Go! I'll stay with your driver. Find Quincey!"

He nodded and ran around the corner onto Wellington Street.

Mina tightened the driver's tourniquet. She was desperate to follow Holmwood, but could not leave this man alone in his injured state. She saw people watching from the windows of a nearby building. "Will someone please come and help?" she screamed. "This man is badly injured! I need a doctor!"

The people in the building turned away and closed their shutters; they could gawk at the disaster but did not want to get involved. She looked back at the driver. She had no choice; her fears for her son's life overrode everything. She left the dying man and limped after Arthur Holmwood.

As she passed the other black and gold carriage, the door suddenly sprang open. All she saw was the flash of dark hair, pale skin, black eyes, and long, white, razor-sharp fangs. Her mind had barely enough time to process that it was a woman who leapt at her . . . and that woman was a vampire.

CHAPTER XXXIX.

Arthur Holmwood shoved his way through the crowd, forcing hapless pedestrians aside. His six-foot-four frame allowed him to see over the crowd, though he had to blink back the smoke. The more he pushed forward, the stronger the current of people pushed back. It was like trying to move through quicksand.

Then at last the crowd parted to make way for three horse-drawn fire brigade steam pumpers. Knowing the cavalry led the charge for the infantry, Arthur positioned himself behind the brigade. Overtaking the pumps, he pushed past the line of people passing buckets of water toward the burning Lyceum Theatre and moments later found himself immersed in the crowd that had formed at the base of the steps, looking dazed, as if hypnotized by the dancing orange flames.

"Move! Out of my way!" he shouted.

He was aided by two firemen carrying hoses, who were trying to force their way though the crowd to the front entrance. The flames and heat were so intense that it was unlikely anyone was still alive inside. Through the broken windows of the theatre, he could see walls collapsing. None of the firemen were going inside: It was simply too dangerous. Then he noticed two of them dowsing the buildings on either side of the theatre with water. This was no longer a rescue, but a holding action.

The Lyceum was lost. Now the strategy was to stop the fire from spreading and consuming the entire street.

Arthur reached the base of the stairs, took a few steps up to get an elevated view, and scanned the throng for Quincey. Hopefully, the boy had never made it inside, and if he had, perhaps he had had the good sense to get out in time.

He saw a small, bespectacled man covered in soot and ash break through the crowd to the firemen.

"Quincey Harker is still inside!" Hamilton Deane screamed. "Please, you have to help him!"

Holmwood's heart sank as a fireman pushed Deane back. "If he's in there, he's already dead," the man said.

Holmwood felt powerless. For a man of action, there was nothing worse. It was the same feeling he'd experienced as he had watched Lucy die, as he had watched Quincey P. Morris die. Not again. Not this time. Not on his watch. He sprinted up the steps to the blazing theatre, flames snapping at him all the way.

A fireman called out, "Get back here! Are you daft?"

The flames receded for a moment, and Holmwood ran forward. The heat was so intense, he was sure he was melting. As he was about to leap past the threshold, the raging inferno beat him back. It was as if he were standing at the gates of hell.

In total desperation, he cried out, "Quincey!"

Quincey's lungs burned. Smoke stung his eyes. He shielded his face from the flames as he made his way backstage.

"Basarab, where are you? Basarab? Answer me!"

He kicked a door open. A sudden wave of hot air knocked him flat. The flames escaped the room and shot up to the ceiling, igniting it. There was a loud yawning sound as fire consumed the surrounding oxygen. Quincey was in the belly of the beast, and he only had moments left before he would be eaten alive. Crawling below the level of the smoke, he made it to the next door, pressed his body against the wall, and touched the doorknob. The skin on his fingertips seared. He yanked his hand back with a cry of pain. The door moaned, its wood expanding, cracking, bulging. Quincey covered his face. The door exploded off its hinges, splintering, the flames shooting out like a fireball. It was useless. The building creaked all around him. It was about to collapse. He had to get out of there now or he was going to die.

He scrambled to his feet to make a run for it, but stopped short. Through the smoky haze, he saw a smoldering body trapped under debris. The body was draped in the burning remnants of what had once been a decorative robe. A broadsword was still clenched in its charred hand.

"Basarab!" Ignoring the hellish heat, Quincey ran to the body. The face was burned beyond recognition. If he had just run out the door, at least there would have been hope. Now the answers Quincey sought were forever lost. Basarab was dead.

Who was this countess of whom Deane had spoken? Quincey had found it difficult to cry for his father, but even though Basarab had lied to him, the tears now flowed easily. Quincey was quickly losing his battle against Dracula. Tears mixed with smoke, blinding him.

Moments later, he heard a horrible creak, and faster than he could react, the ceiling gave way. He didn't even have enough time to raise his arms to shield his face as the heavy wood beams dropped on him. He felt a sharp pain. A beam struck his ribs.

He was trapped.

The dark-haired Woman in White flew out of the black-and-gold carriage, her face wild, her eyes black, fangs glistening. She hit Mina square in the chest and they both toppled back onto the cobbles.

No one on Wellington Street took the least notice: All attention was on the fire at the Lyceum Theatre. Mina was on her own. The Woman in White howled in victory as her clawlike hands pulled Mina's head back, exposing her vulnerable neck to the creature's fangs. The vampire now straddled Mina, holding her fast. Mina struggled, but the Woman in White was strong.

"My countess sends her undying love," the vampire growled as she dipped her fangs toward Mina's throat.

Mina had known the loving kiss of a vampire once before. This was something quite different. The intent was clearly to rip out her throat. "No!" she shrieked. After all she had endured, she was not going to allow herself to be killed now, when Quincey needed her most.

A new rage surged within Mina. Her newfound strength began to surge through her veins. The beast that had lain dormant in her blood, Dracula's blood, for so long was suddenly unleashed. Her heartbeat quickened in a way she had never experienced before, and her blood surged through her veins as if it had a mind of its own, empowering her muscles with unnatural strength and speed. Before the Woman in White ripped open her neck, and before she became completely aware of what was happening, Mina threw her attacker off of her body. The dark-haired vampire flew screaming through the air, her graceful arc ending with a slam against an iron lamppost. The Woman in White hit the cobbles with a hideous thud, and the post cracked in half in an explosion of sparks. The upper half of the lamppost fell on top of the vampire, crushing her beneath its weight.

Mina stared in disbelief at her own hands.

She looked up just in time to see the Woman in White lift the metal lamppost as easily as if it were no more than a broken tree limb and fling it at her. Without thinking, Mina leapt aside, dodging the lamppost with surprising ease. She ran for her sword, now lying on the ground beside Holmwood's overturned carriage. As Mina grasped the handle, unsheathed it, and spun around in one continuous motion, the Woman in White pounced toward her. Mina thrust out with the sword as the vampire drew near. The Woman in White snarled as blood sprang from a a gaping wound on her upper chest.

Blast! I was aiming for her head. Mina swung the katana again: This time, she would not miss. The sword cut the air with a hiss as it angled toward the dark-haired vampire's neck.

With a hideous snarl like that of a wild animal, the Woman in White raised her hand and caught the blade in her fist. Blood spurted from a gash that cut to the bone. The beast twisted the bloody blade and snapped it in two. In an instant, the sword hilt was wrenched from Mina's fingers and she felt her feet leave the earth. The force of the vampire's strike sent her flying through the air, spinning as she smashed into the carriage's wheel, splintering it. The iron axle slammed into the small of her back. Mina fell to the ground, gasping, the wind forced from her lungs.

"You fight like a man," the Woman in White laughed. "I would have thought a prince would choose a more gentle woman to love."

Mina struggled to regain her breath. "Not all women are slaves to their masters."

Offended, the Woman in White roared. One second she was still, the next she was a blur. Mina watched in amazement as the vampire bounded with incredible speed toward her. It was time for the kill.

The image of her dark prince now appeared in Mina's mind; there was panic on his face as he screamed at her, "Move!"

In the second that it took for the Woman in White to reach her, Mina lost control of her body. It was as if Dracula's blood in her veins was answering the command of its general. Mina watched her own hand grab Holmwood's broken walking stick and hold it in front of her like a spearman meeting a cavalry charge. The vampire was moving too fast to check her momentum: She impaled herself through the heart on the sharp, broken end of the walking stick. Mina's face and hands were splashed with ice-cold blood, sending shivers throughout her body. The Woman in White's victorious roar was transformed into a death wail.

Staring at Mina in profound disbelief, she croaked: "How . . . ?"

"Didn't your mistress warn you? I'm Dracula's adulterous whore!" Mina said.

She spun the Woman in White through the air, smashing her into the side of the building. The bricks chipped under the impact, and the vampire slumped to the ground. As her eyes closed forever, her face regained its human form.

Dracula had saved her, but he had also killed her husband. Mina didn't know how to feel. As she retraced her steps only to find Arthur Holmwood's driver dead, she wondered if, deep down, she was just as much of a killer as the vampire prince.

The screams and clanging bells on Wellington Street broke into her thoughts. *Quincey!* Mina unhitched the lead stallion. Etiquette be damned, this was no time for sidesaddle. She hiked up her skirt, flung her leg over the horse's naked back, and straddled the beast. Taking its mane in one hand and its reins in the other, she kicked its flanks with her heels and galloped toward the Lyceum Theatre, forcing the great stallion through the panicked crowd, her primal instincts in full control. She stopped for no one. The horse reared violently as it neared the flaming theatre. Mina should have been thrown, but again her strength saved her. She fought her way to the building's steps, but it was futile. The fire had broken through the roof, showering the ground with burning embers, as if the night were alive with a swarm of fireflies.

She saw several firemen restraining a screaming man.

"Arthur!"

Holmwood shoved them away and staggered down the stairs toward her. There were tears in his eyes as he shook his head, his pale expression one of utter defeat. She had seen that look on Arthur's face only once before. Mina's heart lurched. "What has happened? Where's my son? Where's Quincey?"

Arthur Holmwood had never before backed away from a challenge. But now, as he faced her, he couldn't even meet her eyes. His voice cracked as he said, "Mina, I'm sorry. Quincey's gone."

CHAPTER XL.

◆

It has been said that there is no greater pain for a parent than outliving their own child. Having no heir, Arthur Holmwood thought he'd never have to put that statement to the test. Now he watched helplessly as Mina did just that. Like Lot's wife, she was frozen in place, unable to turn away from the burning theatre. She was completely still. The light went out of her eyes. He imagined her heart had turned to stone. Whatever anger Arthur had felt toward Mina Harker, he would never have wished this tragedy upon her. He had come to like her son, more than he cared to admit. The young man was reckless, but so had he been when he was that age. He had hoped that fate would spare Quincey from the doom that had come to his father and Jack. The doom that seemed to be awaiting them all.

The fire brigade pushed the now-silent crowd back. The firemen had coiled their hoses, and the water pumps had ceased. There was nothing more to do but wait for the inevitable end.

Holmwood took hold of his stallion's reins and moved Mina out of harm's way. He looked at her, and a frightening thought came to him. Would she be so foolish as to throw herself into the fire to be with her son? Walking alongside Mina, he watched her out of the corner of his eye, trying to gauge her intent.

Before they had taken more than a dozen steps, Mina pointed at the entranceway and called out, "Quincey!"

He was certain that Mina had crossed the threshold into madness. Then, turning back, he, too, saw the amazing sight. There was Quincey Harker, stumbling out from behind the curtain of flames. There was a loud, horrible wrenching of splintering wood, starting at the roof. Cracks appeared on the outer walls of the theatre. The structure was collapsing in on itself. Mina quickly dismounted from the horse. Holmwood bounded up the theatre steps, reaching the entrance just as Quincey did. The young man was covered in black soot. His coat was on fire and he seemed dazed.

Holmwood took hold of him by the lapels of his coat and yanked him out of harm's way. "Quincey, run!" He threw Quincey ahead of him down the steps and then leapt to save his own life, just as the rest of the roof of the building gave way. The throngs screamed. A thick cloud of choking black smoke rose from the rubble. Only the theatre's Grecian façade remained standing.

Mina smothered Quincey's burning coat, then ripped it open, searching for wounds. "Quincey, are you injured?"

Quincey was clearly shaken to the core by his harrowing escape. He didn't answer, but he didn't have to. There was not a single mark on his skin.

Holmwood shook his head in shock. He had seen the aftermath of dozens of battles, the effects of carnage on the bodies of brave young men. But he had never seen anything like this. This was not luck: This was a miracle.

A man carrying a doctor's satchel ran out of the crowd, soon to be joined by concerned firemen. Mina looked up at Holmwood, panic on her face. *Don't let them see Quincey.*

Holmwood charged to intercept them. "Stay back. All of you!" The men held their place. He spun back to Mina and Quincey and shouted, "We have to get away from here!"

Tears filled Quincey's eyes. "He's dead. . . . Basarab is dead."

Holmwood could not allow Quincey a moment of mourning. He heard the gasp from the crowd as he helped Quincey to his feet. Those closest to them saw that Quincey was not injured. He did not want to give them the chance to create a scene. He dragged Quincey away from the theatre's ruins while Mina went back for the stallion. Although the crowd might be perplexed by Quincey's amazing escape, Arthur Holmwood knew the reason for it only too well. Mina's youthful appearance was the result of drinking Dracula's blood, and that same blood that had passed into Quincey when he was in Mina's womb now coursed through his veins.

They moved away from the crowd, up the street. For the first time, Holmwood felt a glimmer of hope. Dracula had made his first tactical error. If his blood gave Quincey the power to heal, Quincey might have inherited Dracula's physical strength as well. Dracula might have provided Arthur with a powerful weapon to use against him.

Cotford cursed under his breath. Since the Waterloo fire station closed two years ago, the Scotland Yard fire hall was overworked. Their engines were constantly belting through the streets, their infuriating bells echoing. As the two police carriages made their way along Whitehall toward the Strand, the driver of Cotford's carriage kept pulling aside to allow the fire brigade to pass. The fire, wherever it was, must have indeed been a spectacle. It seemed as if all of London had come out to bear witness to it. Between the fire brigade and the pedestrians, the main streets were practically impassable. If Cotford was to keep his date with the Ripper, then he, Lee, and the handful of armed constables that had joined them on their mission somehow had to find a path to the Lyceum Theatre.

Nervous and impatient, Cotford leaned out of the window and looked back at the other police carriage. It, too, was held back by the chaos. Cotford shouted at the pedestrians clogging the street: "Make way! Move!"

Lee took his cue from the inspector and leaned out of the opposite window. "Official police business, make way!"

Cotford cursed as he saw that the Waterloo Bridge was shut down for repair yet again. He yelled to the driver, "Turn right onto King William Street. We'll go up St. Martin's away from the crowd and double back!"

Cotford sank back into his seat with an all-too-familiar feeling in the pit of his stomach, the same feeling he'd had when he had tripped on the curb, allowing the Ripper to escape twenty-five years ago. With the crowd and detour, his appointment with the Ripper would be delayed by another twenty minutes. If things went wrong tonight, he knew he might never have another chance to balance the scales.

Jostled by the crowds, Mina fought back tears as she watched Arthur Holmwood press ahead with Quincey. She desperately longed to comfort her son. She'd nearly lost him this night, and yet she couldn't find a way to express what she was feeling.

"What is she doing here?" Quincey asked Holmwood, still not acknowledging Mina's presence. "I thought I could trust you!"

That was enough. Mina grabbed hold of her son. "I am still your mother! The only one you'll ever have and I love you."

"We don't have time for family squabbles!" Arthur said firmly. "We have to find Van Helsing! Now!"

Quincey had opened his mouth to protest, but Holmwood pushed him forcefully ahead of him through the crowd. They had already wasted valuable time trying to reach the mouth of Wellington Street, only a stone's throw from the burning theatre, but the intersection was blocked by fire engines and gawkers. It had been like trying to paddle a boat against the current. They were forced to turn around and cross in front of the burning theatre again. The stallion reared in fear, almost knocking Mina over. Holmwood yanked off his cravat and covered his animal's eyes with it, holding fast to the bridle. They pressed on northward, with Quincey recounting what he had just learned.

"You're telling me a countess started this fire to kill Basarab?" Holmwood asked.

Quincey nodded.

Holmwood gave Mina a stern look. She knew exactly what he was thinking. Countess Bathory, the deaths of Jonathan and Seward, and the telegram from Van Helsing all added up to one possibility: that Dracula was alive and back in England. The other possibility was too terrible to think about: that Dracula knew the secret she'd kept from him and was coming to claim what was his by any means necessary, even if that meant working with Bathory and killing her.

"What is it?" Quincey asked, seeing her distraction.

"Dracula is alive. Here in London . . ."

"Mina Harker! Arthur Holmwood!" a familiar voice called out. "Stay where you are!"

Mina looked up to see two police carriages emerging from Tavistock Street. Cotford jumped out of one carriage, Sergeant Lee following suit.

"You are wanted for questioning," Lee said. "Do not move."

Several policemen leapt out of the carriage. Lee led the charge, using his immense frame to cut a path through the crowd.

There was no time to lose. Mina pushed Quincey toward Holmwood and shouted, "Take the horse!"

Holmwood leapt upon his stallion, uncovering its eyes.

Quincey, bemused, cried, "What's going on?"

By way of response, Holmwood took hold of his collar and hoisted him onto the horse.

"Stop them!" Cotford cried. "Do not let them escape!"

Holmwood drew a pistol from his pocket and fired into the air above the heads of the crowd. The onlookers screamed and ran for their lives. A constable raised a rifle, and his finger hovered over the trigger. Sergeant Lee pushed the barrel upward into the night sky. "Don't fire into the crowd, you idiot!"

Holmwood fired the pistol again, clearing a wider path.

"Have you gone mad?" Quincey yelled.

"Many years ago, Master Harker," Holmwood replied with a roguish gleam in his eye. He kicked his heels into the stallion's side. "Hah!" The horse bucked and raced off at a gallop north toward Bow Street.

"Stop!" bellowed Cotford, raising his gun and aiming it at Quincey's exposed back. Now that the crowd had parted, he had a clear shot. From the look in his eyes, he intended to take it.

"No! Not my son!"

Mina ran forward and put herself between the gun and Quincey's back, blocking Cotford's aim.

"Damn it!" Cotford cursed. He shouted to his men. "After them!"

Two policemen gave chase on foot while Lee and the others started back for the nearest carriage.

Cotford stopped Price and another young constable, Marrow. "Hold it! You two stay with me." Then the Irish bloodhound turned his anger on Mina. "Thank you, Mrs. Harker. Now we have a positive identification of your son. Where are they going?"

She drew herself up. "I haven't the foggiest notion. And what does my son have to do with any of this?"

Cotford screwed up his face, preparing to unleash his fury, when an earsplitting shriek froze them all in place. Every head turned to see a woman running down the road.

"Murder! Murder!" she screamed.

Cotford, Price, and Marrow dragged Mina to where the Holmwood carriage had crashed.

This was a night London would never forget. A spectacular fire, a miraculous escape, and now a woman murdered in public, impaled through the heart. Cotford examined the walking stick that was protruding grotesquely from the dead woman's bloody chest.

Playing to the crowd, he announced triumphantly: "The murder weapon bears the Holmwood family crest." He took hold of Mina's arm and spun her around, showing off her blood-spattered clothing. "Would you be good enough to tell me how you managed to get so much blood on you?"

"My son was injured in the fire at the theatre."

"Sir, look at this," exclaimed Constable Price as he picked up the bloodied katana.

Cotford handed Mina over to Constable Marrow and inspected the broken blade. *JONATHAN HARKER. THE ANGLO-JAPANESE ALLIANCE* read the bloodstained inscription. "How very thoughtful of you to use a weapon with your husband's name upon it."

Mina opened her mouth to respond but could find no words that would rationally explain away the evidence.

"Rest assured, Mrs. Harker, I will be thorough," said Cotford with a smile. "We will test blood types and I'm sure it will confirm that the blood on you and on this blade is the same. You murdered that woman." He turned to Constable Marrow. "Fetch the surgeon. This time there will be no cause for doubt. I will oversee the evidence collection myself."

Mina tried hard to keep her expression blank, but she feared that she would soon find herself hanging at the gallows.

Countess Elizabeth Bathory stood upon the green copper dome opposite the ruins of the Lyceum Theatre. Smoke rose, carrying to her the intoxicating aroma of seared human flesh. From her vantage point, she observed the movements of each of the players in her great game. Arthur Holmwood and the boy appeared to have sacrificed the woman to secure their escape. *So much for chivalry.* Inspector Cotford had followed the trail of bread crumbs she had left for him. Her strategy was playing out just as she had hoped. She marveled at the simplicity of the human mind. How easily humans could be manipulated! No wonder God chose to put them above all His other creations.

A wild laughter began low in her loins, rose up through her, and exploded out of her mouth. She was truly a supreme being. By the end of this night, her game would conclude. The losers would be dead, and she'd have another victory over God. Her survival was secure. Without a doubt, she was the fittest.

Bathory gazed at the flaming ruins of the Lyceum Theatre, reveling in her victory over Basarab. "Good night, sweet prince."

With that, she spun away into the night, and to the wild work yet to be done.

CHAPTER XLI.

—•—◇—•—

Quincey's fingers were like iron hooks, holding fast to Arthur Holmwood's coat, barely able to keep his seat on the horse's bare back. Police whistles echoed though the maze of streets. They raced past a fire engine. The firemen aboard pointed them out, and the driver rang his bell to alert the police. Without a moment's hesitation, Holmwood reined in the horse and changed direction abruptly, almost causing Quincey to slip backward onto the cobbles. Quincey felt helpless, hardly the gallant warrior against evil he so wanted to be.

Quincey stole a glance over Holmwood's shoulder to see a police vehicle careening toward them. Once again, Holmwood yanked on the reins, and the steed altered course, now galloping through the Alexandra Gate into Hyde Park. The motorcar would not be able to follow them along the narrow Buck Hill Walk. It seemed that technology had its limitations.

Holmwood halted the stallion at the Serpentine, and Quincey relaxed his grip for the first time in ten miles. Holmwood's eyes scanned the park for the best escape route. "We have to find our way without being detected, and reach Van Helsing."

"That madman threatened my life," Quincey fumed. "I'm not going anywhere near him."

"Don't be a child. Van Helsing has seen Dracula. We need his help."

"The police are everywhere. We don't even know where the bastard is hiding."

Holmwood removed a folded telegram from his jacket pocket and flourished it. "He was at the Great Eastern Hotel. Everything we need to find him is in this tele—" He stopped suddenly, listening to something, still faint in the distance.

Quincey had the same unsettling feeling he'd had when he survived the roof collapse at the theatre. Something was definitely happening to his body, and he did not know what it was. He recognized the approaching sound long before Holmwood. "Dogs!"

"Bloodhounds," Holmwood added after a while.

To Quincey's surprise, instead of galloping away, Holmwood dismounted and pulled Quincey off with him.

"What are you doing? We won't stand a chance on foot!"

"A horse may be swift, but he is most definitely not brave. At the first sight of a snapping dog, he will buck and we'll both end up on our arses." With a sudden yell, he slapped the horse's rear and watched as it galloped wildly through the park. "Follow me," he whispered. He struck out northward with Quincey in tow, at one point breaking a branch from a tree and walking backward, brushing away their footprints, leaving only the horse's trail toward the east. "Our scent will travel in both directions. At best, it will delay our pursuers. At worst, it will at least split them up."

Quincey felt like an uneducated child playing at soldiers. How foolish he was to think he could play the warrior. He followed in Holmwood's footsteps, more impressed by his companion's battle prowess with each passing second.

The two men emerged from the park, crossed the Bayswater Road, and headed for Paddington station. Quincey was not surprised to see that the entrances to the station were teeming with police. They turned their collars up as they crossed Praed Street. A ringing phone in a blue kiosk drew the attention of the constables. One of them took a key from his pocket and unlocked it. It was painfully clear to Quincey that technology was now helping to spread the news of their escape faster than they could run.

Distant barking shattered his train of thought. Holmwood's gambit had been unsuccessful. The bloodhounds were still hot on their trail. The police at the station were now on full alert, searching in all directions. Holmwood gripped Quincey by the arm and steered him away from the station, angling through the adjoining hospital grounds. People were milling about outside, concerned about their loved ones inside. Quincey realized that Holmwood was betting their lives that these people were too preoccupied with their own woes to notice two fugitives slipping through their midst. They tried to walk as slowly and as casually as possible to avoid arousing suspicion as the baying of the hounds drew closer and closer. The family members looked around, their reveries interrupted. Basic survival instincts screamed for Quincey to run.

Holmwood felt Quincey's tension. He held him fast and whispered through gritted teeth, "Don't!"

"We'll never make it through the streets. The police are everywhere."

"We're not going through the streets," his companion replied with a smile. "We're going under them."

A moment later, Quincey suddenly lost his footing and toppled downward, stopping just short of planting his face into foul-smelling water. He found himself in front of a small, urban canal. Holmwood descended beside him and, without a moment of hesitation, marched into the putrid water despite wearing his finest leather shoes. He looked back expectantly at Quincey. Quincey looked down at the canal. It reeked of filth and human waste.

The dogs grew louder. The police were fast approaching.

Holmwood hissed, "The stench of the sewage will throw them off our trail. Move along. Now!"

Quincey clamped his hand over his nose and mouth to ward off the stench and followed him. They were supposed to be the heroes chasing the foul villains, he mused, yet here they were, covered in fifth and pursued by hounds.

Fortune finally seemed to favor them: As they rounded a bend, they discovered a rowing boat that had been discarded on the shore. The weathered stencil on the side of the boat read: METROPOLITAN BOARD OF WORKS. They pulled the boat into the water, and Holmwood took hold of the single oar and began to row. As they approached the War-wick underpass, he surprised Quincey by turning right instead of left, which would have taken them westward and out of the city.

"You're going the wrong way."

Arthur flashed him a glare. "Van Helsing stated in his telegram that Dracula attacked him in his room at the Great Eastern Hotel. The next line is the key: *'Renfield is my sanctuary at the grand house of the patron saint of children. Beside the cross of the king.'* Van Helsing is still in the city."

Quincey didn't care. He placed his hand on the oar, halting Holm-wood's momentum. "We should get away while we can. We can always return when things quiet down."

It was as if a fire were blazing behind Arthur's eyes. There was brav-ery in that fire, and there was something else: a touch of madness. Quincey was reminded of the look he'd seen in Van Helsing's eyes.

Holmwood shoved Quincey's hand off the oar and continued toward the city.

After a while, Quincey noticed a gurgling sound coming from beneath his seat. Of course. The boat had been abandoned because it had a leak. Quincey stared at the rancid water filling the boat and glanced about for something with which to bail out the water. There was nothing. Holding his breath and swallowing back vomit, he cupped his hands together and scooped water over the sides. But it seeped in faster than he could bail it out.

Holmwood paddled as fast as he could, passing unseen through sev-eral tunnels under the streets as the canal continued around Regent's Park. "I should have joined the damned rowing team at Oxford instead of the fencing squad," he muttered.

Quincey soon realized that, even with his bailing, their vessel was not going to hold them afloat for much longer. The water was already well past their ankles. Coming to the same conclusion, Holmwood maneuvered the boat out of the tunnel and back aboveground. They

ABANDONED

abandoned the leaky boat on the shore next to the Gas Works Depot. Quincey followed Holmwood as he walked briskly southward, his waterlogged shoes squelching. His heart grew heavy at the sight of a serpentlike tendril of smoke slithering across the night sky. The Lyceum was still smoldering, as it would for days. The fire had destroyed his dreams as well as the theatre. Basarab would never be able to answer the many questions he so wanted to ask. *Basarab!* Quincey wasn't sure whether he should mourn or curse his mentor. There were so many questions burning in his heart, and the answers were lost in the flames. He felt ruined, and old. Death was approaching, he could feel it.

After a while, he realized that Holmwood was leading them toward St. Pancras station. Quincey broke the silence between them. "You said Van Helsing was still in the city."

"The telegram states 'the *grand* house of the patron saint of children.' Van Helsing has now moved to the Midland Grand Hotel. The one situated over St. Pancras station. St. Pancras is the patron saint of children, and adjacent to King's Cross station."

Quincey did not share his companion's enthusiasm for cracking Van Helsing's code. To get to the hotel, they would still have to pass both stations, which were sure to be swarming with police.

As they neared the hotel, Quincey was awestruck by its size and Italian Gothic splendor. *Grand* was an understatement. Looming against the night sky, it looked ominous and forbidding. Holmwood shoved Quincey behind one of the archways as a police motorcar approached. A tall uniformed officer emerged, holding aloft a drawing for the constables to see.

"Lee," Holmwood muttered, recognizing the officer.

Quincey saw the crude likenesses of himself and Holmwood on Lee's drawing. He would bet his life it was the work of one of the amateur artists working on the Strand, who offered to draw the likeness of passing pedestrians for a shilling.

Holmwood pulled out a cigar and flipped a box of matches to Quincey. Then he lowered his head and ducked under the archway out of the wind. Quincey understood the ruse. He struck the match and cupped the flame as if to block it from the elements. Policemen passed by, carrying the memory of Lee's drawing fresh in their minds. They checked the face of each passing pedestrian but paid no attention to Holmwood and Quincey. It was perfectly plausible that two men would turn their backs to calmly light a cigar. Holmwood took a puff and placed his hand on Quincey's arm to steady him. They waited a moment longer for Lee to climb back into his vehicle and drive off.

"Dracula has manipulated us into danger at every turn," Quincey muttered as he followed Holmwood toward the main door of the Midland Grand Hotel. "Do you really think this crazy old man will hold the key to our survival?"

"Survival?" Holmwood paused at the main door and gave Quincey an odd look. "As long as Dracula dies, what does that matter?" Without clarifying any further, he entered the hotel lobby.

CHAPTER XLII.

——————◇——————

Here lies the body of Bram Stoker, former manager of the greatest actor of any age, Sir Henry Irving.

Bram Stoker tried to push away the image, but every time he closed his eyes, he could see what would surely be his gravestone epitaph. The curtain was about to fall on his life, and there would be no encore. The bitter irony was not lost upon him. He had begun his life as a bedridden child and would spend his last days as a bedridden old man. He had become a prisoner in his own body, paralyzed on his left side, unable to move, or even feed himself. He had to suffer the indignity of having to be bathed and changed as if he were a helpless infant. He had prided himself on being an honest and hardworking man, and could not imagine what he could have done to offend God. To suffer this much failure in one lifetime, it must have been something terrible. It saddened him to know that without his directorial hand in the play, his novel *Dracula* would soon become lost on some forgotten shelf in the back of a bookshop, whilst Oscar Wilde's *Picture of Dorian Gray* would no doubt go on to be known as the greatest gothic novel of its day.

It occurred to him that, somewhere in heaven, Henry Irving must be laughing at him. Irving had left him the Lyceum Theatre, not as a chance to live out his dream, but rather as a slap in the face. When Bram

Stoker reached the pearly gates, a drunken Irving would surely be waiting to gloat, with a Scotch in his hand and a woman on each arm. He
even knew what Irving would say. *I told you so, you untalented oaf. Once a
bean counter, always a bean counter.*

Big Ben, only a short distance away, began to chime. With each
consecutive gong, Stoker knew that the countdown to the end had
begun. Nine chimes, nine o'clock. His wife had retired to her chambers,
as had his nurse. This was the time he hated most, alone, unable to
move, trapped in his thoughts.

He felt suddenly cold, as if the temperature in the room had dropped
by ten degrees. Had the fire gone out? He struggled to prop himself up,
and called out for his nurse. He could only partially move his mouth.

He could barely turn his head to see that the shadows that now
shrouded the room, created by the moonlight spilling past the shade,
began to move. Stoker tried to call out again, but was capable only of a
low grunt.

Stoker's eyes searched for a sign of another soul in the bedroom with
him. There was no one. He strained to listen for any sound of breathing,
but heard none but his own. An odd scratching sound made him hold
his breath. At first he thought it was a mouse burrowing beneath the
floorboards, but the sound grew loud, like a chisel carving wood. His
fear quickened. There *was* someone in the room. A shadow detached
itself from the wall, blocking out the moonlight as it passed the window,
and crept to the foot of his bed. Stoker balled his hand into a fist and
punched at the headboard, struggling to scream. He watched in helpless
disbelief as the shadow began to take on the outline of a human form,
certain he was having a terrible nightmare. He shifted his body so that
he could roll onto his side, trying to use his functioning right arm to
reach for the wheelchair next to the bed. If he could just get into the
chair, perhaps he could escape. As his hand was about to grab the arm-
rest, he heard a *whoosh* of air. Something hit him hard in the chest,
throwing him back onto the bed, the air knocked from his lungs. He
struggled to breathe. An angry growl came to his ears, seemingly coming from nowhere and everywhere at once, as if a pack of wild wolves
had surrounded his bed. The shadow's black mass lunged forward,

enveloping him. It had weight, like another human being pressed down on him, pinning him to his bed. Using what little strength he had, Stoker tried to fight back.

He screamed as something punctured his neck. He felt no pain, but he knew his blood was being drained from his body. The shadow was alive and he would soon be dead.

He had made a terrible mistake. The madman he had met all those years ago in the pub had not merely told him an amusing story. That man had tried to warn him that vampires did exist.

The moonlight from the window once again fell on Stoker as the shadow moved. He could now see what had hit him in the chest. It was his own personal copy of his novel. Scratched across the cover, as if by a savage claw, was the word: *LIES!*

CHAPTER XLIII.

Quincey could never have imagined anything more impressive than the great cathedral of Notre Dame, yet he was awestruck by the immense, ostentatious grandeur of the Midland Grand Hotel. He felt very out of place in his disheveled, stinking, soot-covered attire. He pressed himself against the green marble column as if to blend into the background, keeping distance from any patrons crossing the lobby.

In stark contrast, Holmwood was so sure of himself that he marched straight through the crowd, across the multicolored marble floor, to the hand-carved mahogany front desk. He didn't care what he looked like or smelled like or even that his shoes were sopping wet. He was still Arthur Holmwood, and he commanded respect.

The nervous concierge ran up to him.

"Lord Godalming! What an exquisite surprise. Had I expected you, I would have had a tailor and valet waiting."

Holmwood remained unfazed. "A tailor? Good God, for whatever reason?"

"I could have a suit prepared in less than—"

Holmwood held up his hand to interrupt. "That won't be necessary. I'm looking for a guest by the name of Mr. Renfield."

Renfield is my sanctuary. Quincey finally understood the code hidden in the old man's telegram. Van Helsing was clearly trying to lead them to him. Perhaps he could help them after all.

It was no wonder that the Midland Grand had fallen from its perch as London's finest hotel. The year was 1912 and they still refused to install a lift. And of course Van Helsing, or rather Mr. Renfield, would choose a room on the top floor, no doubt for the advantage of escape routes via the roof.

The climb up the spiraling grand staircase seemed unending. Holmwood made the ascent without once stopping to rest. Quincey, on the other hand, was forced to stop for the second time. As he caught his breath, he craned his neck to see a cobalt blue sky with gold-leaf stars painted on the cathedral-like ceiling. It was as if they were mounting the steps to heaven. In an alcove overlooking the landing, there was a canvas mural of Saint George slaying the dragon. Quincey thought the mural quite appropriate to the quest at hand.

Midway down the hallway, Holmwood stopped and glanced about to ensure they were alone. He discreetly withdrew his revolver and checked that all the chambers were loaded. "We can only assume the telegram was sent by Van Helsing. On the off chance that we're walking into a trap, it is better to be prepared."

"According to Mr. Stoker, shouldn't you be loading silver bullets?" Quincey asked.

"You confuse your folklore. As did Mr. Stoker. Silver bullets are reserved for werewolves, Master Harker," Holmwood replied with a satirical smile.

Quincey didn't share his amusement. If this was a trap, his life would be in just as much risk. Holmwood might not care whether he lived or died, but Quincey still did.

Holmwood went to the farthest door closest to the roof access and whispered, "This is it."

Quincey was about to knock on the door when Holmwood pulled him back, pointing to the space between the floor and the door. Quincey felt stupid. Another mistake. By stepping in front of the door, they allowed anyone on the other side to see the shadows of their feet. He pointed to the doorjamb. The door was unlocked and had been purposely left slightly ajar. This was not a good sign. He nodded to Quincey: *Get ready.*

Quincey's heart was in his throat, but he nodded back despite his fear. Holmwood moved with lightning speed, pushing open the door and bolting into the room, his pistol at the ready. The room was dark, the light from the hallway illuminating ony half of the massive suite. Like the rest of the hotel, the ceiling in this room was abnormally high. The curtains were drawn.

Quincey closed the door behind him. Holmwood whispered angrily, "No, wait." Quincey moved to stop the swinging door. Too late. The door closed, extinguishing the light from the hallway. They now stood in total darkness. He cursed himself under his breath. *Another stupid mistake.*

The floorboards to their left creaked. Footsteps. They were not alone. "I warn you, I have a gun," Holmwood said.

The footsteps came closer. Holmwood spun and cocked his pistol, pushing Quincey behind him.

Quincey found himself so terrified that he had forgotten to breathe, so when a hand reached out from the blackness and touched his shoulder, he jumped in fright.

A deep, sophisticated voice echoed from all around them: "Good evening, gentlemen."

Holmwood raised his pistol.

CHAPTER XLIV.

—•—◇—•—

Considering how long it had taken Cotford to reach the theatre, he should not have been so angry that the police surgeon had been so slow to appear and collect the latest victim. Not wanting to take any risks with the evidence, Cotford followed the surgeon's wagon to the hospital on Carey Street, next to the Royal Courts of Justice, where the autopsy would be performed.

As the police carriage turned south, Cotford savored the flavor of his cigar. The smoke wafted past Mina Harker, who was seated across from him in the police carriage. She fired a disapproving glare at him. Cotford's hand touched the tip of the bloodstained sword triumphantly. He kept himself between this vital piece of evidence and Mrs. Harker. Soon he would prove her involvement in murder. The Crown Prosecution Service whined that they needed more evidence. They would soon have it, and he would at last be vindicated.

The carriage was now close to the alley where Mina Harker's husband and the woman in white had been attacked. Cotford glanced over at his prisoner to see if there was any recognition of this fact, but as in the morgue, her face betrayed no emotion. Was she that cunning or was she innocent? Cotford knew in his bones that Van Helsing had had a hand in orchestrating the death of Jonathan Harker. Cotford thought of the broken oak crates in the alley. It was clear that Van Helsing was no longer young enough to act alone. Undoubtedly, he had recruited new blood to carry out his wicked deeds. The letter from the Ripper, obviously penned by Van Helsing, made it clear that Quincey Harker was the key to unraveling this mystery. In his investigation of Jonathan Harker's life, Cotford had already made some inquiries about the life and behavior of young Quincey Harker. Cotford had discovered that Quincey was a failed actor who had been forced by his father to attend the university in Paris. *Interesting.* Cotford himself had covered the cost of an international telephone call with Braithwaite Lowery, Quincey Harker's former flatmate at the Sorbonne. Mr. Lowery described Quincey as quite mad, "sixpence short of a shilling," and as someone who hated his father. In Lowery's last conversation with him, Quincey had told his old roommate that he had met "someone wonderful" and was leaving his studies at the Sorbonne to "follow his new destiny." A few days later, Quincey's hated father had been found impaled in Piccadilly Circus. The more Cotford learned about Quincey Harker, the more he was convinced that the young man was the natural accomplice in Van Helsing's new string of crimes.

Cotford was prepared to wager his last penny that the "special someone" Quincey spoke of was none other than Dr. Abraham Van Helsing. Quincey Harker was impressionable enough to be seduced by Van Helsing's twisted teachings. He was also young, strong, and very likely mad enough with the bloodlust of his first kill to break the oak crates in the alley. He also hated his father enough to impale him brutally as a final proof of his loyalty to Van Helsing. It all fit together. Cotford was certain the Crown Prosecution Service would agree. He looked out the window at the familiar domed roof of St. Paul's Cathedral poking up through the haze on the horizon as they turned onto Fleet Street, then glanced back at Mina Harker. Her reserve was still solid, but it would not be for long. He would interrogate Mina Harker, and rather than conducting the interview in secrecy, Cotford would now have the full weight of the law behind him. He would be relentless. The bloodhound was back and he would hound her until she broke and revealed the whereabouts of Van Helsing and made a full disclosure of his crimes.

Cotford had long suspected that Van Helsing had recruited followers into his occult beliefs to carry out his bloody work. It was more than likely that Dr. Seward, plagued by guilt, had threatened to expose Van Helsing's crimes. Cotford felt it was safe to assume that Van Helsing was the one who had driven the black carriage that had trampled Seward in Paris, thereby eliminating the first of his previous accomplices. That left Jonathan, Mina, and Lord Godalming as the only living witnesses. It stood to reason that Van Helsing had decided they all had to be eliminated one by one. Jonathan's death had brought them back together.

Cotford surmised that it was Quincey who had set fire to the Lyceum. Perhaps it had been a failed attempt to kill his mother and Lord Godalming. Cotford noted that Quincey had "escaped" with Godalming, and that the young man planned to kill him once away from prying eyes. It was imperative that Sergeant Lee find Godalming before he met his demise. All avenues of escape from the city had been blocked off. Eventually, he would have Quincey in custody. Perhaps that was part of Van Helsing's plan all along. To eliminate everyone—including his newest accomplice, leaving the bastard free to escape justice once again. Everything was falling into place. This night would wash away the years of failure. At last, the scales were balancing. There was only one thing missing from making this night a total triumph. *Where is Van Helsing?*

Constable Price held fast the reins of the horses as the police carriage moved along Fleet Street. The ominous statue of the Fleet Street Dragon loomed ahead of them. The fog shrouded the pillar upon which it was perched, giving the illusion that the dragon was floating in the air with its batlike wings extended. Price glanced over to Constable Marrow, who was sitting next to him, holding the rifle. From the way his eyes were carefully watching the dragon as they passed, it looked as if Marrow was thinking the same thing.

Given the unusual events of this evening, their wild imaginings were unsurprising. For the first time in his police career, they were carrying firearms, which was not usually allowed by London police. Then there was the fire at the great theatre and that poor, brutally murdered woman. He had heard Sergeant Lee and Inspector Cotford whispering a name:

the Ripper. Could it be true? Was he involved in the investigation of the greatest unsolved murders of Scotland Yard? It was more than he could have ever hoped.

As the fog grew thicker, it was becoming more difficult to see the street ahead. He squinted, trying to make out where he was, and suddenly had the overwhelming feeling that their coach was being followed. Constable Marrow must have had the same feeling, for he glanced back as well. The street was empty . . . there was not a single soul in sight. Price blinked. His eyes were surely playing tricks on him, for it appeared as if the fog behind them had turned bloodred. *It must be caused by the new electric street lamps.*

Price's heart almost stopped as he heard an unnerving sound, like the flapping wings of a large bird of prey, perhaps a hawk. But this was louder . . . and far larger. It was coming from above them. And it was getting closer.

CHAPTER XLV.

—◇—

Holmwood's pistol was poised and ready to fire.

"I've been expecting you," uttered the thickly accented voice out of the darkness.

Quincey, with his hand on Holmwood's shoulder, felt his companion's muscles relax. *Why didn't he shoot?!*

The wall sconces suddenly illuminated the room. Standing before them was Abraham Van Helsing, one hand still on the light button, the other supporting himself on his cane.

"Professor!" Holmwood said, pocketing his pistol. "My God, I could have shot you! Thank God you're safe." He rushed to embrace his old friend.

Van Helsing smirked. "You know I can't resist a dramatic entrance."

Quincey winced. The scratch on his neck, caused by Van Helsing only two nights before, stung again. It was as if his body was warning him to be cautious of this old man. He felt a surge of annoyance that Holmwood seemed to have forgotten that the professor had attacked him.

Holmwood hurled questions at Van Helsing, not waiting for a single response before casting the next inquiry. "Are you all right? How did Dracula find you? How ever did you manage to escape?"

"Using my wits and a tactic that he never expected . . ." Van Helsing paused and looked at Quincey, as if hesitating to share this information in front of him.

Holmwood nodded: The young man had been taken into confidence.

Despite this assurance, Van Helsing turned his back on Quincey.

Quincey was angered at this obvious act of rudeness, and further aggravated that Holmwood didn't do anything about it. He also noted that the professor had not answered the question. How had he escaped from Dracula?

"It is good that you have found me," Van Helsing said softly. "I'd hoped Madam Mina had informed you of my telegram."

For someone who had just survived an encounter with Dracula, Quincey thought, Van Helsing seemed unnervingly calm, very different from the frenzied old man he had met in the alleyway. He noticed a table full of weapons, and wondered about the draped window. *Why are we standing here talking?* The longer they waited, the sooner they would be discovered by the police—or Dracula. They needed to plan their next move with haste.

Holmwood introduced the matter of Bathory while he examined the weapons on the table. A collection of crosses sat next to a carpetbag, a wooden stake, a bowie knife, and vials that Quincey could only assume contained holy water. There was, however, no wolfsbane or garlic. The centerpiece was a crossbow, armed and ready.

Quincey watched Van Helsing, who expressed no surprise at the mention of this new vampire, as if he already knew of Bathory. The old man hobbled to the side of the table and, with trembling hands, struggled to open a brandy bottle. He seemed so frail, quite unlike the man who'd bested Quincey in the alleyway only a few nights ago.

At last, Van Helsing addressed him: "So it would seem, Master Harker, that you decided against taking my . . . *advice.*"

The way Van Helsing enunciated the word "advice" made Quincey's teeth clench. He countered, "My willingness to bend to coercion ended with the death of my father."

"All's well," Van Helsing replied with a sly smile. He poured brandy into two glasses. "It's actually fortuitous for me that you are here."

"And why is that?"

Van Helsing made no reply. He picked up one of the snifters with a gnarled hand and shuffled toward Arthur Holmwood, who was examining the bowie knife.

Holmwood slammed the bowie knife into the table and took the glass. "If only I had listened to Seward in the first place," he said. He took a swig in an attempt to wash away the memory. "Perhaps he, Jonathan, and Basarab might still be alive."

"Basarab?" Van Helsing asked, his voice light and curious.

"The Romanian actor," Holmwood said.

Van Helsing steadied himself with his cane and offered the other glass to Quincey.

He was not a drinker like his father. "Not for me, thank you."

Van Helsing set the glass down without comment, but there was something in his body language that seemed distant. *He thinks of me as a rash child.* Quincey thought it best to maneuver the conversation back to what they had learned about Basarab.

"It was through Basarab's correspondence with Dr. Seward that we were led to Dracula and Countess Bathory."

"Basarab," Van Helsing repeated, slowly and deliberately, tasting each letter. He turned his back on Quincey again. "Holmwood, did you learn nothing from our adventures together?"

Confusion fell across Holmwood's face. "What are you getting at?"

"Tell me, have you ever met this Basarab face-to-face?" Van Helsing asked.

"No. Only Quincey has. Why?"

"Ingenious." Van Helsing chuckled.

Growing impatient, Quincey wanted to grab the old man and shake the answers out of him. He faced Van Helsing. "Professor, if you know something, tell us. Do not keep us in the dark."

Van Helsing looked at Quincey for a long moment. Then he sighed. "The dark, gentlemen, is all there is," he said. "You have already lost. His way is the only path left for us."

"Whose way?" Quincey asked.

As if he were in a lecture hall, Van Helsing took one of his wrinkled hands from the cane and, placing it on the lapel of his jacket, held his audience captive. The darkness in his eyes fell directly on Quincey. "*Dracula* is only the title he chose when he became prince. But Dracula's true name is . . . Vladimir Basarab."

CHAPTER XLVI.

---◇---

"**D**o you hear that?" Price asked from his perch on top of the speeding police carriage as his eyes scanned the skies.

Constable Marrow, riding shotgun, wasn't listening. His eyes were focused on the glowing red fog that was gathering in the street ahead of them. "What the devil is that?"

"Look!" Price pointed upward as the low-hanging black clouds in the sky began to churn and converge.

Marrow cocked his rifle. "Something's not right. Have you ever seen red fog?"

Price's growing fear was evident in his quivering voice. "I don't think that is fog. Whatever it is, it's behind us as well."

Marrow turned to see the misty red mass gaining on them from behind, picking up speed. "It's as if it's chasing us."

"I think it's trying to cut us off. It's almost . . ." Price never had the chance to finish his thought. The police carriage's horses came to a sudden, jolting stop, and Price and Marrow had to hold tight to their seat handles to avoid being thrown.

The police surgeon's carriage, ahead of them, also stopped abruptly. Its team of horses began neighing and chomping at their bits as if they could sense danger.

Marrow turned. "It's gaining on us!"

Price slapped the horses with the reins. "Move, you beasts!" But the horses balked, refusing to go any farther.

The bloodred fog now formed a wall in front of the surgeon's carriage. The driver snapped the reins again and again, and at last the horses began to pick up their feet and move ahead.

Marrow grabbed Price's arm. "I think we need to get off this street."

They watched as the police surgeon's carriage broached the barrier of red fog. Price realized he was holding his breath. How foolish he must have looked. It was only fog. Or was it?

Marrow said again more forcefully, "I'm telling you. We need to get out of here!"

Price was not about to disobey orders. "Get a bloody grip on yourself, man. I would remind you, Constable Marrow, that we have our instructions."

With what sounded like the roar of a wild beast from the pits of hell, the police surgeon's carriage suddenly erupted from the red fog, flying through the air, accompanied by severed horses' heads, limbs, and entrails. The carriage itself then imploded in midair, the wreckage crashing to the ground and skidding along the cobbles, igniting sparks and sending a terrible screeching sound into the night.

"Move!" screamed Marrow in panic.

This time, neither Price nor the horses drawing their carriage had to be told twice: Somehow avoiding the wall of red fog, they raced at a gallop into the nearest side street.

Price no longer cared where they were going so long as it was away from there.

Inside the swift-moving police carriage, Cotford and his prisoner were thrown to one side on a sharp turn, and then bounced up and down so violently that Mina hit her head, drawing blood.

"What the hell is going on up there?" cursed Cotford as he pulled himself back onto his seat and peered out of the window. As Mina dabbed at the cut on her brow, she wished there was another window in the carriage; she had no idea what was happening outside, but something told her to be on her guard. Mina was certain she could use her newfound strength to escape any time she wanted. Yet her arrest served as a distraction for Cotford and would hopefully give Quincey and Arthur more time to get away. As she held on to her seat, she wondered if they had found Van Helsing yet.

Her heart sank at the thought of the old professor. She was thankful that he had survived, but was troubled by his telegram. Dracula was still alive? How was that possible? She had seen, through Bathory's eyes, his death in the castle. Was the telegram some sort of ruse by Bathory? Surely not. She refused to believe that Dracula would align himself with the likes of that evil woman. Yet, if Dracula was somehow alive and had learned of Mina's secret, who knew what he might do?

The thought of Quincey and Arthur walking into Bathory's hands now filled her with resolve. She had to escape from Cotford's clutches. She had to rescue them. The carriage lurched violently again and Cotford was thrown against one wall. Mina, thrown against the other, found that she was able to steal a glance out of the carriage window. The instant she saw the red fog, she knew exactly why the carriage was moving so erratically. Her mind whirled in terror. *Was the red fog manipulated by Bathory? Or by Dracula? Or by both?*

"What the blazes is going on?" Cotford screamed. He reached for the door, and then stopped. His eyes met Mina's. Suddenly, his hand moved for the broken katana that he had wrapped in his handkerchief and stuffed into his coat pocket.

Mina almost laughed at the absurdity of this gesture. Right now, she was the last thing Cotford should be worried about.

Suddenly, there was a scream from above them. Cotford lunged to the window, and Mina, peering over his shoulder, saw one of the police constables fall from the carriage, his rifle flying from his hand. Cotford yelled at the top of his lungs, "Price, what the hell are you doing? I order you to stop this carriage now!"

There was no response. Cotford pulled out his key and reached for the door lock. Mina actually felt sorry for him. He had no idea what he was dealing with. Without thinking, she grabbed his arm. "If you value your life, don't open that door!"

"As if I would trust anything you say, Mrs. Harker."

Mina knew there was nothing she could say that would convince him of the evil that lurked in the darkness. She released his arm, allowing him the freedom to seal his own fate. Mina had her own decisions to make, and her son's life hung in the balance.

Marrow heard the sound of flapping wings, but before he could see where the odd noise was coming from, he felt a sharp sting on the side of his head and then he was sent soaring through the air. When he hit the muddied ground, he felt his left shoulder dislocate from the impact. There was a bone-crushing crunch and he thought for a moment that the wheels of the carriage had driven over his legs. He was relieved when he realized that carriage had run over his already-smashed rifle. Somehow he struggled to his feet. *He was alive!* The left side of his head felt cold and damp, searing with pain. He raised his hand to the side of his face and felt a large, hairy flap of his scalp quivering in the breeze. Hot, warm blood poured down his cheek. He was touching his skull.

Marrow stumbled forward queasily. He was in the Temple Gardens, just north of the Thames. He saw the carriage race away with the blood-red fog still in pursuit. He was in terrible pain, and his left arm was useless. Considering the fate of the police surgeon and his horses, though, he was fortunate to have survived. He feared that Price, Cotford, and their prisoner would not be so lucky.

Marrow's respite was shortlived, for a moment later, the red fog headed straight for him and he heard the sound of flapping wings once again. He didn't waste time trying to work out where the sound was coming from. He still had the revolver he had been issued. He drew it and was about to take aim when he felt a sudden gush of wind in his face and a strong tug on his arm. He tried to cock the gun, but his hand wouldn't move. Looking down, he saw a severed hand holding a revolver on the grass in front of him. Confused, Marrow raised his right arm and saw a gushing stump where his hand had once been. He screamed as the horrible pain belatedly registered in his brain.

The flapping wings echoed above him again. In a flash, he thought he saw the sharp talons of a large bird. Then he was shoved backward and heard what sounded like a bucket of water being splashed onto the ground. Feeling cold and unsteady, he looked down. He had been gutted from his chest to his privates, and his innards were spilling out of his body. Marrow felt ill, and a strong urge to vomit. But as he tumbled back, he realized he no longer had the stomach for it.

"Sit down and don't move!" barked Cotford at Mina as he unlocked and flung open the door of the still-moving carriage. He was going out there to get to the bottom of this nonsense. He stepped out of the carriage onto the footrail and grabbed hold of the roof. The wind whipped at him so violently, he thought he would be blown off the side of the carriage. He could see Price, in the driver's seat above him, whipping the horses relentlessly with the reins. "Price! What the hell is wrong with you? Stop this carriage! That's an order!"

If Price heard him, he gave no indication of it. Cotford edged his feet along the footrail, his fingers gripping so tightly to the handrail that his knuckles turned white. As the carriage lurched to the right, his grip slipped, leaving his feet dangling in thin air as the carriage continued to race faster and faster. As a young cadet, Cotford had been able to do one hundred pull-ups: Now he just needed to do one—the one that would save his life. He did not have the strength.

Cotford raised his foot, placed it against the side of the carriage, and pushed with all his might and somehow managed to hoist his other leg onto the bottom stair and pull himself up. Holding fast to the stair rail, he fought the wind and climbed into the driver's seat. From this vantage point, Cotford could see the low black clouds churning violently overhead. Never in his life had he seen such a storm.

Constable Price turned to look at him. His face was splashed with blood and there was a wild look in his eyes. "It keeps coming. We can't get away from it."

It was clear to Cotford that Price had taken leave of his senses. He reached out to grab the reins, but the terrified young man would not let them go. Struggling to pry them loose, Cotford caught sight of something that stopped him cold. A glowing, bloodred fog spread out from under the carriage. Cotford had seen fog like that only one other time in his life, and had never spoken of it to anyone. Price gave a bloodcurdling scream, and Cotford turned to see him yanked from his seat, wrapped in a blanket of red fog. He watched in disbelief as Price flew straight up into the air, disappearing into the spiraling storm clouds.

The memory of Van Helsing's rant about pagan evil echoed in Cotford's ears. There was surely something ungodly going on. But there was no time to dwell on what that evil might be: The horses were racing out of control and Cotford had to take the reins.

Constable Price tried to scream, but the red fog entered his mouth, filling it with the horrid taste of rot. He felt as if his body was being crushed like a walnut. He couldn't breathe. The sound of flapping wings was all he could hear. He thrashed in panic. His flight into the sky seemed to last an eternity as he rose higher and higher. He thought his heart would rupture from fear, but still he continued to struggle.

Suddenly, he felt a sharp pain in his neck—and then he was calm. He felt tired. He wanted to sleep. He understood what was happening to him but had neither the strength nor the will to prevent it. The blood was leaving his body, and he felt wafer-thin, like a feather floating on the air. The mist then simply released him. His horror was brief. The merciless London streets rose up to meet him, and Price felt his bones shatter as he hit the cobbles . . . and then there was blackness.

CHAPTER XLVII.

—·—◇—·—

Disbelieving, Arthur Holmwood spun to look at Quincey Harker. The look of shock on the boy's face confirmed he had heard the same chilling words from Van Helsing.

"Basarab? No, it cannot be." Quincey shook his head in disbelief.

"Fools!" the professor said, mocking them. "Accept the truth as Seward did. As I have. Dracula is not our enemy."

Holmwood stepped back as if Van Helsing's words were physical blows. *As Seward did?* If Seward had truly joined forces with Lucy's killer, then he had betrayed them all. They had nearly been killed while battling to kill Dracula in Transylvania. With his last breath, Quincey P. Morris had plunged the knife into Dracula's chest. Had their sacrifices been for naught? *Lies. Lies! It had to be all lies!* "Quincey Morris did not die in vain!" he shouted.

"Bathory is the true evil," Van Helsing replied earnestly. "After learning of her horrible killings, the Ripper murders, Dracula came to England in 1888 for one purpose—to destroy Bathory. He did not flee back to his castle in fear of us. It was Bathory who fled in fear of Dracula. We interfered in Dracula's pursuit of her, as Bathory knew we would. She tricked us all. The wounds we inflicted on Dracula weakened him and made it possible for Bathory to deliver what she thought was the final blow. Quincey Morris died fighting the wrong villain."

"Dracula murdered my Lucy. He is a demon, and he must die!"

"Rage has clouded your judgment." Van Helsing turned his back on Holmwood, as if disgusted with his former apprentice.

Holmwood grabbed the old professor roughly by the arm. "I will never ally myself with Dracula! If Bathory was the Ripper, so be it, we'll kill them both."

"You are weak-minded and impulsive. You should never have brought the boy here." Van Helsing struggled to pull away from Holmwood's grasp.

Disgusted by the old man's venomous words, Holmwood released him with a shove. Van Helsing stumbled and fell to the floor, facedown.

"Professor!" Quincey exclaimed. He dashed to Van Helsing's aid, shaking the old man. No response. "Professor Van Helsing?" He clutched the old man's wrist, then looked up at Arthur with panic in his face. "I can't find a pulse!"

"Dear God!" Holmwood knelt at Van Helsing's side to verify the horrible truth for himself. His searching fingers could find no heartbeat.

"Help me turn him over," Quincey said.

A moan escaped Van Helsing's lips. Startled, Quincey nearly lost his balance. A slight rocking movement from the old man then caused Holmwood to stand and step back in shock. He was quite sure there had been no pulse. Van Helsing had been dead.

The professor pushed himself up with his rickety arms. His long, disheveled white hair hung forward, casting a shadow on his face. "If you will not join us . . . ," he said in a voice that chilled their blood. The old man was apparently not as frail as he had led them to believe.

Van Helsing spun around, his white hair whipping back—revealing the horrible truth. The professor's eyes were black orbs, and his fangs were long and sharp. He snarled venomously, ". . . then you are against us!"

It was too late to flee. Van Helsing leapt at them.

CHAPTER XLVIII.

—•—◇—•—

"You can't outrun it. This is a fool's errand!" Mina screamed from below.

Cotford knew she was right. The bloodred fog had fallen behind after Price was taken, but now it was on the move again, nipping at the carriage's racing rear wheels. The horses were bathed in sweat: They could not keep up this frantic pace much longer. Cotford needed a plan.

He yanked the reins to change direction, heading back to the main street in the hope of finding a crowd. *Let's see how this red menace reacts when exposed to witnesses.*

Suddenly, he heard that strange sound of flapping wings. For an instant, he saw what appeared to be the great claws of some giant beast reach down from above and he tried to dodge a razor-tipped talon, but he wasn't quick enough. He winced in pain as something sharp tore into his flesh.

Cotford cupped his hand over the wound just beneath his shoulder. It was deep, and the pain was horrible. His blood was pouring out. He drove the team of horses as fast as he could through the maze of back alleys, somehow managing to outmaneuver the crimson fog.

Emerging at last from the side streets, Cotford saw his refuge, like a finish line for a runner: the bold black letters PICCADILLY RLY tiled in brick on the front of a building. Using every ounce of his quickly dimin- ishing strength, he drew the horses to a halt right in the middle of the island on the Aldwych crescent. The few carriages and motorcars still out on the street screeched to a halt as the police carriage blocked their advance. Pedestrians stopped and stared. Cotford leapt from the driver's seat to the ground. He turned back to see that the bloodred fog had not followed them onto the main street. He ran to the side of the carriage and reached out his bloody hand into the opened door. "Get out!"

Mina hesitated for a moment, and then took Cotford's hand as he pulled her from the carriage. She stared at his torn shoulder. Reaching out to touch his wound, Mina knew that she could not staunch the flow of blood. With her hands now covered, she looked up at Cotford. There was nothing she could do. "You need a surgeon."

Cotford's attention was not on himself but on the skies above. The black clouds were gathering, blocking out the moonlight and stars. "Come on!" He grabbed Mina's hand and ran with her to the entrance leading down to the Strand tube station. Both of them stopped as they heard the sound of flapping wings circle above them, hidden within the whirlpool of black clouds. "Underground is your only hope!" Cotford screamed over the growing roar of wind as he pulled out a handful of coins from his pocket and shoved them into Mina's hand. "Tell Van Helsing I was wrong . . . about everything."

"It's me it wants!" Mina protested, trying to push the coins back at Cotford. "You save yourself!"

"My blindness has put both you and your family and friends in ter- rible danger. I see that now. Forgive me."

The sound of the wings above grew louder. The monster was coming.

"Go! Go now!" Cotford shoved Mina to the stairs. He turned back and pulled from his coat pocket the broken katana. From behind him he heard Mina run off and then strangely he heard her whisper in his ear, her voice soft and sweet, "You are forgiven."

For so many years he had been plagued by the deaths of those young women. He knew now why his soul had been so tormented. He'd been lying to himself all along, blocking out the truth. The killer was not human. The night he fell as he chased the Ripper, he had seen the same bloodred fog. It had surrounded him when he lost his way and tripped on the curb. The monster that came for him now was his destiny. If he could save just one person this night . . . then maybe his life's work would not have been in vain.

The monster, swooping low out of the clouds, finally revealed itself. The gargoyle roared, exposing gory rows of sharp teeth, and flashed its glowing red eyes. Its skin was scaly like that of a lizard, and horns curved out of its temples. From its back sprouted two massive leathery wings, and its long muscular tail was serrated and razor-sharp, chiseling bits out of the stone buildings and street as it whipped about. Its talonlike hands opened wide as it sped toward him, ready to embrace him in its vile grasp.

Cotford heard the people on the streets screaming in terror as they scattered for safety, leaving him alone. He prayed for his immortal soul and for courage. It was time to balance the scales. He wrapped the towel around the broken katana to form a makeshift handle as he charged, raising the blade and aiming for the monster's heart as it flew over him, but he was too slow. It was flying so fast that he only managed to embed the weapon in the gargoyle's leg. He heard it howl in pain as it crashed to the ground behind him.

Cotford was about to turn to continue the fight when he saw out of the corner of his eye the deadly tail whipping toward him.

The last thought that entered his mind was Van Helsing's warning: *What you do not see WILL kill you.*

Mina dashed down the stairs to the train platform. Waiting passengers scattered as she approached. She looked down at her hands, covered in Cotford's blood. Her dress was stained with the blood of the Woman in White. As the whistle blew, she ran to the last carriage of the train that had just pulled in. She was about to board when she heard a strange sound, like a child bouncing a ball.

Mina turned back to see Cotford's severed head bouncing down the steps. As it hit the platform with a sickening crunch, it rolled over. She expected to see Cotford's final expression to be one of abject terror. Instead, the old inspector's face was frozen into one of a serene calm. He appeared more peaceful in death than she had ever seen him in life.

A hideous roar shook Mina to her core, and she heard the sound of bricks being smashed. The shadow of a winged beast moved along the stairs.

The second whistle blew. Mina was tired of running. She wanted the battle to begin, but she knew that the longer she kept up the chase, the more time she would buy for Quincey, Arthur, and Van Helsing. The last carriage's metal doors closed in front of her. She reached out and with all her might pried the doors back open and fell in as the train started to move.

Dr. Max Windshoeffel and his wife chose not to board the train after seeing the blood-covered woman and the severed head that had rolled onto the platform. They would wait for the last tube to take them from the Strand to Finsbury Park. Max moved his wife away from the gory sight of the severed head, wondering if he should alert the police. As a doctor, it was his civic responsibility. His thoughts were interrupted by the horrendous sound of breaking bricks followed by an earsplitting screech.

A winged dragonlike creature suddenly appeared, flying out of the stairwell. Both he and his wife were too frightened to scream. The demon's tail, whipping behind it, sliced through the station wall's green and white tiles as if they were tissue paper. The demon then swooped down into the tunnel as if it were chasing the train. Max Windshoeffel had made up his mind. He was going to tell no one what he had seen.

"Get out!" Mina hissed at the few passengers in the carriage. She smashed the seat in front of her and broke off a sharp stake of wood. The combination of this act, her bloodstained appearance, and the gruesome sound now echoing through the tunnel, motivated the other passengers to move quickly forward into the adjoining carriage.

Mina looked back through the rear door to the see the gargoyle in pursuit. She suddenly felt a sensation she had only felt in her dreams for the past twenty-five years. Mina could feel Dracula's presence draw near. *It's him. He's come for me!*

In the tunnel, the gargoyle's wings crumbled a section of the cylindrical wall, leaving shattered bricks and a large dust cloud in its wake. Mina's hand gripped the wooden stake. "That's it. Keep coming. Time is no longer on your side."

There was a sharp gust of wind as a clawed fist smashed in the back door of the carriage. The heavy metal door smashed onto the floor of the train. Mina expected to see the hideous gargoyle in the doorway glaring at her, but to her surprise, she looked up to see only the glowing red mist cascading into the carriage. The mist pooled on the floor, and from within the swirling, blood-colored fog, a human form began to rise.

Thoughts of Dracula seeped into Mina's mind. God help her. What if it was he? The idea of seeing his face after all these years excited her, despite the evil he might have committed this night. She could not help it.

As the fog dissipated, a tall figure, dressed in black, stepped from the mist. Mina's anticipation made her breathless. "Prince Dracula," she whispered.

"Sorry to disappoint," Bathory sneered.

The love rising within Mina instantly curdled to hate. As the countess marched toward her, she noticed that Cotford had impaled Bathory's leg with Jonathan's katana, but the blade did not seem to slow her.

"You will not violate me again, Countess," Mina said, holding the stake before her. "This time I am prepared for you."

Bathory laughed. "Dracula's blood may grant you a modicum of strength, but do not think you are a match for me. I am the queen of my kind."

"You are a twisted, murdering sadist," Mina hissed. "By God, I will see this world free of your evil, or die fighting it."

"Oh, you will die, my sweet. You will die with the knowledge that your son and all your friends shall also perish this night. I promise you, their deaths will be brutal and merciless . . . as shall yours."

The mention of her son enraged her. Mina would never let this monster harm Quincey. She would use the wooden stake to rip the sneer from Bathory's contemptible face. Unleashing a war cry like the one she had heard Quincey P. Morris utter so many years ago, Mina raced forward.

Bathory growled with pleasure as Mina cocked her arm and angled the wooden stake straight for her heart, then merely reached out and caught the stake in midair. She pulled with her incredible strength so that Mina was thrown to her knees, straight into Bathory's clutches. Grabbing Mina by the hair, the she-devil forced her head back, stretching her alabaster neck. Then Bathory drew a blade. Mina recognized it: This curved amputation lancet was the preferred weapon of Jack the Ripper. Her eyes went wide with new terror as she struggled to break free of Bathory's iron grip, but the more Mina struggled, the more Bathory became aroused. Consumed with diabolical passion, the countess raised the blade to slash Mina's neck, savoring each second of the bloody violence to come.

Despite her newfound strength, Mina was no match for Bathory. Nearly four hundred years of drinking human blood had made the countess almost indomitable. Mina had failed to protect Quincey. All that was left was to pray.

With blade poised to strike, Bathory leaned down to lick Mina's ear, whispering sweetly, "Time to greet the Ripper."

CHAPTER XLIX.

—◆—

Van Helsing shot forward, slamming Quincey and Arthur Holmwood into the wall. He was so close to them that he could see his reflection in their eyes and was glad the old myth that vampires cast no
reflection was wrong. He also realized why they were frozen in horror:
His wild look, his pitch-black eyes, and his sharp fangs all stood in stark
contrast to the weak old man they once knew.

When he had drunk Dracula's blood, he'd had no idea just how
empowering it would be. No longer shaky and brittle, Van Helsing now
had the strength of a powerful warrior. He felt young again. He was
whole. He had been reborn.

Quincey recovered more quickly than Holmwood, but Van Helsing
gave him no time to fight back, simply picking up the lad and sending
him flying as if he were a feather pillow. Quincey landed against the oak
wardrobe, smashing its mirror.

Van Helsing laughed to see the look of shock on Holmwood's face.
"It was I who told our story to Bram Stoker. My first feeble attempt at
immortality . . ."

"*You* were the one who betrayed our oath?"

Van Helsing shook his head in dismay. Arthur Holmwood could
only see things in black or white. He was like a trained dog. Grabbing

Holmwood by his lapels, he casually tossed him across the room onto a velvet chaise longue.

Now he had Arthur Holmwood's full attention.

"You were given eyes, but you do not see. Asking Stoker to write my biography was not a betrayal," Van Helsing said. "Through him, I intended to pass on all the wisdom I had gained. My biography was to be a warning to future generations, a guidebook on how to battle the supernatural creatures I had fought my entire life. Instead, Stoker penned a fanciful mockery of the truth."

Van Helsing sensed Quincey's movement beside him and turned to see the boy eyeing the table full of weapons across the room. In that same moment, he felt the mild sensation of a chair being smashed across his back. He would barely have noticed it save for the wooden debris falling noisily about him. Van Helsing returned his attention to the surprised Arthur Holmwood, who was still grasping the broken pieces of two chair legs. He sensed Quincey moving across the room to the weapons. *Two birds with one stone.* Van Helsing picked up and threw Arthur Holmwood straight into Quincey, knocking the wind, and hopefully the fight, out of both of them. He was beginning to enjoy this. He hoped that after this painful demonstration, perhaps Arthur would listen to reason. Instead Holmwood, the old fool, reached into his pocket and brandished a gold cross.

"Every day for the last twenty-five years, I have regretted not joining Lucy in immortality," Holmwood spat. He advanced on Van Helsing, the cross held aloft. "You stopped me. You made me destroy her. You made me drive the stake into her heart to end her 'evil existence,' as you called it!"

"Lucy, Lucy, always *Lucy*," Van Helsing said.

He reached out and took hold of the cross in Holmwood's hand. *Time to teach this fool a lesson.* He was not remotely repelled by the cross. By joining the ranks of the un-dead, one did not necessarily ally oneself with the Devil.

Arthur was frozen in confusion. "Why?"

"Why is the cross not having any effect on me? The same reason the cross had no effect on Prince Dracula. Only a creature that fears God would fear His symbols. Your Lucy feared God." With a snarl, Van Helsing wrenched the cross from Holmwood's hand and threw it across the room. "If Dracula came to you at the moment of your death, Arthur, what choice would you have made?"

Without taking a moment to answer, Arthur dived for the weapons table.

Foolish. Van Helsing pounced to block his path. "It does not have to be this way. You can come with me." He turned to make eye contact with the bewildered Quincey Harker. "You both can."

"Never!" Quincey cried. He lunged at Van Helsing. Holmwood tried to snatch the bowie knife from the table, but the professor knocked him to the floor, spun around to catch Quincey, and twisted him like a rag.

"To face death in the heat of battle is quite different from waiting for it to creep up on you through old age," Van Helsing said. He pulled back Quincey's head, exposing his neck. "I tried to warn you, boy."

Van Helsing did not want to harm a lad he had once bounced upon his knee. Arthur Holmwood was too blinded by a quarter of a century of rage to see reason. But he had hoped he could persuade Quincey to join him. He had made a promise to Prince Dracula not to harm the lad, but to weaken him so he could easily be taken back to his mother. He licked his fangs in anticipation of the first taste of blood he would take by his own hand.

"Hypocrite!" Arthur Holmwood yelled.

Van Helsing heard a bang and felt a sharp pain in his back.

Holmwood's gun ripped a second bullet through Van Helsing's shoulder and sliced into Quincey's arm. The lad cried out in pain, and Van Helsing let him slip to the floor as a third bullet slammed through his body.

"You were our friend!" Holmwood said.

"I still can be," Van Helsing replied. "So can Dracula. It's not too late."

"I will not betray my faith."

Faith? What did Arthur Holmwood really know of faith? It was only when Van Helsing had opened his eyes to the evil that walked the earth that he had found faith. Well, if Arthur was so devout, then he surely knew that God was the creator of vampires. And God gave the un-dead the same freedom of choice that He gave to man: the choice to take the path of good or the path of evil. With incredible speed, he moved to disarm Holmwood. Perhaps without a gun in hand, Arthur would listen. But to the old man's surprise, Arthur would not be relieved of his weapon. Two shots thundered out. Arthur Holmwood's body quaked. A look of astonishment appeared in his pale blue eyes. Both men looked down to see a well of blood pouring from his chest.

With great sadness, Van Helsing whispered, "Only now, in the end, do you understand the fear of death."

"Arthur?" Quincey shouted.

At first it appeared as if Arthur was nodding, but then his eyes rolled back in his head, and the once-great man fell to the floor.

"No!" Quincey screamed. He charged at the professor, but Van Helsing simply caught him by the throat and shoved him against the bureau. He yanked the lad's head back again, exposing his neck, and his mouth gaped abnormally wide as he curled back his lips to reveal his fangs. Then he bent toward Quincey's throat.

CHAPTER L.

━━◇━━

Francis Aytown was not a lucky man. He was never at the right place at the right time. As a photographer, he had worked alongside the much-lauded John J. Thomson, who documented London street life in glorious stills. Thomson had gone to do the same in China, but Aytown had not wanted to travel so far. Thomson went alone and became the photographer of the Chinese emperor and later the British Royal Family. If only Aytown had taken the chance, how different his life could have been.

This evening had become a reminder of his folly. He now earned a shilling per frame by taking still photographs for tourists, especially those leaving the West End theatres. He had been working outside the Globe and Olympic theatres and had not learned of the Lyceum fire until the theatre had been reduced to nothing more than a smoldering pile. What a sum a picture of the flames would have fetched from the *Daily Telegraph* or the *Times*.

He had only just set up on the corner of Wych and Newcastle to take pictures of patrons leaving the nearby theatres when he heard the screams a few streets away. Grabbing his camera, he darted toward the direction of the commotion.

In front of the Strand tube station, there was mayhem. Police vehicles had cordoned off the entrance to the Underground trains. Aytown approached a constable. "What's happened, mate?"

"There's been a murder. Some wild animal escaped from the zoo. A man was killed."

Aytown wondered about this. London Zoo was a fair way north at Regent's Park. How could an escaped animal travel so far without being stopped by the police? Something was not right. His thoughts were interrupted by a shadow moving across the street. Aytown glanced about. Storm clouds shrouded the moon, and the ominous shadow began to move, appearing to vanish into the entrance of the tube station.

Something was definitely not right.

CHAPTER LI.

——◇——

Bathory's grip on Mina's neck felt like the wooden stock of a guillotine. The amputation lancet was the guillotine's blade slicing through the air. Mina threw her hands up to block the deadly strike. Her fingers clasped Bathory's forearm like a shackle, stopping the blade an inch from her skin. Bathory's bloodred lips twisted into a smile and she chuckled low in her throat, pushing her arm against Mina's grip, pressing the blade closer. It appeared she was giving the sadist exactly what she wanted: a fight. The harder Mina resisted, the more aroused Bathory became. At the end of her strength, in a last act of defiance, Mina decided she would deny Bathory this satisfaction. She closed her eyes and released her grip.

There came the sound of thunder. Mina opened her eyes to see the lancet hanging at the countess's side. Splinters of wood and electrical sparks showered down upon them. There was a thud inside the carriage as something heavy landed on the wooden floor. The countess, in a state of shock, was staring upward. Mina followed her gaze to see that the roof of the train had been ripped open. When she looked back, it was to find a dark figure crouched on all fours in the middle of the carriage. The figure's head hung low. He had a thick mane of pitch-black hair. Even bent forward, it was obvious he was over six feet tall. His hands were elegant, the long fingers like those of a concert pianist.

Mina's heart sang. She knew those hands. She had seen them kill, seen them covered in blood. She had also felt their loving caress. Slowly he rose, reaching his full stature, and a yearning surged through Mina's body. She was no longer alone. He had come back to her in the moment of her greatest need. But, after all she had done to hurt him, would he really save her? Could he still love her?

The man raised his head, the black locks falling back from his face. His wolflike eyes narrowed on Bathory, and his fierce expression was just as Mina remembered it. He was at once beautiful and terrible, kind and merciless. He was love and hate. At last Mina spoke the name that she'd held in her mind for a quarter of a century.

"Dracula . . ."

Bathory's hold on Mina's neck tightened at the sound of the name. She focused her hatred on the intruder, hissing, "Your ability to cheat death is most disturbing."

Despite her pain, Mina found joy. Dracula was gazing at her with the same longing she had felt for him. His expression confirmed what she longed to believe. Dracula was indeed a killer, but he was not cruel. The one she loved could never be in league with a sadistic monster like Bathory.

Dracula's black eyes flashed back to the countess, his face contorted into an expression of fury. Bathory would receive all the pain she deserved, and her death would be terrible. His voice was a deep growl spoken through clenched teeth: "Come to me, Countess. Come and die."

Bathory threw her arm back, and Mina felt herself fly through the air. Pain slammed through her head as she hit the metal wall of the carriage. Drifting into unconsciousness, Mina thought, *He has returned.*

Bathory looked upon the man standing before her. How could the infernal prince still be alive? She had killed him *twice.* Her anger boiled. Her desire for vengeance would never be sated. She wished nothing more than to destroy God's crusader, Dracula, once and for all, to bring damnation upon him, upon all of the hypocrites who followed God, even upon God himself. Bathory leapt. She soared through the air, lancet poised, aiming for Dracula's eyes, hoping to blind him.

Before Bathory's blade could find its deadly mark, the dark prince rose to meet her. The combatants clashed in midair. They grappled along the ceiling of the moving carriage, defying all laws of physics. Dracula slammed his knee into Bathory's stomach and she flew off the ceiling and into the window. Glass shattered outward into the tunnel. Dracula lunged to push her out, but Bathory flew back, straightening her body as she shot across the train, becoming a battering ram, hitting Dracula mid-torso. To her great surprise, he cried out in pain as he was thrown into the long bench, splintering the wood as he fell. Wasting no time, Bathory dived on top of him and plunged the lancet into his belly, cutting through his skin like butter. Dracula's precious blood flowed out, and the scent of the kill overtook her. She plunged the lancet again and again into Dracula's flesh and he screamed in unbearable pain. Bathory's confidence soared. He had grown weak!

Bathory had always considered herself queen of her kind. Now she would be king as well. God's champion was ripe for the taking. With Dracula out of the way, the way would be paved for her great plan. She would be benevolent to all of those to whom God showed no mercy. The impoverished wretches, the sexual deviants, the mentally unstable, the sick and the angry, the meek of the earth, the inheritors of the world; all these lowest of the low she would raise up and fulfill their long-suffering dreams. They would become her loyal servants. To those who pledged their loyalty to God and his teachings, she would break their backs on the wheel of her own inquisition. She would feed upon the wealthy and the powerful as they had fed upon the weak. Armies would be crushed beneath her feet. She would tear down the churches with her bare hands and force her blood down the Pope's throat. She was determined to remake the world in her own image, and Dracula's death would strike the first blow to herald her coming.

Bathory grabbed Dracula by the throat. He put up no resistance: He'd lost too much blood, and he was weak. She dug her fangs deep into his neck. Now she would take his blood, all he knew, all he was, all his power, all his strength. When she had still been human, Dracula had drained her and left her bleeding, but he had not drunk the last drop. He could not kill her himself: They were family; he loved her. Bathory was not burdened by such conflict. She planned to drink until the last breath crossed his lips.

Mina's vision was blurry when she regained consciousness. Through the pain in her head and the fog over her eyes, she saw two dark figures grappling on the far side of the carriage. One was clearly stronger than the other. Mina could never relish murder, but this time victory was sweet. She wanted to cry out, *Die, you witch, die!* She wanted Dracula to tear Bathory limb from limb. It would not erase the memory of what Bathory had done to her, but her death would go a long way to making the memory less painful.

Mina sat up, focused on the struggle in front of her, and discovered how wrong she was. Bathory's teeth were in Dracula's neck. He was struggling to escape her bite. He was bleeding from his gut. *How could this be?* For the first time, Mina understood why Dracula had remained in hiding: Bathory was more powerful than he was. If Dracula could not destroy Bathory, then what chance did she, Arthur, and Quincey have, even if they found Van Helsing alive?

Mina looked around for some sort of weapon. A long, thick electrical wire hung from where Dracula had burst through the ceiling. She yanked, and the wire came free. What could she really do with a wire? Tying it about Bathory would be useless. Mina saw the smashed door lying on the floor of the carriage. She tied one end of the thick wire to it and turned back to the battling foes.

With what seemed to be the last of his strength, Dracula grabbed hold of Bathory's face and dug his thumb deep into her eye socket. A viscous, multicolored fluid oozed from the hole where her eye had been. She ripped her fangs from Dracula's neck and wailed in misery. Keeping his hand gripped on her skull, Dracula arched Bathory's head back and twisted, growling like a wild animal as he tried to snap her neck.

Bathory yanked Dracula's hand from her face. A black hole where her eye had been now spewed blood. She slammed him against the floor, arching her head back as she wailed in agony. Mina took this moment of weakness to swing the other end of the wire around Bathory's neck.

The countess spun to face Mina. "You whore!"

Mina replied by kicking the broken door through the hole at the back of the carriage. The door echoed loudly in the dark tunnel as the train clanged along the tracks, igniting sparks as it skidded against the electrical rail. At last, the metal door wedged itself, like an anchor.

Mina relished the look in Bathory's lone eye as the bitch realized what she had done. She tried to run at Mina, but the wire around her neck suddenly pulled taut and Bathory was yanked out through the hole in the train and down onto the tracks.

Mina ran to the hole and stared out, prepared to see Bathory get back on her feet and come chasing after them. Instead, she saw the countess skid along the tracks until the metal blade of the katana, still lodged in her leg where Cotford had struck, caught the electrical rail, causing an explosion of sparks.

Bathory quivered on the tracks as the electricity surged through her. Her entire body glowed a brighter and brighter blue until she suddenly burst into flames. Bathory unleashed an unearthly shriek of pain, thrashing helplessly as the fire consumed her entire body.

Could it be that Mina had done the impossible: killed the vampire queen?

Francis Aytown was down to his last quarter-plate film. He set his camera upon his wooden tripod in the hope that a newsworthy photo would present itself. He had noticed the sheet that covered the victim's body was stained with blood at the top. It occurred to him that the victim might have been decapitated. Perhaps his luck had finally changed.

Aytown positioned himself as close as he could to the entrance of the Strand tube station. A shot of the murdered victim's headless corpse would fetch a good price. Unfortunately, the body had yet to be moved. He overheard the constables mention that no one could locate the police surgeon.

A low guttural sound erupted in the distance. As it drew closer, the pitch intensified, until everyone standing near the station cupped their hands over their ears for protection.

An explosion of red-orange flames spewed from the tube station entrance. Aytown could not believe his eyes. A large creature emerged, shrieking as it thrashed across the Aldwych crescent. Ignoring the deafening pain in his ears, he grabbed his camera and released the shutter. He had no time to frame the shot and hoped he had been quick enough to capture the complete horror of what he saw in his lens. If he had, then his luck really would have changed. The picture would be worth a small fortune. That was no animal escaped from any zoo. It was a living, fire-breathing dragon!

CHAPTER LII.

$\longleftarrow\!\!\!\longleftarrow\!\!\!\diamond\!\!\!\longrightarrow\!\!\!\longrightarrow$

"Professor, in God's name, please," Quincey begged.

Van Helsing regarded the lad with great sadness. "In God's name, I plead with you one last time to join us."

"I cannot," Quincey replied in a quivering voice. "Dracula is the monster that defiled my mother and killed my father."

The professor shook his head, despairing. "You leave me no choice." With one swift movement, he bit deep into Quincey's neck.

To his surprise, Van Helsing suddenly found himself flying across the room, smashing against the table of weapons, which scattered in his wake. Quincey looked down at his hands, frightened of his newfound strength. "God protect me!"

Van Helsing sat up and looked up in shock, trying to understand what had happened. Did this boy really have the strength to throw him across the room? Slowly, Van Helsing began to understand Dracula's desire to keep Quincey Harker alive. The dark prince had clearly thought that he might come to be a great asset in the battle against Bathory. But if Quincey Harker was already so powerful and so full of misguided hate, he could become a liability. It was time to make a decision. Quincey had to die. Van Helsing hoped Dracula would understand.

He grabbed the bowie knife from the floor and went after Quincey with lightning speed, grabbing him by the throat and ramming him against the wall. He drew back the knife to plunge it into Quincey's heart. May Dracula and God forgive him.

Van Helsing heard a *thwack*. He suddenly lost his grip on the bowie knife, and it tumbled to the floor. Quincey's weight became overwhelming. He could no longer hold him. *What was happening?* He felt the familiar sensation of the Reaper's grip. *"No! Nog niet,"* he gasped. "Not yet."

He looked down. A wooden arrow tip protruded from his chest. Van Helsing turned to see a bloodied Arthur Holmwood propped against the far wall, holding the crossbow. Blood streamed from his wounds and his mouth.

Van Helsing had been shot through the heart: Sorrow overwhelmed him. He gazed at Holmwood, with tears stinging his eyes. "I have so many things to do, to learn, to see. I can't die. Not yet."

"Damn you, professor!" Holmwood cried. "Damn you to hell!" With a battle cry, he dropped the crossbow and charged at Van Helsing.

"Arthur, wait!" Quincey yelled.

It was too late. Arthur hurled himself at Van Helsing, and the momentum sent them both crashing through the window. As they plunged the five stories toward the unforgiving ground, Van Helsing realized that, with no other allies at his side, Dracula was too weak to battle Bathory alone. Unopposed, the countess would oversee the end of mankind.

Dear God, why have you abandoned us?

CHAPTER LIII.

—◆—

As the tube approached Finsbury Park station, Mina dashed to where Dracula lay vulnerable and unconscious, propped up against one of the long benches in the carriage. Although he had lost a great deal of blood, she knew he was still alive. The wounds on his neck and abdomen would have killed any mortal, but for him they were already healing.

As if on cue, Dracula's eyes fluttered open. Those pitch-black eyes, filled with such feeling; could they truly be soulless? Mina knelt beside her dark prince, and he reached out for her help. This was just like the moment at the castle gate in Transylvania, when Dracula was burning in the sun, the kukri knife impaling his heart. He had reached for her, and Mina had forsaken him for a more earthly choice: Jonathan. Now Jonathan was dead. The thought made her draw away.

"You killed Jonathan."

Dracula's dark eyes looked up, into what was left of her soul. There was a pain in his eyes as if her words hurt him more than any blow from Bathory. "If you truly believe that, you never knew me at all."

Mina recalled hearing Dracula's voice when she battled the Woman in White. He had saved her. She should have known better than to think he would ever harm her. No matter how terrible his actions,

Dracula had never lied to her. Dracula would not have killed Jonathan. He loved her that much.

Mina took Dracula's hand in hers. The icy cold of his touch sent shivers through her body, like a schoolgirl touched by her first love. She remembered the way he'd touched her that night so long ago, and she yearned for that passion again. Jonathan had been the love of her life, but Dracula was the passion.

A sudden high-pitched wail startled Mina. It was merely the brakes, slowing the Underground train. She looked up to see the other passengers in the next car gawking. Soon they would be surrounded.

It was time to flee.

Even before the train came to a complete stop, Mina and Dracula burst through the doors and bolted onto the platform. He was able to walk briskly but was unsteady on his feet. Mina threw his arm over her shoulder and wrapped her arm around his waist for support. She was frightened: The Dracula she had known was so powerful, and now he was a shadow of his former self. At the same time, Mina felt closer to him than ever before. For the first time, it was clear that he needed her, too.

After struggling up the stairs, they emerged from the station. Mina looked up into the night sky, sensing his thought in her mind. *I know where you want to go. We won't be able to reach our destination before sunrise.*

Dracula nodded. She spied a cart with a single horse hitched to it across the street. There was no driver in sight, but there was a thick woolen blanket in the back. Mina grabbed the blanket and was about to help Dracula into the seat when they were suddenly blinded by bright lights as an open-topped motorcar appeared.

Again, she heard Dracula's thoughts in her mind. *A motorcar will be faster.*

She propped Dracula against the cart, handed him the blanket, and dashed out in front of the motorcar, which quickly screeched to a halt.

"Oi, lady!" screamed the driver. "Watch where you're going. I almost ran you—"

Before the man could finish his rant, Mina snatched him out of his seat and threw him out into the street. The astonished driver quickly scampered away, crying out for help. Mina turned to Dracula. He was smiling.

Mina hoisted the convertible roof and locked it into place, while Dracula stumbled into the passenger seat.

People on the street were staring at them; some started to come forward to assist the driver. It was time to move. Mina jumped into the driver's seat, released the hand brake, put the car in gear, and sped away along the Seven Sisters Road, which would take them northwest out of London.

Mina looked at Dracula and was more certain than ever that she had made the right choice to help him. Bathory had to die, and Dracula, even in his weakened state, was still their best weapon. She thought of Quincey. Dracula's choice of destination was tactically brilliant. There they would own the high ground on familiar terrain. She had to bring her son there, to the only place he would be safe. The only place they would all feel safe, even if right now safety was just an illusion.

CHAPTER LIV.

───◇───

Quincey leaned out of the window of the Midland Grand's upper floor. The battered bodies of Arthur Holmwood and Professor Van Helsing lay grotesquely sprawled on the street outside. The back of Van Helsing's skull had exploded like a watermelon upon impact with the pavement. Dark blood pooled beneath the old man's head and oozed out to the street, filling the cracks between the cobbles. Despite the gore, Van Helsing's face held an expression of pure serenity. The old man appeared wise and scholarly again, as if he had finally found peace. Arthur Holmwood's large frame enveloped Van Helsing's body. His head lay on Van Helsing's chest, sparing him the indignity of a cracked skull.

Through bitter tears, Quincey came to a realization: Dracula had won the war. Like a great military general, he had divided and conquered. Quincey had underestimated his foe, and his blunder had cost Arthur Holmwood his life. Now the foolish boy was the only one left for Dracula to conquer.

A group of morbid onlookers had gathered on Euston Road. Quincey felt the urge to run. The police were still looking for him, methodically searching building by building, street by street. No doubt the gathering crowd would draw them back to the hotel to investigate.

Racked with pain, he made his way down the stairs and through the lobby. The loss of blood from the gunshot wound in his arm should have left him so dizzy he could barely stand. But he did not feel at all weak. It had to be Dracula's cursed blood within him. Quincey wondered if he had ever truly been human.

Out on the street, Arthur Holmwood moaned, trying to move. The crowd of onlookers gasped.

Quincey cried out, "Arthur!" He shoved his way through the astonished crowd, fell to his knees, and scooped Holmwood into his arms, peeling him away from Van Helsing's corpse. Quincey gently cradled his head. He heard the crowd murmuring the word "murder." He sensed a few onlookers breaking off from the pack to run up the streets, surely hurrying off to alert the authorities. He didn't have much time.

Holmwood's chiseled face was pale and swollen. Blood streamed from the wounds in his chest, his nose, mouth, and ears. He was brave and strong, but he couldn't hide the agony he felt. He struggled to breathe.

Quincey fought in vain to hold back his tears. He took hold of Holmwood's hand. Van Helsing had accused Holmwood of being afraid of death. But Quincey saw in Holmwood's face only peace and a small smile. Arthur was at last achieving what he wanted.

Quincey was the one who was afraid and panicked. "Something is happening to me, Arthur. You saw what I was able to do. I'm cursed. I'm *damned*. If Dracula's wretched blood is in Mina, then his blood is in me as well. What am I going to do? You can't leave me, Arthur. Don't leave me."

Holmwood called on the last of his great strength to speak. "It isn't a curse. Don't you see? It can be a blessing. You are as strong as he. You can defeat both Dracula and Bathory." Bubbles of blood foamed out of his mouth. His muscles stiffened and he gritted out one last breath: "Bury me with my Lucy. . . ."

Quincey watched helplessly as the mighty spark that was Arthur Holmwood was finally extinguished. The great lord's battles had finally come to an end. Quincey at last understood why he had sought out death for all these years. In death, he would gain his fondest wish, to be reunited with the love of his life.

Quincey looked at his dirty, bloodied hands. Holmwood had said it was a *blessing* that Quincey was as strong as Dracula, that he could defeat him. But would this power corrupt him as it had his enemy? Would the evil consume him while he tried to hunt down the very creature that cursed him?

"Where it all began."

Quincey was startled by the sound of his mother's voice whispering in his ear. He looked around, but she was nowhere to be seen. There was no one save the crowd of onlookers.

"Where it all began, my son."

This time his mother's voice was crystal clear, unmistakable. Quincey gently laid Arthur Holmwood's body on the ground, unsure of what to do next. He had no plan. He was utterly alone.

"Where it all began, my son. My love."

The vampire blood within Mina was calling out to him. Stoker's novel had described the mental connection between Dracula and Mina. That mental connection was now a triangle. This time, Mina's voice came not only with words but with images as well: a broken-down, centuries-old monastery high upon a cliff, beside a graveyard and a stone chair, with the angry sea lapping below.

It all began in Whitby, at Carfax Abbey. Mina was with Dracula, and they were waiting for him.

Alarm bells rang out around him. He could hear the cartwheels and the horses' hooves on the cobbles. The onlookers who'd broken away from the crowd returned, running beside a police carriage, which pulled up in front of the hotel. Quincey's pulse quickened when he recognized the tall policeman emerging from the coach. He was the one who had the sketch of him and Holmwood. It was time for Quincey's nightmares to end once and for all.

Perhaps it was his destiny to destroy Dracula. Perhaps God had shown Quincey a way to turn his own curse into a blessing. Quincey had nothing left. There was only one option left for him: He had to save his immortal soul. He would go to Whitby, to Carfax. With God at his side, he would confront the demon. If he could kill Dracula, perhaps he could break the curse and save himself and his mother from eternal damnation. If he was to die in battle against such great evil, Quincey prayed the gesture would be enough for God to forgive him.

The tall policeman made his way through the crowd. It was time to go.

As Quincey ran off, he heard the startled cries from the crowd and sensed astonishment from the tall policeman. Then he was running like the wind, faster than any man could possibly run. The curse was unleashed. He was free at last.

CHAPTER LV.

T he sun was rising in the morning sky. Dracula and Mina had been driving all night. During the silence of the drive, Mina's mind had been filled with a cascade of random, anxious thoughts. But over and over again she came to the same conclusion. Zealotry and obsession led to only one place. From her many experiences in life, she knew this to be true, yet Mina could not stop her blood from boiling with rage as they sped north. The violent events of the previous night replayed themselves on an endless loop. The death and destruction caused by Bathory over the centuries were immeasurable, the human wreckage left in her wake incalculable. The more Mina thought about the countess, the angrier she became. The angrier she became, the harder she pressed down on the throttle. She gripped the steering wheel so tightly that the blood was forced from her knuckles. Bathory had violated her, tried to kill her, and most grievous of all, she had threatened Quincey's life. There was no longer any doubt in Mina's mind. For the first time, her human blood merged in perfect harmony with the vampire's. She intended to utterly destroy Countess Elizabeth Bathory.

Mina sped the motorcar around a donkey-drawn milk cart. The animal came to a sudden stop, and pulled back. The cart's driver screamed behind her. Only then did Mina realize how fast she was going. She needed to calm down and sort things out in a rational manner. It was what she did best. She could not let zealotry and obsession blind her or she would be no better than Bathory. In the fifteenth century, a noble had had to be brave to inspire his people to follow him. But it was not bravery that kept peasants in line when the tax season came. It was fear. The peasants outnumbered the noble families by a hundred to one. A nobleman had to be cruel to instill fear in his people, and just as brutal to make his rivals too afraid to attack him. Blood was cheap in the fifteenth century. Murder and death were common. Brutality was an accepted form of control. The only thing that separated the beloved rulers from the tyrants was whether or not their cruelty was justified. It was from these dark ages that Bathory and Dracula had sprung. They were the last surviving relics of a bygone era.

A stalled motorcar suddenly appeared in the middle of the road. Mina pulled hard on the brake, turned the wheel sharply, and drove the motorcar off the road, barely missing a tree. The car shuddered to an awkward stop, and she took a moment to breathe and at last allowed herself to look down beside her. Wrapped in the blanket on the floor, protected from the sun, his body tightly curled to fit the small space, Dracula gave no indication of awareness. Mina was so confused by the man, the creature, beside her. He was capable of such bravery and great love, he was loyal and generous, and yet he could be violent beyond words. She feared what might happen if she allowed Dracula to influence Quincey. He could perhaps protect them from Bathory, but at what cost to Quincey's immortal soul? The daylight hours were the time of Dracula's slumber, when he could heal and rest.

Mina tried to find Bathory in her mind, but all she found were clouds and sky. What that meant, she could not be sure. Obviously, the fact that it was such a small amount of blood she had exchanged with Bathory made it impossible for Mina to obtain a clear picture of her actions. No doubt Bathory had planned it this way. But Bathory had been badly burned, and also needed time to regenerate. The question was, how long?

Mina backed the vehicle onto the road. She had to take herself to a familiar place she could defend, somewhere to regroup with Quincey. She had to go back to Carfax Abbey.

Upon returning to England after her wedding, Mina had learned of Lucy's death. She and Jonathan had not yet consummated their wedding vows, for Jonathan had been too sick from his ordeal in Transylvania, and Mina too overwhelmed by grief. Somehow, though, Jonathan had found the strength to join the band of heroes to find and destroy Dracula's coffins. It was on that night that Dracula had first come to Mina. She had been shocked that Dracula was as much in mourning for Lucy as she was. He blamed her death on Van Helsing. Mina did not know what to believe. She could not match the monster Van Helsing spoke of with the handsome regal prince who now brought her comfort. Not wanting to tell Jonathan that Dracula had come to her, Mina had said that Dracula had explained the true nature of Lucy's death in a dream. Fearing that she had been influenced by the monster, Van Helsing had insisted she be kept out of all their plans. As she wrote in her journals at the time, "It is strange to me to be kept in the dark as I am to-day, after Jonathan's full confidence for so many years."

She had been angry at Jonathan then. Their relationship had been strained. She and Jonathan were staying at Dr. Seward's residence in Whitby when Dracula came to her late in the night. He had professed his love for her, and offered her the realization of all her dreams and desires. While Jonathan lay asleep beside her, she had allowed herself to be swept off her feet, and willingly went away with the prince to Carfax Abbey. That time, alone with Dracula in the abbey ruins, had been the first time in months that she felt at peace, safe and truly loved.

"I have not dared return to Whitby," Mina said aloud now, in the hope she could convince herself that she was doing the right thing. "I have not been to Carfax Abbey since the night we spent together. When we . . ." She couldn't say the words for the flood of mixed emotions that swept through her. *She* remembered how much she'd yearned to relive that night she had spent with Dracula in Carfax.

Mina thought Dracula was asleep, and was surprised when his words emerged from beneath the blanket. "It is fitting. It will end where it all began."

Spoken like a warrior. There was no compromise in him. Bathory had survived for centuries by plotting and retreating. By contrast, Dracula charged in where others feared to tread. But there was a price for his courage, paid by all those around him. Blood always begat more blood. Constant fighting was no way to live: It was not the life lesson she wanted to bequeath to Quincey.

Quincey was the future. Mina needed to ensure that he would survive them all. The blood flowing through her veins gave her the strength to defend him from Bathory, and he needed protection now more than ever. He had never witnessed the full strength of a vampire. She sensed that he had received her telepathic message and was coming to meet them. If she was right in her prediction that Bathory needed time to heal, there was still a chance for him to escape. If Quincey managed to reach Carfax before Bathory found them, Mina could perhaps take a ship to America with her son. Once Quincey was safe and out of Bathory's reach, Mina could return, and instead of being the hunted, she would become the hunter. She and Dracula could track down Bathory, discover where she slept during daylight hours, and destroy her while she lay defenseless in her coffin.

Mina sped across the English countryside, the sun beginning to lower on the horizon. They had been driving for much of the day, giving her time to think it through. Her rationality had won out over her primal instincts. Zealotry and obsession were the tragic character flaws of the likes of Bathory, Cotford, and Dracula. They would not be hers. She and Quincey would survive because they were willing to walk away. They would live to fight another day.

Sergeant Lee opened the wardrobe and peered cautiously into the darkness. There was nothing inside but hanging clothes. Closing the door, he peered out of the adjacent window to inspect the night sky, which was full of rain, distant thunder, and lightning. Lee drew the curtains shut. "All clear. Nothing to be afraid of."

"Under the bed," whispered the voice behind him.

Under the bed. *Of course.* Lee was so tall, he loathed having to crouch down onto the floor, but to keep the peace, he obeyed. Nothing. Not even a stray sock. "All's clear," he announced. "There are no monsters here."

He stood up and looked into the relieved eyes of his five-year-old son, turned and smiled at his four-year-old daughter. Both children were curled up in their beds under the covers. Lee hated to lie to his children. No one knew better than he that there really were monsters in the world. Not the kind that children imagined, goblins and the like, but real monsters—those that prowled the darkened streets of London, looking to do others harm. The kind of monsters he had sworn to bring to justice. It was better that children remained innocent of such real-world horrors for as long as they could.

Lee smoothed the covers as he leaned over and kissed his children on their foreheads. "Good night. Sweet dreams."

"Don't forget the door, Daddy," his daughter whispered urgently.

"I'll leave it ajar as always." Lee smiled. "I love you." His children believed that the light from the hallway sconces repelled monsters.

If only it were that simple.

He stepped into the hall to see his wife, already in her nightclothes and cap, waiting to say good night, and recognized the look of concern on her face. He took his wife by the arm and led her into the living room. He needed to talk, and he wanted to ensure it was out of earshot of the children.

"What are you going to tell them?" she asked with grave concern.

"I don't want you to worry yourself. It will be all right," Lee said. He had been beside himself with sadness since receiving the telegram from Scotland Yard earlier that evening, and his wife had been on the verge of panic. The telegram was an official confirmation, but Lee had already heard the sad news from Inspector Huntley, who had been to the area surrounding the Strand tube station that morning. Inspector Cotford, the police surgeon, Constable Price, and the policemen who had accompanied them were dead. Scotland Yard's top brass had many unanswered questions, and Lee was to commence his night shift with a summons to the deputy commissioner's office to describe his part in the actions of Inspector Cotford. He brushed the dust from his knees and tucked in his crisp white shirt.

Upon learning that Cotford had died for his beliefs, Lee's initial instinct had been to pick up the sword from his dead friend's hand and continue the charge. But, as Lee forced his rage aside, he realized he could not allow himself to give way to vengeance. He could not allow himself to be consumed like Cotford. He refused to travel down that dark path. It was hard for him to admit it, but Van Helsing and Cotford were opposite sides of the same coin. Both had been consumed by a dark quest. In the end, telling the truth would never bring Cotford back, nor would it prove the identity of Jack the Ripper. Lee's superiors would reprimand him, possibly even discharge him from duty for taking part in Cotford's unwarranted and foolhardy investigation. He could not risk his career by telling his superiors what they didn't want to hear. Without his job, how would Lee support his family? Providing as best as he could for one's family is what a man should be measured by—not by how many felons he'd collared. On this point, he differed greatly from the late Inspector Cotford. There would always be delinquents roaming the street: It was a never-ending battle. Lee looked back down the hallway to his children's room and imagined them drifting into peaceful sleep. He felt no guilt as he decided what he had to do: He would betray Inspector Cotford. He would lie to his superiors and go on record to state that Cotford was as mad as the March Hare, and had lost all sense of reason. It would not be a complete lie. Cotford was a fanatic, and it was his downfall. Lee would testify that he realized Cotford's folly, and that was the reason he refused to join the inspector in his new investigation into the Ripper murders. Yet, he respected the chain of command and did not go behind Inspector Cotford's back to report him to their superiors. After all, Huntley had given his word that he would never implicate him. Being a former army man, as Lee was, the deputy commissioner would accept this explanation and respect his loyalty. He believed that this course of action would even help his career by positioning himself as a man who could be trusted.

After pulling on his overcoat, putting his hat on his head, and kissing his wife, Lee ushered her to bed. Once he heard the master bedroom door close, he hurried into his study and unlocked the lower desk drawer. He pulled out the old Ripper suspect profile that Cotford had taken from Scotland Yard. Reading the name on the file gave Lee a shudder: DR. ABRAHAM VAN HELSING.

Lee returned to the living room and stoked the fireplace with the poker. The moment of truth. His guilt rising again, he attempted to justify his action. He had deduced from the evidence at the Midland Grand Hotel that Arthur Holmwood had pierced Van Helsing with an arrow and that both men had fallen to their deaths. If Cotford was right and Van Helsing was Jack the Ripper, then it was truly over. Cotford was never one to seek glory. He'd sought only justice, and justice had been done. As for Mina Harker, no evidence remained to tie her to any crime. Lee was certain it was Quincey Harker he'd seen hovering over the body of Holmwood outside the Midland Grand. Regardless of what he thought he saw, he would stick to the facts. The facts were . . . he had no real evidence against Quincey Harker. Besides, the alley murder case, the one that had started all of this, belonged to Inspector Huntley. Let it be on Huntley's head.

Lee tossed the Van Helsing file into the fireplace and watched the papers darken, smoke, and burn. He had had it with Jack the Ripper. He begged God to forgive him. Right or wrong, Lee's part in this story was finished.

The clouds churned and rolled quickly over the moon, plunging the English countryside into darkness. Quincey's horse charged along the coast, panting, heaving, and sweating. It flinched at the roar of distant thunder. An angry jag of lightning ripped through the sky, causing Quincey's mount to stop in its tracks and then suddenly bolt. Quincey dug in his heels and held tightly to the reins, trying to retain his balance. At last getting the horse under control, Quincey patted its neck, reassuring it. It was as if the weather was throwing everything at him to slow his progress. Didn't Stoker mention in his novel that Dracula could control the weather? There was hardly a soul left to ask whether Stoker's assumptions were true.

Dracula knows I'm coming.

Quincey gripped with his legs and sent the horse charging forward again. It was the blood. Whatever he knew, so did Dracula. Surprise was out of the question. Quincey understood that the odds were not in his favor, but he would not waver in his pursuit. Dracula had to die.

If Quincey had been asked about his belief in the supernatural two months ago, he would have laughed out loud. Now he knew different. It was up to him to finish the grim task the brave band of heroes began twenty-five years ago.

As Quincey raced across the moors, he became convinced that this had always been his destiny. For the first time in his life, the road he traveled was free from guilt, remorse, fear, or question. Quincey was resolute. It is said that those who deny their best destiny can never find success. He had applied this logic in his choice to become an actor. Now the consequences were much greater.

He raced on, ducking beneath a tree branch that nearly unhorsed him, so lost in thought that he hadn't seen it coming. It was only his newly enhanced senses that saved him from having his face smashed in. *What a stupid way to die that would have been!* Quincey never thought much about his own death. He was young and, until a few days ago, still thought himself invincible. If only that were true. He felt his quest for blood swell with the incoming storm. He was reminded of a line from *Macbeth*, a role he now knew he would never have a chance to play onstage. *"Yet I will try the last. Lay on, Macduff; And damn'd be he that first cries, hold!"*

Bathory swooped down to the steps of the Basilique de Saint-Denis as the night sky began to dissolve into the translucent blue of dawn. If anyone were awake to witness her arrival, it would have appeared as if one of the stone gargoyles had fallen to the ground. The dark-hooded cloak Bathory wore to conceal her charred skin blended almost perfectly with the stone.

Bathory walked toward the entrance to the church. She was in torturous pain. The flames had burned deep into her flesh, causing her muscles to harden and constrict. With each new movement, she could feel her flesh tearing and slowly regrowing. She longed for rest, and for the loving embrace of her Women in White. They would have been eager to tend to her wounds. Bathory missed their devotion to her.

They were dead now. Two more reasons for Dracula and Mina to suffer.

Her remaining eye spied the stone-carved Trinity over the entrance. Bathory could have easily walked through the door as any visitor would, but this was God's church. She wanted to make an entrance that would remind Him of her strength. Her charred hand smashed through the heavy wood-and-iron door. Drawing back her hood, Bathory walked defiantly through the mammoth great hall of the Gothic church known as the Royal Necropolis of France, the final resting place of all the monarchs. Her eye fell on the statue of Christ dying on the cross. Even His son was weaker than she.

Vibrant colors appeared in the stained glass as the sun rose to caress the windows. She ignored the pain that enveloped her entire body as she walked past the statues of the last Bourbon kings to the tombs. The carved-stone room housed onyx grave markers on the floor. Louis XVI supposedly lay beneath the center stone on the right, and Marie Antoinette under the center stone on the left. Gold letters on the black onyx read: MARIE-ANTOINETTE D'AUTRICHE 1755–1793. Bathory knew that Antoinette wasn't under there. Well, not all of her anyway. Bathory turned her attention to the unmarked onyx stone beyond the dead queen's tomb. Gritting her fangs, she smashed her blackened fist through the stone, breaking a hole large enough for her arm to fit through. Her crooked hand reached beneath the floor and pulled out an ivory box with a cross on it. Bathory felt tears of blood swell in her one remaining eye, causing steam to rise from her flesh, which was still hot from the fire. The box itself was a gift from someone Bathory had once loved. Dracula had called Bathory a monster that could not love. If only he knew. In truth, she loved so deeply that she had been willing to burn down the world in revenge when she lost what she loved. The box contained what Bathory had at one time considered her greatest possession. The last time she had stood in this church, she'd lifted the onyx stone and carefully placed the box beneath it. It was her gift to her beloved, a sign that her death had been avenged. It was also a promise that the whole world—and God Himself—would pay for what they'd done.

Dismissing the agony shooting through her fingers, Bathory

wrenched open the ivory box's lid. The secret inside caught the reflection of the candles in the crypt. Bathory ran her fingers gingerly along the object within: a kukri knife, stained with dried blood. It was the same knife that she'd driven to its hilt into Dracula's chest twenty-five years ago. To seal the promise that she now made to herself, Bathory licked the dried blood from the still-sharp blade. It was Dracula's blood, and it was delicious. This knife would deliver the final deathblow to her enemy.

Bathory replaced the ivory box. She dwelled on the error of her last encounter with Dracula. She had miscalculated him and misjudged Mina. She would not make that mistake again. It was clear that Mina Harker had Dracula's blood in her veins, as well as Bathory's own. Bathory smiled to herself, this time not minding the pain in her charred face. She, too, had drunk from Dracula. She would skewer him to the wall with the kukri knife and make him watch as she ripped Mina's head from her neck. Before Dracula died, he would see Bathory bathing in Mina's blood.

Bathory no longer had the immortal's luxury of time. If she were to succeed, she had to move quickly. Dracula was still weak, but she sensed that he would try to persuade Mina to join the ranks of the un-dead. To claim her prizes, Bathory needed to reach them before that happened. She needed to strike, and strike quickly.

She turned on her heels and marched toward the exit. There was one other mortal who carried Dracula's blood: Quincey Harker. Mina's son had to die as well. Without Mina and Dracula to protect him, the boy was no more than a gnat waiting to be swatted. When they were gone, there would be none left to challenge her. God's world would be her plaything.

"Que faites-vous?" a male voice called. She spun to see a young monk holding a lantern. A look of horror fell across his face as he beheld what was left of Bathory. She could smell the fear in his blood from across the hall as he cried out, *"C'est le Diable!"*

He called her the Devil. She smiled. *Not quite.* Although Bathory admired Lucifer for having the courage to break with heaven, he had failed. She vowed never to be cast down.

Bathory drew closer. The monk held up his cross and cried, *"Sanctuaire!"*

What a fool! There was no sanctuary from Countess Elizabeth Bathory. She lunged forward.

"Antichriste!"

Her fangs sank into the monk's throat, silencing his cry. After tasting the bouquet of Dracula's blood, the monk's was like a cheap altar wine. It mattered not. He would sate her thirst until she returned to England.

Upon draining the body, she cast the monk's corpse across the nave, smashing it into the rows of votive candles. Then she pulled the hood of her velvet cloak over her bald, blackened head to protect her from the sun, left the church, and moved quickly through the streets of Paris. There were very few people out and about at this early hour, and those who saw her would see no more than a passing shadow. Before the sun's direct rays filled the sky, Bathory would be back in England. Her feet had already left the ground. Rising through the blanket of clouds, she saw the land disappear beneath her as she soared over the English Channel. A few seconds more and she would be safe within her black carriage. While she slept, she would heal further. As she slumbered, her mares would race across the English countryside to Whitby. There, in a ruined abbey, her obsession would reach its zenith. How perfect. God's warrior would die in a ruined cathedral. Dracula and his bloodline would come to an end. She would pick up the spark that Satan had once used in his attempt to burn down heaven, bring it to earth, and ignite the flame that would consume the world.

CHAPTER LVI.

───◆───

As they passed the old Westenra summer home, Mina slowed the car to gaze back in time. She half expected Lucy to come running out the front door.

Mina remembered the day she had met Lucy, back when they were adolescents. Mina's parents owned one of Whitby's two shops, and Mina had been forced to work at the shop after school and all summer to help her family make ends meet. She had never known the normal childhood joys. Lucy was the rich girl on the hill, but she, too, felt isolated, though not due to lack of friends. Lucy had an insatiable curiosity and wanted to experience everything life had to offer. Sneaking away from her estate one warm summer morning, Lucy had traveled alone into town to investigate how what her mother called the "common" people lived. Her adventure had brought her, with a handful of coins, into Mina's parents' shop with the mission of gorging herself on sweets. Mina at first assumed it was pity for the sad, lonely "common" girl that had caused Lucy to offer her friendship; but Lucy's heart was more kind than that.

As the motorcar sped on, Mina's eyes drifted to the cliff that overshadowed the town. Upon those treacherous rocks loomed her destination, Carfax Abbey. She saw the stone seat on the cliff's edge, where she had found Lucy sleepwalking, with what she had thought were two pinpricks in her neck, pinpricks that Mina had believed she had made while fastening Lucy's shawl for her. That was the terrible night when the *Demeter* had crashed ashore and Dracula had come into their lives.

A sound of distant thunder interrupted Mina's reflection. Dark clouds were spewing up from the south. The sea had become choppy. A storm was fast approaching. Mina needed to get to the top of the cliff before the rains swelled the river, washing out the road. The car passed the one hundred and ninety-nine steps that led up to the cliff's summit. As children, Mina and Lucy used to race to the top, with Lucy usually getting caught up in her petticoats but still winning. At the stone seat on the summit, Lucy had told her all about her three suitors. Mina thought of Quincey Morris and Dr. Jack Seward. God rest their souls.

The motorcar passed a hotel that had once been the stately Holmwood summerhouse. As the rain began to fall, Mina maneuvered the car onto the wooden bridge that ran over the now-churning River Esk. She thought again about that first night when Dracula had arrived in Whitby, and images started to flash in her mind. He'd happened upon Lucy after having been trapped on the *Demeter* without any nourishment. The sailors had been besieged by plague, making their blood too poisonous for Dracula to drink. He couldn't even feed on the rats, as they, too, carried the plague. A starving man would make a glutton of himself after fasting for so long, and Dracula should have drained Lucy to the death. Despite his hunger, he had consumed only enough to sustain himself and had left her on the stone seat for Mina to find. In Dracula's own way, he had been merciful.

Creak. The rotting horse bridge objected to the weight of the motorcar. Mina considered reversing. The bridge protested more fiercely as it began to sway. The storm clouds had not fully obscured the sun, which meant Mina could not abandon the car and leave Dracula defenseless. The bridge was not going to hold much longer; Mina had to decide quickly. She was about to put the car in reverse, when Dracula reached out from under the blanket and slammed her hand down on the throttle, sending the car forward at top speed. The motorcar thundered across the last few feet just as support gave way. The rear wheel had barely landed when the bridge collapsed into the river. Dracula drew his hand back under the protection of the blanket.

The motorcar grumbled up the steep incline of Green Lane until the wheels started to spin uselessly on the rain-muddied road. Finally reaching the fork in the road, Mina decelerated and turned onto Abbey Lane. The familiar sight of what had once been Dr. Seward's asylum caught her eye. Poor Jack. He had been the kindest soul.

They neared the grounds of the abbey and here she noticed anew how the trees simply disappeared, as if the land was so cursed it could not sustain life. Storm clouds smothered the sky. She drove on and suddenly there it was, their destination. Carfax Abbey sat broken, haunting the cliffs above the sleeping town of Whitby. Its Gothic towers scratched the skies and its long-empty cathedral-like windows kept a silent and solemn watch over the mist-filled graveyard next door. The last time Mina had set foot in the abbey was the night when she had come to bid farewell to her dark prince, twenty-five years ago. Now she was here to do so again.

Mina's plan played itself out in her mind. She would leave Dracula behind to face Bathory's wrath, buying time whilst she smuggled Quincey to safety in the New World. Mina understood that Dracula would not refuse her, but that leaving him to fight alone would mean his demise. She shuddered. Could she be that cold and calculating? For Quincey's sake, she knew she could.

She steered the motorcar to a stop at the western gate. "We've arrived," Mina said, the engine coughing into silence. "The sun's gone."

Dracula pulled himself onto the seat and opened the door and, slowly unfolding himself, emerged from the car, allowing the worn-out blanket to tumble from his broad shoulders onto the ground. Leaning his head back in the rain with his eyes closed, he breathed in deeply, letting the night fill him. Lightning exploded in the sky, illuminating Dracula's strong face. He showed no signs of ever having been injured, though he had lost much blood. He seemed as Mina had always remembered him: regal and forbidding. It was as if returning to Carfax had somehow rejuvenated him.

A lonely howl—a dog or wolf?—sounded in the distance, floating on the wind. Dracula turned at the sound. Mina could not discern from his stony look whether the cry was a welcoming or a warning.

Rain pounded the ground as Dracula reached out to Mina. The moment of her dreaded decision was upon her. She took Dracula's hand and they raced through the rain toward the shelter of the abbey.

Bathory's black carriage raced northward. She leaned out to see that darkness now covered the land. The driving rain beat in rhythm with her mares' thundering hooves. She had slept for hours. The flight to France and back on the night wind had taken a great amount of effort. Bathory looked in the mirror at her ravaged face. The blood of the monk had restored her strength but had not begun to heal her wounds. *So much the better*, she thought. Her ghastly injuries would lull Dracula into a false sense of superiority. In the battle to come, she would use this to her advantage. Oh, how she enjoyed the game!

Bathory cackled. Dracula had always thought too much of himself. Last night she had proved what she had always believed to be true. Dracula was and had always been weaker than she. By only partially draining Lucy Westenra, Dracula had left a living witness to expose himself to the band of "heroes." A near-fatal lesson had been learned. Now he rarely allowed himself the rich nourishments of human blood. This was his greatest weakness—that he would not accept what he truly was. Dracula was a vampire, yet he continued to think of himself as human. He was more than five hundred years old, and he had still had not learned to embrace, without guilt, the powers of the un-dead.

The carriage stormed along the coastline, and Bathory dreamed of a time when she would reign without challenge. It was close: She could feel it.

CHAPTER LVII.

——◆——

Surveying Carfax Abbey, Mina Harker felt that it was a reflection of her life. There had been a time when it had been grand and beautiful, full of virtue, hope, and promise. Now time had eroded it to an empty shell. Even the dust-covered cobwebs filling the corners had been abandoned by the spiders that had built them. The wind from the intensifying storm outside made the abbey's corridors wail, as if the spirits from the past were calling out to be set free. These walls had witnessed many bloody conflicts, from the Roman-Celtic war and the invasion of the Vikings, to the Saxon-Norman wars. In her youth, Mina had been too afraid of the many phantoms said to haunt the vicinity to venture onto the abbey grounds at night. The large stone room in which she now stood had once been the library where monks would study in silence. It was the first room that Prince Dracula had attempted to make his own when he had come to Whitby twenty-five years ago. Forgotten furniture covered in dust cloths stood like forsaken ghosts around the room. Tomes written in every imaginable language filled the rotting wooden shelves. The dust upon them was so thick that Mina could hardly discern the color of the covers, let alone the titles. She glanced up at the cracked mirror hanging over the fireplace. A young woman looked back at her. Even so, Mina felt as old and hollow as this decaying abbey.

She saw the walnut linen chest she had brought back with her to Whitby in 1888, from her flat in London. She had spent that summer with Lucy while Jonathan was in Transylvania. After her adulterous liaison with Dracula, she had arranged for that chest to be secretly transported to Carfax Abbey, planning to flee England with her lover. Later, she had forgotten the box in her whirlwind haste to leave Dracula and put her betrayal of her marriage vows behind her. It was both sad and ironic that now she was reunited with Dracula and the chest. It was as if fate had known her destiny long before she ever had.

She opened the chest and found in it a dress that Lucy had given to her. Mina had never worn it; the style was far too provocative for her. But, twenty-five years later, it seemed to fit perfectly the woman she had become. Mina looked at the black, matronly dress she was wearing. She had dressed like a middle-aged woman for years to appease Jonathan. There was no longer a need to do so. She unbuttoned the black dress and allowed it to crumple to the rubble-strewn floor. Then she lifted the youthful garment from the chest and slipped its soft, elegant fabric over her body. It made her feel beautiful. A pang of guilt hit her: She wished she could have dressed like this for Jonathan, but it would have been pouring salt over a wound that would never heal. She looked in the mirror, and the small gold cross resting above her pale bosom caught the flickering light from the fireplace.

Unable to face her reflection any longer, Mina walked to the cathedral-like window. Her steps echoed like a slow, deliberate drumbeat. She peered into the night. Lightning flashes lit the cemetery below, casting long shadows among the gravestones. She could sense Quincey was fast approaching, and hoped he would reach the abbey before the storm unleashed its full fury. Once he arrived, Mina would confront Dracula and launch her plan.

"That dress suits you," a voice said from behind her. She hadn't heard him enter and was afraid to turn to him, lest she lose her resolve. Or worse, give in to her darkest desires. She could hear the hunger in his voice as he said, "You are a feast . . . for the eyes."

"I found my old trunk," Mina stammered. She looked down at her own voluptuous form. The dress exposed a lot of flesh. "I left much behind here."

Given the uncomfortable moment of silence, the meaning behind Mina's words did not go unnoticed by Dracula. At last he said, "This home, like me, belongs to you."

His voice was just as she remembered, melodic and hypnotic. Mina realized how much she'd missed its soothing sound. *No!* She could not think of herself. She had to think of Quincey. Her son's escape was all that mattered, something Dracula might not understand.

In her mind's eye, she had an image of Quincey riding a horse. His clothes were bloodstained. . . . Had he been shot? Mina felt the flames of rage consume her. She snapped back, turning to Dracula, like a lioness prepared to defend her cub. "How could you send Quincey into danger? He could have been killed by Van Helsing."

"Van Helsing tried to secure his place in history by naming me a villain through Stoker's pen," Dracula replied unapologetically. He took a step toward her, trying to close the gap between them, but refusing to accept any sort of advance, Mina turned away from him. The dark prince sighed. "I never sought revenge on your husband and the others for trying to kill me. Their misguided cause was indeed chivalrous, as they were only trying to protect you. But Van Helsing crossed the line."

His voice softened as he came up behind her. Mina looked back over her shoulder and saw how Dracula's eyes turned to the dark horizon as the beacon of light from the lighthouse flashed across the window. "Quincey has made Van Helsing pay for his transgressions," he said.

Mina felt her blood turn cold. She heard the meaning behind his words. And the way he said the name of her son—she could sense his purpose. Dracula had other plans for Quincey. "You would take from me my only son?"

"In order to survive what is coming, Quincey must embrace the truth. He must embrace what he is."

Mina's heart slammed against her ribs. "Quincey's destiny is not for us to decide."

Quincey's horse raced along Robin Hood's Bay. Waves crashed hard against the rocks. The cold April wind had grown stronger. Thunder trumpeted and lightning whipped around him. The heavens were signaling a call to battle.

Quincey's horse bucked and reeled, stumbled and then collapsed on the muddy shores, sending him through the air and onto the ground. Pushing himself from the mud, he stumbled to the horse, fearing the steed had broken a limb. He knelt down beside the animal and saw that it was drenched with foaming sweat and heaving for air. His mount was near death with exhaustion.

Again, lightning punched across the night. In the distance, Quincey could see the ruins of the abbey on the cliff overlooking the sea. He was drawing closer.

The horse tried to stand, but collapsed again, its legs unable to support its own weight. Quincey did not have time for the animal to recover. He stroked the horse's mane. He was prepared to die for his cause, but he could not ask for this horse to sacrifice itself as well.

Without a moment to spare, he continued on foot down the slippery, rocky path to his destiny.

CHAPTER LVIII.

"The time of using children as pawns of war has long passed. Leave my son alone," Mina challenged. She was on thin ice, and she knew it. It was dangerous to bring up the suffering Dracula had endured as a child. Centuries ago, the Turkish sultan had taken Vlad Dracula and his younger brother, Radu, as political prisoners. The years away from his family had scarred Dracula in ways one could never measure. Dracula had been kept prisoner until his father had been killed in battle. He had then inherited the throne of Wallachia and become a warrior for God. He had spent the rest of his mortal life seeking revenge. In his un-dead existence, he continued to carry the same banner, believing that he was still a warrior for God, and those like Bathory were his greatest foes.

But Mina could not allow Quincey to become a casualty in Dracula's never-ending war. "Quincey deserves a normal life. It is best that I take my son away from here. Away from England. Away from Bathory."

Dracula's face bore an expressionless stare. Of course he knew her deepest thoughts: He had known this moment was coming. Without breaking eye contact with her, Dracula caressed the scar tissue on his neck. The marks bore little resemblance to the gaping wound he'd suffered the night before from Bathory's fangs. He'd healed quickly. "Bathory drank my blood, too," he said. "We are all now connected.

Wherever we run, Bathory will find us, and Quincey. It is time to make our stand."

"You are not powerful enough to face Bathory. She nearly killed you."

His granite stare cracked into a frown. For a moment, Mina was certain she saw a look of pain in his eyes. Then he turned away from her, took a deep breath, and opened his mouth. No words came out. Dracula closed his eyes as if steeling himself and at last spoke softly. "Twenty-five years ago, I was nearly destroyed. First by Harker and then by Bathory. My wounds have not yet healed." He turned back to her and tore open his shirt.

Mina gasped at the horror she beheld. "Oh, God!"

Dracula's chest was emaciated; Mina could count his ribs. The scarred flesh was stretched tightly over his bones, and she could see the scars from where Morris and Jonathan had stabbed him. She could see the wounds from the attack she had seen through Bathory's eyes on his body, too, and remembered Bathory's boot driving the kukri knife deep into his chest. She was unable to turn away from the grisly spectacle, or to stop the tears of pity from streaming down her face. For the first time, Dracula had exposed his own fear and weakness to her. Mina understood how difficult it must be for him to share such vulnerability: It was an act of pure love. Now there could be no secrets between them. Mina's love for Dracula had always been passionate, but with this revelation, Dracula moved into her heart, into the space where Jonathan had once resided. Mina reached out to her dark prince, her hands trembling as they stretched to caress his disfigured chest. "This is why you needed Seward's help," Mina said, understanding at last. All the pieces of the puzzle were falling into place. She gingerly stroked the marred skin over Dracula's heart, the place where Morris's knife had once pierced, and the place from which she had once drunk his blood. Dracula gently placed his cold hand over Mina's, and their fingers intertwined.

"I did everything I could to protect you and Quincey from Bathory," he whispered. He raised her chin to allow her to look deep into his dark eyes, as if begging her to see the soul within. "But now there is no escape. She will kill us all unless you come back to me, Mina."

He was presenting Mina with a choice . . . but Mina could not forsake her faith. It was all she had left. She had to fight her urges.

"I may look like the young girl you remember," she countered without breaking eye contact, "but I have grown wiser these many years. No matter how sweet your words, or gentle your touch, you are a monster. A murderer."

Dracula's back straightened and his face became proud. "I am a knight in the Holy Order of the Dragon. Stoker and Van Helsing left me no choice but to—"

"These are not the Dark Ages. You cannot simply kill a man because he slandered you in a story," Mina interrupted.

"In life, I was God's hand," Dracula said, defiant. "I fought to protect all of Christendom. Brutality and death was all I ever knew. I yearned for a second life, a new chance. When the opportunity came, I pursued it, regardless of the consequences. Yes, I rose from my own death, but I do not kill for sport. The blood I need to survive is taken only from animals, murderers, rapists, and thieves. I am still doling out God's justice."

His eyes opened wide. Mina remembered that hypnotic stare. She felt his blood coursing through her brain and, with it, a flood of images. He was allowing her to see through his eyes, to see the deeds he had done in God's name, the monsters dispatched, the innocents saved. . . .

Their mental connection complete, he continued, "I was made in God's image, but I am of a higher order. Does not the wolf feed on sheep? As all great hunters, I am alone. There is no sound sadder than the cry of the wolf, alone in the night, reviled by man, hunted to the point of near-extinction."

His lips came close to her ear so that she could feel his icy breath. She longed to feel a kiss from his lips. At the selfsame time, she wanted to tear herself away and run.

"Please understand, Mina, without you I am lost," Dracula whispered. "My sole crime is that I am unschooled in the ways of this modern age. Can any man who loves you as much as I do be truly evil?"

Mina turned away, unable to face him. "Once, long ago, I would gladly have left Jonathan and gone away with you. Now my son is all that matters to me. Our time has passed." She knew there was no conviction in her words, which meant Dracula knew it as well. Lying was futile.

He spun her back to face him. "Stop this!" he commanded. "You're deceiving yourself. I know you still love me. Give in to your passions. Come to me. Be with me. Enlighten me. Only together can we save the world from Bathory."

"You are asking me to accept your dark gift. To become as you are."

"If you flee with Quincey to America, we divide our forces. Tonight, we are together and we own the high ground. Even if I should fall in battle tonight, I will leave Bathory severely weakened. Though newly minted, you will be a vampire born of my ancient blood. You will be able to protect Quincey. Your powers will be a match for a wounded Bathory."

Mina clutched the cross hanging from her neck. "I cannot."

Dracula removed his hands from her, his expression hardening. "Then the Devil has won."

He turned abruptly and left the room, leaving Mina more alone than she had ever been.

At the window, she looked into the moonless night. Where was her son? She needed to make a decision, and it would be easier if she knew he was safe. There was a loud crack of thunder. Mina had never been frightened of storms, not even when she was a child. Now she was terrified, as if the thunder was a warning for her alone.

A moment later, Mina detected a presence. She knew exactly what that meant. Bathory was drawing near.

Bathory smiled as she watched two whaling ships struggling to dock in Whitby Harbor while the heavens opened up. Floods of rain fell upon the earth. The roaring winds announced her arrival. The townsfolk dashed for cover, securing their houses against the storm. She could hear the familiar shrieks of horror as her carriage drove by the small stone houses. Somehow, even the lowest of the low could sense when the power of evil was approaching. Through the carriage window, Bathory made eye contact with a wrinkled, toothless old woman and reveled in the look of fear in the old hag's eyes. Bathory loved to feed off the fear of humans: It warmed her blood, made her heart race. Invigorating. *Intoxicating.*

The carriage's horses suddenly came to a halt. Bathory leaned out to see that the wooden bridge over the Esk River had collapsed and her horses could not cross the raging river. The effort needed to fly to the abbey from here would sap some of her strength, and she needed all the power she had for the battle to come. Bathory reached out with her mind to her mares, and they stamped and tossed their manes with understanding. Bathory would double back and take a longer route to the stone steps at the base of the cliff. The night was still young.

Bathory's solitary eye glared at her objective—the towering abbey high upon the rocky cliffs. In a window of the west wing, Bathory could see the silhouette of a woman bathed in a warm, flickering light. She licked her fangs in anticipation; she would taste the bitch's flesh and bathe in her blood by morning.

CHAPTER LIX.

Mina knew what had to be done. Outside, she could hear the storm brutalizing the walls. Carfax stood strong against the torrent; so would she.

She descended a short stone stairway to where the old monks' living quarters had once been. A series of doors along a narrow hallway ended with a large oak door, leading to what had once been the abbot's private quarters. As she walked along the hallway, passing each door in turn, her choices narrowed until only one door remained.

Dracula had claimed many times that a vampire was not evil by nature. He did not believe that by becoming un-dead, a soul was automatically damned. Good or evil resided in the choices one made. Mina had seen that a newly formed vampire's unquenchable thirst for blood could corrupt. She knew that Lucy had lured young children into her clutches, but Lucy never had the choice; unprepared, she had become a monster. Mina prayed Lucy's sad fate would not become her own.

She could feel Bathory closing in. She knew there was only one choice. She would have to sacrifice her soul to save her son.

Resolved, Mina placed the lantern she was carrying on the floor and swung the large oak door open. Dracula stood before the great hearth, in which a fire was roaring. He turned to her. With the fire and the flickering light of dozens of candles, the room was alive and vibrant. Dracula gazed at Mina with yearning and hope. She crossed the threshold.

"Quincey's destiny must be his own. You cannot choose his path for him," Mina said, her voice stern. There would be no bargaining on this point.

Dracula nodded. "If that is the price, so be it."

He moved slowly toward her, and her heart raced at the idea that soon his hands would be on her body. With great trepidation, she reached for the small gold cross on her neck and pulled. The necklace's thin gold chain broke and the cross fell to the floor. The hunger in Dracula's eyes grew.

His hands on her shoulders were cold, and added to the shiver running through her body. His kiss was gentle on her lips. He swept her into his arms, never taking his eyes away from hers. "Together," Dracula whispered, his lips caressing her ear, "we shall see nations rise and fall. Together, we shall witness eternity."

He carried Mina to the bed and laid her down. Touching her in ways that Jonathan never had, his hands and lips explored her body. He made her feel like a woman. For all of his strength, Dracula was gentle. He slipped her dress from her body and gazed upon her nakedness with a mixture of avarice and awe. He lived in a world of darkness, yet he did not extinguish the candles as Jonathan used to before he made love. Dracula desired the sight of every part of her. Mina's heartbeat quickened as he kissed her neck. It was not fear that she felt, but complete surrender. She wanted him. By the way he caressed her, the way he entered her, she knew that her pleasure was more important than his own. She felt him inside her and with each movement was brought closer to pure joy than she had ever known.

Dracula whispered into her ear, his breath upon her lobe, "We shall take the world by the throat and drink from it what we desire."

All her life, Mina had fought against repression. Accepting Dracula's eternal kiss would break those chains. No longer would she be bound by rules or laws, other than those she made for herself.

His hand slid between her legs; she could not hold back any longer.

She wrapped her arms around him and pulled him closer. Suddenly, in the heat of passion, all became clear. All of her conflicts, her dualities, fell away in an instant. It was as if the clouds had parted to reveal a clear sky. She loved Dracula, loved him in the way she never could love Jonathan. Together, she and Dracula made a whole being.

"God forgive me, I want you still," she said.

Dracula opened his mouth, revealing his fangs, but Mina raised her hand to stay his bite. There was no anger in him as he paused. He wanted the choice to be hers.

"There's something I have to tell you. I kept a secret, all these many years."

He shook his head slowly. "I have always known."

Mina smiled, free at last from the weight of her guilt. She turned her neck, exposing her vein to her lover.

Dracula bit down hard. Her body convulsed as he drank, swooning from an erotic cocktail of pleasure and pain. She no longer cared, as her blood drained out, if her soul did as well.

Dracula drank the hot blood and clutched his chest, convulsing. Something was happening to him. He was in pain. He reared back, breathing heavily. Then he cried out and tore away his ripped shirt. His scarred, emaciated chest rippled as if he were being reborn before her eyes. He looked at Mina with wonderment. "My pure blood, the blood that you drank from me so long ago, is healing me."

Mina was his savior. The blood she had once called *cursed* would save Quincey and defeat Bathory.

"The blood is the life. The blood is *our* life."

Mina gasped. She took hold of his head and pulled his fangs deeper into her neck, inviting him to finish. The time had come for her to die in his arms and be reborn. In ecstasy, Mina closed her eyes forever to her human life.

Quincey approached a fisherman who was tying up his small wooden boat. "Carfax Abbey! Which way?"

"Carfax Abbey? Now, lad, you mean Whitby Abbey."

"No, Carfax Abbey. Do you know it?" Quincey roared impatiently.

The fisherman nodded. "Aye. But you stay far from there!"

"Whitby Abbey, Carfax Abbey, damn you! Which way?"

The fisherman crossed himself, with fear in his eyes. Quincey realized that he must be a sight, soaked by the rain and covered in mud, blood, and God knew what else. "Forgive me; it's a matter of life and death! I must get to Carfax Abbey!"

The old fisherman shook his head and pointed to a path leading to the forest. "God be with you, lad!"

Quincey ran for the path. The wind was so strong, it seemed to be pushing him back. The rain fell in stinging darts. Quincey wondered if Dracula was responsible for the storm, using the weather to try to slow him down. He could no longer sense his mother's thoughts. This in itself terrified him.

He trudged along the path through Stainsacre woods. The rain made each step more difficult than the last, the mud slipping beneath his feet. At last he found himself in front of the abandoned shell of what had once been Dr. Seward's asylum. A mass of moss, ivy, and weeds had wrapped themselves around the stone remains of the buildings, as if nature were trying to erase the torment that had once existed there. According to Stoker's novel, this was the field that Renfield would have raced across to find sanctuary in Carfax Abbey. The wealth of Quincey's family had been acquired as a result of Mr. Renfield's anguish. While his parents had cursed Dracula, the truth was that they had directly benefited from his crimes. Quincey wondered if the suffering he and his family endured was God's justice.

Carfax loomed solemnly in the night, much larger than Quincey had imagined. A flicker of light illuminated a solitary window. A beam from the lighthouse offshore swung past intermittently, casting long, gruesome shadows upon the ruined walls.

The wind and rain grew stronger as he pressed across the open field. Refusing to be defeated, he summoned his strength and charged forward with all of his might.

Quincey reached the abbey's ornate wooden door at last and leaned against it in exhaustion. To his surprise, the door was unlocked and he slammed face-first into the hall. Scrambling to his feet, he forced the abbey door shut, locking out the storm. He looked out the windows to see if anyone was watching him but saw only lonely gravestones illuminated by flashes of lightning. There was no one outside but the dead.

Quincey tore through the abbey's winding corridors and in time came to a long corridor lined with many doors. At the end was one door that was partially open and a stream of light crept from behind it. Quincey steadied his nerves and ran toward the light. He burst into the room.

He found no one.

Dozens of candles had melted down to pools of wax; there was an empty, unmade bed in the corner. Dying embers in the fireplace cast the only light in the room. There was a heap of clothing beside the bed. He turned, and felt something underfoot. He glanced down and his heart skipped a beat. He'd stepped on his mother's cross lying on the floor. He knew she would never have willingly removed it. Enraged, he snatched up the small, gold cross and took to his heels, with no idea where he was going. He tried every door, but they were all rusted shut.

It would soon be dawn. Dracula would need to find a resting place. If there were any truth to Stoker's novel, it would have to be where no sunlight could ever reach.

He found the main stairwell and descended quickly through the abbey. The stairwell was damp and rank with the stench of decay, and the deeper he traveled in the darkness, the closer he felt to his reckoning.

He found himself in a cavernous hall. Looking around, Quincey saw that he was in a mausoleum. Rows of shelves lined the walls. Within each alcove was a skeleton. Hundreds must have been buried here.

An ancient oil lamp sat beside the entrance. Quincey took it up. The glass was still warm. Someone had just entered this place. He searched through his pockets for the matches Arthur Holmwood had given him, praying they would be dry enough to ignite. His prayers were answered; Quincey struck flame to the wick, and the lantern sparked to life.

He walked to the center of the room, shining the lantern onto three large stone sarcophagi. The name upon the first was etched in Latin: *ABBOT CARFAX*.

A wooden crate beyond this was marked: PROPERTY OF VLADIMIR BASARAB.

Basarab! The name was now poison. Frantically, Quincey surveyed the area with the lamp, and his eyes fell upon a rusted shovel leaning in one corner. Placing the lantern on top of the sarcophagus, he grasped the shovel's wooden handle and slammed it against the stone wall, shattering it into two pieces. With his newly fashioned stake in his hand, Quincey attacked the crate, using every ounce of his strength to pry open the lid.

As the lid ripped open, Quincey shouted in victory. Remembering the grave error his namesake had made in Transylvania, he kept his eyes shut, lest he be skewered by Dracula's hypnotic gaze, and raised the sharpened stake, ready to strike into the vampire prince's heart. He opened his eyes at the last second to focus on his target and froze in place as if his heart had stopped, unable to believe what he saw.

His mother lay dead inside the crate.

Quincey threw away the broken shovel handle and reached out to touch the face that had smiled at him, the lips that had kissed him. Those lips were cold now and lifeless. There would never be a chance for reconciliation or repentance now. Dracula had won.

Quincey's fingers were bleeding from tearing open the crate. They left small droplets of blood on Mina's pale lips. In a silent good-bye, he placed his hand on his mother's chest and was shocked when he felt her chest heave suddenly. In absolute horror, he watched as his mother licked the droplets of his blood from her lips. Her eyelids flew open. Her gentle blue eyes had been replaced by pitch-black orbs. Her lips curled back, revealing long, sharp fangs. The scream that issued from her mouth was both terrifying and deafening. Before Quincey could react, Mina's clawlike talons reached out and grabbed him by the throat.

CHAPTER LX.

***

Tears from heaven poured to the earth as if God knew that tonight his reign would finally end. The waves of the North Sea pitched high. Lightning ripped through the darkness. Thunder roared.

Bathory's carriage bounced violently as it charged through the rain along the broken cobbles of Church Street. The roads leading to Carfax Abbey were muddy, and quickly becoming impassable. The carriage drew to a stop beside the one hundred and ninety-nine steps leading to the summit. Bathory's carriage could go no farther. From here, she would have to climb the steps that were carved into the side of the cliff on foot.

She emerged from the carriage into the deluge. The raindrops on her bare scalp were a bitter reminder of how her raven-black locks had been burned away. The cold water on her still-hot flesh evaporated into steam immediately on contact.

Her solitary eye caught sight of a shadowy figure standing on a great boulder with its back to her, gazing out at the raging North Sea. He seemed unaware of her presence or even of the beating rain. Bathory bared her fangs. As slowly and as silently as she could, she snaked toward him. *The rain will hide the sound of my footsteps.*

No sooner had that thought passed through Bathory's mind than the rain suddenly stopped. The clouds parted and the full moon cast its light upon the figure on the boulder.

"It is time to answer for all your sins." Dracula's baritone voice carried on the wind as he turned toward her. "Erzsébet."

She hated the sound of her name in her native tongue, on Dracula's lips. He said it not as a greeting but as a curse. Every cell in her body wanted to leap upon Dracula and tear him limb from limb. Bathory had waited centuries for this moment. She could afford to indulge him in a few more of his little games: What were a few more moments when an eternity lay before her? She sated her rising bloodlust by imagining herself ripping out Dracula's flapping tongue and wearing it on a chain like a pendant.

As Bathory stepped into the moonlight, she saw Dracula's eyes betray some alarm. Her newly hideous appearance had obviously caught him off his guard. If Bathory had had lips, she would have smiled. But, like her nose and eyelids, they had been eaten away by the flames in the Underground.

"With words of love, you ripped out my throat and left me to die," Bathory hissed. "But now, with the powers of all the devils behind me, tonight I stand before you. I swear you will not cheat death again."

Dracula stood upon the rock looking down at Bathory. With total confidence, he replied, "Be warned. God fights beside me."

"It is your blind devotion to your God that will be your undoing."

Dracula pulled back his cloak with one hand and cast something forward with the other. A glint in the moonlight marked the passage of two swords, which arced through the darkness before sticking, point first, into the earth.

"The old way," Dracula challenged.

Bathory gazed upon the two weapons. "Your father's sword?" she asked, nodding to the closer of the two.

"Yes," Dracula said. "And the other is one of many that belonged to my brother."

"You flatter me."

Bathory approached the swords, studying them. Both had been beautifully crafted, in a style that had been common five hundred years ago. From the notches along the blades it was clear that both weapons had seen combat and spilled blood. How fitting. There was too much history between them to use virgin steel. Bathory picked up both blades, clenching them in her gnarled, skeletal hands. One had a hilt of wood with a pointed pommel that could be turned and used to stab. The other sword had an ivory hilt with a rounded pommel, but its quillion was bent like a *V*, with the tip facing the handle. A superior fencer could use this shape to weaken the lower portion of the opponent's blade. This was Radu's blade. This was the weapon for her.

Without warning, Bathory threw the other sword to Dracula, at the same time leaping forward to slice at Dracula's head.

With a speed that would have shamed lightning, Dracula caught his father's sword in midair, shifted his weight to one side, and dodged Bathory's attack. He assumed a fighting stance with the hilt of his sword at his abdomen and the point aimed directly at Bathory.

Bathory's ravaged face contorted into what passed for a smile, and Dracula, always the showman, spun his sword about as if he were onstage.

Bathory sighed. She thought about the second stranger. Her mentor. How Bathory wished he could be here to witness Dracula's demise. "Have you ever wondered, Vlad," she said, unable to resist the urge to open old wounds, "who it is that hates you more than I?"

A brief look of confusion crossed Dracula's face. "Whether human or from within our own ranks, how many enemies does one make in a lifetime?"

"All these years, Vlad, haven't you ever wondered, after you left me to die, who it was that set me on my path of revenge?" Bathory continued. "Who bestowed upon me the dark gift?" Bathory sensed Dracula entering her mind, searching for the identity of her mentor, the one who had made her a vampire. She did not resist. She wanted to destroy Dracula's confidence and watch his anger consume him. Indeed, she reveled in this moment of truth. "I am not alone in my war against God, but am only one of many. Perhaps you consider yourself brave to stand alone against the coming onslaught. You are an arrogant fool to think you can turn the tide of the world's fate."

Dracula snarled. He had captured from her mind the face of her mentor. He knew the mentor's name all too well. The hate between them was legendary. Fury flashed in his eyes. He shouted to the heavens as he raised the sword high and leapt off the broken boulder to engage her. Bathory raised her sword to meet him. She was shocked by the ferocity of Dracula's attack. He was driven by pure rage. Their blades clashed with such tremendous force that sparks flew. The crossed metal rang out like the chimes at midnight signaling the end of all things.

Mina could smell human blood. She opened her eyes, and was assaulted by the intense light from an oil lantern. Her eyes were newly sensitive. She could barely make out the silhouette of a man before she was forced to shut her eyes again. Fortunately, the scent of blood was so pungent, so intoxicating, that she was able to find and grasp her first victim with ease, even though she couldn't see him. Mina drooled with anticipation. *Blood is life!* She would drink her fill. She opened her mouth wide, her tongue brushing against the tips of her newly formed fangs. She could hear herself growl like a beast as she sensed the rhythm of her victim's heart, guiding her strike. She drew her head back like a cobra ready to pounce.

"Mother?"

Mina heard the trembling voice. It was barely a whisper, but to Mina's un-dead ears, it resounded like thunder. She stopped. The voice sounded like that of her son, Quincey. The light from the lantern was still blinding, but she fought the pain and forced her eyes open. Within seconds, her eyes adjusted. She was in awe of what she beheld. Everything seemed to be more vibrant, clearer; she could actually *see* the heat emanating from the body before her. The shadow gave way to a face she loved. It was Quincey, here at last, alive and safe. But she was denied a joyous reunion. She could see upon his face a look of complete horror. At once, she felt an overwhelming guilt and shame, emotions stronger than she had ever endured before. "Quincey, forgive me." She felt her fangs retract back into her gums as her mind became more focused. The expression on Quincey's face was heartbreaking. The need to comfort her son overwhelmed her. Dracula had told her the truth. If she could still feel, if she could still experience love, pain, and guilt, then she still had her soul. She was not a demon.

"My mother is dead," Quincey said, moving away from her.

"No! That's what Van Helsing taught. It is not true!" Mina pleaded, her mind racing to try to find the right words. She watched as Quincey flinched at the mention of Van Helsing's name. She could see the torment in her son's eyes. She had to make him understand. "Van Helsing was wrong. I am still your mother, Quincey." She opened her arms to her son, hoping for forgiveness.

Mina saw the energy radiating from her son's body suddenly change color from a benign white and light blue to a deep, heated red. The expression on his face changed as well. Quincey's logical mind was overruling his natural emotion.

"No!" Quincey cried. He pushed her away from him. The force was so strong that she fell back into the crate, smashing the side, and collapsed onto the cold, wet stone floor, still weak from her transformation and in great need of blood.

She struggled to pull herself up. Quincey backed farther away, shaking his head in disbelief and pure disgust. Now the energy emanating from him turned black. Mina could see the focus building in his eyes. In his mind, one single thought raged: *Kill.*

"Quincey, no!" Mina screamed as she stumbled toward him. "Do not even think it!"

He turned away from her and retrieved the broken shovel. His fists gripped the handle of the stake so tightly that the blood from his wounded fingers began to flow again. Mina forced herself to step away from the sweet aroma.

Tears streamed down Quincey's face. Without another word, he turned and ran away with incredible speed.

"Quincey, wait! It was my choice," Mina shouted after him. "We did what had to be done to save you from Bathory!"

She stumbled a few more steps and collapsed. She would never be able catch her son in her present state, nor stay his hand from making a deadly mistake. She needed blood for strength. She needed to get to Quincey before he faced Dracula, for she had made him swear that he would not take her son. She knew that Dracula would not betray his word, even in self-defense. But she feared Quincey's naïveté. In his ignorance, Quincey could align himself with Bathory, hoping to mete out the revenge he so desired against Dracula.

Mina's newly sharpened senses were overwhelming her mind, hindering her ability to chase after her son. She could smell the decay of the bodies in the tombs, the mold growing on the stone, animal droppings, the dampness of the air, and the sounds of Quincey's footsteps echoing as they ascended the stairs. She was deafened by the din of small droplets of water exploding into a puddle in the corner. She understood how poor Lucy might have gone mad from this. Lucy had fallen into a coma after Van Helsing's botched blood transfusion and then had suddenly awoken in her coffin, confused, disoriented, and burning with an inexplicable thirst for blood. She did not have guidance. While fleeing the band of heroes, Dracula couldn't instruct Lucy in the ways of the vampire. Mina understood why Lucy had feasted from the first victim she found—a child. The thirst was unbearable, but Mina was determined to remain focused. Dracula had prepared her. She was aware of what was happening to her and she knew what she had to do in order to stop Quincey.

She needed blood. This hunger was not just in her stomach, but in every inch of her body. The venom that had transformed her was directly feeding the cells of her body, and the more her cells feasted, the more the venom in her heart waned. The vampire blood was being consumed by her own body. She needed more, before she ate herself alive.

The noise of small rodents scurrying by now rang in her ears. Mina spun her head around as her fangs extended and her eyes went black. She focused on a group of rats. Putting aside her revulsion, she pounced on the rodents, scooping them up with her hands, ripping open their throats with her fangs. The high-pitched screeching hurt her ears. And yet she drank. She had no choice. *Blood is life!*

CHAPTER LXI.

— ◇ —

Dracula's ferocious attack took Bathory off guard. The power of each thrust pushed her farther back. Each clash of steel caused vibrations to shoot through her entire body. She could barely block each of the savage blows, and now she found herself retreating backward up the slippery steps of the cliff face with each swing. She had been right in her decision to take her coach and conserve her strength. She would need all of it now. So much the better. She would give all she had to see Dracula defeated.

Dracula, eyes wide, teeth clenched, looked every inch God's madman as he drove Bathory up the stairs. She gritted her fangs, but she would not let Dracula know the level of agony he was inflicting upon her. The words of her mentor rang through her mind: *We learn from pain.* This was not the Dracula she'd faced in the Underground. He was stronger. Surely, Mina had helped to heal him. She would take care of her later.

Bathory's strength declined with each of Dracula's blows, which only made him bolder. Hacking ever more violently, he forced her up the stairs, but a plan was formulating in her mind. He might be stronger than she for the moment, but he couldn't keep up his pace for much longer. And she knew she was faster than he.

Dracula unleashed a series of wild attacks. Steel bit steel with such force that Bathory could barely raise her arms to parry the attack. The look of victory upon his face was infuriating. She had no choice but to turn and run up the stairs to the next landing, her sword trailing behind her, appearing weak and ready for the taking. She waited as Dracula advanced slowly upon her, savoring each moment, believing that each step brought him closer to victory. His arrogance was such that he no longer even held his sword before him but let it hang by his side as if she no longer bore any threat.

Come to me. Come and die.

When Dracula reached the landing upon which Bathory stood, he made no move to strike but simply stood there, looking at her ruined beauty. She watched as the anger seemed to drain from her enemy's face, leaving only sadness behind. She hated to admit it, but she understood what he was thinking. When he killed her, he would be killing part of himself. They were cut from the same cloth, immortals who led solitary lives. They could have been allies, companions. But, because Bathory had chosen to turn her back on God, Dracula had to turn his back on her. She watched as his expression changed and saw that he now resigned himself to closing the book on their long-standing feud. He had decided it was time to end her life. *The fool.*

Dracula raised his sword, poised to remove Bathory's head in one blow. Always the better one, he would show her the mercy of a painless death.

At the last second, Bathory put her plan into action. Before the steel of Dracula's sword sliced into her neck, Bathory used the advantage of her speed. In one swift motion, she bent her knees and curved her spine backward. His blade swiped a hairsbreadth above her nose and not finding the target, forced him forward with its weight and momentum. Now Bathory moved so fast that no human eye would have been able to detect her, trapping Dracula's sword in the hilt of her weapon, and pushing his blade into the wet earth beside the stone stairs. Bathory pivoted, twisting the sword and exposing Dracula's chest, then reached into her cloak for the kukri knife. She had him.

Bathory slammed the curved blade into Dracula's body, dug deep and sliced from his abdomen upward across his chest. Dracula screamed and fell back, blood spouting, baptizing Bathory. He needed both his hands on the wound to stem the red tide.

Bathory dropped her sword and raised the curved blade, displaying it for Dracula. "Remember this?"

The flash of horror that sparked in Dracula's eyes was all the answer she needed. "Your time has come. Our battle is over, and I am victorious. At last I will rule the world as the superior being that I am. Man will fall at my feet, begging God for help. And just as God turned his back on me in my time of need, he will turn his back on man. God took from me everything that I ever loved, including my children. God's laws turned my family against me. God's laws made my husband torture me. God's laws made my own people shun me. Well, I spit on God and his laws. And I spit on you, God's champion. You came to my aid, yes, but when I could not change what I was and sought my just revenge, you tried to kill me. Did I not deserve revenge? Well, I have it now. God has no place in the world I will create."

Quincey P. Morris's blade was mere metal, but the memories connected to it were powerful. Bathory turned it, allowing him a clear view of the very same weapon she had used in Transylvania. He stared as if entranced. Once again, Dracula had misjudged his opponent's cunning.

"This time, the Texan's blade will finish the job," Bathory purred.

Dracula retreated, clutching his wound. It was not only the fear of Bathory that drove him back. There was something else. His eyes were looking beyond Bathory, at something behind her.

She turned. Dawn was approaching. Time was running out for both of them.

A high-pitched cry now pierced Bathory's eardrums. She turned back to find her enemy racing toward her. His shoulder hit her square in the chest, throwing her back against the stone stairs. Dracula took up Bathory's dropped sword, launched himself into the air over her head, blood from his wound spraying her as he soared past. His boot heels thudded on the stairs above her and he chopped down in an attempt to cleave her head in two.

Has he learned nothing? Bathory rolled her head to the side as Dracula's blade embedded itself in the stone step. The steel cracked when it hit the stone, for the battle's many blows had weakened the blade. She lunged for Dracula's sword, still buried in the earth, and Dracula wrenched Bathory's sword from the stone in the same moment in which Bathory drew the other blade from the earth. They had exchanged weapons. Raising the sword before her, Bathory turned to run at Dracula, knowing victory was near at hand.

Dracula's eyes had become those of a reptile, his skin an ashen green, his ears pointed. His mouth widened, filled to overflowing by gory fangs protruding outward in a hideous snout. His face became thus when he wanted to instill fear in his mortal enemies and when he was in danger. But it would have no effect on Bathory. There was nothing mortal left in her.

Bathory lashed at the creature, driving Dracula back with the ferocity and speed of her attack. As she drove him up to the summit, the rock face receded, exposing his back to the rising sun. The sun's rays would hit Dracula first. Bathory intended to stand in his shadow, protecting herself from the sun's fire. Tonight, she would rise, and God's champion would fall.

Bathory felt Dracula weaken more and more with each blow of her sword. He was backing up the stairs, his blood draining from the wound she had inflicted. The sun began to beat on his back. Bathory's sword struck his blade, again and again, faster and faster. Only a few more blows and she would render him defenseless: Then she would strike through his heart.

Mina stumbled through the winding corridors of the darkened abbey. Despite the darkness, she could see clearly. No longer a creature of light, she had become a nocturnal predator.

Her body was in turmoil. She was alternately fighting pangs of hunger and bouts of nausea. Suddenly dizzy, Mina fell against the cold wall, unable to stand. She felt a wrenching in her chest and vomited blood. Was her body rejecting the blood of the rats? Perhaps, as a new vampire, only human blood would suffice.

All around her was the sound of the storm, but there was another sound as well. It was far in the distance, but Mina could hear it clearly. She recognized it as the sound of rain and wind on wood. The outer door! It had to be. Mina ran, the new sound guiding her, threading her way through the catacombs. She could smell the damp, the smoke from distant candles, even the decaying rats she had left behind. She could smell Quincey. Her son had come this way. At last she understood what Dracula had meant when he had said that vampires existed on a higher plane than mortals. Even though she was weak and fragile, she was much more than a human being. Though, in her fear for Quincey's life, she was still all too human.

Led by scent and sound, Mina found the large wooden doors at the front of the abbey. She swung them open and was overwhelmed with fright and pain so strong that it forced her back into the shadows. *The sun!* It was rising into the sky. Her instincts told her to retreat back into the darkness and hide from the light, but her need to save Quincey forced her out again. The sun's rays were like a million needles puncturing her skin. It was painful, but bearable.

Mina ran blindly across the field until her eyes finally adjusted. She felt weak again, and the nausea returned. She stumbled and fell to the ground. When she looked up, she saw Quincey standing amidst the graves and heard what sounded like the clanging of swords. Her eyes burned in the light, forcing her to squint. She looked to where Quincey was gazing.

Two figures silhouetted in the light were battling on the stone stairs, crossing swords. Mina knew it was Dracula and Bathory. She could sense that Quincey was choosing his next move, whether or not to intervene. She scrambled to her feet. She had to reach Quincey before he made a move.

Quincey stood there, transfixed by the battle going on in front of him. Dracula was in retreat. The skeletal creature that attacked him was lightning fast, relentlessly driving him toward the summit of the cliff, into the slowly rising sun. It was all there for Quincey to take. All he needed was the courage. But he could not move.

The charred creature fighting his mortal enemy had to be the countess that Van Helsing had warned him of, Jack the Ripper herself. If he charged in now to join her, with Dracula on the retreat, he could attain victory. Instinct told him to be wary; but reason said: *The enemy of my enemy is my friend.*

Bathory hissed through her lipless mouth. Centuries of obsession had driven her to this moment. Victory was at hand. She beat at Dracula's sword, feeling her foe losing strength with each moment as the sun rose in the sky. His breathing was becoming labored; blood was pouring from his wound. Now was the time to strike hard. Bathory dug deep within herself and called upon all the memories of pain and suffering she had endured in her long life. As they came to the final steps at the summit of the cliff, she used her fury to ignite the last of her strength and land one final blow.

The cracked steel in Dracula's sword finally gave way, Bathory's final stroke shattering his blade and sending him to the ground. Her remaining eye bulged with the anticipation of the kill. She felt Dracula's fear. If she'd had the time, she would have wept bloody tears of joy. With the kukri knife still in her left hand, Bathory raised her sword with her right, over her head, holding it as she would a spear, and drove it down toward her enemy's heart.

Dracula was caught without room to maneuver. His death was sure. In mid-strike, Bathory saw the creature's expression turn from one of fear to a twisted smile. With her blade only inches from his heart, he reached out and clasped the double-edged sword in his fist, slowing the deadly thrust. The razor-sharp blades sliced his fingers from his hand, the digits spinning through the air as he shoved Bathory's blade aside.

Sparks erupted as the sword embedded itself in the stone of the final step, missing Dracula completely. Bathory's momentum sent her falling forward toward her mortal enemy. In that moment, Dracula dug in his heel and, with his other hand, plunged his broken sword into Bathory's belly. The splintered blade tore through charred flesh and exploded out of her back, the hilt halting her fall.

Bathory had gambled and lost. Where was her justice? This was not the way it was supposed to happen. All her schemes, all her machinations, all her plans were just ashes blowing on the winds of time. Through the unimaginable pain, she was forced to gaze upon the smiling face of Dracula, now transformed back to human appearance. She had been played by the master. He had looked into her soul and understood her rage, her arrogance. Most of all, he had understood her obsession. It was not by chance that Dracula had picked up her cracked sword, nor was it anything more than a ruse when he had feigned fear. Dracula had played his part like the actor he was. She had forgotten her mentor's golden rule of combat: *Never underestimate your opponent.*

Dracula withdrew the sheared blade from Bathory's belly and tossed the sword aside. He looked down on her with no gloating or happiness. "Once the gauntlet has been thrown, no knight of God who is true can lose in single combat to one who is false."

The name of God filled her with fury. With a cry from the depth of her hellish soul, Bathory forced herself upright and, with the kukri knife in her free hand, slashed at Dracula's throat. Blood erupted like a geyser. Forgetting her own unbearable pain and loss of blood, Bathory exploded into uncontrollable laughter. The look of shock on Dracula's face as he raised his fingerless hand to his neck to stem the blood was just too precious.

Dracula's face contorted with rage. He balled his intact right hand into a mighty fist, which he slammed deep into Bathory's belly. She heard the sickening sound of her charred flesh crunch, crackle, and tear. She could feel his fist inside her body ripping upward, smashing organs as he reached between her ribs.

"God loved you," he growled. "You chose to kill because you would not accept His love. You are responsible for your own crimes."

Dracula's hand closed around her heart. And squeezed. Then he wrenched his arm from her body. Bathory stared at her own still-beating black heart clenched in his fist.

Howling a death wail, she plunged the kukri knife into Dracula's chest. She knew she did not have enough strength left to drive the knife home through his heart. But the loss of blood from the wounds she inflicted and the rising sun at his back would surely finish him. Their duel was a draw. They had both won and they had both lost.

With her last breath, refusing to die at Dracula's feet, Bathory pushed herself away, and the weight of her body sent her falling back down the stone steps. She heard her bones breaking the entire way down, but she felt no pain. Dracula would soon be dead, and though she would not help to lead it, her murder of God's champion would clear the way for a new world order. As she died, her last thought was that Countess Elizabeth Bathory—reviled, abused, discounted, and terrorized—had risen from her own death and become the implement that would lead to the destruction of the world: a befitting epitaph for one on whom God had turned His back.

Quincey watched Bathory fall, leaving Dracula alone with the curved knife still protruding from his chest. In a few more moments, the sun's rays would be directly upon him.

Quincey clenched his fist tightly around the broken shovel in his hand. It was time for him to act. Dracula must die. He started forward.

"Quincey, wait!" Mina shrieked from somewhere behind him.

The sound of his mother's voice only served to fuel his bloodlust. Quincey ran on. It was time to bring justice to the man who had brought ruin upon his family. "Dracula! Face me!"

CHAPTER LXII.

◆

The sun was not yet high in the sky, and Mina's skin was already burning. Her mind told her body to get up and stop Quincey, but her body was slow to respond. Using the headstones of the graveyard for support, she dragged herself forward. The lack of fresh blood was making her weak. In desperation, she cried out, "Quincey! Stop! Wait!"

Quincey unleashed a war cry and raised the broken tip of the shovel over his head. He ran at Dracula with unnatural speed. But Dracula did not turn to face him. Puzzled, Quincey stopped. There was no honor in stabbing his mortal enemy in the back.

Honor be damned, this was life and death! He drew back his arm and steadied the shovel to strike. A searing pain, like a nail driven through his skull, stayed his hand. He heard a voice in his mind: *Can you really kill me, Quincey? I whom you loved?*

Quincey was frozen, wrestling with the thoughts in his head. It was as if he no longer had control over his own brain or body. Clouds converged, blotting out the rising sun. He understood now why his enemy hadn't turned to face him: Dracula was concentrating his powers on the skies and on Quincey's brain. Only now did Dracula turn to face him.

In his zeal to destroy his enemy, Quincey had not anticipated the fact that when he looked upon Dracula, he would also gaze upon the face of Basarab. With his throat and abdomen slit, his fingerless hand a bloody stump, and his chest bleeding from the kukri knife, the vampire looked so weak and frail that Quincey was suddenly pierced by compassion. Not compassion for Dracula, who had murdered his father and violated his mother, but compassion for Basarab.

"It *is* you. Van Helsing told me . . . and yet I hoped beyond all hope . . ." No longer able to withstand the wrestling match in his head, Quincey reluctantly let the shovel fall from his grasp. He stepped back, defeated. "I can't do it."

The voice in his head grew louder, more confident. *Dracula or Basarab . . . I am still the man who loves you.*

Dracula's pain was intense, but he gritted his teeth and forced out the words: "I was sorry to deceive you, but Bathory had to think I was dead. I became Basarab so that I could hide in plain sight."

Images exploded in Quincey's mind, showing him the truth, or a version of it. Bathory, the countess, was the real villain. And Dracula's actions, for better or for worse, had had one purpose: to protect Quincey and his mother. He did not know what to believe. Were the images in his head real? Had Dracula been his ally all along? The realization that Basarab had lied to him spurred him to rage: "I loved you. Trusted you! You used and betrayed me!"

The sun fell full upon the dark prince now. Dracula's skin began to dry and shrivel. His bones rose like the peaks of sand dunes beneath his flesh. As he decayed, his powers grew weaker. The clouds began to melt away.

"Ask yourself why you cannot kill me," he wheezed. "You are what I am. You cannot kill me without killing yourself."

Quincey shook his head against the thought. It did not matter if Bathory was a villain or not. If Dracula's evil had not come to England, if he had not invaded Quincey's family like a cancer, Bathory would never have come. Whether it was Dracula who had struck his father down or Bathory who had impaled him so grotesquely, it did not matter. It was Dracula who had started this.

It was no longer the Basarab he loved who stood before Quincey, but a living corpse, evil to the core. Quincey was free at last of any confusion in his mind. He grabbed Dracula by the cloak and drew him in so that they would be eye to eye, with only the length of the embedded kukri knife between them. "You murdered my father!"

He had expected a fight. Instead, Dracula smiled at him. Flakes of burned flesh fell away from the upturned corners of his mouth. "Quincey, you are not a fool," he said calmly and earnestly. "Do you not yet see the truth? I did not murder the man you knew as your father, Quincey. *I* am your father."

The shock was immense. Quincey released Dracula, and the vampire fell back against the stairs. Then he lunged forward, placing both hands on the hilt of the kukri knife. "You lie!"

Dracula offered no resistance. He spread his arms, offering Quincey control over the kukri knife in his chest, and free reign over his life or death. "Do it, if you dare," he challenged.

This final show of power must have drained all of Dracula's remaining strength, for now the clouds parted and the sun's rays fell directly upon him.

The moment that Van Helsing had warned Quincey of had arrived. Was he still a weakling child, or was he a man with the wisdom and strength to do what had to be done? He stared at the man he had always thought of as his enemy; the man now claimed to be his father. Steam seeped from under Dracula's clothes and the exposed flesh of his limbs. Quincey vacillated. Should he drive the kukri knife to its hilt, he would become a murderer like the demon before him. Was that what God intended for him?

"You wanted to know the truth, did you not?" Dracula rasped out. "The secret they were all so desperate to hide from you? I lay with your mother before your father ever did. You are the fruit of my seed. My blood flows through your veins."

The pain flooded back into Quincey's head, and he fell back, releasing his hands from the kukri knife. The voice he heard this time was Mina's. *Forgive me, my son. He speaks the truth.*

Quincey's entire existence had been a lie. He stared at Dracula. His skin was melting, but Quincey was not affected by the sun's rays. He was still human. . . . That meant he still had free will. He had a choice.

"I am the son of Jonathan Harker, and a child of God."

Dracula gazed toward Mina, his expression one of resignation.

Then he lifted himself off the ground, launched himself over the edge of the cliff, and burst into a ball of flame.

The sun had done the job. The light had destroyed the darkness.

Quincey could only watch helplessly as the flaming body that was Dracula fell three hundred feet from the cliff and crashed into the foaming sea. Behind him, he heard his mother scream. He felt nothing.

Mina shrieked as she watched Dracula's body fall. In an instant, he was gone, leaving behind a trail of black smoke. She had battled so long against the truth of her love for Dracula, wasted so much time. Their love was meant to be eternal, and now it was over.

Smoke rose from her hands. The sun's rays were now falling upon her body, inflicting searing pain. Mina stumbled a few steps through the graveyard before her body rebelled against her and she fell. She crawled on her hands and knees, clawing her way along the ground, trying to get to Quincey. Perhaps now that he knew the whole truth, he would understand her choice and offer the forgiveness she needed.

But he would not turn to look at her and simply stood there, staring out over the cliff, lost in his thoughts.

"Come away with me now, my love," Mina implored. "There is much to tell you. Much I must prepare you for."

Quincey looked down at his hands, bloodied and unwashed. The words he spoke were more deadly than any stake he could have driven. "My mother is dead." And with that, he turned his back on her and ran away, never looking back.

Mina watched him go, feeling a desperate emptiness inside her. She had saved her son, and the victory had come with a heavy price. It was worth it: Quincey could still choose his own destiny. But now she was alone. The only people she'd ever loved were dead. She had not chosen to face eternity on her own. What was the point of immortality if she had no one to share it with?

The flames licked at Mina's feet as she trudged toward the cliff's edge, but she felt no pain, only the sensation that her life had almost run its course. She yearned to see Jonathan, Lucy, and all her friends again. She yearned to be reunited with her dark prince. The journey had been long and hard. It was time to go home. She raised her arms to the sky and commended her soul to God. She hoped He knew the truth in her heart and, in His infinite wisdom, could forgive her.

For a moment, she teetered on the edge. Then she leaned a little farther forward and an instant later she was falling.

The water and treacherous rocks rose up to meet her. For an instant, she saw her flaming reflection, then darkness. A sleep well earned.

CHAPTER LXIII.

◆

Able Seaman John Coffey was exhausted. He'd put in a late night of drinking belowdecks with his fellow crew members, and now he was paying the price.

It was a cloudy day, but the sun was struggling to break through. The weather was causing a heavy chop on the sea. Coffey wondered how his hangover would fare if the weather turned. The massive ocean liner was anchored at Roches Point, two miles off the coast of Queenstown, being too damn big to fit into the local dock. He wondered why the hell they built ships so bloody huge. Who were they trying to impress? Certainly not the crew: On a ship like this one, a sailor had to do more work for the same meager pay.

It was common practice that when anchored offshore, the liner's crew would accompany passengers on the ferry, taking them to and from the port. It was just John Coffey's luck that he was assigned this brisk morning to the *PS America*—one of the steamer ferries used to taxi passengers. Queenstown was Coffey's hometown, but despite being so close, he would not have a chance to set foot there. He was under orders to make this trip as quickly as possible. The ocean liner was on its maiden voyage, and its owners and captain were determined to break all speed records to New York. There was no time to be wasted.

Coffey had been at sea for over two years, working his fingers raw for little pay. The job on this new ocean liner was the best he'd had, but his wages didn't allow for any savings.

The PS *America* raised its anchor and unleashed itself from the great ocean liner, ferrying seven passengers on their way to the port. As it made its way across Cork Cove to the pier, Coffey's bloodshot eyes were drawn to the Cathedral of St. Colman, nestled near the top of the hillside. Construction on it had begun over forty years ago. By the look of the scaffolds adorning the bell towers, it was almost complete. Coffey smiled at the sight. This seaport had become the gateway to America since 1891, when the SS *Nevada* began taking thousands of Irish immigrants across the sea on their way to a new life. Coffey had been to New York many times but always found himself longing for his quiet sea town. To add insult to injury, the PS *America* would be dropping off its seven passengers to Pier 13. Such an unlucky number. Once again, Coffey wished he could say a prayer in the church before setting off on the massive ocean liner. He sighed and gazed out over the approaching pier, where over a hundred third-class passengers waited to board the liner. These men and women had come from all over Europe for a chance to make a better life for themselves. God knew what they would find when they got to America.

Once Coffey had finished checking every ticket and marking the names on the manifest, he and the other seamen began loading cargo.

A voice called from the shore: "Wait!"

Coffey looked up to see a disheveled fellow careening across the weathered planks toward the ferry. By the look of the man's ragged clothes, Coffey wagered he was some homeless wretch trying to steal passage to America. "Ahoy, where do you think you're going?" he demanded.

"Forgive me," the vagabond stammered. His accent was English and well-to-do, which was surprising, and he had a hollow, possessed look in his eyes. Coffey felt there was something not quite right about him. He had seen that look before—it was his father's look, that of a man who had been to war and had seen and done terrible things. Another surprise: The man handed over a paper bearing the familiar bright red letters in the center: BOARDING PASS.

"B Deck, First Class?" Coffey asked dubiously as he looked at the vagrant's rags. He read the name on the boarding pass. "You're telling me that you are Dr. Fielding?" He had also noticed that this filthy lad appeared to be younger than he, too young, surely, to have a medical practice. He had obviously stolen the ticket from the real doctor. Coffey looked down at the suspicious-looking satchel, hanging off the man's shoulder. "Am I to believe that is your medical bag?"

"Ah . . . I had an accident, as you can plainly see from my appearance. I lost my medical bag," the lad replied, tightening his grip on the bag's leather straps.

"Lost? Along with your luggage?" Coffey asked. He now expected the lad to run, the game over. The young man gave Coffey a look that sent a chill down his spine. "Let me see your license and passport," Coffey said.

The vagabond produced a wallet from his pocket and handed it to Coffey. Inside, Coffey was shocked to see a green banknote. It had an odd design. After only an instant, Coffey recognized it as American. The number 20 was printed in bright yellow, as were the words IN GOLD COIN. Coffey blinked. His fingers flipped it over nervously to see if it was real, and only then did he realize that there were five banknotes. One hundred dollars. It was more money than he made in a year. Coffey looked back at the vagrant. This money was his chance for a new life, but at what cost? Swiftly, he made a decision.

"Your papers seem to be in order," he said. "You just made it, doctor. Come this way."

There was a stack of crates piled on the dock, cargo to be transported onto the ocean liner. As Coffey and his fellow seamen finished loading the cargo onto the ferry, he promised himself that he would make a confession of his sinful behavior at the Cathedral of St. Colman before the day was out.

"Dr. Fielding" disembarked the *PS America* and boarded the mighty ocean liner. He made his way up the grand staircase and out onto the promenade deck, walking along the stern railing. The pompous elite of high society scoffed at his appearance. He was surprised that no one had reported him, thinking he was a steerage passenger who had wandered somewhere he didn't belong.

Peace, at last a moment of peace. Dr. Fielding was as good a name as any other for a man who no longer knew who he was. He had once been the namesake of Quincey Morris, a brave man who'd died battling evil for the good of mankind. Quincey Harker felt he no longer deserved to carry that name. He remembered running for what had seemed like hours from Carfax Abbey. He remembered the moment he had sensed that his mother was dead, utterly dead.

Alone, he had wandered aimlessly for days, with no idea where to go or what to do. Was it by a miracle or pure luck that he happened upon the horse he had stolen in Whitby, after taking a train from London? He had shown mercy to the beast when it had collapsed. How the horse had found him, he did not know. Quincey had not noticed the satchel on the horse's saddle before, so focused had he been on his journey. Now God had shown him a path.

Upon opening the satchel, he had found the doctor's wallet containing three hundred American dollars and a first-class ocean liner ticket for New York City. Quincey's first instinct had been to seek out the good doctor and return his property, as well as his mount. He would have liked to have been a man of strong moral fiber, even if he was the son of Dracula. Despite this, Quincey had found that after all he was a coward.

But now as he stood on the deck of the mighty ship, he could not help but feel that his great adventure was about to begin.

Having assisted the one hundred new steerage passengers off the *PS America* and onto the ocean liner, Coffey began his final task of the morning. As ordered, he would unload the cargo from the ferry into the liner's hull. Then, once the grand ship was casting off, Coffey would stow away on the *PS America* and return to Queenstown. He would head directly to church to make his confession, and then disappear to begin his new life.

Coffey attached a rope to the two crates that remained to be loaded onto the liner. He tugged on the ropes as he and his fellows hauled the crate across the gangplank, through the cargo hull door, and into the hold. Stenciled on the sides of both crates were the words: PROPERTY OF VLADIMIR BASARAB. QUEENSTOWN, IRELAND. TO NEW YORK CITY, UNITED STATES OF AMERICA.

The crew closed the doors of the cargo hold. Coffey's moment of freedom had arrived. He backed away from his fellow seamen and scurried into the PS America's lower deck. There, he found a discarded canvas oost-bag and hid beneath it. He patted the money in his pocket, relieved to find it was still there. Coffey raised the edge of the canvas sack so that he could spy through the porthole. He watched his fellow crewmen run up the gangplank and enter the mighty ship; and then the PS America cast off from the ocean liner and steamed back toward Queenstown. Coffey was almost home.

As the PS America pulled back into Pier 13, Coffey took one last look at the name painted on the stern of the ocean liner as it drifted out of sight, then pulled the canvas tarpaulin back over his head and resolved that he would wait until dark to make his escape. For some reason, he was overcome by a feeling of dread. Something told him that the future of the vagrant, and all the other souls aboard the liner, was in peril. He prayed that the grand ocean liner, the *Titanic*, was as unsinkable as the captains of industry believed it to be.

AFTERWORD

———◆———

Abraham (Bram) Stoker was born in Clontarf near Dublin, Ireland, on November 8, 1847. His father, John Abraham Stoker, was a clerk with the British civil administration in Ireland. His mother, Charlotte Thornley, from Sligo in western Ireland, was an active social reformer. The Stokers were Protestants who attended the Church of Ireland. Bram was the third of seven children: He had four brothers (William Thornley, Thomas, Richard, and George) and two sisters (Margaret and Matilda).

Bram was a sickly child, but no explanation for his mysterious illness has ever been provided. During these early years, his mother filled many of his hours with stories and legends from her native Sligo, including supernatural tales and narratives of disease and death. Whatever the nature of his illness, by the time he entered Trinity College (Dublin) in 1864, Bram Stoker was a strong young man who excelled at university athletics, notably football, footraces, and weight lifting. He also received awards for debating and oratory, and was president of the Philosophical Society.

Upon graduating, he followed in his father's footsteps and accepted a position in the Irish civil service. During these years, he wrote theatre reviews for a local newspaper. One of these, a review of *Hamlet*, led to a meeting with Henry Irving, who would later be acknowledged as one of the greatest Shakespearean actors of the Victorian age. The two became friends. In 1878, shortly after his marriage to the Dublin beauty Florence Balcombe (who had also been courted by Oscar Wilde), Stoker accepted an offer of employment as acting manager of Irving's new Lyceum Theatre in London, a position he held until Irving's death in 1905. Much of his writing, including *Dracula*, was done during whatever spare time his exceptionally busy schedule allowed. His primary responsibilities included organizing the company's provincial seasons and overseas tours, keeping financial records, and acting as Irving's secretary. He was a vital part of the Lyceum's eight North American tours, during which he befriended Walt Whitman (whose poetry he had admired for many years) and Mark Twain. Working at the Lyceum with the prominent Henry Irving (who was knighted by Queen Victoria in 1895) brought Stoker into contact with many of the leading figures of his day. Numbered among his friends and acquaintances were Alfred Lord Tennyson, Sir Richard Burton, and William Gladstone. But most significant was the influence of Irving himself; in *Personal Reminiscences of Henry Irving* (1906), Stoker would write at length a glowing tribute to the man for whom he felt great affection and loyalty.

Though he is best known for *Dracula*, Bram Stoker was the author of several other novels and collections of short fiction. He died on April 20, 1912 (just five days after the sinking of the luxury liner *Titanic*), having suffered from Bright's disease and two separate strokes. His cremated remains are located at Golders Green in London. An obituary in the *Times* (London) observed that Stoker would be best remembered for his association with Henry Irving. That, as we know, was not to be the case.

Dracula was published in London in 1897. We know from his Notes[1] that he worked on the book intermittently for over six years, including while he was on vacation and while on tour with the Lyceum Theatre in North America. The original title for the novel was *The Un-Dead*. On May 18, just a few days prior to publication, a dramatic reading was staged at the Lyceum in order to protect the theatrical copyright. Entitled *Dracula; Or The Un-Dead*, it was performed for a small group of

1 See *Bram Stoker's Notes for Dracula: A Facsimile Edition*, transcribed and annotated by Robert Eighteen-Bisang and Elizabeth Miller (McFarland, 2008).

theatre employees and passersby. Lasting about four hours, it comprised large segments of the novel apparently cobbled together by Stoker in haste. The final decision to use *Dracula* as the title was made virtually at the last minute.

Whether Bram Stoker ever intended to write a sequel to *Dracula* is a matter of conjecture. The rumor has persisted that he had "planned to bring Dracula over to America in a different story."[2] No supporting evidence has been unearthed. The ending of the novel is, however, sufficiently indeterminate to support the concept of a sequel in which the count reappears. The method of Dracula's destruction is at variance with the prescription and procedures outlined earlier in the text: a stake through the heart, followed by decapitation. Instead, the vampire is dispatched with two knives: a kukri and a bowie. Furthermore, it is unclear whether Harker's knife (the kukri) actually cuts off Dracula's head. Further ambiguity is present in Mina's statement that the vampire's body "crumbled into dust." Does this clearly indicate his final destruction, or is the crumbling yet another manifestation of the count's shape-shifting powers? Another factor that leaves the door open is that Stoker (or his editor) changed the originally planned ending, which was to have Castle Dracula disappear completely in a massive natural explosion. Was the change made to make the ending more ambiguous? We do not know. Of course, given that the text of *Dracula* is replete with inconsistencies, this may all be the result of sloppiness, of a rush on Stoker's part to finish his book. Whatever the explanation, Stoker's novel has generated a number of prequels and sequels, yet another testimony to its enduring appeal and power.

Dracula the Un-Dead is a multifaceted sequel to a multilayered novel. Dacre Stoker and Ian Holt follow the lives and fortunes of the surviving characters: Dr. John Seward, Arthur Holmwood (Lord Godalming), Abraham Van Helsing, Jonathan Harker, and Mina Harker. All have suffered irreparable damage in both their personal and their professional lives as a result of their past encounters with Dracula. Seward has succumbed completely to morphine addiction. Arthur has unsuccessfully

2 Roger Sherman Hoar, as quoted in David J. Skal, *Hollywood Gothic* (Faber and Faber, 2004).

sought relief from his grief over the loss of Lucy in another marriage, isolating himself from his former friends. Van Helsing, now an old man, is still obsessed with tracking down the monster. Jonathan and Mina's marriage has been irreparably strained by their respective memories of Dracula.

Through these characters' present lives, we relive some of the key events of their earlier experiences as recorded in Stoker's novel: the death of Lucy, the madness of Renfield, Mina's "baptism of blood," the chase to Transylvania, and the final confrontation with Dracula. The unifying element is provided by Quincey Harker, the son of Jonathan and Mina, who's "bundle of names links all our little band of men together." Mentioned briefly in Jonathan Harker's "Note" at the close of the novel, Quincey is the first member of the next generation.

Dracula the Un-Dead is set in 1912, a year chosen deliberately. It permits an appearance by Bram Stoker himself (he died on April 20, 1912). Even more crucial to the story is that the authors can dovetail their conclusion into the sailing of the *Titanic* (which also occurred in April). This essential link lays the trail for a sequel to the sequel, with the distinct possibility that Dracula will indeed find his way to America.

This decision necessitated altering the dating of the events in Stoker's original narrative. The story of *Dracula* has been clearly established as being set in 1893, based on evidence both from the Notes and from references within the text itself. In order to use an adult Quincey Harker as the catalyst (and to set their own story in 1912), Stoker and Holt found it necessary to resituate the plot of *Dracula* to an earlier year. The selection was 1888, as fortuitous a choice as 1912. It was during the period from August to November 1888 that Jack the Ripper murdered five women in the Whitechapel district of London. That Stoker knew of these murders is without question; in fact, he refers to them directly in the preface he wrote for the Icelandic edition of *Dracula*, published in 1901. Revealing the identity of the notorious Ripper becomes a subplot in *Dracula the Un-Dead*.

The Dracula we meet in this novel is much more than the vampire count of Bram Stoker. For starters, he is clearly identified as Vlad the Impaler, the fifteenth-century Romanian *voivode* (warlord) notorious for his atrocities. Merging Stoker's Dracula with Vlad is hardly new, having been popularized by Raymond McNally and Radu Florescu in their best-selling *In Search of Dracula* (1972) and making its way from there into fiction and film. In reality, the connection in *Dracula* is much more tentative. Nowhere is the name "Vlad" mentioned in Stoker's novel (or in his Notes), nor are there any references to the atrocities for which he became notorious. Indeed, recent scholarship has clearly demonstrated that Stoker knew very little about the real Dracula, other than his nickname, that he crossed the Danube to fight against the Turks, and that he had an "unworthy brother."[3] For many, the fact that Vlad has permeated the Dracula story to such an extent has made the two Draculas inseparable. Vlad's appearance here is almost to be expected.

But Stoker and Holt do something quite creative with their Vlad/Dracula. In their novel, he comes to England as Basarab (the name of the royal family to which Vlad the Impaler belonged), a Romanian actor who is taking Europe by storm. Quincey brings Basarab to England, just as his father had paved the way for Count Dracula to undertake a similar journey. Stoker's original intention as shown in his Notes was to have the count arrive through Dover, the port of entry used by Basarab. The change to Whitby occurred after Stoker visited the town on England's northeast coast and decided to make it a major setting in his novel.

One immediately recognizes that Basarab is in part homage to Sir Henry Irving, whose death in 1905 excludes him from an active role in the narrative. The resonances of Irving are pronounced. Quincey Harker is drawn to Basarab much as Stoker himself was to Irving. Quincey hopes that Basarab will play the role of Dracula in a stage version of the Stoker novel; Stoker may have had similar aspirations. The revelation that Basarab is indeed Stoker's Count Dracula plays cleverly on the widespread (albeit readily challenged) view among scholars that Stoker deliberately modeled his vampire on his domineering employer.

Obviously, not all of the characters in this novel are drawn from Stoker's *Dracula*. Yet those "in the know" will recognize many examples of intriguing intertext. Some are minor, as with Braithwaite Lowery,

3 See Elizabeth Miller, *Dracula: Sense & Nonsense* (Desert Island Books, 2006), Chapter 5.

Quincey's roommate at the Sorbonne. This name actually appears in *Dracula* as one of the names on the headstones pointed out by Mr. Swales in the Whitby graveyard. In fact, that is exactly where Stoker found it. Another example is a character listed in an early outline for *Dracula* (and later discarded) as a detective named Cotford. In *Dracula the Un-Dead*, this character is resurrected as Inspector Cotford, who had worked the Ripper case under the mentorship of Chief Inspector Frederick Abberline (a real person) and is still obsessed with making up for his earlier failure by solving it now.

Stoker and Holt incorporate a number of other real people in their narrative. Most obvious is Bram Stoker himself. Due to the restrictions resulting from the choice of narrative time, the authors have had to take certain liberties with the facts of Stoker's life. Here, as owner of a still-operating Lyceum Theatre, he is active for a while, overseeing a proposed stage production based on his own novel. He admits that *Dracula* was the result of the merging of his own vampire story with what he thought was a fantastical tale told to him by an old man in a pub. In a confrontation with the titular character (which, incidentally, precipitates his stroke), Stoker faces Basarab's challenges of some of the "facts" in his novel, as the Romanian actor decries its inconsistencies and false presumptions.

Another historical personage who finds her way into the text is Elizabeth Bathory, the Hungarian countess infamous for bathing in the blood of murdered maidens. As with Vlad the Impaler, her name has been inextricably connected with Stoker and his novel. There is in Bathory's case even less evidence of a connection with Stoker and his book. But her appearance gives *Dracula the Un-Dead* much of its power, allowing the authors to shift some of the "absolute evil" away from Dracula and onto another entity.

Among the many nuggets in this book are cameo appearances by several characters who are clearly nods (some only in name) to individuals connected with the theatre and/or the Dracula story throughout the twentieth century: for example, Hamilton Deane, Tom Reynolds, John Barrymore, Raymond Huntley, Vincent Price, Christopher Lee, and Louis Jourdan. Others, unrelated to Stoker and his novel, ground the text clearly in 1912. There was, for example, a person named Henri Salmet, an early aviator who flew from London to Paris in March of that year. But arguably the most ingenious is the inclusion of Able Seaman John Coffey. Though he had no connection with Stoker or his novel, he has become part of history as the worker who left the *Titanic* at Queensland because of a superstitious fear of what lay in store for the great liner.

In shaping a sequel that is grounded in its predecessor, Stoker and Holt take liberties with both fact and fiction, ranging from the fire at the Lyceum to the location of Seward's asylum in Whitby. They also create backstories for several of the characters in Stoker's novel, such as Renfield's prior association with the Hawkins law firm, Jonathan and Mina's courtship in Exeter, and the establishment of Seward's asylum. On one occasion, they even manipulate a key date in the original novel— postponing Dracula's flight from London back to Transylvania by a few days so that his presence in London on November 9 can make him a suspect in the Ripper murders.

A purist might indeed be occasionally shocked by the introduction of such "errors" into the original text. While it might seem that the coauthors are only sacrificing accuracy for artistic purposes (a completely legitimate enterprise), something else is taking shape. They reestablish the "true" text of *Dracula*, which in turn forms the basis of this sequel; at the same time, they recognize in that sequel that there is no single *Dracula* but many *Dracula*s, ranging from Stoker's earliest Notes to the latest Hollywood adaptation, and that the boundaries between them are blurred indeed. The urge to reclaim and reshape *Dracula* is a mark of the novel's enduring power and influence. To quote Professor Abraham Van Helsing in Bram Stoker's 1897 novel, "And so the circle goes on ever widening, like as the ripples from a stone thrown in the water."

—Elizabeth Miller
Toronto, February 2009

Elizabeth Miller, Professor Emerita (Memorial University of Newfoundland) is recognized internationally for her expertise on Dracula, both the novel and the historical figure. Coeditor (with Robert

Eighteen-Bisang) of *Bram Stoker's Notes for Dracula: A Facsimile Edition*, she has also published *A Dracula Handbook* and the award-winning *Dracula: Sense & Nonsense*. She lectures regularly on both sides of the Atlantic and has participated in numerous radio and television documentaries. At the World Dracula Congress in Romania in 1995, Dr. Miller was granted the honorary title of "Baroness of the House of Dracula." Her Web sites—Dracula's homepage and the Dracula Research Centre—are both accessible through www.blooferland.com.

AUTHORS' NOTE

Dacre's Story

Since I am a Stoker, it is not surprising that I have had a lifelong interest in the work of my ancestor. Bram's youngest brother, George, believed to be the sibling with whom he had the closest relationship, was my great-grandfather, so I am Bram's great-grandnephew. In college, I wrote a paper on my great-granduncle, examining what may have motivated him to write *Dracula*. My research opened my eyes to how, from my family's perspective, the history of the book *Dracula*, is pretty tragic.

Bram Stoker died without ever seeing *Dracula* become popular. The sales of the novel were so limited at the time of his death that his widow, Florence, thought she would never benefit financially from Bram's "wasted" seven years of research and writing. With Bram's other fiction and nonfiction books out of print, Florence was convinced she would live out her days on a tight budget.

It was ten years after Bram's death when his literary imagination finally caught up with that of the public. The vampire/horror genres had begun heating up, which sparked sales of *Dracula*. Posthumously, Bram started to receive recognition as the progenitor of the modern vampire/ horror novel.

In 1922 Florence was confronted with the knowledge that a film based on her late husband's book had been made without her consent. She was dependent on what little income was to be derived from *Dracula*, and as inheritor of Bram's copyright, she should have benefited from this and any other film versions.

Florence went to court, suing the German company Prana Films for copyright infringement for their unauthorized adaptation of *Dracula* into the movie *Nosferatu*. The case was extremely complicated and it dragged on through numerous appeals over a three and a half year period. She finally prevailed in 1925, only to find out that Prana Films was bankrupt, so although she recovered her legal fees, Florence never received any cash settlement.

Florence's only accomplishment after the legal nightmare was the satisfaction that all copies of the film *Nosferatu* were ordered destroyed—or so she thought. To her great dismay, she soon discovered that a copy had survived and begun to appear in film houses in London in 1928 and in the United States in 1929. Frustrated, Florence gave up her fight over the film.

Florence did, however, enforce her copyright and give her input to stage adaptations of Bram's *Dracula* in the United Kingdom, for which she received percentages and royalties. She later benefited from the sale of movie rights to Universal Studios in 1930, but payments were not easily forthcoming.

After the film deal with Universal, it came to light that for some reason Bram had not complied with one small requirement of the U.S. copyright office, therefore rendering *Dracula* public domain in the United States since 1899. From this point on, Florence would have to be satisfied with U.K. royalties only.

With the U.S. copyright lost, Hollywood, corporate America, and anyone else was free to do whatever they wanted to Bram's story and characters. The Stoker family was never again asked for input or approval of any of the hundreds of incarnations of *Dracula* over the next century.

As a Stoker growing up in North America, I saw firsthand how the entire copyright issue impacted our family. My father's generation had a negative feeling for all things Hollywood and *Dracula*—except, of course, for Bram's original novel. I didn't write about these issues in my college paper, but they were always on my mind. I felt it was a shame that my family could not control the legacy of my great-granduncle. I also felt that it was important for the Stokers to somehow lay claim to the character of Dracula as he was more and more embraced by popular culture. Unfortunately, for much of my life I had no idea how I could help make this happen.

It was many years after college that I met an interesting character, Ian Holt. Ian is a screenwriter who has been obsessed with all things Dracula since childhood. Ian, being a true idealist, had a plan that inspired me to not accept the frustrating history of *Dracula*. He wanted to change history. Ian's plan was simple: to reestablish creative control over Bram's novel and characters by writing a sequel that bore the Stoker name. To my surprise, none in my family had ever considered this. Intrigued, I decided to join Ian on a roller-coaster ride as coauthor.

In writing *Dracula the Un-Dead*, I felt a strong sense of duty and familial responsibility. I hoped to work with Ian to represent Bram's vision for the character of Dracula. We aimed to resurrect Bram's original themes and characters, just as Bram conceived them more than a century ago. So many books and films had strayed from Bram's vision—and thus our intent was to give both Bram and Dracula back their dignity in some small way.

I am very proud to have the support of my extended Stoker family to reclaim *Dracula*. I think Bram would be proud that a family member has taken this initiative, and finally done justice to the legacy he created.

Ian's Story

I am not ashamed to say it, I LOVE horror films. As a child there was no horror film I loved more than the Bela Lugosi-Tod Browning 1931 classic, *Dracula*. When I was ten years old, my mother bought me a record for Halloween with Christopher Lee narrating the story of *Dracula* by Bram Stoker. Reading that record sleeve changed my life, for it was then I learned that Transylvania was an actual place and that Dracula was a historical figure. As a ten-year-old boy, I swore I would travel to the land and seek out the old count.

Inspired by the record, I then read Bram Stoker's *Dracula*. I was surprised at how different the novel was from the films—and I had seen every Dracula film ever made. The novel was more intelligent, astute, and dark. The novel had more intricate and exciting characters than I could have ever imagined. I felt cheated by Hollywood. I vowed revenge!

Fifteen years later, my opportunity came. Flipping channels one night, I came upon a program on the making of Francis Ford Coppola's *Bram Stoker's Dracula*. On the program, Coppola held up the 1972 book *In Search of Dracula* written by Fulbright Scholars Professor Raymond McNally and Professor Radu Florescu (Prince Dracula's actual descendant). Coppola had used the professors' research of the historical Prince Dracula's life as inspiration for the opening sequence of his film.

Before taking a breath I was on a plane to Boston College to meet the professors. After showing them some notes on the screenplay I planned to write based on their book, the professors sold me the rights for one dollar and became my partners, mentors, and great friends.

The friendship I forged with McNally and Florescu has borne fruit in many ways. I soon began traveling with the professors giving lectures on the impact of Bram Stoker's novel on our culture. This garnered me an invitation to speak at The First World Dracula Congress in Bucharest, Romania, in 1995 — a gathering of Dracula/horror scholars from around the world. At last I had made it to Transylvania. There I spent a night in the ruins of Dracula's castle in Poenari and traveled to his palace in Tirgoviste—it was here that I stood on the balcony of Dracula's Chindia tower, where Prince Dracula had looked out upon his Forest of the Impaled. I also visited Dracula's birthplace in Sighisoara and his "empty grave" at Snagov Island Monastery. I had finally made the dream I had as a ten-year-old come true.

Thanks to the friends I made at the First World Dracula Congress, I was asked to join the Transylvanian Society of Dracula—a scholarly organization dedicated to the study of all things Dracula. Through friends in the society I met Professor Elizabeth Miller, the world's foremost authority on all things vampire, Dracula, and Bram.

Professor Miller asked me to speak at the Dracula convention in Los Angeles in 1997, where we celebrated the 100th anniversary of the release of Bram's novel. It was a horror geek's dream. It was there that I conceived a sequel to Bram Stoker's *Dracula*. This was not new, but there had never been a sequel made with input from a member of the Stoker family. Securing that input became my goal.

I then reached out to the Stoker family patriarch. Still scarred by the *Nosferatu* copyright affair and years of being ignored and abused by Hollywood, the members of this generation of the Stoker family wanted nothing to do with me. But I wouldn't give up. I simply kept building up my film-writing résumé and Dracula connections, preparing for the day when the younger generation of Stokers came to forefront. Five years later, I met Dacre Stoker—Bram's great-grandnephew. I pitched him my sequel idea, which at the time I had been planning as a screenplay. Dacre was enthusiastic and suggested that the proper way to proceed was with a book first. I eagerly agreed to a writing partnership.

Dacre contacted numerous members of his extensive family and presented them with our sequel proposal. Once it was understood that this would be a labor of love, our intentions honorable, and that our plan was to restore to the world Bram's original vision and characters, the Stokers offered support, at long last.

Dracula the Un-Dead is the culmination of my lifelong dream and years of hard work. It is my gift to every horror nut out there. My greatest wish is we have created a book that is close to Bram's original gothic vision—while modernizing it at the same time. Believe me, I realize how lucky I am. I have been truly blessed that in some small way, my name will be linked with that of my hero, Bram Stoker—the man who invented modern horror.

Writing the novel

DACRE:
When Ian first asked me to become involved in this project, I laughed. I thought to myself, *How can I write a book, especially one of this magnitude?* Ian reassured me that, even though I had never written a novel

before, I could do it. We would cooperate and share writing duties completely, each being responsible for half of the workload. Our editors would help. Ian also knew of an award-winning historical researcher, Alexander Galant, who could aid in our attempts to be true to the time period of the story.

The next hurdle was that we had to craft a good story. Ian enthusiastically and seamlessly merged his story ideas with my own. This task was much easier than either of us thought—due to the fact that both of us drew our ideas from Bram Stoker himself. At times it was as if Bram were in the room with us, guiding us through the numerous hints he left behind, like bread crumbs for us to follow.

Ian and I both deduced from writings Bram left behind that he, or his publisher, always intended there would be a sequel to *Dracula*. Our primary evidence for this is Bram's publisher's typewritten manuscript, recently sold at auction at Christie's, which has a different ending. In that version, the story ends with a volcanic eruption and Dracula's castle falls into a river of lava. This sequence was cut in the final version for the current, more ambiguous ending. In addition, Dracula's "death" at the end of Bram's novel does not follow the "rules" that the Van Helsing character shares on how to kill a vampire. Van Helsing states that a stake must be driven through the heart, followed by decapitation. At the end of the novel, Dracula is stabbed through the heart and his throat is slit. We felt that these were telltale signs that a sequel had been part of Bram's plan.

As a Stoker, I felt Bram needed to be a character in this story, so we could finally give him a share of the limelight. Ian had read Bram's preface to the Icelandic edition of *Dracula* from 1901, where Bram claimed the events he wrote of "really took place." We both seized on my great-granduncle's whim and saw this as the centerpiece of our story. We would use the idea that the events of Bram's book were "fact" as a building block in our own tale.

The next question you may ask is, Why drag Jack the Ripper into a sequel to *Dracula*? Again Ian and I drew our inspiration from my great-granduncle. To quote another section of Bram's 1901 Icelandic preface, "[Dracula's] series of crimes has not yet passed from the memory—a series of crimes which appear to have originated from the same source, and which at the same time created as much repugnance in people everywhere as the murders of Jack the Ripper." It seems that Bram was hinting that the Ripper's crimes were of the same nature of Dracula's. This we used as a launching point for one of the aspects of our story, and it was amazing how easily all the pieces fell into place.

Once we knew that our villain was going to be Jack the Ripper, Ian and I needed to identify the elusive serial killer. Ian had read Bram's short story *Dracula's Guest*, which was published after Bram's death. Many scholars believe this story was part of the original novel, but had been cut by Bram's publisher. Some even think Bram intended to use this short story as a basis for a sequel. In this story, the character Johann happens upon a tomb with an iron stake on the roof. The grave marker reads COUNTESS DOLINGEN TO GRAZ IN STYRIA SEARCHED AND FOUND DEAD 1801. Also engraved, in Russian, is THE DEAD TRAVEL FAST—a clear marker that in this grave is a vampire. The theory exists among some scholars that Bram was influenced by the historic Countess Elizabeth Bathory's bloody deeds when writing *Dracula* and that Bram made Dracula a count based on the name given to Countess Bathory, "Blood Countess." It is also assumed by some that the countess in *Dracula's Guest* somehow represents Bathory herself. That theory appealed to us and we decided to expand upon it.

One of Ian's sources suggested that Bathory was a distant relative of Dracula. We decided that this would serve our purpose well, and we have incorporated it. According to stories passed down mainly by Saxon scribes, Prince Dracula was guilty of performing many bloodthirsty acts. The same can be said of Countess Bathory, who was known to bathe in the blood of her victims. We found it interesting that the two most well-known figures in history that people today (rightly or wrongly) associate with vampire legends might have been related. As Bram did in 1897 when he introduced us to his lead villain, a fictional count based loosely on an historic figure, we in 2009 have done the same with with our Countess Bathory.

As we continued to hammer out our plot, Ian suggested that I travel to the Rosenbach Museum in Philadelphia to research the notes Bram used to write *Dracula*. In the notes I found a character that Bram had planned for, but had deleted early in the process. This was a detective named Cotford. It had always been perplexing to me that Bram, being as thorough as he was, would not have included a police investigation into the strange deaths caused by Dracula. We decided to make Bram's character of Detective Cotford our own, and use his detective work as a way of leading our readers through the mystery at the heart of our novel.

IAN:

Dacre and I now focused our attention on Bram's character of Count Dracula. Here was a major dilemma. When Bram was writing *Dracula* in the late 1800s, the historic Prince Dracula was a little-known figure in the West, mostly forgotten to history. Bram cobbled together a few facts regarding Prince Dracula and merged them with his own fiction. Was this done by Bram intentionally, to separate his Count Dracula from the historic Prince Dracula? Or, was it that Bram couldn't find Prince Dracula's complete story in his research and simply filled in the gaps using his imagination?

For guidance, we returned to Bram's writings. The Dracula character that Bram created in 1897 was a mysterious, refined, and complex being. He displayed conflicting attributes: At times he appears a nobleman of culture and learning, deeply in tune with his country's past, yet at other times a wild animal displaying basic survival instincts. He was a man of the fifteenth century trying to relate to the nineteenth-century world around him, at times embracing modernization, and at others times rejecting it. He displayed a moral compass, which caused struggle as he tried to justify his need to take human life. He killed only when necessary and, to his mind, for the greater good.

I immediately sensed that the character, if not the backstory, of Bram's Count Dracula was very similar to the descriptions of the historical Prince Dracula. Prince Dracula was a man also fighting against changing times, seeking to drive the world back to the dark days of the crusades. Prince Dracula also had a way of always justifying his dark deeds, claiming he did what he did because he had no other choice, or that his victims had chosen their own fate by their actions.

If Bram wanted to make his count synonymous with the historic prince, it would have been impossible at the time he was writing his novel. But we both felt that the similarities between the character of the historical Prince Dracula and Bram's Count Dracula were not mere coincidence.

Since the 1972 release of *In Search of Dracula*, the line between the historic Prince Dracula and Bram's Count Dracula has been irreversibly blurred for the public at large. The two forever merged in pop culture in the opening sequence of Francis Ford Coppola's *Bram Stoker's Dracula*. Based on the similarities in Bram's character and the historical record, and the weight of the public's awareness of the historical prince, Dacre and I felt we had no choice but to once and for all merge the count with the prince. We are also confident that if Bram was writing *Dracula* today, with the wealth of historical information now available on Prince Dracula, his meticulous nature and attention to detail would result in a character that reflected the historic record.

Some may read our novel and astutely point out that our character of Dracula is not, as in Bram's novel, the absolute villain. In Bram's novel, Dracula was only described through the view of his enemies, the journals, letters, etc. of the band of heroes. In our sequel we decided that we would give Dracula his say. This allowed us the chance to merge Prince Dracula with Count Dracula and present the Dracula of our sequel as a complex antihero. Others still perceive him as evil, but by allowing him to speak to his own experience he presents a different side. We therefore do not change Bram's vision, we just present another view. This also served to keep our story fresh and vital.

We have long stated that one of the key reasons for writing this sequel was to remedy the cannibalization and bastardization of Bram's novel by Hollywood and other authors. This is not to say we dislike the other versions. It is just that from a literary standpoint, none of the films or books fully captured the complete essence of Bram's novel and characters. Even in the Tod Browning-Bela Lugosi classic—the only film to have input from the Stoker family—the character of Arthur Holmwood was left out, and Renfield travels to Castle Dracula in the opening of the film instead of Jonathan Harker.

The problems truly began when Hollywood wanted to make a sequel to that film based on *Dracula's Guest*. The story goes that Florence Stoker would not sell the rights unless she was guaranteed more input in the creative process. It was in the midst of these negotiations that Bram's copyright was declared void by the U.S. Copyright Office. This left Hollywood free to develop the sequel as they wished. With Florence demanding more control and Bela Lugosi demanding a large pay increase to reprise the role of Dracula, the decision was made to hire John Balderston to write *Dracula's Daughter*, thereby cutting Bela and Florence out of the process completely. The film failed, but the die had been cast. Everyone was now free to write a Dracula novel or make a Dracula film any way they wanted. And oh, they did.

Now, here's the rub. We know there is a *large* segment of Dracula fans that have only seen the movies and have never read the book, and of course we wanted to inspire many of those folks to read Bram's original. Our dearest wish is all Dracula fans—of the book and of the films, will read and enjoy our sequel. To this end there are several areas which we felt that film fans had so embraced and had become so ingrained into Dracula legend that we could not overlook them. To the literary purists we apologize, but we feel this is a necessary concession, made in the hope of once and for all harmonizing all Dracula fans.

The concessions are as follows: the romance between Mina and Dracula; the ability of vampires to walk in daylight, fly, and transform themselves; the weapons used to destroy them; and the location and names of certain geographical sites.

As for the Mina-Dracula romance, Dacre and I agreed that this would have to be handled with greater care than in any of the films, and deal with the fact that Bram never clearly wrote that a romance occurred. With this in mind, we went to a passage in one of Mina's journal entries from Bram's novel that we felt was conspicuously ambiguous. The passage comes after Mina writes that she believes Dracula has come to her in a dream and reads: "It is strange to me to be kept in the dark as I am to-day, after Jonathan's full confidence for so many years."

Dacre and I found it strange that Jonathan's and Van Helsing's reaction to Mina's dream is to cut her out of their plans to combat Dracula since heretofore she had been an equal member of the band of heroes. This was before Mina drinks Dracula's blood from his chest. To our minds, this was the perfect place to insert the Dracula-Mina romance without recasting Bram's narrative. As we envisioned it, during this "dream" Dracula comes to Mina to explain his side of the story in the hopes of encouraging the brave band of heroes to back off their pursuit. Mina, not wanting to admit to the others that she had spoken to Dracula because they had made a romantic connection (not physical yet), claimed instead that he had only visited her in a dream. Jonathan and Van Helsing naturally find this suspicious and cut Mina out of their plans. Mina's reaction to this slight by her husband and Van Helsing then sends her back into Dracula's arms and to an eventual physical liaison. By thus weaving the Dracula-Mina romance into the fabric of Bram's writing, we were able to stay true to Bram and our literary fans while at not alienating our film fans.

In Bram's novel, Count Dracula can walk about in daylight, but is weaker during daylight hours. A vampire being destroyed by the light of the sun was an invention of F. W. Murnau in *Nosferatu*. Yet, vampires burning to ash in the sun is such a part of modern vampire lore that many reading Bram's novel for the first time claim that he is "wrong."

This, like many other aspects of vampire lore has also evolved over the past century. Bram's vampire lore is no longer cutting edge, and we have tried to address this in our sequel. Therefore, we decided to turn to science and fringe science to, with great care, modernize Bram's vampires. We did nothing here that Bram had not foreseen and even expected would one day occur. Our proof for this again comes from the 1901 Icelandic preface: "And I am further convinced that [these events] must always remain to some extent incomprehensible, although continuing research in psychology and natural sciences may, in years to come, give logical explanations of such strange happenings which, at present, neither scientists nor the secret police can understand." In other words, Bram wrote that the strange events that occurred in his novel, at the time he wrote them, are unexplainable. He goes on to write that he fully expects for science in years to come to provide a logical explanation.

Thus, Ian and I have taken the position that vampire's burn to ash in the sun due to an allergic/chemical reaction to the viral vampire blood that transforms the vampire's DNA. Of course in 1912, the year in which our sequel takes place, the terms "DNA," "virus," or "flu" had not yet been discovered. In their place we used the term "venom." The vampire virus changes the DNA of a human into a vampire. Part of that transformation is the ability to control the approximately 70 percent of our brains, which we do not yet use or know much about and thus allows for nonhuman powers. We explained the transformation of vampires into mist and gargoyle, etc. as a telepathic illusion created through mind control. As for the ability of the vampire to "travel fast" by soaring through the air, we turned to the study of telekinesis or levitation—the ability to move objects or one's self with the mind. With the increased brain power due to the vampire virus, it is easy to understand in our fictional realm how these things could be possible.

We have also clarified the weapons that could be used against the vampire. Again we turned to science, and in some cases merged religion with the science. To explain why in our novel religious icons, such as the cross, work to repel some vampires and not others, we turned to psychology. Those vampires who in life believed in God but have committed evil deeds would naturally have a guilty conscience and fear religious icons as a symbol of their soul's ultimate damnation. Vampires who did not believe in God in life would have no fear of religious icons. The burning of the skin that occurs when a "guilty conscience" vampire comes in physical contact with a religious icon or is splashed with holy water is due to a supercharged psychosomatic reaction.

When it came to vampires and mirrors, we could not find any justification in science for this phenomenon, so we used our sequel to discredit it. As for garlic, we felt a vampire could be allergic. The same for wolfsbane. As for silver, this has long been relegated in modern pop culture to werewolves, and that is where we left it.

The final concession is the location and names of certain geographical sites. Bram spread his story over many locations from Transylvania to London, Exeter, and Whitby. When Deane and Balderston wrote their play it became unfeasible to have so many set changes. The solution was to set the play in only two main locations: Transylvania and Whitby. This simplification was duplicated by numerous film versions of the story, thus confusing fans for a generation. In Bram's novel, there was not a Carfax Abbey, which is shocking to the scores of film fans who've never read the book. Bram did write that Dracula bought a house called Carfax, placing it in Purfleet about twenty miles east of London. To add to the confusion, there are the ancient ruins of Whitby Abbey from which Bram drew inspiration while writing parts of the novel in Whitby. Again hoping to resolve conflicts by blending the stories of the films, play, and original novel, we merged Carfax and Whitby Abbey into one location: Carfax Abbey in Whitby.

This same idea of compromise was used to finally address the long-standing confusion over the locations of the Westenra summer home and Dr. Seward's asylum. We placed them both in Whitby, as they are in the play and many of the films. In our story, we explained why the character Bram made his decision to locate the asylum at Purfleet in his novel this way: At the time Bram didn't know that the events he was recounting were real. He thought they were the ravings of a madman who had told him a tall tale in a pub. Thus, Bram felt he was free to make whatever changes he wanted for the purposes of his fictionalized account. In our novel, Bram discovers that the story is indeed true, and the liberties that he took with the tale come back to haunt him. Literally.

DACRE:
When researching Bram's notes at the Rosenbach Museum, I found a few more exciting tidbits that we decided to include. First, Bram originally scribbled many different title ideas before settling on the title for his novel to be *The Un-Dead*. Later, possibly based on the suggestion of his editor shortly before publication, it became just *Dracula*. This explains the inspiration for our title.

In the Rosenbach notes I also found a list of potential character names that Bram compiled but never used for whatever reason. Ian and I decide to give these names to some of our lesser characters. These names are: Kate Reed, who discovers the impaled body of Jonathan

Harker; Dr. Max Windshoeffel, who witnesses the gargoyle flying down the tube tunnel; and Francis Aytown, the photographer who witnesses "the flaming dragon" outside the tube station.

In the writing of *Dracula the Un-Dead* we have included many hidden references to Bram's *Dracula* and some of the best Dracula adaptations in the hope that the true Dracula enthusiasts and scholars will discover and enjoy them. Many of the characters who pop up in our sequel are also real historic figures.

Look to the name of Quincey's roommate at the Sorbonne, Braithwaite Lowery. That name in Bram's novel was pointed out by Captain Swales on a gravestone in Whitby. Our Braithwaite Lowery mentions he is the son of fishermen, implying he is the grandson of the Braithwaite Lowrey buried in Whitby. The name of Cotford's partner, Sergeant Lee, is homage to the actor Christopher Lee. There is also Lieutenant Jourdan of Le Surte, our tip-of-the-hat to Louis Jourdan, who played Dracula in the excellent BBC 1978 miniseries that Ian and I believe is the closest adaptation of Bram's novel. Look for Dr. Langella, a reference to Frank Langella's excellent, erotically charged Dracula. Inspector Huntley is based on actor Raymond Huntley, who was the first to play Dracula in Hamilton Deane's stage production. These are just to name a few.

As for historical figures that appear in our sequel, see Henri Salmet, a French aviator who made the first flight from London to Paris in March 1912. Look for Lord Northcote, who in 1880 was elected to the House of Commons as MP for Exeter. Frederick Abberline was lead investigator in the Jack the Ripper murders in 1888. Ivan Lebedkin was assayer for the czar of Russia 1899–1900. Of course, Hamilton Deane was the writer-producer of the stage production of the play *Dracula*. John Barrymore was a legendary actor of both stage and screen and is the great-grandfather of actress Drew Barrymore. Tom Reynolds was a well-known British stage actor who, as a member of The Lyceum Theatre Company, portrayed Van Helsing in Hamilton Deane's production. Able Seaman Coffey was an actual crew member on the *Titanic* who mysteriously had a premonition of danger while the ship was docked in Queenstown, Ireland. A. S. Coffey jumped ship, had his fifteen minutes of fame, and disappeared into mists of history. In addition, we have followed Bram's lead in relying on actual time period train routes and schedules, street names, and locations that in many cases still stand today.

The last bit of business Ian and I had before we could begin writing was to decide whether we were going to answer many of the lingering questions left unanswered by Bram in his novel. Due to Bram's use of journal entries, letters, etc. to tell his story, he was limited in his ability to fully explore his famous characters' backstories. This left huge plot holes that fans have been arguing over for decades. Ian and I felt it was imperative to at last answer the following enduring questions of how Lucy and Mina first met and forged their lifelong friendship, how a Texan met and became close friends with an English lord's son and a doctor of middle-class birth, how all three men became friendly rivals in pursuing Lucy's hand, how Mina and Jonathan first met and fell in love, how the character of Renfield first came under Dracula's influence, and why Renfield was so important to Dr. Seward and the brave band of heroes. We hope you agree that these issues are well addressed in *Dracula the Un-Dead*.

In the end it was our most important goal with this sequel to right the wrongs done to Bram's original classic. We have worked hard on this front. In this way, I, as a Stoker, and Ian, as Dracula's greatest living fan, hope to apologize for losing the copyright and control of Bram's magnificent and immortal story for almost a century.

Then again, all the terrifying events Ian and wrote of in our novel may, as Bram once suggested, have really taken place.

Pleasant dreams.

DACRE STOKER AND IAN HOLT

The following pages are taken from the collection of Bram Stoker's handwritten notes for *Dracula*. Dacre Stoker and Ian Holt consulted these notes while conducting research for their book, *Dracula the Un-Dead*.

If you look on the page labeled "31b," for example, you will find the inspiration for the title. The page labeled "1" features Bram's early draft of his character list. Many of the characters do not appear in *Dracula*, but they do in *Dracula the Undead*, including, most importantly, the detective Cotford. The page labeled "38a" features Bram's ideas for the characteristics of the vampire.

Count Drakula
Peter Hawkins
Jonathan Harker
Mina Murray
Sir Robert Parton
John Seward
Quincey P. Adams
Hon Arthur Holmwood son of Viscount Godalming
Dr Van Helsing
Mrs Westenra
Lucy Westenra
Dr Vincent ii North Hospild

Mem
none. He Un-Dead —
or
The Dead Un-Dead.

Count Dracula

Dracula **Historie Personae** Dracula

o Doctor of mad house — — Seward
  Girl engaged to him — Lucy Westenra Schoolfellow of Mrs Murray
o Mad Patient (theory of getting able - instinct is goes for Count & follows
                  up idea with mad cunning.
o Lawer ~~Arthur Abbott~~ ~~John~~ Peter Hawkins Exeter.
o His Clerk — — — — — — Jonathan Harker
o Fiancee of above ~~Pupil teacher~~ Wilhelmina Murray (called Mina)
~~Lawyer~~
~~piscator~~
o ~~Doctor~~ ~~man~~
  Friend & ~~schoolfellow~~ of above — — — Kate Reed
  The Count — — — Count ~~~~~~ Dracula
  A Deaf Mute woman } English
  A Silent ~~man~~   } Servants of
                       the Count
o A Detective — — — — — — Cotford
o A Psychical Research Agent — — — Alfred Singleton
~~An American Inventor from Texas~~
o A German Professor — — — Max Windshoeffel
o A Painter — — — Francis ~~Pl~~ Aytown
o a Texan — — — Brutus M. Maris

                              Mem
o ~~~~ note dinner of 13   Secret room — ~~~~~~

Vampire

memo(s)

~~no ... glasses, in buck house~~

never can see him reflected
in ... — no shadow?
lights arranged & give no
shadow —

~~Never eat, nor drink~~

Carried or led over threshold

enormous strength —

see in the dark

power of getting small or large

Money always old gold — traced to
Salzburg banking house

at Munich dead house see face among
I.2 flowers - think corpse - but is alive
III.. (afterwards when white moustache grown is
same as Count in London

Doctor at Dover Custom house sees him
in Corpse —

Coffins selected ... latch over — one
empty we thought —

ACKNOWLEDGMENTS

Ian Holt

First and foremost, I would like to thank my parents, Dolores and Sonny. Without your unwavering support and encouragement, I couldn't have gotten through the rough times. I love you.

I would like to offer this book in loving memory to Ruth and Bob Kaufman, J. Boyce Harman, Jr., and Professor Raymond McNally. Their love, friendship, support, and guidance over the years helped make this book possible. Through me you all live on, for I will carry you with me the rest of my days. God bless you all.

To Professor Radu Florescu. You took a chance on a nobody. Your genius, dedication, trust, and friendship helped create a somebody.

To my old friends John Florescu and Sir David Frost, who helped me realize that it is a good thing to be fearless and rush boldly in where others hesitate to tread. Your early support gave me the tenacity to never give up.

To Professor Elizabeth Miller, who kindly made the introductions that made this dream a reality.

To Laura Stoker, and the late Nicolae Paduraru, founder and president of The Transylvanian Society of Dracula and a gentleman and a scholar. You two were the first to believe.

To Jenne Stoker, who made the call and brought us all together.

To Dacre Stoker, my writing partner, business partner, brother, and friend. You are my Dr. "Bones" McCoy. Flesh of the original flesh, blood of the original blood—WE DID IT!

To Bela Lugosi, Tod Browning, Hamilton Deane, John Balderston, Bud Abbott, and Lou Costello, for fueling the nightmares of a young boy that became an enduring quest.

To Bela Lugosi, Jr., for sharing the story of his father's pain, and his own childhood struggles with me.

To Frank Langella, W. D. Richter, and John Badham. Your film inspired a young boy to take chances and encouraged me to reimagine Dracula as the romantic, hero knight he was.

To Christopher Lee, for making the record that changed the course of my life. You bring dignity to the horror genre, sir. I would be remiss to praise Mr. Lee's accomplishments without also recognizing the talents of Peter Cushing and the works of Hammer Horror.

To Jan de Bont, whose mentorship, mighty vision, and fearlessness inspired me to greater heights than I thought possible. To Chris Stanley of Blue Tulip, whose damn good eye for a hot property got the ball rolling.

To Ernest Dickerson, one of the nicest people and finest directors I know.

To Ken Atchity, Chi-Li Wong, and Mike Kuciak of AEI, my managers and friends, for their hard work, talented guidance, experience, and connections. Thank you for being steadfast believers who always had my back.

To Danny Baror of Baror International, our foreign agent, who made it rain and rain.

To the entire talented, brilliant, patient, understanding, even-keeled, and dedicated Dutton team, and especially our fearless leader, Brian Tart, and our mother hen, guidance counselor, psychologist, friend, and incomparable editor, the amazing Carrie Thornton. Every author should be lucky enough to work with you all. You all have my thanks, appreciation, and gratitude.

To Ron Gwiazda and Amy Wagner of Abrams Artists, my agents and friends. You two give agents a good name—nobody does it better.

To Shannon Mullholland of MODA Entertainment, our L&M guru and agent. You are so cool, bat-lady.

To Peter Fields, our guardian muscle—with you and your team at our side I never worry.

Special thanks to Alexander Galant, Spock to my Kirk, my film writing and business partner, friend, and brother who rode shotgun the entire bumpy journey. Your brilliant research, selfless sacrifice, and amazing talent were invaluable to making this work a reality.

To Carmen Gillespie, who provided the women's perspective and designed our logo by resurrecting the lost Victorian art of the braid. If you don't see the bat-logo, it's not official Bram Stoker Dracula merchandise.

To Cynthia Galant, who allowed me to steal her daddy for a few hours every day.

To Doctor Dre, my best friend and brother, for all your support, encouragement, wisdom, and the hours you spent patiently listening to my worries during the dark days.

To Graig F. Weich, one of my closest and oldest friends, whose truly scary original artwork for this novel did not survive the final edit due to length constraints. Look for Graig's Un-Dead art on our Web site www.draculatheun-dead.com and be sure to check out Graig's too-cool-for-words artwork on www.beyondcomics.tv.

Dacre Stoker

I would like to offer *Dracula the Un-Dead* to all who carry the Stoker blood, originating in Ireland and now all over the globe.

Special thanks to my children, Bellinger and Parker, who will one day think it is pretty cool to carry on these genes.

To my late father, Desmond, and to his brother, my uncle Paddy, our Stoker family dinosaur.

And to my late godfather, my namesake, Henry Hugh Gordon Dacre Stoker, the WWI submarine commander who influenced history at Gallipoli.

My efforts on this book would not have been possible without the support and encouragement of my wife, Jenne, whose research unearthed troves of Stoker lore.

I am grateful to the Bram Stoker Society, for their efforts to raise awareness of Bram's literary legacy; Douglas Appleyard, our family genealogist, and all who support the Dublin Irish Gothic Literature and keep the Stoker torch burning bright; John Moore, for providing access to his Bram Stoker Dracula collection; John Stokoe at the *Whitby Gazette* and Suttcliff Studios, for providing inspirational historical location photos; to John Stoker, for introductions made; and to Elizabeth Miller, the "Dracula Police."

Thanks to the twenty-first-century "Band of Heroes": Ian Holt, whose enthusiasm continues to be unparalleled; Alexander Galant and his extensive knowledge of the Victorian period; and Carrie Thornton, who redefined patience and understanding during our editing process.

Special thanks to the staff of the Rosenbach Museum and Library, in Philadelphia, for graciously making Bram's notes available.

9th March 1912

Dear Quincey,

My dear son, all your life you have suspected that
there have been secrets between us. I fear that the time
has come to reveal the truth to you. To deny it any
longer would put both your life and your immortal
soul in jeopardy.

Your dear father and I chose to keep the secrets of our
past from you in order to shield you from the darkness
that shrouds this world. We had hoped to allow you a
childhood free from the fears that have haunted us all
our adult lives. As you grew into the promising
young man you are today, we chose not to tell you what
we knew lest you think us mad. Forgive us. If you are
reading this letter now, then the evil we so desperately